ANITA AND ME

ANITA AND ME

MEERA SYAL

Flamingo
An Imprint of HarperCollins*Publishers*

Flamingo
An Imprint of HarperCollins*Publishers*
77-85 Fulham Palace Road,
Hammersmith, London W6 8JB

Published by Flamingo 1996

9 8 7 6 5 4 3 2 1

ISBN 0 00 225340 2

Set in Linotron Baskerville at
the Spartan Press Ltd, Lymington, Hants

Printed and bound in Great Britain by
Caledonian International
Book Manufacturing Ltd Glasgow

For my parents and brother
with gratitude and love

And for Shekhar and Chameli, as always

ANITA AND ME

I do not have many memories of my very early childhood, apart from the obvious ones, of course. You know, my wind-swept, bewildered parents in their dusty Indian village garb standing in the open doorway of a 747, blinking back tears of gratitude and heartbreak as the fog cleared to reveal the sign they had been waiting for, dreaming of, the sign planted in tarmac and emblazoned in triumphant hues of red, blue and white, the sign that said simply, WELCOME TO BRITAIN.

And then there's the early years of struggle and disillusion, living in a shabby boarding house room with another newly arrived immigrant family, Polish, I think would be quite romantic; my father arriving back from his sweatshop at dawn to take his place in the bed being vacated by Havel who would be off to do his shift on the McDouglas Biscuits assembly line, my father sweeping away crushed garibaldi crumbs from the communal pillow before sliding gratefully into oblivious sleep, my mother awake at his side, counting the kicks from the daughter inside her who would condemn her, marry her to England forever.

I slept in a drawer, probably, swaddled in back copies of the *Daily Mirror*. My mother only found out about Kennedy's assassination two weeks after the event, when she read the reversed newsprint headlined on my damp backside. She didn't follow the news, no telly, no radio, no inclination, being a simple Punjabi girl suffering from culture shock, marooned and misplaced in Wolverhampton.

Of course, this is the alternative history I trot out in job interview situations or, once or twice, to impress middle-class white boys who come sniffing round, excited by the thought of wearing a colonial maiden as a trinket on their arm. My earliest memory, in fact, is of the first time I understood the punchline to a joke. I was watching some kind of Royal Variety television show on ice – I remember that because it was a balmy summer evening and I wondered how they had managed to keep the floor so cold. A man in a lime green jumpsuit raised a gun and took aim at a fat female ballerina who was gliding towards him like some vast, magnificent galleon, pink tulle emanating in a cloud from around her strong marbled thighs like ectoplasm. The man raised the gun, fired once, twice, and the ballerina fell dramatically to the floor to hilarity and applause.

'Oh my dearie,' said the man. 'I think I shot her in the tutu.'

My mother said I laughed so much that I threw up and at one point, called in Mrs Worrall from next door who put her teeth in and solemnly declared that I'd probably 'had a turn.' But I've always been a sucker for a good double entendre; the gap between what is said and what is thought, what is stated and what is implied, is a place in which I have always found myself. I'm really not a liar, I just learned very early on that those of us deprived of history sometimes need to turn to mythology to feel complete, to belong.

1

'I'm not lying, honest, papa!' I pleaded as he took my hand and pulled me towards the kerb, briefly checking for traffic along the twisting country lane. It was hot and I could feel beads of sweat and fear threading themselves into a necklace of guilt, just where my itchy flesh met the collar of my starched cotton dress. Papa did not look angry, he had the air of a man on a mission. He was walking along with that jaunty air that my mother said had made her fall in love with him, a hop of optimism in his walk that belied a sensitive, introspective-looking face. His features effortlessly combined those same contradictions of vulnerability and pride, the sharp leonine nose that swooped down towards the generous questioning mouth, meeting in what looked like the fleshy imprint of a single teardrop.

I scuttled after papa along the single road, bordered with nicotine-tipped spiky grass, the main artery which bisected the village. A row of terraced houses clustered around the crossroads, uneven teeth which spread into a gap-toothed smile as the houses gradually became bigger and grander as the road wandered south, undulating into a gentle hill and finally merging into miles of flat green fields, stretching as far as the eye could see. We were heading in the opposite direction, northwards down the hill, away from the posh, po-faced mansions and towards the nerve centre of Tollington, where Mr Ormerod's grocery shop, the Working Men's Club, the diamond-paned Methodist church and the red brick school jostled for elbow room with the two-up-two-downs, whose outside toilets backed onto untended meadows populated with the carcasses of abandoned agricultural machinery. There was only one working farm now, Dale End farm, bookending the village at the top of the hill, where horses regarded the occasional passers-by with mournful malteser eyes.

From the crest of the hill, on a clear day, you could see the industrial chimneys of Wolverhampton, smoking like fat men's cigars, and sometimes glimpse the dark fringes of Cannock Chase, several square miles of thick conifers bristling with secrets and deer, where every so often, forgotten skeletons of ancient victims were discovered by local courting couples. But the horizon gradually disappeared as we marched down the hill towards Mr Ormerod's shop, down into the valley of . . . I wished I'd never gone to Sunday School, I wished I did not know the name for what I was now feeling. Sin. One word, three letters, eternal consequences. Unless I confessed all now. I swallowed and looked around, as if for help. There was my home, halfway down the hill, standing on the corner of the crossroads, one of the miners' tithe cottages huddled around a dirt yard which was the unofficial meeting place for our small community. There was the small overgrown park next to the Yard, where the swings and ricketty slide were watched over by the witch's hat of an ancient metal roundabout.

I could see children riding their bikes, screeching in and around the parked cars and lines of washing, practising noisy manoeuvres which threw up clouds of dust, punctuating each skid like exclamation marks. I could see my mother, even at this distance her brown skin glowed like a burnished planet drifting amongst the off-white bedsheets of her neighbours. She was wearing one of her slop-around outfits, a faded Punjabi suit whose billowing trousers rippled in the breeze, mercurial wings fluttering at her ankles. She paused, gathering some bundle from a basket at her feet, and then with one motion shook out a peacock-blue sari which she began tacking to the washing line. It puffed outwards in a resigned sigh between her hands. She looked as if she was holding up a piece of the sky.

Maybe someone from the Big House would come out and save me. The Big House, as gloomy and roomy as a set from a Hammer horror film, was the only building set apart from the main road and lay at the end of an uneven track which began five hundred yards from our front door. The Big House occupied its own island of private grounds, shielded by high mournful trees and a barbed wire fence. Two ancient, lopsided wooden signs declared NO TRESPASSERS! and BEWARE OF GUARD DOGS! The latter featured a slavering Doberman frothing at the mouth, except the paint had peeled around his muzzle, replacing what were once ferocious teeth with flaking splinters so he looked like he was chewing on a loo brush.

On windy nights, the trees around the Big House, a thicket of towering chestnuts and poplars which sometimes blocked the sun and filtered damp green light into my bedroom, would talk to me urgently, telling me to open the window, spread my arms and flap over the fields to their waiting branches. At least that's what I told my mother when she found me crouching on the windowsill with a copy of the *TV Times* in my hand. I tried to explain what the trees had whispered, that the *Golden Shot* was a fix and Bob Monkhouse, the devil himself. I was not allowed to watch any television for two weeks after that.

The Big House, as usual, seemed deserted. I noticed papa was unconsciously clenching and unclenching his fingers around mine as we walked, and I wondered if it would be a good or a bad move to take away my hand. Then I got distracted, noticing a kestrel hovering behind the old pithead of the mine, visible just behind the grey green slates of the Big House's roof. The Tollington mine had once employed the whole village; it had been feted as a small but plucky contributor to the Black Country's industrial growth, not as technically impressive as the nearby Cannock Pit, not as imposing and thrusting as the one further afield in Wirley, but a respectably productive enterprise all the same.

Our adjoining neighbour, Mrs Worrall, had once shown me a yellowing newspaper cutting commemorating the day the Mayor of Wolverhampton had come to visit Tollington mine. It must have been during the war, for some of the grainy bystanders were decked out self-consciously in their Home Guard uniforms and a coalman's dray was parked in the left hand corner of the photograph, where a shire horse lurked with pricked ears. The mine and the village had been as intertwined as lovers, grateful lovers astonished by their mutual discovery; you could see it in the stiff backs of the men and the proud smiles of the women. Mrs Worrall had pointed to an indistinct blob whose elaborate hat was just visible behind the mayor's jowly face, 'Me, that is,' she said grandly. 'That hat cost two weeks' egg rations,' claiming her moment of fame by association.

Then the mine suddenly closed down in the late Fifties, no one seemed to know why. A few of the luckier miners were offered temporary jobs in the adjoining pits, but most of the able-bodied men with families had moved on to look for work, leaving behind a gaggle of wheezy old geezers and dozens of stout, dour-faced miners' widows who had nowhere else to go. It had been a community of tough, broad-armed women and fragile old men until a few new families started moving in, drawn by the country air and dirt-cheap housing – families like us.

But no one, not even Mrs Todd who was eighty-five and kept her colostomy bag in a sequinned pouch under her pinafore, not even she could remember seeing anyone ever going in or coming out of the Big House since the mayor's visit. The owner in those days was a ruddy bouncing ball of a man, who in the newspaper cutting is holding onto the mayor's hand with two fat fists whilst a woman I presumed was his wife, in a shapeless smock, stands at his side looking faintly embarrassed.

However, a few years later, someone else bought the mine: someone who never cared to mix with his neighbours or his work force but delegated all his duties to faceless officials; someone for whom the pit closure apparently had no repercussions, or at least not any that would make him want to emerge and share the grief and confusion; someone who presumably still lived there because we would occasionally see smoke curling out of the chimney. There were occasional flurries of excitement, when every few months a delivery van from one of the posh stores in Wolverhampton would back up to the peeling gates, and discharge siege-worthy supplies of groceries. Some of the local women would gather around the van, shaking their heads at the sod-off grandeur of the delivery, muttering at the parade of wines, preserves, spices, monogrammed biscuits and extra soft toilet roll, each item taken as a slap in the face from a stuck-up stranger. But despite their unashamed snooping and straining to glimpse through the always drawn curtains, the Big House's inhabitants remained a mystery so incomprehensible that it was no longer even discussed.

The kestrel gave out a faint cry, sharp and forlorn all at once, and plummeted from view. Papa quickened his pace. I realised, sadly, that whoever lived in the Big House would not break their solitude to save a little Indian girl who had been caught telling lies.

We passed Mr Topsy standing outside his postage stamp garden, a riot of blazing rhododendrons and grinning gnomes trying to burst out of their fenced-in borders. Nearly everyone's garden was like this, making up in content what they lacked in space, every frontage crammed full of miniature ponds and stone clad wishing wells, tiny porches stuffed with armouries of shiny horse brasses and copper plates, a row of Santa's grottos all year round.

It was a constant source of embarrassment to me that our front garden was the odd one out in the village, a boring rectangle of lumpy grass bordered with various herbs that mama grew to garnish our Indian meals. 'This is mint, beti,' she would say, plucking the top of a plant and crushing the leaves under my nose, 'This one *thunia* . . . coriander I mean . . . this lemon verbena, you can make tea from this . . .' I did not want things growing in our garden that reminded me of yesterday's dinner; I wanted roses and sunflowers and manicured hedges and fountains where the blackbirds would come and sip. I wanted to see mama in a big hat doing something creative with a pair of pruners. I looked at Mr Topsy's garden and felt furious. Suddenly, somehow it was his fault that I was standing here in front of him waiting to be tried and punished by a jury of grinning gnomes with no genitals and fishing rods.

'How you doing, Topsy?' Mr Topsy had christened me thus as he claimed he could not pronounce my name, and I returned the favour by refusing to ever learn his. He talked out of the side of his pipe, like Popeye, and had a bullet shaped face softened with a dusting of white and grey whiskers. He scratched his belly absent-mindedly and I became suddenly fascinated by the size of his trousers. There was enough material in one leg to build a den and his fly stretched all the way from knee to navel like an operation scar.

'Alright, Mr Kumar?' My papa paused and exchanged pleasantries, still holding tightly onto my hand. I could not speak, as by now my teeth were embedded in the strawberry tarmac of a penny chew which I had sneaked from my dress pocket. I thought I might be able to swallow the evidence of my crime before we reached Mr Ormerod's shop. I hurriedly unwrapped another and stuffed it in, gagging on the goo. I looked up at papa. His silhouette momentarily blocked out the sun and his eyelashes seemed spiked with light. He could traverse continents with a stride and hold the planets in the palm of his hand. He was going to kill me.

We reached Mr Ormerod's shop and stopped outside the window. The display had been the same for years: a huge cardboard cut-out of a Marmite jar dominated the space, bleached on one side where the sun had caught it, the Player's Capstan cigarette display behind it, featuring a saturnine sailor's face in the centre of a lifebelt. A few days earlier, Anita Rutter had told me that this sailor was in fact her father.

I had been in my usual spot outside Ormerod's window having a visual affair with his sweet display when she had sauntered past, arm in arm with her two regular cohorts, Sherrie, who lived at Dale End Farm and Fat Sally. As they came nearer, they began exchanging excited stage whispers and clumsy dead-arm punches. I had instinctively stiffened and busied myself with reading the small print on the Marmite jar, my heart unaccountably flipping like a fish. Anita stopped and looked me up and down, her top lip beginning to rise.

She pointed at the Player's Capstan sailor and said, 'That's my dad, that is. He wuz in the Navy. He got medals for blowing up the Jerries, like . . .' I wondered why he had taken a particular dislike for men with this name but before I could ask, Sherrie and Fat Sally burst into side-hugging laughter. Only the big girls laughed in this way, malicious cackles which hinted at exclusivity and the forbidden. I knew they were all at senior school, I had seen them round the village in their over-large uniforms, customised with badges and crop-ped-off ties. I was nine but felt three and a half as this particular day, mama had had one of her 'You Always Look Like A Heathen' moods and had forced me into a dinky pleated dress, which despite my efforts at ripping and rolling in mud, still contained enough frills and flowers to give me the appearance of a bad tempered doily.

I shot Anita a haunted look, I told her silently that this was not me. She paused and then spun round, scowling, the other girls' smiles melted and slowly trickled out the side of their mouths. Then Anita broke into a beam of such radiance and forgiveness that my breath caught and my throat began to ache. They linked arms again and walked away, leaving questions buzzing around my head like a heat-hazy fly. It had been the first time Anita had ever talked to me and I had wondered what I had done to deserve it.

The day after this encounter, I happened to see Anita's dad, Roberto, standing at the village bus stop. He had his blue Dunlop tyre factory overalls on and was dragging deeply on a butt end. He did not look much like his photograph any more, but maybe it was the trauma of his wartime experiences that had caused his beard to fall out and his eyes to change colour. I ambled past and smiled at him. He winked back, 'Alright, chick?'

I stood before him for a moment, waiting for courage to open my mouth. He smiled at me again and dropped the butt into the road, squinting up the hill for any sign of the asthmatic single-decker which would take him to town.

'Mr Rutter,' I squeaked, 'do you miss the sea?'

'Ey? Rhyl you mean? Oh ar, was alright.'

He did not want to remember. I could see pain and confusion contorting his face. I changed tack. 'Have you got any tattoos?'

He smiled proudly and rolled up the sleeve of his oily overall, stabbing a finger at his forearm. 'Look at this, chick.'

The flesh looked like the exam paper of an unhappy dyslexic; a row of names in blue fuzzy ink ran up his arm like a roll call, Brenda, Deirdre, Janice, Gaynor, just legible under unsuccessful attempts to cross them out with what looked like blue marker pen. He tugged the sleeve up further to reveal the name perched on top of an undulating muscle, still pristine and untampered with, three letters set in a faded red heart, MUM. 'That's who I miss, chick. No one could replace her. No bugger alive.' He sniffed loudly and rearranged his Bryl-cremed quiff. Suddenly he raised a hand to his eyes, scanning the top of the hill, and shouted, 'Bus, ladies!'

All at once, several cottage doors flew open like airholes on a concertina and blew various women out of their houses adjusting headscarves, closing handbags, shouting at husbands, voices hoarse with cigarette smoke or muffled by herbal cough sweets but all dipping and rising in that broad Midland sing-song where every sentence ends in a rhetorical swoop. 'What you done to your hair, eh? Dog's dinner or what, aaar! Am you gooing up bingo tonight or what, eh? Mouthy wench, that Sharon, aaar? Ooh, yowm looking fit today, Roberto duck, getting it regular then, aaar?'

These women were commonly known as The Ballbearings Committee as they all worked at a metal casings factory in New Town, an industrial estate and shopping centre and our nearest contact with civilisation. The factory had opened, by way of compensation, soon after the mine closure, and everyone had assumed that the jobs would be given to the ex-colliers. But it was not the men they wanted; they wanted women, women who would do piecework and feel grateful, women whose nimble fingers would negotiate their machines, women who, unlike their husbands, would not make demands or complain. So it was that in the space of a few months, the hormonal balance of Tollington was turned upside down. There must have been a time when women waved their men off on doorsteps with lunch boxes and a resigned smile, but I could not remember it. It seemed to me that they had always run the village and they had always been as glamorous and shocking as they were now.

There was not much room for dialogue with these women, whose communal tone of voice said, I know the answer but I'll ask you anyway but make it quick, chick. They appeared ensemble as coiffured maenads in belted macs and bright lipsticks who all worked together, lived together and played together, and bounced off the village boundaries like a ballbearing against the sides of a pinball machine. Too much energy and nowhere to put it, and though I knew some of their names, Mrs Dalmeny, Mrs Spriggs, Mrs Povey, they seemed to exist and function as a group.

Indeed, their husbands were incidental; all I knew of them was what I would glimpse through half-open doorways on these regular morning panic runs from porch door to approaching bus, men in vests and braces, with rumpled hair who clutched half-read papers and fiddled absent-mindedly with their testicles whilst their wives flung them hurried goodbyes. I noticed there was never any show of affection, no hugs or kisses, not like my parents for whom every leavetaking was accompanied by squeezes, contact numbers on the journey in case of breakdown or terrorist kidnap and always a folded white hanky. Maybe, I told my mother once, they did not love their husbands, that was why we never saw them out together. 'Oh no,' my mother replied. 'They do. They work so their husbands can eat. Their husbands must feel like ghosts. Poor men. Poor women.'

I did not think they were impoverished, watching them teeter across the road, shouting and laughing until they met and merged together like mercury. The bus coughed to a halt and Roberto made a great show of holding the automatic doors open for the women. They all flew past me in a tornado of perfume and smoke and shiny snappy handbags, pinching my cheek, ruffling my hair, 'Alright chick? . . . Ooh, she's a little doll, in't she? . . . Them eyes, eh? Ey Roberto, gooing to come and sit by me, aaar?' They drew energy from me like a succubus and I deflated as the bus doors closed with a sigh and pulled away. I could see Roberto chatting and flirting with the women but only I knew how bravely he concealed his terrible tortured past. I envied him. I wished I was a tortured soul.

My eyes travelled from the sailor's grimace to the rows of sweetjars above his head. I knew my father was waiting for me to say something. I took in the plump, cloudy bonbons, snug in their glass jar, the cherry lips smiling back at me, the flying saucers whose paper surfaces dissolved into acid on your tongue, the humbugs and rainbow drops and Blackjack chews, adorned with the face of a grinning piccaninny. Wouldn't anyone be tempted? I wanted to say, but I didn't.

'Well,' said papa. 'Are you going to tell me the truth? Or shall we go inside and ask Mr Ormerod what happened?'

I glanced at the brass crucifix in the centre of the window display and then shot my father a look. We both knew this was an empty threat. No one instigated conversation with Mr Ormerod if they wanted to get home before their next birthday. A sentence as innocuous as 'How much is the thick-sliced Sunblest?' would result in a chirpy monologue which took in Harold Wilson, global disaster and the price of peas, somehow always ending in a hallelujah chorus about the glory of God. Mr Ormerod was hyperactive in the local Wesleyan Methodist church, the only church in the village, the centre of over-organised events we laughingly termed a social life, and the best way he knew how to make us feel at home was to continually try and convert us to the ways of Jesus Christ, his Saviour.

'Have you seen this leaflet, Mr Kumar?' he would enquire innocently, thrusting a flyer into papa's hands with his change. 'Lovely speaker we've got for the Harvest celebrations, Mr Delaney has just come back from Rhodesia. In Africa. We're having a collection. They asked for a plough but we thought a few tins and preserves would tide them over for a bit.' You could see it in his face, he'd made the connection, Africa was abroad, we were from abroad, how could we refuse to come along and embrace Jesus for the sake of our cousins? Papa always did refuse but with such grace that Mr Ormerod never lost hope; he just filed us away under 'Waverers', rearranged the pens in the breast pocket of his brown overall, and waited for next time.

'Now,' said papa. 'For the last time, did Mr Ormerod give you those sweets for nothing? Or did you take that shilling from mummy's bag and spend it on yourself?' I was mute with shame and anger. I hated him for forcing me to stoop to such a grubby act; if he had listened to me in the first place and just given me the sodding money, I would not have had to steal anything. I lifted up my head slightly, saw the ice in his expression and felt doomed. If papa was so angry now, what would he be like when he found out what had happened to me at school only last week?

I had been publicly beaten in front of all my class mates whom I now hated without exception. It had been during a Modern History lesson, when our bullfrog-faced teacher, Mrs Blakey, asked us if we knew why the area we lived in was called the Black Country. Peter Bradley, who had a stammer and a predictable habit of deliberately dropping pencils so he could peer up the girls' dresses, raised a sleeve covered in snail trails of snot and said, 'B . . . b . . . because so m . . . many darkies . . . live here, miss?' I laughed along with everyone else but the next time I heard Peter snuffling around under the desk, pencil in hand, peering optimistically past reinforced gussets and woolly tights, I aimed a quick kick and was surprised to see him emerge with a fist clamped over a bloody nose. As Mrs Blakey karate-chopped the back of my legs with a splintered wooden ruler, I tried to explain that we were the only Indians that had ever lived in Tollington and that the country looked green if anything to me.

My humiliation had been compounded by the fact that mama was an infants' teacher in the adjoining school; we were separated by a mere strip of playground, and I knew it would only be a matter of time before she got to hear of my behaviour. I knew I should tell papa everything now, Confess said the Lord and Ye Shall Be Saved. Papa's expression made me wonder if this only ever worked with English people, but I had to say something because if we entered Mr Ormerod's shop, my crime would become public shame as opposed to personal failure and that, I knew, was something papa hated more than anything.

Somewhere a front door slammed shut. It seemed to reverberate along the terrace, houses nudging each other to wake up and listen in on us, net curtains and scalloped lace drapes all a-flutter now. Everyone must have been watching, they always did, what else was there to do?

'Right then. We'll ask Mr Ormerod what happened.'

Papa pushed open the door of the shop, the brass bell perched on its top rang jauntily. Its clapper looked like a quivering tonsil in a golden throat and it vibrated to the beat of my heart.

'I was lying,' I said in a whisper.

Papa's face sagged, he looked down and then up at me, disappointment dimming his eyes. He let go of my hand and walked back towards our house without looking back.

2

I sat on the front step and finished the rest of my sweets, feeling the bile rise as I chewed with the pace and rumination of a sulky cow. I knew I would end up feeling ill but I had already paid for my haul in shame and saw no point in wasting good food. It would serve them right if I did choke on a raspberry poppet and had foaming convulsions right here on the step. As I tried to unstick my jaw, I remembered the mad dog that had wandered into our communal yard some years ago, whose drunken walk and white-flecked muzzle had sent the mothers screaming for cover, clutching their protesting children to them. I managed to find an airhole in the folds of mama's trousers and had gazed on the object of all this terror, a mottled, scrappy mutt of a dog who seemed proud of his madness, freed by it, whose expression was one of unconcerned, off-the-planet bliss. I really envied him, or rather the effect he was having on the local harpies who, in normal circumstances, would arm wrestle each other for a parking space. If what that dog had was madness, I wanted some of it. Even then, I felt I spent most of life saying sorry.

I also knew what it was like to almost choke to death. It had happened two years ago, we had celebrated my seventh birthday with a trip to Wolverhampton, where we saw *Bedknobs and Broomsticks* and then went for a rum baba in the nearby Stanton's cake shop. I had been promised a party but at the last minute, my mother had been taken ill. Papa found her lying on her bed, crying. He'd said it was a migraine and then talked softly to her in Punjabi, which I knew was a sign that something was a secret and therefore, probably bad news. I still recognised a few words in between mummy's sobs – mother, money, and then a furious invective in Punjabi with 'bloody fed up' stuck in the middle of it. (Swearing in English was considered more genteel than any of the Punjabi expletives which always mentioned the bodily parts of one's mothers or sisters, too taboo to sit on a woman's lips.)

But I was relieved; I did not want a party as I would not have had anyone to invite, anyone interesting anyway. In the village I was stuck in between the various gangs, too young for Anita's consideration, too old to hang around the cloud of toddlers that would settle on me like a rash every time I set foot outside my front door. Going out with the grown-ups was much more exciting, although lately, mama's moods had begun to intrude upon every family outing like a fourth silent guest, whom I saw as an overweight sweaty auntie with lipstick-stained teeth and an unforgiving expression.

In Stanton's, after the film, I could tell that whatever had been upsetting my mother was still going on. She sat silent and moist-eyed, looking down into her cup of weak tea, running her finger round and round the edge of its rim. She was dressed in a dusty pink sari with small silver lotus blossoms on its borders, whilst my father wore his blue serge suit and a tie striped like a humbug. Whenever we went 'out', out meaning wherever English people were, as opposed to Indian friends' houses which in any case was always 'in' as all we would do was sit in each others' lounges, eat each others' food and watch each others' televisions, my parents always wore their smartest clothes.

My mother knew from experience that she would get fewer stares and whispers if she had donned any of the sensible teacher's trouser suits she would wear for school, but for her, looking glamorous in saris and formal Indian suits was part of the English people's education. It was her duty to show them that we could wear discreet gold jewellery, dress in tasteful silks and speak English without an accent. During our very special shopping outings to Birmingham, she would often pass other Indian women in the street and they would stare at each other in that innocent, direct way of two rare species who have just found out they are vaguely related. These other Indian women would inevitably be dressed in embroidered *salwar kameez* suits screaming with green and pinks and yellows (incongruous with thick woolly socks squeezed into open-toed sandals and men's cardies over their vibrating thin silks, evil necessities in this damn cold country), with bright make-up and showy gold-plated jewellery which made them look like ambulating Christmas trees. Mama would acknowledge them with a respectful nod and then turn away and shake her head. 'In the village, they would look beautiful. But not here. There is no sun to light them up. Under clouds, they look like they are dressed for a discotheque.'

But she was quiet now, no light in her face. Papa said, 'Have something to eat. A cake. Have one of those . . . what you like . . . those meringue things.' 'She won't,' I chipped in, scraping my fork into the spongy belly of my rum baba. 'You know what she will say, I can make this cheaper at home.' My mother never ate out, never, always affronted by paying for some over-boiled, under-seasoned dish of slop when she knew she could rustle up a hot, heartwarming meal from a few leftover vegetables and a handful of spices. 'I bet you couldn't make this at home,' I continued. 'How would you make a cake? How would you get it round and get the cream to stand up and the cherry to balance like this? You have to buy some things, you can't do everything you know . . .'

'That's enough!' barked papa. 'Mind your manners now or we're going home!'

My mother shook her head at him and put her hand over mine. I snatched it away and finished my cake in silence.

My father showed he was sorry by buying me a hot dog on the way home. I sat in the back of the Mini and concentrated on licking the tomato sauce off my fingertips whilst singing 'Bobbing Along on the Bottom of the Beautiful Briney Sea' in between slurps. Mummy and papa were talking again, soft whispers, sss sss sss, my mother's bracelets jingled as she seemed to wipe something from her face. This was my birthday and they were leaving me out again. I squeezed my hot dog and suddenly the sausage shot into my mouth and lodged firmly in my windpipe. I was too shocked to move, my fingers curled uselessly into my fists. They were still talking, engrossed, I could see papa's eyes in the mirror, darting from my mother's face to the unfolding road. I thought of writing SAUSAGE STUCK on the windscreen and then realised I could not spell sausage. I was going to die in the back of the car and somewhere inside me, I felt thrilled. It was so dramatic. This was by far the most exciting thing that had ever happened to me.

The car went over a bump in the road and the offending chipolata slipped out of my mouth and into my lap, leaving a red stripe across my yellow satin dress. When my mother looked round, my face was wet with tears and I was panting and pointing the sausage at her like a gun. 'Just look what you've done to your dress! Can't you be careful?' I did not tell her what had happened. This was my near death experience and I would make damn sure I'd use it on her one day.

Mama rarely raised her voice but when she did get angry, she looked like one of the ornamental statues I had seen on my Auntie Shaila's shrine. The goddess she resembled most when in a strop, the one that both terrified and fascinated me, was Kali, a black-faced snarling woman with alarming canines and six waving arms. Every hand contained a bloody weapon and she wore a bracelet of skulls around her powerful naked thighs. And her eyes, sooty O's of disbelief and also amusement that someone insignificant had dared to step on her shadow.

Mama could look like that at me sometimes, when she had caught me tearing carefully sewn ribbons off my dresses, cutting up earthworms in our back yard with her favourite vegetable knife, and most usually, when I was lying. The size of lie never made a difference to her reaction; it could have been one of my harmless fabrications (telling a group of visiting kids in the park that I was a Punjabi princess and owned an elephant called Jason King), or one of my major whoppers – telling my teacher I hadn't completed my homework because of an obscure religious festival involving fire eating . . . She was always furious at the pointlessness of it all; stealing was understandable if distressing, violence anti-social yet sometimes unavoidable, but lying? 'Why do you do this, Meena?' she would wail, wringing her hands unconvincingly, a parody of a Hindi movie mama. 'You are only four/seven/nine . . . Isn't your life exciting enough without all these stories?'

Well naturally the answer was no, but I did not want to make mama feel that this was her fault. Besides, I enjoyed her anger, the snapping eyes, the shrieking voice, the glimpse of monster beneath the mother; it was one of the times I felt we understood each other perfectly.

Of course, no one else outside our small family ever saw this dark side of mama; to everyone else, she was the epitome of grace, dignity and unthreatening charm. She attracted admirers effortlessly, maybe because her soft round face, large limpid eyes and fragile, feminine frame brought out their protective instincts. Tragedy, amusement and bewilderment would wash across her face like sea changes, flowing to suit the story of whoever she was listening to, giving them the illusion that they could control the tides. She was as constant as the moon and just as remote, so the admiration of the villagers was always tempered with a deferential respect, as if in the company of minor royalty.

'Oh Mrs K,' Sandy, the divorcee two doors down, would sigh, running her fingers through her hennaed hair, cocking her head to one side whilst widening her bright blue eyes, giving her the air of a startled parrot, 'you are a duck.'

This was after my mother had lent her butter or given her a

lift down to the shops or taken her son, Mikey, in for some pop and crisps when Sandy missed her bus back from work.

'You're so lovely. You know, I never think of you as, you know, foreign. You're just like one of us.'

My mother would smile and graciously accept this as a compliment. And yet afterwards, in front of the Aunties, she would reduce them to tears of laughter by gently poking fun at the habits of her English friends. It was only much later on that I realised in the thirteen years we lived there, during which every weekend was taken up with visiting Indian families or being invaded by them, only once had any of our neighbours been invited in further than the step of our back door.

The Aunties all had individual names and distinct personalities, but fell into the role of Greek chorus to mama's epic solo role in my life. Although none of them, nor their husbands, the uncles, were actually related to me by blood, Auntie and Uncle were the natural respectful terms given to them, to any Asian person old enough to boss me around. This was an endless source of confusion to our English neighbours, who would watch tight-lipped as mama and papa's friends would phut-phut into the communal dirt yard and heave themselves and their several kids out of their hatchbacks, unfurling shimmering saris and clinking with jewellery, holding up their embroidered hemlines from the dirt floor. As I dutifully kissed every powdered or stubbly cheek with a 'Namaste Auntie, Namaste Uncle' and led them towards our back door, I could see our neighbours shift uncomfortably, contemplating the apparent size of my family and the fact we had somehow managed to bring every one of them over here.

I once tried explaining to our next door neighbour, Mrs Worrall, why my parents seemed to have so many siblings. 'It's just being polite, see,' I said. 'Like saying sir or madam, to call them Auntie and Uncle. 'Cos we have different words for proper relatives, like my dad's younger brother is called a *Chacha*, his elder brother is called a *Thaya*. But me mom's sister is called a *Masee*, and my dad's sister a *Buaji* . . . So you know the difference between pretend ones and real ones.'

It was a litany I knew well, from being sat down in front of photos from India and forced to memorise my parents' many brothers and sisters by name, occupation, and personality quirks. 'This is your *Thaya*,' papa would say. 'Clerk, sweet tooth, married, prone to crying over nothing in particular . . .' as if committing them to memory would make up for not being with them.

Mrs Worrall listened carefully to my monologue and then said, 'Yow must be mad. What do yow want *more* relatives for? Yow want extra, tek a few of mine. Selfish sods, all of em,' and lumbered back into her kitchen.

But I could not imagine existing without them, although I hated the way they continually interfered in my upbringing, inevitably backing up my parents' complaints. 'Look at you, like a "*jamardani!*"' mama would exclaim when I tumbled into the lounge smelling of pig dung after a good rambling session. 'Hah, a sweeper!' the Aunties would mutter in stereophonic sound. 'Spoiled your lovely smock and all . . .' But it would never end there. This was a moral marathon, and they took up the baton with pride, passing it amongst themselves long after mama and papa had run out of breath and were having a cold drink on the sidelines.

'Why behave like a boy all the time? . . . Stand with your legs together . . . Are those nose drippings on your sleeve? . . . Why don't you grow your hair, do you want to be a boy, Meena?' And so in a few short phrases I had progressed from a slightly messy girl into a potential sex change candidate, all done in this jocular caring way, as they showed how much they loved my parents by having a go at me on their behalf. And then suddenly the session would be over and I would be enveloped in crackling silk bosoms and rough clumsy hands, fed morsels off over-loaded plates and shunted away to sit in the Kids' Room, which was wherever the television was, all recriminations forgotten.

I rarely rebelled openly against this communal policing, firstly because it somehow made me feel safe and wanted, and secondly, because I knew how intensely my parents valued these people they so readily renamed as family, faced with the loss of their own blood relations. I understood this because of the snippets of stories I would hear when the grown-ups would sit around on the floor, replete and sleepy, exchanging anecdotes that reinforced their shared histories, confirming that they were not the only ones who were living out this unfolding adventure. 'I got off the train at Paddington,' papa would begin, stifling a satisfied burp, 'sick as a dog from that damn boat, twenty-five pounds in my pocket, and I looked up across the platform and I saw . . .' 'Me!' my Uncle Amman would say proudly. 'Va, you looked like a film star, Kumar-saab, that Jimmy Cagney suit and all.' 'So, naturally, I go up and introduce myself, and . . .' 'And we found out our cousins had gone to the same college! So we went back to my home and that was that!' Uncle Amman would finish with a flourish, as if it were perfectly natural to meet a total stranger and within ten minutes, find him a meal, a home and a list of Situations Vacant.

During this particular story, mama would always listen with a patient, fond look, absorbing the history she had not been around to witness. Papa had left her in Delhi whilst he tried his luck in England, promising to send for her as soon as he had discovered the promised gold beneath the dog shit on the streets. We have the photograph taken on the day of his departure, it looks like a still from one of the old black and white movies I used to watch on Saturday afternoons (after the football and before the wrestling). Papa is leaning out of a steam train window in a brilliant white shirt, an overcoat slung over his waving arm. The smoke rises like cold-morning breath around his face and he is backlit by a rising sun. He is smiling his gap-toothed smile, though his eyes are intense. Mama stands on the platform, the fingers of one hand slightly raised, as if she is afraid to wave him goodbye. She is impossibly young and utterly bereft, her long chiffon *dupatta* is frozen in mid-curl, lifted by the wind. Even in such a small photograph her longing is palpable, the way her fingers say what her mouth cannot.

This was always one of my favourites, this image of my parents as epic, glamorous figures, touched by romantic tragedy. I knew there was plenty more where that came from too; I have heard the excited whispers between the Aunties whenever my parents' marriage was mentioned, odd words from which I concocted a whole scenario – '. . . Saw her riding her bike round college . . . At first sight it was . . . Her parents, of course . . . Long negotiations . . . Such a love story!' I was in a fever of excitement the first time I eavesdropped on these juicy morsels. My parents in a love story! I kept myself awake imagining them chasing each other around old Indian streets (which were basically English streets with a few cows lounging around on the corners), mama on a bicycle laughing loudly as papa tried to grab onto her saddle and haul himself beside her whilst various old people looked out of half-shuttered windows and tutted under their breath.

But when I confronted mama about her courtship adventures, her face closed up like a fan. 'Don't be so silly!' she sniffed. 'We were introduced by an uncle. It all was done through the proper channels. Listening to your elders' conversation again . . .' And that was that. I did not have the courage to ask her why there was only one single photograph of their wedding, when all the other Aunties each had a van load of nuptial albums, which they would whip out at the slightest excuse, and sigh over their eighteen-inch waists and demure demeanours, neither of which would ever return. In my parents' album, this single photograph is given a page all on its own. Mama and papa are seated in the back of a car. Papa wears a turban with strings of pearls attached to the front which obscure his face, except for one guarded eye. Mama is in the foreground, her delicate neck seemingly bent under the weight of a heavily encrusted *dupatta*. She looks up into the camera lens with the expected posture of all new brides, a victim's pose showing passivity and bewilderment, stressing the girl would much rather stay with her family than drive off to a bed with her new husband. But mama is not crying, although her head is bowed, her gaze is direct and calm, and there is a light in her pupils which papa said was the camera flash, but which I recognise as joy.

Individually, the Aunties were a powerful force, my mother was an Auntie to several kids in her own right too, but together they were a formidable mafia whose collective approval was a blessing, and whose communal contempt was a curse wrapped up in sweet sari-shaped packages. I found myself continually surprised at how these smiling women who would serve up their husband's food first with such wifely devotion, could also be capable of such gentle malice.

For example, when I once confronted my mother about the Front Garden dilemma, I unwisely did this in front of the Aunties. Under their benevolent gaze, I tried to explain to her what a social embarrassment it was to have such a bare, ugly display in front of our house and could she not possibly consider buying an ornamental well, make some effort to fit in with the neighbourhood? Mama shot her posse a knowing look and explained that all this garden frippery, gnomes, wells and the like, was an English thing. 'They have to mark out their territory . . .' It was on the tip of her tongue to add '. . . like dogs', but the Aunties recognised their cue and launched into their own collected proverbs on English behaviour. 'They treat their dogs like children, no, better than their children . . .' 'They expect their kids to leave home at sixteen, and if they don't, they ask for rent! Rent from your kids!' 'They don't like bathing, and when they do, they sit in their own dirty water instead of showering . . .' 'The way they wash up, they never rinse the soap off the dishes . . .' 'You know that barmaid-type woman from up the hill has run away again, this time with the driving instructor. He is called Kenneth and wears tank tops . . . It's the children I pity . . .'

At this point I would be sent on a non-existent errand so my mother could finish the latest piece of yard gossip whilst the Aunties would listen wide-eyed, ears flapping, moustaches quivering, glad they had made the perilous journey from the civilised side of Wolverhampton to catch up on the peculiar goings on of the 'gores'. There was much affectionate laughter, but laughter all the same, tinged with something like revenge.

But mama was not laughing today. The sun was hot now and I felt sick with all the sugar I had consumed; every sweet had tasted only of one thing, Guilt. Through the open front door, I could hear my parents having what they called one of their 'discussions', which began as a stilted, almost embarrassed conversation as if two neighbours who barely knew each other had met on the steps of a VD clinic, progressed to a strangely musical monologue by my father, accompanied on percussion by mother banging down various pots and pans, and always ended with a male vocal explosion and a tangible female silence which invaded the house like a sad damp smell. I wondered vaguely if they were arguing about the house.

Whenever my father got sick of our three-up-three-down with its high uneven walls and narrow winding stairs, sick of the damp in the pantry, the outside toilet, the three buses it took to get to work, taking a bath in our bike shed and having to whisper when he wanted to shout, he'd turn to my mother and say, 'You wanted this house, remember that.'

My mother grew up in a small Punjabi village not far from Chandigarh. As she chopped onions for the evening meal or scrubbed the shine back onto a steel pan or watched the clouds of curds form in a bowl of slowly setting homemade yoghurt, any action with a rhythm, she would begin a mantra about her ancestral home. She would chant of a three-storeyed flat-roofed house, blinkered with carved wooden shutters around a dust yard where an old-fashioned pump stood under a mango tree.

She would talk of running with her tin mug to the she-goat tethered to the tree and, holding the mug under its nipples, pulling down a foaming jet of milk straight into her father's morning tea. She spoke of the cobra who lived in the damp grasses beneath the fallen apples in the vast walled orchard, of the peacocks whose keening kept her awake on rainy monsoon nights, of her Muslim neighbours whom they always made a point of visiting on festivals, bringing sweetmeats to emphasise how the land they shared was more important than the religious differences that would soon tear the Punjab in two.

Yet, in England, when all my mother's friends made the transition from relatives' spare rooms and furnished lodgings to homes of their own, they all looked for something 'modern'. 'It's really up-to-date, Daljit,' one of the Aunties would preen as she gave us the grand tour of her first proper home in England. 'Look, extra strong flush system . . . Can opener on the wall . . . Two minutes walk to all local amenities . . .' But my mother knew what she wanted. When she stepped off the bus in Tollington, she did not see the outside lavvy or the apology for a garden or the medieval kitchen, she saw fields and trees, light and space, and a horizon that welcomed the sky which, on a warm night and through squinted eyes, could almost look something like home.

At first I would listen entranced to this litany of love, imagining my mother as I had seen her in those crumpled black and white photographs hoarded in a shiny suitcase on top of her wardrobe. She was skinny and dark then, all eyes and stick insect limbs protruding from a white pyjama suit with paper-sharp creases in the legs. She retained this image, of a country girl lost in the big city, throughout her teens and early twenties, only the costume changed. Here was mama in a school play, a coat hanger for a home-sewn robe, mama winning a race as All Delhi College Champion, running in full length *salwar kameez*, mama as a lecturer, standing in front of a class of bored Delhi teenage girls, looking younger than all of them. On paper her achievements were remarkably impressive – actress, athlete, teacher – incarnations from other lives, trumpeting talents I would never see fully realised. But I still found it comforting that in every face she wore, I still saw the incredulity and bewilderment she so often turned on me. I liked knowing I could still surprise my mother.

But gradually I got bored, and then jealous of this past that excluded me; she had milked goats, stroked peacocks, pulled sugar cane from the earth as a mid-morning snack. She had even seen someone stabbed to death, much later on when the family had moved to Delhi and partition riots stalked the streets like a ravenous animal. A man in a rickshaw, she said. The driver gave him a *bidi*, took one himself and indicated he needed a light. As the customer fumbled in the pockets of his ill-fitting suit (and this memory seemed to upset her greatly, remembering how his shirt sleeves protruded from worn linen elbows), the driver reached into his *dhoti* and brought out a knife which he plunged into his fellow smoker's head, a lit match still in his victim's twitching hand.

That was my favourite, but she would not repeat it more than twice. The last time I had asked her to tell me the Rickshaw Story, she looked at me much as I imagine Damien's mother looked when she gave her smiling baby his first shampoo and found three sixes curled up like commas behind his tiny pink ear. But the story did not fascinate me because of the violence, what obsessed me was this meeting of two worlds, the collision of the epic with the banal. A shared cigarette and a hidden knife, a too-small suit, probably borrowed from a brother who was expecting it back that evening, and a bloody betrayal. I listened to this tale and heard huge boulders moving somewhere, my centre of gravity shifted and I saw the breath of monsters gathering on the horizon. Terrible things could happen, even to ordinary people like me, and they were always unplanned.

I recognised this feeling; it was the same feeling I had when I had almost asphyxiated in the back of our car, that a birthday treat could end with a screaming headline in the *Express and Star*, TOT CHOKES ON UNCOOKED SAUSAGE! BIRTHDAY RUINED, SAY WEEPING PARENTS! Death itself did not frighten me; I had grown up examining the crushed slippery bodies of baby sparrows who had fallen prematurely from their nests to land under our gables, filmy eyes and bloody beaks open with surprise, maybe with their last thought that mama had made flying look so easy. We local kids regularly gathered round the mangled corpses of cats, foxes and badgers left at the side of the road, their fur patterned with tyre marks, their bluey-white entrails trailing the murdering vehicles' exit like accusing fingers. What frightened me was the excitement I felt when death became possible, visible, bared its teeth and raised a knife in Indian moonlight. There was so much more I wanted that I could not name, and brushing mortality, all those hot dog moments, helped me name it. Was this all there was? When would anything dangerous and cruel ever happen to me?

3

A shadow fell over my T-bar sandals and I looked up to see Anita Rutter staring at me through squinted eyes ringed in bright blue eyeshadow. She broke off a twig from our privet hedge and thrust it under my nose, pointing at a part of the branch where the leaves were not their usual straight darts but were rolled up in on themselves, neat and packaged as school dinner sandwiches. 'See them leaves?' She carefully unrolled one of them: it came away slowly like sticky tape, to reveal a sprinkling of tiny black eggs. 'Butterflies' eggs, them is. They roll up the leaf to hide them, see.'

She stripped all the leaves off the twig in one movement and smelled her fingers, before flicking the naked branch at my ankles. It stung but I did not pull my legs back. I knew this was a test.

'What you got?'

I held out my crumpled bag of stolen sweets. She peered inside disdainfully, then snatched the bag off me and began walking away as she ate. I watched her go, confused. I could still hear my parents talking inside, their voices now calmer, conciliatory. Anita stopped momentarily, shouting over her shoulder, 'Yow coming then?'

It was the first day of the long summer holidays and I had six whole weeks which I could waste or taste. So I got up and followed her without a word.

I was happy to follow her a respectable few paces behind, knowing that I was privileged to be in her company. Anita was the undisputed 'cock' of our yard, maybe that should have been hen, but her foghorn voice, foul mouth, and proficiency at lassoing victims with her frayed skipping rope indicated she was carrying enough testosterone around to earn the title. She ruled over all the kids in the yard with a mixture of pre-pubescent feminine wiles, pouting, sulking, clumsy cack-handed flirting and unsettling mood swings which would often end in minor violence. She had the face of a pissed-off cherub, huge green eyes, blonde hair, a curling mouth with slightly too many teeth and a brown birthmark under one eye which when she was angry, which was often, seemed to throb and glow like a lump of Superman's kryptonite.

Although she always had a posse of 'littl'uns' tagging after her, all saggy socks and scabby elbows, her constant cohorts were Fat Sally, a shy lump of a girl from one of the posh semis, and Sherrie, the farmer's daughter, lanky and gamine, who, it was rumoured, had her own pony. I would watch them strolling round the yard, arms linked, feet dragging along in their mothers' old slingbacks, and physically ache to be with them. But they were much older – 'Comp wenches' – and I never expected them to even notice me. Until today.

We stood on the corner of the crossroads a moment whilst Anita rummaged around for another sweet, tossing a discarded wrapper to the floor. I knew my mother would be picking that up later when she did her early evening sweep of the front garden path and pavement. We walked slowly, me half a yard behind, past my front door and along one side of the triangle of houses of which my house was the apex, past the long dark alleyways which led into our communal dirt yard at the back of the cottages.

I hesitated as we passed the first 'entry' as we called them; they always spooked me, these endless echoing corridors, smelling of mildew whose sides always seemed to weep and covered you with shiny scales and bullet black slugs the size of a fingernail if you bumped against them, running from daylight through night and then back into the safety of the yard. Anita suddenly veered off and turned down the entry next to Mr Christmas' house, still chomping away.

Mr Christmas always dressed like it was midwinter; it had
to be at least a hundred degrees before you'd see him without
his muffler and V-shaped cardigan, standing outside his back
gate scattering old cake crumbs for the starlings, his wrinkles
creasing into kind smiles as they pecked round his carpet
slippers. I knew Mrs Christmas was 'poorly', the yard had
talked of nothing else when the news first came out some
months ago.

I was not sure what was wrong with her exactly, but it must
have been serious, the way the women huddled together over
their washing lines, talking in whispers accompanied by much
pointing to a general area around their laps, only referred to as
'down there . . .' I tried to listen in but it was as if there was an
invisible volume knob which someone turned up and down at
certain points in the conversation. 'Course, they took her in
and opened her up but you know, once they got to her, you
know . . .' Their voices would disappear, their lips would still
be moving but only their hands talked, making strange
circular shapes and cutting motions, which caused half the
women to shake their heads and the others to cross their legs
and wince in sympathy. Of course I asked my mum, the
oracle, and she told me Mrs Christmas had got something
called cancer, yes, she would probably die and no, it was
certainly not infectious, poor lady.

Standing at the mouth of the entry, I suddenly realised that
I had not seen Mrs Christmas for a long time. The last
occasion had been the Spring Fayre, when Uncle Alan, the
youth leader from the Methodist church, had sent us hapless
kids round to knock on everyone's door in the yard and ask
them if they had 'anything spare' for the bring-and-buy stall.
None of our neighbours liked giving anything away, materi-
ally or otherwise, and by the time I had reached the
Christmas' house I remember feeling completely de-
moralised. After two hours of knocking and being polite, all I
had had to show for my efforts was a bunch of dog-eared back

issues of the *People's Friend*, two tins of sliced pineapples, a toilet brush cover in the shape of a crinoline-clad lady, whose expression was surprisingly cheerful considering she had a lav brush up her arse, and a scratched LP entitled 'Golden Memories; Rock'N'Roll Love Songs with the Hammond Singers'. (And even that had been difficult to prise away from Sandy, until she had remembered it had belonged to her 'ex-bastard', as she called him, and flung it at me with a flourish.)

Worse still were the women's expressions when they had opened up their back gates expecting to see Uncle Alan and found me instead. Uncle Alan was the nearest thing we had to a sex symbol in a ten-mile radius. He seemed ancient, at least twenty-eight, but he did have chestnut brown curly hair, a huge smile, an obscene amount of energy and a huge dimple right in the centre of his chin which looked like someone had got a pencil, placed it on his skin and slowly twirled it round and round on the spot. (I knew this because I had spent many a happy hour creating dimples in my arms using this very method.) We kids always braced ourselves if we saw him bounding across the yard from the vicar's house, eager and slobbery as a Labrador, because we knew he'd be looking for volunteers for another of his good-egg schemes. 'Well lit-tl'uns!' he'd gasp, rubbing his hands together in what he thought was a matey, streetwise kind of manner. 'How about we get together and do something about this litter, eh?' And the next thing you know, you'd be wearing one of his canvas aprons with 'Tollington Methodist Tinies' plastered all over it and picking up fag butts from underneath parked cars.

But we never said no; though we would rather die than admit it, we actually enjoyed trailing after him, gathering blackberries for the 'Jam In', washing down the swings in the adjoining park with Fairy Liquid, even sitting in on his Youth Chats every Sunday afternoon, in which we'd have two minutes of talk vaguely connected to Jesus and then get on with making up plays or drawing pictures or playing 'Tick You're It' in and around the pews. Frankly, there was nothing else to do, as many of us were not privy to the big boys' leisure activities which were mainly cat torturing or peeing competitions behind the pigsties, and he knew it.

'Oh I could give him one,' Sandy had once said to Anita's mother, Deirdre, as they watched Uncle Alan leap across the yard. 'Don't he wear nice shoes? You can always tell a bloke by his shoes.'

'Gerrof you dirty cow,' said Deirdre. 'He's a vicar or summat. Yow wouldn't get to touch him with a bargepole.'

'He could touch me with his bloody pole anyday,' said Sandy, dreamily, before both of them collapsed into screeching guffaws.

I had pretended not to hear this as I trailed after him with an armful of leaflets, but had mentally stored it away. At least I now knew what a sex symbol was supposed to look like, and could understand why I was considered a poor second choice when it came to donating bric-a-brac.

So by the time Mrs Christmas had reached her back gate, wheezing her way from her yard door, her slippers slapping the cobbles, I did not expect much of a booty. But she had swung the gate back and all I could see was her shock of white hair peeking over a huge armful of clothes she held in her hands.

'Meena chick, I've been expecting you,' she said. 'Where do you want this lot?'

I had helped her pile the clothes into my wooden pull-along, parked at her gate (it had been an old play trolley of mine which used to be filled with alphabet building blocks. Perfect, my mother said archly, for door-to-door begging.) Mrs Christmas had straightened up carefully and I examined her face, rosy pink with delicate veins running from her huge nose like tributaries, surprisingly sparkling and deep blue eyes with an expression that made her look like she was always about to burst into laughter, or tears. She had looked healthy enough to me and I felt relieved.

'You can have all this lot. I shan't be needing it, chick. Not where I'm going.'

I had knelt down and rifled through the cart; there must have been at least a dozen dresses, all one-piece tailored frocks with baby doll collars, darted sharply at the waist, many of them with belts and full pleated skirts. But the fabrics, I could not take my eyes off them, all delicate flowers, roses and bluebells and buttercups set against cream silk or beige sheeny muslin, ivy leaves snaking around collars and cuffs, clover and mayblossom intertwined with delicate green stalks tumbling along pleats like a waterfall. It was as if a meadow had landed in my lap.

They were so different to the clothes my mother wore, none of these English drawing room colours, she was all open-heart cerises and burnt vivid oranges, colours that made your pupils dilate and were deep enough to enter your belly and sit there like the aftertaste of a good meal. No flowers, none that I could name, but dancing elephants, strutting peacocks and long-necked birds who looked as if they were kissing their own backs, shades and cloth which spoke of bare feet on dust, roadside smokey *dhabas*, honking taxi horns and heavy sudden rain beating a *bhangra* on deep green leaves. But when I looked at Mrs Christmas' frocks, I thought of tea by an open fire with an autumn wind howling outside, horses' hooves, hats and gloves, toast, wartime brides with cupid bow mouths laughing and waving their hankies to departing soldiers, like I'd seen on that telly programme, *All Our Yesterdays*. And then I had glanced at Mrs Christmas' saggy belly straining at her pinafore, the belly which even then had been growing something other than the child she said she had always wanted but never had, and I had wondered how she had looked when she had worn all these frocks and whether I would have recognised her.

Mrs Christmas had rummaged in the front pocket of her pinny and brought out a furry boiled sweet which she popped wordlessly into my open mouth. It tasted sooty and warm. Then she suddenly leaned forward and kissed me. She did not have her teeth in and I felt as if she was hoovering the side of my cheek. 'You've always been a smashing chick, you have.'

My face felt damp and I wanted to wipe it but realised that would be rude, and at the same time, suddenly felt desperately, bitterly sad. I managed to mumble 'Thank you, Mrs Christmas,' through the sweet and stumbled out of the yard, tugging my now heavy cart behind me. I had not wanted to look back but I had to, and she was still watching me across the yard. She had waved her massive red hand and I had not seen her since.

Before I could ask out aloud if Anita had seen sight or sound of Mrs Christmas lately, Anita chucked the packet of sweets, still half full, to the ground and began running down the entry, whooping like an ambulance siren. The echo was amazing, deep and raspy and rumbling like a dinosaur's cough, it bounced off the high entry walls and made me shudder. She stopped, panting for breath at the far end of the passage, a stick silhouette, seemingly miles away. 'Yow do it. Goo on then.'

I took a deep gulp of air and began running, gathering speed, opened my lungs and bellowed, no pattern or tune, just pure sound swooping up and down the scale, so much of it I felt it was pouring out of my nose and ears and eyes. The echo picked me up and dragged me along the slimy walls, the harder I shouted the faster I moved, it was all the screams I had been saving up as long as I could remember, and I reached sunlight and Anita at the other end where we both laughed our heads off.

Suddenly a gate scraped open beside us and Mr Christmas emerged in his vest and braces, his face blue with fury. His hair stood on end, straight up like he'd put his finger in a socket, and there was drool gathering on one side of his mouth. 'Yow little heathens! What yow think yow'm playing at?' he hissed. 'I got a sick woman inside. Yow think she wants to hear yow lot honking around like a lot of animals?' He was pointing a shaky finger at his sitting room window, the one that overlooked the yard. Through it, just visible, was the top of Mrs Christmas' snowy head. It seemed to be propped at an awkward angle, it looked like she was watching the tiny black and white telly sitting on top of the sideboard.

I felt mortified, more for not going to visit Mrs Christmas than for shouting down the entry, forgetting that its walls were also the walls of half of the Christmas' home. 'I shall tell your mothers on you, that I shall,' Mr Christmas continued. My belly contracted. That wasn't good news, not today, when I'd already been exposed as a petty thief and a liar. My mother let me get away with mouthy behaviour and general mischief around my Aunties, she never had to worry about policing me because guaranteed, one of them would raise a fat hand jingling with bangles and cuff me into place, no questions asked. Scolding each other's kids was expected, a sign of affection almost, that you cared enough about them to administer a pinch or nudge now and then. But to be told off by a white person, especially a neighbour, that was not just misbehaviour, that was letting down the whole Indian nation. It was continually drummed into me, 'Don't give them a chance to say we're worse than they already think we are. You prove you are better. Always.'

'Don't tell, Mr Christmas,' I pleaded pathetically, only just realising with shock that he had not got his V-neck on today. 'We're really sorry, aren't we Anita?'

Anita had not moved or spoken. She was twirling her privet switch round and round in the dirt, her eyes unblinking and fixed. She sighed and said in a flat, bored voice, 'Tell me mom. I don't care.'

I gasped. This was treason. Why hadn't I said that?

'Right. I will then, I'll go round right now . . . No, not now, Connie needs her medicine first, but after that . . .'

Anita was already strolling away, dragging her feet deliberately, a wiggle in her thin hips. 'Goo on then. I dare ya. Soft old sod.'

45

The sky did not crack. It was still clear, blue, unbroken. Anita Rutter, the cock of the yard, had not only answered back a grown-up but sworn at him and invited him to tell the whole thing to her own mother. Mr Christmas' shoulders sagged slightly. He turned his gaze to me, a hard look, unforgiving. 'Nice friends yow've got now, eh chick?' He shuffled back into his yard and slammed the gate. A moment later I heard the TV volume go up to full blast.

Anita was now outside her own back gate. Her little sister, Tracey, was sitting on the stoop, looking up at her with huge red-rimmed eyes, a plastic toy basket lay on its side next to her feet, spilling out a few scrawny, unripe blackberries. If Anita was a Rottweiler, Tracey had been first in the whippet line up in heaven. She was a thin, sickly child, with the same cowering, pleading look you'd get in the eyes of the stray mutts who hung round the yard for scraps, and soon fled when they discovered they would be used for target practice in the big boys' spitting contests. Whereas Anita was blonde and pale, Tracey was dark and pinched, the silent trotting shadow whimpering at her big sister's heels, swotted and slapped away as casually as an insect. Her dress hung off her, obviously one of Anita's hand-me-downs, a faded pink frilly number which on Anita must have looked cheerful, flirty, and on gangly, anxious Tracey gave her the air of a drag queen with a migraine. 'What'm yow dooing sitting out here, our Trace?'

Anita poked Tracey with her switch as she talked. Tracey edged further away along the stoop and wiped her nose with the back of her purple-stained hand. 'Mom's not here,' she said, resignedly. 'I went blackberrying with Karl and Kevin and when I came back, she wasn't here.'

'Probably gone up the shops, love,' Hairy Neddy called over from his car.

Hairy Neddy was the yard's only bachelor and, as Deirdre

put it, just our sodding luck, the only available man and we get a yeti. When Hairy Neddy first arrived he looked like a walking furball, one of those amorphous bushy masses that the yard cats would occasionally cough up when the weather changed. As legend has it, the day he moved in he roared into the yard in his Robin Reliant, which at that time had NED DEMPSTER AND HIS ROCKIN' ROBINS painted on one side, and on the other, WEDDINGS, PARTIES, THE HOTTEST RIDE THIS SIDE OF WOLVERHAMPTON. Except he'd miscalculated how long Wolverhampton was going to be and the TON was small and wobbly, squashed hurriedly against the side of the windscreen. Everyone came out to see who their new neighbour was going to be and was confronted by this vision of decadence, a plump, piggy-eyed man in tattered jeans coughing through the dust he'd churned up: at least they could hear the cough but couldn't quite make out where his beard ended and his mouth began, as his flowing locks and facial undergrowth seemed to be one huge rug interrupted slightly by his eyes and nose.

Since then of course, The Beatles had come into 'vow-gew' as he used to say, and Neddy's facial fuzz had disappeared, revealing underneath a surprisingly pleasant, blokey kind of face topped with a sort of bouffant hairdo that respectably skimmed the back of his collar. But inevitably the name Hairy Neddy stuck; first impressions were the ones that counted in Tollington, and he even adopted it into his stage act when he formed yet another band with which to set the West Midlands a-rocking. The Robin Reliant now sported the slogan HAIRY NEDDY AND HIS COOL CUCUMBERS, which of course gave the bored women in the yard lots of unintentional pleasure. 'Come here our Ned, I could do with a good cucumbering today!' Or 'It's hot today, Ned, make sure yowr cucumber don't droop!' or usually, just in passing, 'Goo on, get your cucumber out, Ned, I could do with a laff.'

We only ever saw the other members of Hairy Neddy's band, the Cucumbers themselves, on one occasion when the Robin

Reliant had overheated and was lying in various stages of disembowelment in the yard. (I suppose Neddy was the one who ferried everyone around, but he'd tried to take the big hill on the way to Cannock at fifty miles per hour in second gear with all the equipment in the back and the 'poor old bint' had just died on him, mid-splutter.) On that day (it must have been last summer because I remember my hands were sticky from the Zoom lolly I'd just ingested in one gulp), a purple Ford Cortina entered the yard on two wheels and came to a halt beside Hairy Neddy's back gate. I could make out two men in the front seats: they were laughing, each had an arm casually hanging out of the open window beside them, two male arms, hairy with surprisingly long, nimble fingers, and as they laughed, clouds of cigarette smoke billowed from their mouths.

The man driving sounded his horn: it played a tune I vaguely recognised, a rumpty tumpty, jolly sort of marching sound which made Mrs Lowbridge's cat yowl and scarper into the innards of Hairy Neddy's autopsied car and inevitably set the back gates a-swinging as various yard inhabitants poked their heads round to see who was bringing their bloody noise into their space. Hairy Neddy emerged a moment later, staggering under the weight of his Bontempi organ. He was wearing a smart blue jacket with a tiny string of a tie, ironed trousers which were supposed to go with the jacket but were obviously older and therefore a few shades lighter, and weird shoes, as long as clown's shoes, but which ended in a kind of point. The two Cucumbers got out of the car and made whistling and 'Wor!' noises as Hairy Neddy did a mock pirouette.

'It's pure Troggs, Ned,' said Cucumber one, a tall skinny, ginger man who did not seem to have any eyelashes.

'Aar,' said Cucumber two, a small fat man, blond and ruddy, his belly straining at his buttoned-up jacket.

'Yow got to look the part, in't ya? The wenches wet their knickers over a bloke in a suit, aar? Yow got to dress up before yow even get a feel of their tits nowadays . . .'

Hairy Neddy shushed him, indicating the crowd of kids, including me, who were now standing round them in a semicircle, waiting for something to happen. 'Giz a hand with this, lads,' said Hairy Neddy, straining and puffing as they pulled the Bontempi between them to the boot of the car. Ginger opened it up with his keys and the three of them spent at least five minutes trying to wedge the keyboard into what looked like an impossibly tiny space.

'Wharrabout the back, Keith?' grunted Hairy Neddy.

Keith, blondie, shook his head, the veins standing out in his temples as he turned redder, shifting the weight around fruitlessly. 'Got me Fender back there, and Wayne's drumkit. Took us three hours to unscrew that, and all.'

Sandy looked up from hanging her lacy bras out on her line and shouted, 'Ey Ned, yow shouldn't have such a big organ, should yow?'

Suddenly, Kev lost his grip and the Bontempi slipped lower, Hairy Neddy grabbed at it and the yard was suddenly filled with the pulsing electronic rhythm of a bossa nova. All of us kids gasped a moment and instinctively jumped back, then a few of the older lads started laughing. Sam Lowbridge, the wild boy of the yard (he'd already been up for shoplifting and nicking bikes), started doing a mock sexy dance, thrusting his hips and making boob shapes with his hands round his chest and pretty soon, all of us were gyrating around to the fabulous sound of Bontempi. Little did I know this was the nearest I'd get to a disco for the next ten years.

Hairy Neddy left the sound on whilst they tried various kamasutra positions for his organ. Whilst they pulled, pushed and swore, we jumped and jiggled to what seemed like a hundred different beats, the waltz, the samba, the jazz riff, the African drums, until we and the Cucumbers were all out of breath and still nowhere near getting to their gig. 'We'll have to drive with the boot open. We ain't got no choice, lads.'

'Got some rope then?'

Hairy Neddy shook his head sorrowfully and sunk to the dirt floor.

'Bugger. I ain't missed a gig in ten years, not even that time I had that infection and I was coughing up stones . . .' He looked as if he was going to weep. All us kids fell silent. It wasn't fair, I thought, a man with so much talent, so much to offer, who lived for giving people the kind of pleasure and release he'd just given us, and he couldn't get to his party because of a stupid bit of rope.

'Hee-y'ar, try these.' Sandy, the divorcee, was standing over Hairy Neddy smiling wickedly. She was dangling a pile of old stockings over his head. 'They're extra long, I've got a thirty-four inch leg, see,' she said silkily.

Hairy Neddy suppressed a gulp and wordlessly took the stockings off Sandy, hurrying to the boot. He and the other two men began lashing the Bontempi into the open boot, securing nylon to metal, tucking it in carefully like a child at bedtime. Halfway through, Hairy Neddy looked up at Sandy who was still standing near his gate with a strange expression on her face, amusement maybe, tender certainly, almost motherly. 'Yow er . . . yow sure yow don't need these, Sandy love?' he stammered.

Sandy shook her head and continued smiling. In less than five minutes, the Bontempi was in and secure, Hairy Neddy clambered into the back, squeezing himself between large black instrument cases, and with a sound of the horn, which I later found out was a tune called 'Colonel Bogey', the purple Ford Cortina chugged carefully out of the yard. We all waved Hairy Neddy off, the boys giving him thumbs up signs as if he were off on a mission. But he didn't see us. Hairy Neddy's face was squashed up against the back windscreen and he was staring helplessly at Sandy.

Since that incident, we had all noticed that Hairy Neddy had sort of avoided Sandy, as much as you could when you lived next door to each other and could hear each other's toilets flushing in your respective backyards. Sandy's response to these tactics had been somewhat confusing: for a few brief weeks, she had taken to wearing make-up and a frilly peach housecoat when hanging out her wash, instead of the grey moulty slippers and towelling dressing gown she usually threw on for such brief public appearances.

One morning, I had caught her doing something very peculiar; I watched her pour a nearly full bottle of milk into her outside drain, and then run and drag Mikey out of her kitchen. He looked moon-faced and sullen and was still clad in his Captain Scarlet pyjamas, and Sandy thrust the empty bottle into his hands. 'Now goo on, ask Ned for a pinta. Say we've run out . . .' Then she looked up and visibly jumped when she saw me hovering in the Yard. 'Oh hello Meena chick . . . yow'm up bloody early . . . go on then Mikey . . .' she muttered, scurrying backwards and shutting the gate in my face.

Whilst this strange one-sided tango was going on, the Yard gossip was that Sandy and Hairy Neddy might be getting married, although it seemed to me that no one had told Hairy Neddy about this. Sandy was making monumental efforts to impress him which we all enjoyed from a distance. Not only did her dressing gowns become shorter and fluffier by degrees, her hair changed colour every few days; she moved from simmering redhead through to mahogany brown whilst her eyebrows got progressively thinner and more arched until they reached an expression of extreme alarm. Maybe this was because Hairy Neddy did not seem to notice her at all; his response was to lock his back gate whenever he was in, and to spend the rest of his time with his head stuck inside the innards of his apparently permanently sick car. And then, quite suddenly one day, Sandy gave up. The next morning, she was back in the towelling dressing gown, acting as if nothing had happened.

There were sniggers and whispers after this of course, but if Sandy did hear them, she never showed that she cared. No one in the Yard, particularly the women, ever showed that they were upset or hurt. There was once a dreadful fight between Karl and Kevin's mum and Mrs Keithley, in which Mrs K (the fecund divorcee), had told the twins' mum that her boys were no better 'than sodding bloody heathens! What kind of little bastards leave turds on people's back stoops, eh?' It began venomously and ended with both women being held back by some passing menfolk whilst they exchanged wild swinging blows and spat out words I did not understand but knew somehow I should not repeat at home when I recounted the incident. And yet, whenever the two women met, which was practically every day in such a small circular space, their instinctive reaction was to grow three feet in height, snarl and send death rays to each other through narrowed eyes.

I knew this was the expected Tollington stance, attack being the best form of defence, and never ever show that you might be in pain. That would only invite more violence because pity was for wimps and wimps could not survive round here. This made me very concerned for my mother, who I would regularly find in front of the television news with tears streaming down her face. 'Those poor children . . .' she would sniffle, or 'Those poor miners . . . those poor soldiers . . . those poor old people . . .'

Papa seemed to enjoy these sentimental outbursts of hers and would smile fondly at his sobbing spouse, glad that he was married to someone with enough heart for the rest of the world.

But it irritated the hell out of me. I had to live amongst my neighbours' kids, who were harder, tougher versions of their parents, and I needed back-up. I had already been in quite a few 'scraps', where I felt obliged to launch in with fists and kicks to show I was not one of the victims that would be chosen every so often by the bigger lads for their amusement. And whilst I hated the physical pain and the nervous nausea of these ritual 'barneys', what I hated even more was having to hide my bruises and tears from my mother. I knew I would end up with her sobbing on my shoulder, crying on my behalf, whereas what I longed for her to do was rush into the yard in curlers and a pinny and beat the crap out of my tormentors. But mama wasn't a Yard Mama, so I learned early on there were some things I would have to do for myself.

It comforted me slightly when I realised that Tracey the whippet was a much bigger coward than me. She cowered in front of her sister, Anita, trying to control her quivering bottom lip. 'But she's supposed to be here! Where's me mum? I'm hungry . . .'

'Shut yer face, our Trace,' snapped Anita, who was concentrating on aiming her switch right at Hairy Neddy's backside.

He was still bent over his open bonnet, the gap between the end of his T-shirt and the beginning of his jeans revealing an expanse of very tempting builder's bum. 'Yow can come in for a piece at our house, if yow'm hungry, chick,' called Hairy Neddy, a 'piece' being a peculiar Tollington word for sandwich which my mother had banned me from saying in the house. 'Just because the English can't speak English them-selves, does not mean you have to talk like an urchin. You take the best from their culture, not the worst. You'll be swearing and urinating in telephone boxes next, like that Lowbridge boy . . .'

But mama's voice did not have its usual resonance today, this tinnitus of conscience forever buzzing in my ears the minute I even thought about doing anything she might disapprove of. Because today, everything was fuzzy and unformed except for Anita, what she looked like, what she did, the way she made me feel, taller and sharper and ready to try anything. She winked at me and edged her switch nearer and nearer to Hairy Neddy's bum. She aimed the point of it right at his cavernous crack and raised her eyebrows, daring me to dare her. I was about to nod my head when a screaming siren sounded from the other end of the yard.

'Anita Rutter! Yow put that down now before I give yow a bloody hiding!'

Anita's mum, Deirdre, tottered into the yard on her white stilettos, her pointy boobs doing a jive under a very tight white polo neck sweater. She looked like she had been running; beads of sweat stood out on her upper lip and brow, her mascara had run slightly and she tugged at her lacquered helmet of hair with short fat fingers glinting with rings. Tracey threw herself at Deirdre's legs but she pushed her off, irritated, pausing only to cuff Anita on the side of the head. Anita laughed.

'Have these two bin driving you barmy, Ned?' she asked him.

Hairy Neddy shook his head, not looking up. 'Yow'm alright, love,' he said from under the bonnet.

'Where you bin?' whined Tracey, who started to gather up her spilled blackberries from the dirt.

'Shopping.'

'What you got us?' asked Anita.

Deirdre glanced at her empty hands and patted her hair again. 'Window shopping. You want fishfingers for tea?'

'Yeah!' yelled Tracey, happy again, all those hours of anguish and abandonment instantly forgotten.

I was happy, too. I loved fishfingers, we hardly ever had them at home, mum somehow found it quicker to make a fresh vegetable *sabzi* than fling something from a packet into a frying pan. And of course I would be invited in for tea because that's what all the yard mums did, if you'd been playing with their offspring and you happened to be nearby when the call to the table came.

Of course, you didn't always strike it lucky; once I'd been at Kevin and Karl, the mad twins' house, and their mum had put what looked like an ordinary white bread sandwich in front of me. I took a huge bite and promptly threw up all over her fortunately wipe-clean vinyl tablecloth.

'What's up with yow?' asked Karl. 'Don't yow like lard sandwiches?'

When I told my mother what I'd eaten, she made me drink

a cup of warm milk and ordered me to sit on the toilet for fifteen minutes, all the time muttering, '*Bakwas lok!*', which roughly translated means 'Bloody weird people . . .'

But actually, the food you ate was less important than being asked, the chance to sit in someone else's house and feel grown up and special, knowing you weren't just playing together, you were now officially socialising.

Deirdre unlocked the back gate of her house and handed the bunch of keys to Tracey who ran up to the back door and fumbled for the lock. Anita stood behind Deirdre and smiled at me, so I took a step forward. Deirdre looked at me for the first time. I had forgotten how scary the bottom half of her face was. The top bit was like everyone else's mum's face, soft eyes, enquiring nose, eyebrows asking a million questions. But the mouth was not right, not at all; those huge bee-stung lips always on the edge of a sneer and grandma, those big teeth, far too many and far too sharp, which gave what could have been a beautiful face an expression of dark, knowing hunger. Deirdre looked me up and down as if making a decision, then turned on her heel and tip-tapped into her yard. Anita let her pass, pressing her body away from her mother to avoid contact, then whispered, 'See you tomorrow' before closing the gate in my face.

I wandered slowly back through the yard towards my house, wondering what I had done wrong. The sun was just beginning its slow lazy descent and I could see the glittering sliver of a fingernail moon hanging over the rooftops near my house. I passed Sam Lowbridge's back gate. There was an accusing space where his moped usually stood, a flattened oval of pressed dank earth.

Sam Lowbridge was generally considered the Yard's Bad Boy. He'd managed to acquire a criminal record by the age of sixteen and supplemented it with wearing black leather and an obligatory sneer. Most of the littl'uns were scared of him and gave him a wide berth when he came out for one of his wheelie sessions in the adjoining park, but for some reason, he'd always been polite, even kind, to me. His mother, Glenys, had the distinction of being our oldest single parent (followed by Sandy, our most desperate, and Mrs Keithley, the youngest and most fertile with three children under the age of eight). None of us had ever seen Sam's father, whoever he was he never visited, but the general opinion was good riddance to bad rubbish, 'cos he must have been full of bad seed to spawn a sprog like Sam.

Glenys was standing on her stoop, wringing her hands, with her characteristic expression of someone who has sniffed impending doom and knows no one is going to believe her. I'd seen a similar *moue* on the face of the mad soothsayer in Frankie Howerd's *Up Pompeii* on the telly. The soothsayer was depicted as an old wild-eyed woman dressed in rags who began every entrance with the litany, 'Woe! Woe! And thrice Woe!' This never ceased to crease me up because *Wo Wo* was our family Punjabi euphemism for shit, 'Do you want to do a *Wo Wo*?' and 'Wipe properly, get all the *Wo Wo* off . . .' The first time I'd heard the soothsayer's lament I'd said, 'I think she must have constipation!' which made my papa laugh proudly and my mother hide her smile under an expression of distaste. When I repeated the joke in the playground the next day, I realised it lost a lot in translation and vowed I would swot up on a few English jokes before I undertook challenging Vernon Cartwright again for the title of school wit.

Glenys wrung her hands a bit more and began chewing the ends of her bottle blonde hair, a sad dishrag of a haircut, but I guessed she'd long given up trying. I'd always assumed she was about fifty, in her shapeless sweaters and crimplene trousers with the sewn-in crease on each leg. But mama informed me, rather proudly I thought, that Mrs Lowbridge was not even forty, and that smoking and bad luck had chiselled all those weary dragging lines around her eyes and mouth. 'That's why you must always count your blessings, beti, and never think negative thoughts. If your mind is depressed, your body will soon follow. Me, I don't even dye my hair.' I went around for days after that, smiling so much that my cheeks ached and Mrs Worrall next door asked if I'd got wind. I was terrified that my body would betray my mind and all the anger and yearning and violent mood swings that plagued me would declare themselves in a rash of facial hives or a limb dropping off in a public place.

'Meena chick, have yow seen our Sam today?'

'No, Mrs Lowbridge,' I answered. 'Maybe he's gone up the shops,' I added helpfully.

'He shouldn't be up the bloody shops, he should be here. He knows I'm gooing up bingo tonight . . .' She sighed and chewed a bit more hair. 'Ey, yow'm on the corner, int ya? If yow see him gooing past, give us a knock will ya, chick?' She trudged back inside her yard and propelled by the growling waves of hunger cascading around my stomach, I ran home.

Mama was rummaging about in what we called the Bike Shed, one of two small outhouses at the end of our backyard, the other outhouse being our toilet. We'd never had a bike between us, unless you counted my three-wheeler tricycle which was one of a number of play items discarded amongst the old newspapers, gardening tools, and bulk-bought tins of tomatoes and Cresta fizzy drinks. Of course, this shed should have really been called the bathroom, because it was where we filled an old yellow plastic tub with pans of hot water from the kitchen and had a hurried scrub before frostbite set in, but my mother would have cut out her tongue rather than give it its real, shameful name.

'Found it, Mrs Worrall!' she shouted from inside the shed. Mrs Worrall, with whom we shared adjoining, undivided backyards, stood in her uniform of flowery dress and pinny on her step. She had a face like a friendly potato with a sparse tuft of grey hair on top, and round John Lennon glasses, way before they became fashionable, obviously. She moved like she was underwater, slow, deliberate yet curiously graceful steps, and frightened most of the neighbours off with her rasping voice and deadpan, unimpressed face. She did not smile often, and when she did you wished she hadn't bothered as she revealed tombstone teeth stained bright yellow with nicotine. But she loved me, I knew it; she'd only have to hear my voice and she'd lumber out into the yard to catch me, often not speaking, but would just nod, satisfied I was alive and functioning, her eyes impassive behind her thick lenses.

She would listen, apparently enthralled, to my mother's occasional reports on my progress at school, take my homework books carefully in her huge slabs of hands and turn the pages slowly, nodding wisely at the cack-handed drawings and uneven writing. Every evening, when she came to pick up our copy of the *Express and Star* once my papa had finished reading it (an arrangement devised by my mother, 'Why should the poor lady have to spend her pension when she can read ours?'), she'd always check up on me, what I was doing, whether I was in my pyjamas yet, whether I was mentally and physically prepared to retire for the night. At least, that's what I read in her eyes, for she never spoke. Just that quick glance up and down, a slight incline of the head, a satisfied exhalation.

I wondered if she was like Mrs Christmas, childless, and maybe that was why she was so protective of me. But mama told me, with a snort of disgust, that she had three grown-up sons and a few grandchildren also. 'But I've never seen them! Do they live far away?' I persisted.

'Oh yes, very far. Wolverhampton!' she quipped back.

It had seemed quite a long way to me when we had driven there for my birthday treat, but I guessed by my mother's flaring nostrils and exaggerated eyebrow movements that she was being ironic, the way Indians are ironic, signposting the joke with a map and compass to the punchline.

'But why don't they come and see her then?'

My mother sighed and ruffled my hair. 'I will never understand this about the English, all this puffing up about being civilised with their cucumber sandwiches and cradle of democracy big talk, and then they turn round and kick their elders in the backside, all this It's My Life, I Want My Space stupidness, You Can't Tell Me What To Do cheekiness, I Have To Go To Bingo selfishness and You Kids Eat Crisps Instead Of Hot Food nonsense. What is this My Life business, anyway? We all have obligations, no one is born on their own, are they?'

She was into one of her Capital Letter speeches, the subtext of which was listen, learn and don't you dare do any of this when you grow up, missy. I quite enjoyed them. They made me feel special, as if our destiny, our legacy, was a much more interesting journey than the apparent dead ends facing our neighbours. I just wished whatever my destiny was would hurry up and introduce itself to me so I could take it by its jewelled hand and fly.

She paused for oxygen. 'I mean, Mrs Worrall is their mother, the woman who gave them life. And she on her own with Mr Worrall, too. I tell you, if my mother was so close, I would walk in my bare feet to see her every day. Every day.'

She turned away then, not trusting herself to say anything more. There was still something else I wanted to ask but I knew it would have to wait. I had grown up with Mrs Worrall, I had seen her every day of my life, but I had never seen or heard Mr Worrall. Ever.

My mother emerged from the shed holding aloft an old dusty glass vase which she blew on, and then scuffed with the sleeve of her shirt before handing it to Mrs Worrall who took it with a pleased grunt. 'Please, Mrs Worrall, have it. We never use it.'

Mrs Worrall nodded again and cleared her throat. 'He knocked mine over. I was in the way, in front of the telly. *Crossroads*. He likes that Amy Turtle. So he got a bit upset, see.'

Mama nodded sympathetically. 'How is he nowadays?'

Mrs Worrall shrugged, she did not need to say, same as always, and went back inside her kitchen.

'Mum, I'm starved, I am,' I wheedled. 'Give me something now.'

She busied herself with shutting the shed door, not looking at me, her face drawn tight like a cat's arse. 'There's rice and daal inside. Go and wash your hands.'

'I don't want that . . . that stuff! I want fishfingers! Fried! And chips! Why can't I eat what I want to eat?'

Mama turned to me, she had her teacher's face on, long suffering, beseeching, but still immovable. She said gently, 'Why did you take money for sweets? Why did you lie to papa?'

'I didn't,' I said automatically, blind to logic, to the inevitable fact that my crime had already been fretfully discussed while I'd been having the best day of my life being Anita Rutter's new friend.

'So now you are saying papa is a liar also? Is that it?'

I pretended to take a great interest in a mossy crack in the yard concrete, running my sandal along it, deliberately scuffing the leather. I knew how I looked, pouting, defiant in the face of defeat, sad and silly, but I could not apologise. I have still never been able to say sorry without wanting to swallow the words as they sit on my tongue.

Mama knelt down on the hard floor and cupped my face in her hands, forcing me to look into her eyes. Those eyes, those endless mud brown pools of sticky, bottomless love. I shook with how powerful I suddenly felt; I knew that with a few simple words I could wipe away every trace of guilt and concern ebbing across her face, that if I could admit what I had done, I could banish my parents' looming unspoken fear that their only child was turning out to be a social deviant. 'I did not lie,' I said evenly, embracing my newly-born status as a deeply disturbed fantasist with a frisson that felt like pride.

After my mother had retreated back into the kitchen, Mrs Worrall came out and stood in her doorway, wiping her large floury hands on her front, watching me kick mossy scabs across the yard. 'Come and give us a hand, Meena,' she said finally. I hesitated at the back door; I'd seen glimpses of her kitchen practically every day, I knew the cupboards on the wall were faded yellow, the lino was blue with black squares on it and the sink was under the window, like in our house. But I'd never actually been inside, and as I stepped in, I had a weird feeling that I was entering Dr Who's Tardis. It was much bigger than I had imagined, or it seemed so because there was none of the clutter that took up every available inch of space in our kitchen.

My mother would right now be standing in a haze of spicy steam, crowded by huge bubbling saucepans where onions and tomatoes simmered and spat, molehills of chopped vegetables and fresh herbs jostling for space with bitter, bright heaps of turmeric, masala, cumin and coarse black pepper whilst a softly breathing mound of dough would be waiting in a china bowl, ready to be divided and flattened into round, grainy chapatti. And she, sweaty and absorbed, would move from one chaotic work surface to another, preparing the fresh, home-made meal that my father expected, needed like air, after a day at the office about which he never talked.

From the moment mama stepped in from her teaching job, swapping saris for M & S separates, she was in that kitchen; it would never occur to her, at least not for many years, to suggest instant or take-away food which would give her a precious few hours to sit, think, smell the roses – that would be tantamount to spouse abuse. This food was not just something to fill a hole, it was soul food, it was the food their far-away mothers made and came seasoned with memory and longing, this was the nearest they would get for many years, to home.

So far, I had resisted all my mother's attempts to teach me the rudiments of Indian cuisine; she'd often pull me in from the yard and ask me to stand with her while she prepared a simple *sabzi* or rolled out a chapatti before making it dance and blow out over a naked gas flame. 'Just watch, it is so easy, beti,' she'd say encouragingly. I did not see what was easy about peeling, grinding, kneading and burning your fingers in this culinary Turkish bath, only to present your masterpiece and have my father wolf it down in ten minutes flat in front of the nine o'clock news whilst sitting cross-legged on the floor surrounded by spread sheets from yesterday's *Daily Telegraph*.

Once, she made the fatal mistake of saying, 'You are going to have to learn to cook if you want to get married, aren't you?'

I reeled back, horrified, and vowed if I ended up with someone who made me go through all that, I would poison the bastard immediately. My mother must have cottoned on; she would not mention marriage again for another fifteen years.

'Shut the door then,' said Mrs Worrall, who swayed over to the only bit of work surface that was occupied, where a lump of pastry dough sat in a small well of white flour. Otherwise, all was bare and neat, no visible evidence of food activity here save a half-packet of lemon puffs sitting on the window sill.

'What you making?' I asked, peering under her massive arm.

'Jam tarts. Mr Worrall loves a good tart. Mind out.'

She bent down with difficulty and opened the oven door, a blast of warm air hit my legs and I jumped back.

'What's that?'

'What yow on about? It's the oven.'

I'd never seen my mother use our oven, I thought it was a storage space for pans and her griddle on which she made chapatti. Punjabis and baking don't go together, I've since discovered. It's too easy, I suppose, not enough angst and sweat in putting a cake in the oven and taking it out half an hour later.

'Yow ever made pastry?' I shook my head. I'd always wondered what the crispy stuff on the bottom of jam tarts was, and here was Mrs Worrall making it in her own home. I was well impressed. 'Hee-y'aar,' said Mrs Worrall, putting a small bowl in front of me in which she poured a little flour and placed a knob of lemony butter. 'Always keep your fingers cold. That's the secret. Now rub your fingers together . . . slowly. You wanna end up with breadcrumbs . . .' I squeezed the butter, feeling it squash then break against my fingers, and started to press and pummel it into the flour like I'd seen mama do with the chapatti dough.

'No! Too hard! It'll stick! Gently, dead gentle . . .' I slowed down, tried to concentrate on feeling each grain of flour, made my fingers move like clouds, and saw a tiny pile of bread-crumbs begin forming at the bottom of the bowl.

'I'm doing it! Look! Pastry!'

Mrs Worrall grunted. 'Not yet, it ain't . . .'

She left me to it whilst she quickly rolled out the large lump of pastry into an oval and pressed a cutter over its surface, slipping the tart cases into a large tin tray. Her fingers moved swiftly and lightly, as if they did not belong to those flapping meaty arms. She then took my bowl off me and stared at the contents critically. 'Not bad. Now binding. Use warm water, not cold. But the fork has to be like ice, see . . .'

She poured in a little liquid from a steel, flame-blackened kettle and handed me a fork from a pan of cold water in the sink. I pressed the crumbs together, watching them swell and cling to each other, until they gradually became a doughy mass.

'It's like magic, innit?'

'No. Your mum does that,' she said. 'This is your one. Alright?'

I nodded, and she quickly rolled out my dough, which I noticed stuck to the rolling pin much more than hers, cut out a small shape and placed it onto the tray before shoving the whole thing in the oven.

As Mrs Worrall began washing her hands, a low uneven moaning drifted in from the room at the other side of the closed kitchen door. It sounded like an animal, wounded, like the time a juggernaut lorry had swerved right across the crossroads outside our house, and missing our gate by inches, had ploughed instead into the fields opposite, mortally wounding a chestnut bay called Misty. One of my earliest memories is of feeding old bits of chapatti to Misty, I must

have been tiny as papa had to hold me up whilst I held out my
hand, palm flat as he instructed me, and felt Misty's soft
whiskery muzzle lightly nibble and suck the bits off my hand.
'Now she's a real Punjabi horse, eh?' nodded papa with
satisfaction, patting her lightly on the neck before letting me
down. He talked to her softly, in Punjabi, I presume, though I
could not tell what exactly he was saying, and he smiled when
her ears pricked up and she snorted, rolling her eyes, as if she
now understood every word.

And the next time I saw her was from my bedroom window,
when she was lying on her side in the grass as Mr Ormerod
and my papa and a few other men ran wildly around the field,
dragging the driver from his steaming cab. Mrs Lowbridge
and Mrs Worrall stood nearby in the requisite Tollington pose
for witnesses at a disaster, one hand cradling the cheek, the
other on the hip, and a slow, disbelieving rhythmic shake of
the head. No one seemed to notice Misty flung in a corner of
the field, her muzzle just visible above the clover stalks,
emitting this terrible, haunting moan for help. And now I
heard it again and I knew who was making it and I was afraid.

'Can I have lemon curd in my one, Mrs Worrall?' I
jabbered, eager to distract her. She did not answer but wiped
her hands on her pinafore and said, 'Come and say hello to Mr
Worrall.' She opened the door leading into the sitting room
and I blinked rapidly, trying to adjust my eyes to the gloom.
The curtains were drawn, split by a bar of red sunset light
where they did not quite meet, and the small black and white
television set sitting on the dining table was on full volume.
Opportunity Knocks was on, one of my very favourite programmes where ordinary people who felt they had a great untapped
talent could try their luck at singing, impressions, unicycling
whilst juggling hatchets, whatever, and if the great British
public voted them the best of the acts, could return again and
again every week, gathering more acclaim, accolades and
possibly bookings at dizzying venues like the Wolverhampton
Grand until they were finally knocked off first place by the new

64

young pretender to the variety throne. The unicyclist is dead, long live the fat man from Barnet doing Harold Wilson impressions!

From the first time I watched that show, I knew that this could be my most realistic escape route from Tollington, from ordinary girl to major personality in one easy step. But I'd never seen anyone who wasn't white on the show, not so far, and was worried that might count against me. Hughie Green was doing his famous one-eye-open, one-eyebrow-cocked look right down the camera and he announced, 'Let's see how our musical muscle man, Tony Holland, does on our clapometer!' An oiled, bulging bloke in micro swimming trunks appeared briefly and rippled his belly muscles into animal shapes as the audience whooped and hollered and the clapometer began at fifty and rose and rose, climbing slowly along until it nudged ninety and there were beads of sweat forming on Tony's undulating diaphragm.

Mrs Worrall suddenly switched the TV off and another wail of protest came from a far dark corner. 'Later. Say hello to Mrs K's littl'un first, eh?' She pushed me forward and I suddenly became aware of the smell of the room which seemed to be at one with the gloom, the smell of a sick room, unaired and lonely, of damp pyjamas steaming, sticky-sided medicine bottles, spilled tinned soup and disinfectant under which there hovered the clinging tang of old, dried-in pee. A shape took form before me, thin useless legs in clean striped pyjamas, the toes curled and turned inwards, passive hands with fingers rigid and frozen as claws, a sunken chest making a bowed tent of the pyjama top, and finally Mr Worrall's face, wide blue-blue staring eyes and a mouth permanently open, asking for something, wanting to talk, with the bewildered, demanding expression of an unjustly punished child.

Mr Worrall moaned loudly again, nodding his head vigorously, a few drops of spit fell onto his chin which Mrs Worrall expertly wiped away with her pinafore hem. She took up his hand and placed it on mine, his fingers seemed to rustle like dry twigs but, amazingly, I could feel the pump and surge of his heartbeat throbbing through his palm. I wanted to pull my hand away but I looked up to see Mrs Worrall's eyes glittering behind their bottle bottom frames. 'Hello Mr Worrall,' I said faintly. Mr Worrall jerked his head back violently and gave a yelp. 'He likes you,' Mrs Worrall said, the glimmer of a smile playing round her mouth. 'It was the shells. In the war. He got too close. He was always a nosey bugger.'

I felt it was maybe alright to pull my hand away now, and I carefully replaced his back onto his lap, like replacing a brittle ornament after dusting. Mr Worrall jerked forward, I felt his breath on my face, it was surprisingly sweet-smelling, like aniseed, like Misty's warm steamy mouth used to smell. 'That's enough now,' said Mrs Worrall, pushing him back into his chair and gathering his blanket around his knees. 'It's nearly time for your wash. You want a wash, eh?' Mr Worrall seemed tall, even sitting down. He must have been over six foot before the shells got him. Now I knew two war veterans, him and Anita's dad. I felt annoyed that my papa had not done anything as remotely exciting or dangerous in his youth, or if he had he'd kept it quiet.

'How do you get Mr Worrall upstairs? Have you got a lift or something?' I asked as she busied herself with removing his socks. 'Ooh, we never use the upstairs, do we? No. Not been up there for twenty-two years.' My gaze travelled to the small door leading onto the stairs, the same as in our house, which fooled people into thinking there was another bigger room leading off from the lounge. It was padlocked from the outside, its hinges rusted.

All this time when I had run up and down our landing and imagined the Worralls ambling about on the other side of the wall, tutting about the noise, our adjoining bookends, I had never realised that next door were empty rooms, cobweb-filled, echoing, unused rooms. I felt queasy, my hunger had become nausea; Mrs Worrall was attempting to kneel, her fat knees cracking, and I suddenly saw what the last twenty-two years of her life must have been, this endless uncomplaining attendance of a broken, unresponsive body, the wiping of spittle and shit, the back-breaking tugging and loading and pulling and carrying, all the nights in front of the television whilst the Deirdre Rutters and the Glenys Lowbridges were putting on lipstick and waltzing off to pubs and bingo and dances and Mrs Worrall's big treat was an extra lemon puff in front of *Crossroads*, whilst her husband dozed off.

Not all the English were selfish, like mama sometimes said, but then again, I did not think of Mrs Worrall as English. She was a symbol of something I'd noticed in some of the Tollington women, a stoic muscular resistance which made them ask for nothing and expect less, the same resignation I heard in the voices of my Aunties when they spoke of back home or their children's bad manners or the wearying monotony of their jobs. My Aunties did not rage against fate or England when they swapped misery tales, they put everything down to the will of Bhagwan, their karma, their just deserts inherited from their last reincarnation which they had to live through and solve with grace and dignity. In the end, they knew God was on their side; I got the feeling that most of the Tollington women assumed that He had simply forgotten them.

'I've got to go,' I mumbled, backing away on Bambi legs, 'Mum's waiting . . .'

Mrs Worrall wordlessly helped me into the kitchen which now smelt like a bakery, yeasty and welcoming and warm. She retrieved the metal tray from the oven on which stood ten perfect tartlets and one which resembled a relief map of Africa. Nevertheless, she filled it with lemon curd from a twist-top jar, and threw in another two tarts for mama and papa, warning me, 'Wait a minute, or that curd'll tek the skin off yer tongue.'

I carried the three trophies on a napkin carefully to the

door, and then paused to call out, 'Bye Mr Worrall!' as cheerily as I could manage. I did not expect an answer but I felt Mrs Worrall's eyes gently guide me to my back door.

4

Mama and Papa were sitting on the mock leather yellow settee, a bad idea if you wanted to have a serious or unnoticed conversation because your every shift would be accompanied by a symphony of leathery farts and squeaks. It was especially thrilling to welcome a new overweight relative to the house, who would invariably be received in our 'front' room with its tie-dye Indian hangings and brass ornaments, as opposed to the 'lounge', our telly and flop room next to it with its worn flowery suite and ricketty dining table. I got hours of pleasure seeing corpulent uncles parp their way through their starters or alarmed roly-poly aunties vainly hold onto their sari petticoats as they slowly slipped backwards into the marshmallow cushions.

So I knew, when I entered, by the hurried scrapings and scuffles, that mama and papa had been sitting together and talking about me. I decided to adopt my cute over-achiever face as I held my jam tarts aloft. 'Mrs Worrall taught me to bake. Next week we're making rum babas!'

Mama got up slowly and brushed past me into the kitchen. I had not seen papa since this morning, a hundred years ago, when he'd dragged me to Mr Ormerod's shop to extract a confession.

'Come here, beti,' he said.

I obeyed, and sat down carefully. The settee pushed me into his side, I caught his smell, Old Spice and tobacco, and sighed with relief as he slipped his arm round my waist. 'Beti, if you want something in future, you must ask us. Don't we give you enough? Do you feel deprived?' I shook my head sorrowfully. I desperately wanted to eat my jam tarts.

'You have heard the story of the boy and the tiger?' I shook my head again and snuggled into the crook of his arm. I loved his stories, I loved the timbre of his voice and the places it took me, effortlessly. 'Once a young boy was gathering wood in the forest and he decided to get some attention for himself. So he shouted to the village that he had seen a tiger. All the villagers came running with axes and torches and *lathis* and when they got to the forest, there was no tiger. "I did see a tiger," said the boy. "It must have run away . . ." The next day . . .'

I felt cheated. This was The Boy Who Cried Wolf! I had read it hundreds of times in my *Golden Anthology of Fables and Tales*. Did he think I would swallow an old story dressed up in Indian clothes? I closed my eyes, pretending to listen, and imagined myself in lime hot pants and blonde hair singing 'Let's Go Fly a Kite' whilst Hughie Green sobbed unashamedly into a large white hanky and the clapometer needle shot off the scale and flew out of the television, shattering the glass . . . 'And the tiger had eaten the boy. All that was left was one *chappal*. So you see, if you tell lies too often, no one will believe you when you are telling the truth.'

'I'm sorry, papa,' I said, almost meaning it. I left a suitable pause and then asked, 'Papa? Were you in the war? Like Mr Worrall?'

'No, beti,' he laughed. 'I was only nine when the war started. Besides, it was not really our war. We were fighting different battles . . .'

'What battles? Did you have a gun? Did you . . .' I was going to say 'ever kill anyone', but I remembered mama's expression when I asked for a rendition of the rickshaw murder story and thought better of it. '. . . Did you do anything dangerous?'

Papa hesitated a moment, looking at me protectively. I could see he was rifling through possibilities, wondering how much he could give away. There was something leonine in his expression, that long noble nose and steady eyes, that tiny teardrop shape above his lips, replicated exactly in my face. I stroked my finger into the well beneath my nose. I liked looking like him. 'Well, there was one occasion . . .' He checked the kitchen quickly, making sure mama was still occupied, 'when we lived in Lahore, just before Partition . . .'

I knew something about Partition, about the English dividing up India into India and Pakistan, and of some people not knowing until the day the borders were announced, whether they would have to move hundreds of miles away, leaving everything behind them. However, I had fallen upon this information inadvertently, during one of papa's musical evenings.

Papa's *mehfils* were legendary, evenings where our usual crowd plus a few dozen extra families would squeeze themselves into our house to hear papa and selected Uncles sing their favourite Urdu *ghazals* and Punjabi folk songs. Once the mammoth task of feeding everyone in shifts was over (kids first, men second, then the women who by then were usually sick of the sight of food), the youngsters would be banished to the TV room. A white sheet was spread in the lounge upon which the elders sat cross-legged, playing cards, chatting, until someone would say, '*Acha* Kumar saab, let's go!' Then papa would take down his harmonium from the top of the wardrobe, unwrap it from its psychedelic bedspread, and run his fingers over the keys whilst the other hand pumped the back, and it coughed into life like a rudely-awakened grumpy old man.

Then the fun would begin; papa would start off slowly, practising scales maybe, then playing a simple folk song with a chorus that everyone could join in with. '*Ni babhi mere guthe na keree*' . . . he would intone, singing in the voice of a young unmarried girl who is begging her sister-in-law not to do her hair as the long oily plaits remind her of snakes . . . Why she was worried about dreaming about snakes, I did not figure out till I was much older. The men would shout the refrain to the verse, holding their hands to the sky, as if expecting gold to be thrown in the face of their massive talent. The Aunties would grab nearby utensils, spoons, pans, even using the bangles on their wrists, to keep a beat going, performing mock blushes and flirty reprimands in the face of their husbands' smiling innuendoes.

Then suddenly the mood would change. Papa would wait for the laughter and joking to die down, and close his eyes, drawing breath deeply from down in his stomach. And then he would open his mouth and a sound came out which was something between a sob and a sigh, notes I could not recognise hung in the air, so close in tone yet each one different, a gradual ascent and then pure flight as his throat opened up to swallow the room. Then the words, words always about love, a lover departing or arriving and how the heart bled or bloomed in response, a whole song about the shadow cast by a lover's eyelashes on her cheek, a single line which somehow captured life, death and the unknown.

During these *ghazals*, my elders became strangers to me. The Uncles would close their eyes with papa, heads inclined, passions and secrets turning their familiar faces into heroes and gods. The Aunties would weep silently, letting the tears hang like jewels from their eyelids, tragedy and memory illuminating their features, each face a *diya*. The only sound besides papa's voice came occasionally from one of the Uncles who would raise their hands and simply shout, '*Wah!*' The word had no literal meaning, mama told me later, but what word would there be for these feelings that papa's songs awoke in everyone? I did not often stay for these mournful *ghazals*, preferring to creep off to bed unnoticed whilst my younger cousins slept in milky heaps like an abandoned litter. There was no point in my being there; when I looked at my elders, in these moments, they were all far, far away.

And it was during one such evening when I was awoken by shouting. I jerked awake to the sound of a man's voice berating someone, something. I checked out of the window, all the cars were still there, parked haphazardly on the sides of the country lane, so I knew the Uncles and Aunties had not left yet. I crept slowly along the darkened landing and down past the bannisters, avoiding the creaks on the third and seventh stairs, and was relieved to see that the door separating the winding staircase from the front room was slightly open. It was my Uncle Bhatnagar shouting, I recognised his gravelly boom even from that distance.

'But it was a damn massacre!' he was spluttering, and then he talked in Punjabi of which I recognised a few words, 'Family . . . money . . . death . . .' and then, 'They talk about their world wars . . . We lost a million people! And who thought up Partition? These "gores", that's who!' Then everyone launched in, the whispers squeezed through the gap in the door and I could make out familiar voices saying such terrible and alien things.

'My mother and I, the Hindus marched us through the streets . . . our heads uncovered . . .' That must have been my Auntie Mumtaz, one of our few Muslim friends. 'They wanted to do such things to us . . . but we had left the house for them and everything in it, and my father . . . he was a judge, he had been so good to them . . .' There was a long pause, I thought I heard someone sniff. 'All the time we were walking, mama and I, papa was lying dead, his head cut from his body. They found it later lying in the fallen jasmine blooms . . .'

'We all have these stories, *bhainji*,' Uncle Bhatnagar again, addressing her as his sister. 'What was happening to you was also happening to us. None of us could stop it. Mad people everywhere.' There was a murmur of consensus, subdued, fearful maybe because of all the old wounds being reopened. 'We were on the wrong side of the border also when the news came, none of us knew until that moment if we would be going or staying. My whole family, we walked from Syalcote across the border . . . We maybe passed your family going the other way. The bodies, piled high . . . the trains pulling into stations full of dead families . . . *Hai Ram*. What we have seen . . .'

73

My heart was trying to break out of my chest. I had to hold onto the bannister to steady myself, terrified I would be discovered and they would clam up and deny me more. Were these my Uncles and Aunties speaking? Were these stories truly theirs? How could they have kept all this from me for so long? Then a sob broke into the low chatter, I knew immediately it was my Auntie Shaila. The fattest, noisiest and most fun of all the Aunties, she could only express herself in extremes of emotion, banshee howls of disbelief or ear-splitting yodels of joy. That and a taste for loud bright saris with over-tight blouses underneath always guaranteed she was the centre of attention. But I had never heard her sound so broken as this.

She struggled for words through the sobs. 'Sister . . .' she gulped. '*Meri bhain* . . . Sumi . . . We were walking, along the river, trying to find the road to Delhi . . . We could see the Muslims on the other side . . . Don't look, *mamaji* said, don't look . . . Sumi looked and they were crossing the river on horses . . . mad men, mad eyes, sticks with red tips . . . They just took her. She was too beautiful. They took her. Where is she? *Hai mere dil* . . . where is she now?'

The whole room seemed to be sighing, I could make out mama's soft weeping, it was muffled. She must have been negotiating the complicated geography of Auntie Shaila's cleavage. No one said 'I am sorry,' like an English person might have done. In the silence that followed, I felt a hundred other memories were being briefly relived and battened down again.

It was papa's voice which finally broke it. He was deliberately upbeat. It was his host's voice, he knew it was his job to steer his friends away from the rocks that might shipwreck them all. He spoke in his characteristic blend of Punjabi and English, but enough for me to understand. He said he and his family had all been living in Lahore, which became Pakistan within a split second of the announcement. His parents then had the job of smuggling eight children across the border. They decided to head for Delhi. 'We just left our house where it was, we took nothing. We split up, all of us. Some in carts with Muslim friends, some of us by train. I went with my father on the train. It stopped suddenly, a tree on the track.' He described how the whole carriage began panicking as it became clear they were being hijacked, but no one knew if it was by Hindus or Muslims.

'There was a Muslim in our carriage. He began praying. A Sikh next to us began cutting off his hair quickly. He offered to shave the Musselman's moustache but he refused. "Allah will save me," he said. The Hindu *goondas* entered the carriage . . .' Papa paused a moment. 'They looked at us, my father quoted the Gita at them, the only time I have ever heard him quote any religious script. They tore the trousers off the Musselman, saw he was circumcised, and cut off his head . . .'

Papa must have realised then that his plan of jollying up the party had gone sadly wrong. He cleared his throat. 'I celebrated my seventeenth birthday in a refugee camp with only what I stood up in. But I thank God, because if I had not gone to Delhi, I would never have met Daljit . . .' Then the room broke into cheers and relieved laughter. The Uncles began teasing papa for his admission, the Aunties, I could hear, were tittering away and no doubt poking mama in the ribs.

After this, I remember climbing slowly back to my bed and swathing myself in my heavy Indian *rajai*. My sleep that night was full of blood red trains screaming through empty stations, scattering severed limbs as it whistled past, of beautiful sisters in churning rivers, and old men's heads in flowerbeds. I wanted to know so much more, but now I was afraid to ask. I realised that the past was not a mere sentimental journey for my parents, like the song told its English listeners. It was a murky bottomless pool full of monsters and the odd shining coin, with a deceptively still surface and a deadly undercurrent. And me, how could I jump in before I had learned to swim?

75

So as I sat in papa's arms, heard that word, 'Partition', and I held my breath with delight, not daring to exhale until he began. This was a gift to me, this was his way of saying he had forgiven me for lying and I accepted it gratefully. 'On this occasion,' continued papa, 'my friend and I . . . Kishan it was, we met some policemen, at least they said they were police. But these were the stupid days, everyone waiting to see if Partition would go ahead, all kinds of ruffians and rogues wandering about . . .' He smiled, 'Like us, I suppose. We wanted to sniff the air, maybe become heroes, freedom fighters, you know? These men, they called us over. Gave us a parcel and some money, just a few *annas* but a lot to us. They asked if we would go and deliver the parcel to some building, not far away. A merchant's house, I think . . .'

Papa swallowed slightly, he held me tighter. 'We walked through the streets with this package, we stopped to boast to our friends, we were on some kind of mission, we had money. We did not hurry. When we got to the merchant's place, there was nobody in. A big place, he was a rich man, Muslim, well known. Well respected. So we just left the parcel in the doorway. What did we care? We had our payment. When we reached the end of the street . . . there was a huge bang. An explosion. We fell to the ground, people began running, screaming for cover. There was smoke everywhere, falling stones. We looked back. The merchant's house had gone. It was dust.'

Papa exhaled deeply and I sighed with him. 'A bomb!' I breathed. My father had planted a real live bomb! I wanted to go round to Anita Rutter's right now and spit on her father's crummy tattoos. 'Of course, we did not know. We could have been killed. Those *goondas* did not care about us. But they must have been Hindu, like us . . .'

'Was anyone in the house?' I asked, couldn't help myself this time.

'I don't . . . No. Of course not. No,' said papa, with a final note that meant the story was over.

I was so grateful that I kissed him hard and said, 'I'm sorry' again for good measure, meaning it fervently and forever.

Papa kissed me tenderly on my head. 'Now eat. Mummy's made you something special . . .' As if on cue, mama came out of the kitchen holding a plate upon which was a large pile of fishfingers and homemade chips.

It was the ambulance siren that woke me up, in my dreams it sounded like laughter but I soon guessed what was happening by the voices outside and the flashing blue light throbbing behind my drawn curtains. I quickly pulled them apart and saw that the ambulance was parked outside the Christmas' house, its back doors wide open. I spotted Mrs Lowbridge, Sandy who was clinging onto Hairy Neddy, Mrs Povey, in her curlers and nightie, Mr Ormerod in his brown overall over his pyjamas, papa, who looked pale and strange in the strobing blue pulse, and Roberto who was comforting a hysterical Deirdre, fully made-up in pink mules and a minidress.

Everyone suddenly stopped talking as two ambulancemen struggled through them carrying a stretcher with a body on it, covered in red blankets. Mr Ormerod closed his eyes and began muttering a prayer but no one bothered to join in. It was only then I noticed the two policemen who came strolling out, flanking a gently smiling Mr Christmas, still dressed in his tank top and vest. He paused to wave shyly at everyone before being carefully helped into the police car parked behind the ambulance. I jumped as my bedroom door opened and mama entered, in her nighttime *salwar kameez*.

'What are you doing?' she said sharply and then, 'What are they saying?' She leaned over me and opened the window, letting in with a blast of cool night air the renewed babble of voices, the loudest of which was, predictably, Deirdre's.

'I went over . . . 'cos, you know, Mr Christmas had said summat to my Nita . . . and he asked me in . . . and I saw her . . . like in front of the telly . . . no face left. Gone. Eaten away.'

Sandy piped up, 'The ambulance blokes said she's been dead for weeks . . .'

'We should have known. Shocking. Bloody shocking,' said Hairy Neddy, holding Sandy closer.

'Indeed,' intoned Mr Ormerod, 'what happened to neighbourly love? They should let the poor old man go now. He didn't know what he was doing . . .'

'He always doted on her, ar,' said Mrs Lowbridge, shaking her head. 'Sixty years married. I couldn't manage six months, me . . .'

I didn't hear much else; my head began swimming, the back of my neck suddenly turned to sticky ice and I slumped down on the bed. I had seen a dead body. I had seen Mrs Christmas' poor white head poking out from the top of her settee and all that time . . . I had wanted to touch tragedy and it had come and smacked me on the cheek, and if it had not been for Anita Rutter shouting down the entry . . .

Mama knelt down next to me and felt my brow. 'You should not listen to such things. I am sorry.' She closed the window smartly and made me lie down, tucking the leaden quilt around me. 'Mrs Christmas did not suffer. She's okay now. Do you understand?'

I nodded, and then whispered, 'I saw her. Today. I saw her head. She was watching telly . . .'

Mama's eyes narrowed, 'Don't you think you've done enough lying for one day, Meena?' I opened my mouth to protest but caught the steel tempered with concern snapping in her eyes. I imagined having to retell the whole story, about meeting Anita, the yelling, Mr Christmas' fury, and then maybe the police would get involved and maybe, and the thought hit me in the solar plexus, maybe Mrs Christmas had been alive until we ran down the side of her house and our banshee wails had shaken her walls and burst the thing in her stomach. Maybe me and Anita Rutter were murderers. It did not matter that it had all been her idea, I had gone along with it, I had done it, and now we were joined in Sin, and we would have to carry around our guilty secret until we died.

'I meant . . . last time I saw her. She had the telly on. Ages ago.' Mama nodded satisfied, and patted me reassuringly before retreating and gently closing the door. I heard engines revving up. I had to see. I got up and went to the window, just in time to catch the ambulance and police car pulling away at high speed and the group of onlookers slowly dispersing. Amongst them, grinning and shivering with cold, was Anita Rutter. For some reason, she looked up suddenly, straight into my eyes, and I could have sworn that she winked.

Three weeks later, having just returned from a short spell in hospital, Mr Christmas died in his sleep. He was buried with Mrs Christmas, whose body had just been released from autopsy, in a pre-booked single grave in the grounds of the Anglican Church in the neighbouring village. This deeply upset Mr Ormerod who had assumed all these years that the Christmases were Wesleyan Methodists like the rest of the community, and thus they had selfishly deprived Tollington and our church of its first funerals for five years.

My mother attended the funeral; she was taking Mrs Worrall anyway in our family Austin Mini, a feat of spatial engineering in itself with Mrs Worrall's bulk plus her bodyweight again contained in her huge black hat. Mama agonised for hours whether to wear white, as in traditional Hindu mourning, and thus risk upsetting the conventional mourners, which was everybody, or stick to black, the only black garment she possessed being an evening sari shot through with strands of shimmering silver thread, not quite the garb for a midday gathering on a windswept former slagheap. 'For God's sake, it does not matter what you wear. That won't bring the poor old man back, will it?' snapped my father, who had been strangely depressed since this tragic double whammy.

Mama eventually plumped for a grey trouser suit, the nearest shade she could get to a compromise, and returned from the funeral red-eyed and subdued. She flopped down on the flowery suite next to papa who had not moved the whole time she had been away, but sat glued to the television screen not seeing what he was watching. It was almost the end of the summer holidays, the last week there would be cartoons on in the daytime, all day, *Scooby Doo*, *Wacky Races*, *Captain Scarlet*, *Stingray*, my favourite programme, with the deliciously pouting Troy Tempest who was in love with the indifferent, amphibious Marina, for whom I developed a deep, passionate hatred. Could she not see how much Troy loved her? Why did she emit bubbles instead of speaking to him? How could she turn this macho marionette down? (I suspect here began my taste in remote, handsome wooden men. Troy Tempest has a lot to answer for . . .)

Normally, papa would have switched off this marathon fayre of inanimate drama after an hour and ordered me to get a book or go outside and get some fresh air, but today, he just left me to get on with it. Mama moved closer to him, she seemed swollen and bovine, and laid his head on her shoulder, talking softly to him in Punjabi, soothing but firm. It never ceased to amaze me how expertly she rode and reined in my father's moods, the long silences and intense looks which would send me into a panic and force me to scuttle round him, scanning his face for the return of that tender familiarity.

At times like this, mama operated just like the men on the Waltzer ride in the travelling fair that came to the village every autumn. While we tossed around, shrieking, in our high-sided whirling cars, these men, nonchalantly chewing or smoking, would straddle the heaving wooden floor like they were walking on water, still cocky centres in a screaming storm, tilting their bodies away from every twist and heave so that they remained perfectly upright. Although papa's moods were unsettling, I never felt they were directed at me, unless I'd done something specifically naughty, and even then I knew forgiveness was never far away. He always seemed more angry at himself for allowing the big black crow to settle on his shoulder and make itself comfortable. When I was upset I was like mama, we cried instinctively and often. But I had never seen papa cry and wondered if he would feel better if, occasionally, he could let himself go.

I caught a few English phrases, half-listening as I fixed on the flickering screen: '. . . can't worry about them, worrying won't do anything . . .' Mama whispered. Papa said, 'When they go, we won't be with them. We will get a letter, or a phone call in the middle of the night . . . everything left unsaid.' They were talking about their parents, the grandparents I had never seen except in the framed photographs that hung in my parents' bedroom.

Mama's mother, my Nanima, looked like a smaller, fatter version of her, all bosom and stomach and yielding eyes, whilst her husband, Nanaji, towered over her, erect and to attention, regal in his tightly wound turban and long grey beard. Papa's parents seemed more relaxed, more used to the camera. My Dadaji was smiling toothlessly into the lens, a tall man but stooped by years of tap-tapping at a desk in a faceless government office, who supplemented his existence as a clerk with passionate literate articles in the left-wing press, which he composed on his daily walk to the market for fresh vegetables. And my Dadima, an ocean of goodness contained in a loosely wound sari, a carefree grin belying the suffering that had touched all of that generation.

Papa had got the best of both his parents: Dadima's generous mouth and affectionate eyes, Dadaji's pride and cheekbones. And while papa spoke copiously about his mother, her sweetness, her courage, her patience, his references to Dada were less frequent and always more surprising. Once, after we had watched footage of Russian tanks parading past some half-dead leaders on the TV news, papa said casually, 'Your Dada was a communist. That's why I never learned any of the prayers, but I can tell you what the GNP of Kerala is . . .'

I did not understand all of this, though it made mama laugh

until she cried, but I did gather that it was somehow Dada's fault that we did not have a homemade Hindu shrine with statues and candles on top of our fridge like all my other Aunties.

On another occasion, another *mehfil*, after papa had just finished a song to rapturous *Vas!*, my Auntie Shaila leaned over to papa and squeezed his arm playfully, her breasts hanging over the harmonium so that they brushed the keys and played a discordant fanfare. 'Kumar saab,' she shouted, 'you should have been in films!'

'I was offered a contract, when I was younger,' papa smiled back, 'but my father refused to let me go. Mindless rubbish, he said, give people politics not songs . . .' There was a brief pause and then papa laughed uproariously, cueing Auntie Shaila to join in, turning a father's edict into an anecdote.

Oh but in that pause, what possibilities hovered! Papa could have been a film star! There was no doubt he had the looks; even then the Aunties would waggle their heads appreciatively when he sang, enjoying his noble profile and almond eyes in a proud, proprietorial way. Mama would sigh at the framed photograph of the two of them which hung above their bed, taken in some small Delhi studio where they looked as if they had had their picture taken through vaseline. 'Look at your beautiful papa,' she would say. 'What did he see in a dark skinny thing like me?' Funnily enough, papa would often ask me the same rhetorical question about mama. I presumed that this was what love meant, both people thinking they were the lucky one.

But once I had heard about Dada's film ban, I became obsessed with what I had missed out on, being the daughter of a famous film hero. Maybe I would have grown up in a palace, had baby elephants as pets and held my papa's hand as he Namasted his way through crowds of screaming fans who pressed forward to garland him with marigolds . . . But if I was disappointed, I could not begin to imagine how papa must have felt. Maybe this was why he never talked about what he did for a living, all I knew was that he went to an office every day and came back with a bulging briefcase full of papers covered with minute indecipherable figures.

But whatever he did to make money was not what papa really was; whilst my Aunties and Uncles became strangers when listening to him, papa became himself when he sang. My tender papa, my flying papa, the papa with hope and infinite variety. And then one day I made a connection; if my singing papa was the real man, how did he feel the rest of the time? This hurt me unbearably, and I stopped hanging around the adults to see him perform. I somehow felt it was my fault and not Dada's, that papa never got into the movies.

Mama and papa were holding hands now, the tension in the room had somehow abated and I began to breathe a little easier. It struck me suddenly how mama and papa had somehow managed to retain something I did not see in most of the Aunties' and Uncles' marriages, an openness, a flirty banter which both fascinated and embarrassed me. I knew everyone began this way, I'd seen the same dance of hands and eyes going on between the big boys from Sam Lowbridge's gang and their interchangeable girlfriends. They would occasionally invade the local park, which conveniently began at the end of our communal Yard, taking over the swings or roundabout, equipped with bottles of cider and endless cigarettes. The boys would begin by teasing the girls, always loudly, aggressively, more for the benefit of their mates than the girls themselves. The girls would feign indifference, sulkily dodge the boys' attempts to grab them and corner them, but always would end up sitting in between the boys' lanky denim legs, sharing drags and slurps, rolling their eyes at the boys' exaggerated swearing and spectacular gobbing in a fond, possessive manner. Their commitment seemed infinite, so it was always a surprise to see the same boys with completely different girls the following week, playing out the same rituals of devotion with the same apparent conviction.

I always watched them from a safe distance, hiding in the

hollyhocks and nettles around the old pigsties at the far end of the yard. Their intimacies unsettled me. I knew that nice girls should not behave in this way. (I got scolded for showing my knickers when I did handstands, and sitting between a boy's legs was presumably much worse.) But despite the fuzzy commas of bumblebees hovering around my ears, and the tall nettles pricking my bare legs, I always had to watch Sam's gang and their girls. They looked so complete, in on a secret which I worried I might never discover.

I got this same feeling looking at the photographs of mama and papa when they were first married, and living in Indian government quarters in New Delhi. Papa had completed a college degree in Liberal Arts and Philosophy (when I asked him what these were exactly, he had said, 'A damn waste of time in this country as it happens' and I did not ask again), and was doing something clerical for the government. Mama had just begun her first teaching job and they lived in a whitewashed single-storey flat-roofed house. I knew this from one of the photos, where they are sitting on a bed in a court-yard, a low bed strung across with hessian mesh which bends under their weight. Just visible on the stone courtyard floor is a dull stain the size of an orange, which papa told me happened when he squashed a passing scorpion under his *chappal*. Papa sits behind mama, has his arms around her just like Sam Lowbridge with his 'wenches' in the park. They are both in white cotton which catches the sunlight and emphasises the nutty brown of their skin. They are laughing, they are at that moment exactly where they want to be.

What I did not understand was why this yearning had not worn off yet. Other parents did not behave like they did; if any of the Uncles attempted to put their arms around their wives in public, this always provoked a chorus of shrieks and mock-naughty-boy slaps from the Aunties. '*Sharam Tainu Nahin Andi hai?*' the women would laugh, demanding to know why their men had no shame and were admitting in public that they sometimes touched, despite the fact that all of them had at least two kids each and therefore must have touched a few times before, even if it was in the dark. They contacted each other through their children, their hands met as they hugged their sons, tickled their daughters, their fingers intertwined as they ate chapatti from the same plate. But I never saw any of them volunteer kisses and hugs like my parents did, contact which I knew had nothing to do with me.

As for our married English neighbours, I sometimes had difficulty matching up the husbands to the wives as their lives seemed so separate. They were the women, like the Yard women, who stayed home whilst their menfolk slipped out to work, too early for me to catch them. And then the others like the Ballbearings Committee, whose men waved them off to work and then gathered together in the evenings in the local pub, the Mitre, or the Working Men's Club, leaving their wives to create havoc together at the rival female venues, the bingo hall, or the Flamingo Nightclub near their factory.

The Flamingo was a converted chapel with tinted windows and screaming pink paintwork, which I had occasionally glimpsed through the car window on my way to school. A big neon sign above the door declaimed, 'Ladies Only Nites, Free Cocktail Before Ten O'Clock!' You'd always know when the women had been 'down the 'mingo', because you would hear them piling off the night bus on the corner of the crossroads, shrieking with laughter and cursing as they negotiated the potholes in their slingbacks. 'Yow dirty cow, Maisie! I seen ya eyeing that fella up!' 'I never! He was gagging for it any road, he had his hands in his pockets all bloody night!' 'Oh me head . . . Malibu's a bloody killer, innit?' 'Don't yow chuck up near me, Edie! This wet-look top ain't waterproof, ya know . . .' 'I wonder if my Stan's up . . . probably not. Our chaps are never up when yow need em up, know wharr-I mean, girls!'

I gladly woke up for these nocturnal dramas, their fun was infectious and laced with Sin. I knew if I could hear them, so could most of the Yard, and I wondered what their husbands made of these public dissections of their capabilities. But there was no way of knowing as I hardly ever saw them together, and as for the Yard couples, I only managed to put husbands to wives on Saturday mornings when couples piled into their cars to go shopping.

What mama and papa had was special maybe, certainly different to the other couples I observed. But with the English people, Sam and his wenches, the Ballbearings Committee, there was something that intrigued me, the brazenness of their behaviour, an absence of sentiment and a boldness of self which I could not see in my parents' almost claustrophobic connection. As I looked over at them now, exchanging whispers on the settee, I could not imagine how I might one day be capable of such sweetness. I could only see myself tripping up in a pothole, clutching my shoes and laughing to the moon.

Papa had stopped discussing his parents; mama was sitting quietly next to him, darting glances at his brooding face. I turned back to the TV screen, ears on radar, waiting for the outburst or the apology, with papa it could go either way for no apparent reason. Papa always got into these moods whenever mortality flitted near our doorstep. The loss of a distant parent would be the final proof, that they had left them and would not be returning. Mama shook herself visibly, snapping into her practical mode. She plumped up the cushions behind papa's back, he did not move to make it easier for her, and then she snuggled closer to him, a girlish smile playing on her lips.

'Darling, no more of this, huh? We will have someone else to think about soon. We should not get so upset, *jaanoo* . . . We should also tell Meena.'

My ears pricked up at this, I turned round expectantly, accusingly, waiting to hear this secret, another secret, they had added to the list of things they had kept from me. Papa cleared his throat and smiled at me reassuringly. 'Meena beti . . . er . . . your mama is having a baby soon, a little brother or sister for you to play with. Would you like that?'

A loud cracking sound filled my head, my vision blurred and I turned away hastily, fixing my eyes on Troy Tempest, willing him to steady my voice. It came out hard and distant. 'No,' I replied, without turning around.

5

Mama's belly was a proud high football by the time I bumped into Anita Rutter again. It was late October and Tollington had discarded its usual duffle coat of red brick and dirt, and was prancing around in its ostentatious autumnal cloak. Huge fat leaves of blood red and burnt gold covered every available surface, the pavements, the small neat gardens, the hedges and fields were clogged and carpeted with a blazing crunchy floor which we kids jumped and stamped through, snorting with effort through our assorted layers of woollies.

Anita and I seemed to have avoided each other through unspoken mutual understanding since the Christmas' demise. I had seen her from afar, strolling up to the tadpole pools near the Mitre pub at the north end of the village, arm in arm with Sherrie as Fat Sally waddled after them pathetically trying to keep up, snuffling and wiping her nose on her cardigan sleeve. I noticed Anita often did this, played off one girlfriend against the other, so it was rare that all three girls walked together, in the same harmonious pace. Whatever the scenario, it was always Anita leading the way with Sherrie or Fat Sally at her side, favoured and blessed, whilst the scapegoat of the hour sulked and straggled behind. I wondered what would happen if I joined the group, if the foursome would split off into twos who would then declare all-out war. But it would be hard to imagine any of us having the courage to actually take sides against Anita, even the thought felt uncomfortably close to sacrilege.

I had seen Tracey, Anita's skinny sister, gambolling about

the yard with the family's newest acquisition, a stringy black poodle who yapped and widdled excitedly around her knees. Hairy Neddy had already warned Tracey to keep that 'runty rat' away from his motor, whose wheels were already becoming the official toilet area for the various mutts in the vicinity. But as Tracey's dog seemed to keep up a constant stream of pee, regardless of where it happened to be standing, this was not really a problem.

I disliked the animal on first sight; compared to the other neighbourhood dogs – Blaze, the mad collie who raced alongside cars as they passed the park, only just missing their wheels, Patch, Karl and Kevin's ancient retainer mongrel who did nothing much but sit in a corner and drool and Shandy, the Mad Mitchells' perky white hound – Tracey's dog was a characterless apology for an animal, no personality, no menace and no fun. 'Mum got it!' Tracey told me, trying to kiss its ratty muzzle. I stepped back slightly, even though I was in my red wellies, not wanting to get sprayed, and wished that Butch had been around to see off this canine catastrophe. Butch, that was the name we had given him, had been a psychotic stray who had wandered into the yard just as the new school term had started. It had been a mad blissful few weeks when Butch had run havoc, tearing down washing, crapping on Mrs Lowbridge's step and finally biting Sam Lowbridge on the leg when he'd tried to kick Butch 'into the bloody middle of next week.' As Mrs Povey had put it, 'Any dog that takes a chunk out of that bugger is alright by me.'

From that point on, Sam had waged a ruthless vendetta against the dog who had torn a hole in his new black leather motorbike trousers, and spent most days chasing Butch out of the yard on his moped, whooping like a cowboy, until one day, Butch had simply not returned and we mourned him deeply.

'He's nice,' I said, half-heartedly, not wanting to dim the love shining in Tracey's eyes. 'What's his name?'

As if on cue, Deirdre appeared on her stoop and leaned over, patting her hands on her chubby knees to beckon the dog. 'Nigger! Nigger! Here, darling! Come to mummy!'

My mummy nearly choked when I told her what the Rutters' new pet was called. She told papa and he laughed uproariously. 'It is not amusing, *Shyam*! These no good ignorant English, what kind of a name is that to say in front of your children, anybody's children?'

'They don't know it is an insult!' papa replied. 'You remember when we went into that paint shop, they had a colour called Nigger Brown and you complained? The shopkeeper was most apologetic . . .'

'Black, brown, what does it matter?' mama continued. 'Just because we are not black, it is still an insult! Have you seen any white paint called Honky With a Hint of White, heh?'

'You ask any man on the street to tell the difference between us and a Jamaican fellow, he will still see us as the same colour, Daljit,' papa finished off, returning to his paper.

From that day on, mama decided that Deirdre would not be one of the many beneficiaries of her impeccable manners and warm social chit-chat. Of course, to the untrained eye, mama did not treat Deirdre any differently, she still smiled and nodded when they passed each other in the yard to hang out washing, or when we were returning from parking our Mini in the garages near the old pigsties, but I knew what mama's polite smile meant, what the layers of subtext beneath it were.

Not that Deirdre seemed to notice or care that she and mama hardly exchanged five sentences per month, a minuscule amount for neighbours in Tollington, she always seemed very busy for a woman who claimed not to have a job. Every morning she would leave the house around ten o'clock and not return until early afternoon, just before Anita and Tracey came back from the village school. Sometimes she carried shopping, but most of the time she was empty-handed and flushed, bustling with secrets and self importance.

There was an air about Deirdre that prevented the gossips

from asking her outright what she was up to, a haughty, menacing defensiveness that stopped even Mrs Lowbridge and Mrs Povey from launching their usual two-pronged verbal assault. However, whenever Deirdre strutted past them in her stilettos, boobs like two heat-seeking missiles guiding her forward, they would shake their heads conspiratorially and whisper, 'She's got it coming to her, that one. Mark my words . . .'

Unfortunately, my information about Deirdre's dog had now put my relationship, if that was what it was, with Anita into question, at least in mama's eyes. The day the autumn fair arrived in the village, a convoy of swaying caravans and belching trucks pulling heavy metal equipment barnacled with light bulbs, dead as fish eyes, Anita knocked on my front door to ask, 'Coming to see the men unload then?'

Mama looked up from dusting and her eyes narrowed slightly on seeing Anita. She straightened up with difficulty, her hands instinctively resting on her heavy, low stomach, straining the material of her old cotton *salwar kameez*. 'Why do you want to see that? Nothing much to see, you'll just be in the way.' I knew if I pestered her, she would say yes, I could hear fatigue and defeat in her voice.

Mama had been cooking and cleaning for weeks it seemed because today was Diwali – 'Our Christmas, Mrs Worrall,' mama had told her, not wanting to go into huge detail about the Hindu Festival of Light and why the date changed each year, being a lunar festival, and how we did not give presents but put on all the lights in the house and gambled instead to welcome the goddess Lakshmi into our lives, hoping she would bring luck and wealth with her. Christmas was not the best comparison to use in front of me because I naturally expected a carload of presents and the generally festive, communal atmosphere that overtook the village somewhere around late November and continued into January.

But no one else in the world seemed to care that today was our Christmas. There was no holiday, except it happened to be a weekend so mama and I were off school and papa was only working a half-day, no tinsel or holly or blinking Christmas trees adorning the sitting room windows in Tollington, no James Bond films or Disney spectaculars on the telly, and nobody, not one person, had wished me a happy Diwali, despite the fact I had hung around the yard all morning with what I hoped was a general expression of celebration.

Everyone's indifference had stunned me, and I now understood why my parents made an effort to mark Jesus' birthday, despite the remarks made by some of my Aunties and Uncles. 'Meena would feel left out . . . It is not fair, when all the other children are getting presents. Besides, we all get the day off, so why not?' This was a typical example of Hindu tolerance, the reason, my mama told me, why so many religions happily co-existed in India – Buddhism, Christianity, Judaism, Sikhism and especially Islam. 'There are more Muslims in India than there are in Pakistan!' mama told me proudly. 'Every path leads to the same god, that is what we believe, beti . . .'

Papa would have to repeat these arguments to my Auntie Shaila who held her ears and whispered, '*Thoba!*' when he once told her that I was a regular visitor to Uncle Alan's Sunday School at the Wesleyan church. 'They just read and play, nothing much religious really . . .' he offered. 'All the kids go there, it keeps them out of the cold and out of mischief.'

'But really, Shyam-saab, you want your daughter to come home reciting hymns and what not?' Auntie Shaila cried. 'All that boring sitting around and amen this and that, no joy and those damn hard seats and that awful organ music, like a donkey in pain. Besides, you will confuse the girl.'

Papa did not let on that he was as confused as I was about Hinduism; because of Dadaji's beliefs, religion had never been an integral part of his upbringing, and his experiences around Partition had removed any lingering religious instincts he might have kept through suspicion or habit. 'I have seen what we do in the name of religion,' he once told mama. 'What I do, how I behave, I will do in the name of humanity. And that is that.' All the same, I continually mourned the fact that we did not have a shrine.

Auntie Shaila's shrine took up all of the top of her fridge, where Lord Rama and Shri Krishna and Ganesha, the plump, smiling elephant-headed god, my favourite, sat in miniature splendour, surrounded by incense sticks, *diyas*, fruit offerings and photographs of departed loved ones. I never saw mama or papa bow their heads in prayer or sing one of the haunting, minor key *aartis* that Auntie Shaila would regularly perform with closed eyes and a long-suffering, beatific look, I suspect, for my benefit. After the prayer, she would bring the *diya* to me, holding my hands above the flame, showing me how to waft a blessing over my head. 'The fire will purify you, beti. Go ahead, have another go.' I wafted furiously, trying to accrue enough good karma to last me until the next visit.

'You know,' Auntie Shaila confided, 'that we believe whatever you do in this life will come back to you in the next. If you are good, you will come back as a good-hearted, rich person. If you are not, you will have to pay, at some point. Like with the bank, you know?' I thought back on my lying and murderous thoughts and knew I would be booked in to reappear as a slug in my next reincarnation unless I did some serious damage repair. As soon as we got back from Auntie Shaila's, I burst into tears and flung myself at papa, sobbing, 'Why haven't you taught me any prayers? I want to go to a temple! I want to come back as somebody famous!'

Once I had managed to blurt out what Auntie Shaila had said, papa transferred me to mama's lap where I sat sniffling whilst he went and phoned somebody. I could only hear fragments of the conversation, which was polite, serene even, '. . . don't scare her, she is very imaginative . . . Well, that is our choice, Shaila . . . Of course, I know you were only trying to help . . . We will . . .' Afterwards, he sat me on his lap and said, 'Beti, do you know what a conscience is?' I shook my head; whatever it was, it sounded like I should have one. 'You know when you do something wrong, when you upset someone, or break something, or even if you are thinking about doing something wrong and you hear a little voice in your head that says, "Meena, you should not do this . . ."'

I stiffened, alert now. Had he been reading my mind? How did papa know about this irritating other me that sat on my brain and kept confusing me at points of crisis? 'Well, that voice is your conscience and God gave you that voice to help you . . . be good. And it will always be there, no matter how many temples you go to. Do you understand?' I nodded, a sinking sensation overtaking me. So it would always be there, that's what he said. I was stuck with it. 'As long as you listen to this voice, it will lead you to God. Even if you do something wrong, if you feel sorry, God knows that too. So don't worry about being punished. That is what we are here for . . .' he added, as an afterthought.

Later on, mama, who had been very quiet during this early crisis of faith, declared that she was taking me to the *gurudwara* in Birmingham the very next day. This was something of a major announcement on two counts; firstly, because mama also had never shown signs of being overtly religious. Of course, she invoked the name of Bhagwan in times of pain or exasperation, and had often praised the virtues of Sikhism to me, how it was a very fair religion that believed totally in equality. 'We Sikhs do not believe in the caste system at all,' she said proudly, and then muttered, 'Of course, now we have different snobberies, who has the biggest Mercedes and the fattest gold necklace, as if the biggest show-off is the most holy . . .'

And secondly, (the most worrying aspect of this planned pilgrimage) because the only *gurudwara* in the Midlands was at least twenty miles away, and that therefore meant that mama intended to drive us there. We had acquired our first car, a green Austin Mini, a few months back and mama had passed her test a week before Auntie Shaila's attempted exorcism. I knew very well that papa was working the next day, and therefore I was to be the guinea pig on my mother's first journey as a solo driver.

Mama tried to be a careful motorist, but drove so slowly that the amount of blood pressure she provoked in anyone unlucky enough to be stuck behind her, cancelled out all her good intentions. I had seen her having lessons from papa around the village, caught glimpses of her crawling around a gentle corner or tackling a minor slope as if it were the north face of the Eiger, whilst papa sat impassively next to her, his fingers gripping the dashboard in a parody of a fighter pilot bracing himself for a blast of G-force.

The journey started off pretty much to plan; papa had drawn a detailed map which mama taped to the dashboard, and she packed a thermos of *haichi* tea and a few parathas wrapped in silver foil in case we became delirious with hunger or thirst along the way. My job was to read out from the other list of instructions which complemented the visual map with precise details of landmarks we would be passing. 'After this roundabout, which should see a betting shop and a petrol station, the one we filled up at last time we went to Uncle Trivedi's place for his daughter's first birthday . . .'

Mama would nod, like a spy who has just been given the right coded password in a public park '. . . the daffodils are out in Gdansk early this year . . .' and rev up all the way into second gear for a few yards, confident at least that the next stage of the trek had been accounted for. Usually we chattered constantly in the car, playing I-Spy or singing songs, but this time mama was in no mood for pleasantries. Her eyes never left the road and her knuckles, clamped around the steering wheel, never got beyond a pale yellow colour. But then we got to Coal Hill, a notorious junction just outside Wolverhampton where five sets of traffic lights and a one-way system met on the incline of an extremely steep slope. If you made the lights, you were laughing, straight down the hill the other side, a clear run to the dual carriageway stretching all the way to Birmingham. But if you didn't, you knew you were stuck for at least five minutes in a huge queue, doing an A-level in clutch control.

Of course, we would have made the lights had we got above ten miles an hour and if mama had not slowed down at the junction, waiting for the green to possibly change to amber and therefore catch her out, which is exactly what happened. We juddered to a halt to the accompaniment of several angry car horns and mama pulled up the handbrake with a grunt, flicking her eyes to the mirror to check the growing line of vehicles behind her. I decided feigned nonchalance was the best approach, and attempted a whistle as I scanned a facing billboard. On one side of it was a huge caption, GO TO WORK ON AN EGG! with a prancing lion beneath it, and on the other, a poster advertised the forthcoming pantomine at the Grand Theatre, Tinga and Tucker, everyone's favourite koala bears, starring in *Babes in the Wood*, with Auntie Jean Morton and a host of TV favourites!

I was about to ask if we could go to see the show when I noticed that the koalas seemed to be moving forwards, and mama's scream confirmed that actually, we were moving backwards. 'Get out! Tell the bus driver to go back! Quickly!' I had never seen mama so panicked before, her feet were slipping off the pedals, those strappy sandals were not a wise choice I remember thinking as I leaped out of the car and began a fifteen minute exercise in ritual humiliation. The bus driver was pragmatic enough, perhaps because he was Indian and had no doubt seen much worse back home, and I did preface my pleading with the word 'Uncle', which seemed to do the trick. But in order for him to move back, twenty other drivers had to be similarly charitable, and none of them looked like they wanted to be related to me.

The truck drivers, the taxi drivers, the fat men squeezed into small cars and the thin women rattling around in hatchbacks, all wore the same weary amused expression, as if my mother's driving had only confirmed some secret, long-held opinion of how people like us were coping with the complexities of the modern world. Putting the car into reverse was, for them, an act of benevolence, maybe their first, as well-intentioned as any of Mr Ormerod's charity parcels to the poor children in Africa.

I had expected aggression, some name calling, the kind of hissed comments I occasionally endured from the young lads on the council estate near my school, the school where mama taught. But I believed by the end of the queue, I had won them over with my cheeky charm, a sort of Well, What A Mess But It's Not My Fault expression, and my deliberately exaggerated Tollington accent, thus proving I was very much one of them, they did not need to shout to make themselves understood or think they could get away with muttered swearing and I would not understand, that I belonged.

By the time I reached the last car, a Hillman Imp containing a sweet-faced elderly woman, I was almost enjoying myself, swept up by the drama of the occasion, imagining how I would recite and embroider the story for my friends at school the next day. I tapped on the window and the old dear slowly rolled it down. 'Sorry, but me mum's at the top of the hill and she's rolling down, ar . . . can yow move back just a bit? Ta.'

She blinked once and fumbled with the gear stick and said casually, 'Bloody stupid wog. Stupid woggy wog. Stupid.'

I backed off as if I had been punched and began running up the hill to our Mini, where mama was waiting with the door open and the lights were green. I jumped into the front seat and mama shot off, from nought to thirty in five seconds in first gear, just as the lights changed to amber behind us, trapping the bus which tooted furiously at our retreating bumper. We did not speak at all until we pulled into the car park of the *gurudwara*, a converted church in an anonymous, treeless side street. Mama said, 'Wipe your nose,' and handed me a tissue and we went inside.

I don't remember much about the rest of the day; there were lots of women, some of whom mama obviously knew, who pinched my cheek and sang along loudly and sharply to the *bhajans*, led by a solemn turbanned priest. There was a draped canopy beneath which sat the Holy Book, the poles support-ing the tented roof were spiralled with fairy lights, and portraits of the Gurus engaged in various bloody acts of martyrdom adorned the walls. There was a small anteroom with a sectioned, open cupboard which contained hundreds of pairs of shoes, which everyone had to remove on entering, and a small cracked sink where we washed our hands before leaving.

But I never left mama's side the whole time and although she may have intended to talk me through every aspect of the worship, explaining the rituals, translating the elaborate Punjabi, teaching me one of the hymns, she seemed to be preoccupied. I knew she was already thinking about how she would handle the long journey back home, and my mind was too full of the old lady to think about God.

Later that evening, papa pulled me onto his lap and asked me what I had learned that day. I wanted to tell him about the old lady, but then I looked at his face and saw something I had never seen before, a million of these encounters written in the lines around his warm, hopeful eyes, lurking in the furrows of his brow, shadowing the soft curves of his mouth. I suddenly realised that what had happened to me must have happened to papa countless times, but not once had he ever shared his upset with me. He must have known it would have made me feel as I felt right now, hurt, angry, confused, and horribly powerless because this kind of hatred could not be explained. I decided to return the compliment. 'I learned,' I replied, 'that mama is a really good driver.'

But today was our Christmas. My parents were celebrating it as they celebrated nearly everything else, with another *mehfil*. This was perfect for them but a major disappointment for me and all my other 'cousins' who wanted presents thrown in as part of the package, at least a nod towards what Christmas meant for the English. But I wanted to give myself a present, as no one else would, I wanted to see the fair. I knew mama did not want me to go, especially with Anita Rutter, but she assented with a slight nod of her head, and added as I rushed out of the door, 'Be back by five o'clock. I want you to help me cut the salad . . .'

Anita was peeking over my shoulder as she stood in the doorway, checking out the simmering pans and mountains of chopped vegetables crowding the kitchen. As we walked out of my gate, she said, 'Is it someone's birthday today?'

'No,' I replied. 'It's like our Christmas today. Dead boring.'

'Yow have two Christmases, do ya? Lucky cow.'

I had not thought of it this way before and suddenly felt elevated.

'I'm getting a pony for Christmas,' Anita said airily. She was wearing one of her old summer dresses and a cardigan I guessed must have been her mum's as it hung off her in woolly folds. I felt babyish and cosseted, wrapped up in my hooded anorak and thick socks and realised Anita must have been a lot older than I had previously thought.

'I'm gonna keep it at Sherrie's farm. In summat called a paddock. And then me and Sherrie am gooing to share a flat together. In London.'

I felt blindingly jealous. Sherrie was still her best friend then, and they had mapped out their life together already. I imagined them living in a penthouse flat in a place called the Angel (my favourite stop on the Monopoly board as it sounded so beautiful). They both wore mini-skirts and loads of black eyeliner and were eating toast whilst they looked out of their window. Before them stretched Buckingham Palace, the Tower of London, the Houses of Parliament and several theatres, all lit up, throwing coloured flashes onto their laughing faces, and tethered to a post attached to the breakfast bar was a sleek chestnut bay that looked just like Misty.

We passed the Big House which, as usual, showed no signs

99

of life, save a thin twisting line of smoke curling up from its huge red chimney. Anita crossed herself quickly as we passed, muttering to herself.

'What yow dooing?' I asked.

'Quick! Do this! Do the cross over your heart!'

I hurriedly copied her, and broke into a trot behind her. We did not stop until we'd passed the grounds.

'Yow got to do that every time yow pass. Didn't yow know a witch lives there?'

I shook my head dumbly. I should have guessed, it explained everything. The sense of menace surrounding the place, the fact no one ever saw visitors or inhabitants arriving or leaving, or any lights blazing at night.

'It's a woman. She killed her kids and husband, but they could never prove it, see. She wants kids, needs the blood to keep alive. Remember Jodie from up the hill?'

Jodie Bagshot was a four-year-old girl from the top end of the village who had gone missing for three frantic days a few summers ago, and whose body was found caught in the bulrushes round Hollow Ponds, the deep water-filled old mine shafts at the back of the Big House. While she was missing, the village seemed to hold its breath. Mothers stopped their children playing anywhere except the yard and the adjoining park, where everyone could see them from their kitchen windows. Police cars and officers scoured every field and hedgerow with long sticks and alsatians, even going on into the night where we could see their torches flashing through the cornfields, like cyclopic aliens calling to each other under the high-domed summer sky. The radio was on constantly in every home, waiting for the latest newsflash, aware as they listened that the news itself was being made on their own doorsteps, with a dumb sense of shame that Tollington had finally been put on the map in this tainted way.

When Jodie's drowned body was discovered and the swift conclusion reached that she had tragically wandered off, a horrendous accident, no one else involved, Tollington breathed again. Pity for the girl's family was mingled with relief that it had not been some sick stranger roaming the village, an outsider bent on destroying the easy trust and unhampered wanderings of the village children. Those things happened to other people, people in cities, people who did not know their neighbours, not the good, reliable, nosey inhabitants of Tollington.

But soon afterwards, a rumour began, started by Sam Lowbridge who had made sure he was in the front row with the press when the body was hauled out of the water. 'Her was blue,' he said. 'Like every bit of blood wore gone from her little body . . .'

I remembered his testimony now, and shivered, seeing the triumph growing in Anita's face.

'Ar, the witch is after more kids now. Shame she can see right into yowr bedroom window, in't it?'

I swung my gaze across the fields and saw that our house was indeed directly, diagonally across from the Big House's gates.

'I don't care!' I blurted out. 'My mom knows loads of prayers anyway. She says them every night in my bedroom, before I sleep.'

Anita laughed. 'Them's no good! The witch is English, in't she? Yow need proper English prayers. Like Uncle Alan knows.'

The only one I could remember offhand from my Sunday sessions was the chant we uttered in unison which heralded the appearance of two plates of custard creams and paper cups of weak orange squash – 'For what we are about to receive, may the Lord make us truly thankful. Amen.' Me and Anita said it together, all the way to the Old Pit Head.

The fairground trailers were parked in what must have been the former car park attached to the old mine. A small brick office building near the base of the pit head had long crumbled away, and frost-withered hollyhocks and dandelions had broken through the concrete floor. This usually desolate rectangle was now a hive of activity as various stubble-brushed, burly men yelled to each other in smokey voices as they heaved around large lumps of machinery which would eventually become the Waltzer, the Octopus, the Helter Skelter and several sideshow stalls offering such delights as a free goldfish with every fallen coconut.

A row of caravans was parked alongside the back fence where a fire burned in a metal brazier and children's clothes hung stiffly on a makeshift washing line strung between two door handles. A group of pin-thin children were playing with some scrawny kittens near the brazier, whilst a tired, washed-out woman in a hairnet, stood leaning against her caravan door inhaling deeply on a cigarette. I was fascinated by these travelling people, envied them their ability to contain their whole home in a moving vehicle, and imagined how romantic it must be to just climb in and move off once boredom or routine set in. How many countries had they visited, I wondered, how many deserts and jungles had they driven through, setting up their rides and booths on shifting sands or crushed palm leaf floors. Maybe they had even been to India.

I suddenly had a vivid picture of all my grandparents, dressed as they were in their photographs, being sedately whirled round in their waltzer cars. Dadima holding a goldfish in a plastic bag, Dadaji sucking on a candy floss, whilst Nanima sang along to the thumping soundtrack of 'All You Need is Love' and Nanaji kept time with a tapping sandalled foot, holding onto his turban with long brown fingers . . .

'Don't goo up there,' Anita warned me, indicating the caravans. 'Them's gippos, them is. Tinkers. Yow'll catch summat. Mum told me.' Then she waved and whooped at Fat Sally and Sherrie who were standing watching three young blokes putting the dodgem car floor down. They waved back and indicated we should come over.

As I got closer, I realised why I had not recognised them straight away. Sherrie was shivering in a short denim skirt and high heels, and had applied mauve eyeshadow all the way up to her eyebrows. Fat Sally was squeezed into a psychedelic mini-dress with a shiny scarf tied round the waist, and her lips looked wet and shimmery, like a goldfish.

'That's nice!' said Anita, pointing her finger at Fat Sally's mouth. 'Giz sum. Mom locked her door today, couldn't get nothing off her dressing table. Mean cow.'

Sherrie and Fat Sally giggled, Fat Sally rummaged in a pocket and brought out a small tub of Miners Lip Gloss which Anita grabbed and began smearing over her lips with a practised finger. They did not seem to have noticed me.

All three girls then scrutinised each other's faces, toning down a streak of blusher here, wiping a wet finger over a lipline there, whilst the three by now sweaty blokes stopped work and straightened up, looking over at us curiously. Anita, Fat Sally and Sherrie immediately pouted to attention, flicking their hair and digging each other in the ribs. Not to be outdone, I took my anorak hood down and wiped my nose. I could see the three musketeers clearly now, in a uniform of dirty denims and skinny rib sweaters, streaked with engine oil. The tallest of the three, a lanky, mousey youth with a poetic mouth, scratched his crotch absentmindedly, and muttered something to his companions, a short Italian-looking guy and a stockier blonde bloke with a smear of acne lying across his chin like scarlet porridge. They must have been about Sam Lowbridge's age, eighteen or so, just growing into their clumsy long limbs and carefully groomed bum-fluff upper lips.

Anita hissed, 'I'm having the tall one, roight?' and sauntered over towards them, her thin hips swaying to some far off radio which was playing 'This is the captain of your ship, your soul speaking . . .' I wondered if a soul was the same thing as a conscience and if Anita Rutter was following or ignoring hers at this moment in time. She sat down on the half-erected stage, right in the midst of them, and began talking to the Poet, each question punctuated with her short barking laugh. Pretty soon, all three guys were smiling along with her; I stood open-mouthed in admiration, wondering what spell she had cast, to turn these boy-men, whom I would have crossed streets to avoid had I seen them hanging around any corner near my school, into grinning, pliant pets.

Sherrie and Fat Sally were similarly impressed. 'Her always gets the best one,' muttered Sherrie, pulling her skirt down so that it momentarily covered her goosepimpled thighs.

'Look! He's only putting his arm round her! Cow!' breathed Fat Sally, who pulled her scarf tighter around her belly, as if constant optimistic pressure would finally reveal a waist as tiny and perfect as Anita's.

Anita suddenly seemed to remember we were waiting, and after a brief exchange with her new admirers, beckoned us over. I hesitated at first, wondering if it was five o'clock yet and if I should be getting back. But I sniffed something unfamiliar in the crisp late afternoon air, something forbidden and new, and I did not want to miss out.

'These am me mates, Sherrie and Sally . . .' Anita said, her hand resting proprietorially on the Poet's knee. 'This is Dave, that's Tonio, he's Italian like me dad, and Gary . . .'

Sherrie immediately plonked herself next to Tonio, once she realised she towered over him by about six inches. They seemed as relieved as each other to have not drawn the short straw and ended up with either spotty Gary or Fat Sally, who now faced each other sullenly over an empty dodgem car. There was an uncomfortable silence in which anger and pity overtook both their faces as they realised fate and their appearance had consigned them, inevitably, shamefully, to each other. If spotty Gary and Fat Sally had any illusions that they deserved better, they only had to look across and see their own miserable reflection in the other's eyes.

For one brief, mad moment, Gary's gaze flickered round

wildly, seeking an alternative, hoping there might be someone else on whom he could hang his rapidly diminishing status. He came to rest on me, took in the winter coat, the scabbed knees, my stubborn nine-year-old face, and dismissed me with amusement and yes, relief. He had not got the short straw after all and I knew, I knew that it was not because I was too young or badly dressed, it was something else, something about me so offputting, so unimaginable, that I made Fat Sally look like the glittering star prize.

The Poet whispered something into Anita's ear which made her scream as if she'd been pinched.

'What? What!' hissed Fat Sally and Sherrie in unison.

Anita pulled them unceremoniously to one side and they huddled in a group, inches from my shoulder. I might as well have been invisible. The three lads did not seem surprised at this sudden withdrawal. This was obviously part of whatever ritual they were all going through and from which I was excluded, this gathering in of the troops to discuss tactics. The lads fell into their expected stance; they raised knowing eyebrows at each other, puffed out their chests and sat with their legs as wide as possible so that their jeans strained at the seams. I had seen the dogs in the yard do something similar when one of the bitches padded past. They would cock their legs in her face as if to say, 'Well, gerra load of this then, baby!' I was beginning to realise that what was happening in front of me was somehow related to this.

'What he say, goo on, tell us!' panted Fat Sally, almost salivating with anticipation.

'He said,' drawled Anita, 'he wanted to shag the arse off me!'

Fat Sally grabbed Sherrie in a bear hug and squealed madly. Sherrie began a squeak of delight and then stopped suddenly, pushing her off, realising that Anita was playing cool in the face of this compliment. I assumed it was a compliment by her smug expression. Now Anita was looking at me, inside my head it seemed. She knew exactly what I was thinking and even wrapped up in my duffle coat, I felt suddenly naked.

'Hey Meena,' Anita said almost tenderly. 'Know what that means, that he wants to shag the arse off me?'

I shrugged in what I hoped was a non-committal, I-Might-Know-But-I'm-Not-Telling-You sort of way.

'It means,' she continued, coming right up to my face, 'that he really really loves me.'

I nodded wisely. Of course, I had known this all along. Fat Sally and Sherrie turned their faces away, their shoulders shaking slightly. I didn't care. They were only jealous that Anita had taken time to let me in on their secret and I felt blessed.

'Ey! Nita!' called the Poet. He was holding up a packet of cigarettes, and suddenly all three girls had left me, falling upon the boys like puppies, giggling uncontrollably. It was only when I started walking away that I realised Anita had not even introduced me, they did not even know my name. I glanced back; the Poet was holding out the now open cigarette packet. Anita slipped one expertly into her mouth. It seemed that her lip gloss reflected the dying sun. I ran all the way home, crossing the road when I got to the Big House, muttering my prayer and desperate to be inside and anonymous.

I reached my front door at exactly the same time as papa. His suit looked crumpled at the knees and elbows and his tie hung loosely around his neck. He put his briefcase on the front step and lifted me up, nuzzling my neck. 'How's my beti?'

'Fine,' I lied. I opened the door to see mama on her knees, trying to push the windy yellow settee back against a wall.

'What the hell are you doing, Daljit?' barked papa, striding inside and pulling her up. 'Are you mad?'

'I was not going to lift it,' mama said weakly, surrendering herself to his embrace.

'Couldn't you wait?' papa shouted angrily. 'You will damage yourself like this.'

He sat mama down on an armchair and ordered me to fetch her a glass of water, which she sipped slowly, watching papa shove the settee into a corner and lay out a clean white sheet on the floor, ready for the evening's *mehfil*.

He glanced into the kitchen. The pans were heavy and silent on the stove, a large bowl of chapatti dough stood untouched at the counter.

'You haven't even made the roti yet,' he said. 'We should cancel tonight. Too much work.'

'Don't be silly, darling,' mama sighed. 'Everyone is coming. How will it look?'

This was one of her favourite get-out clauses, the mantra for her self-imposed martyrdom – what will people think?

'You could have waited till I got home,' papa continued, plumping up cushions. 'You don't have to do everything yourself.'

'Who else is there?' mama muttered, and then I remembered I was supposed to cut the salad. I went into the kitchen and opened the fridge where a huge tupperware full of freshly-cut tomatoes and cucumber stared back accusingly at me.

The first guests began arriving around seven o'clock. I was admiring myself in mama's dressing table mirror, deciding whether I liked this unfamiliar reflection staring back in a purple *salwar kameez* suit, stiff with yellow elephant embroidery around the cuffs and neckline. I liked the suit, but it did not quite go with the pudding basin haircut and chewed-down fingernails. I spotted mama's modest cache of make-up, a couple of Revlon lipsticks with round blunt heads, a gold-plated compact case which when opened, played 'Strangers in the Night' in a tinkly offhand manner, and a tiny stub of black eyebrow pencil. I picked up one of the lipsticks, Pink Lady, and applied it carefully around my mouth, startled to see a glaring cerise grin appear on my face, seemingly hovering above it like the Cheshire Cat smile I had seen in one of the ink drawings in my Alice in Wonderland book. To finish off the stunning effect, I rifled through mama's jewellery case, a blue leather box with delicate filigree clasps, and chose a gold chain upon which hung a single teardrop-shaped diamond. Even though I was sure mama would not mind, I hid it under my vest.

'Meena?' mama called from downstairs. 'Door please!' I hurriedly opened the compact case and stuck my finger into its belly. The powder was surprisingly soft and crumbly, and I wiped a few smears around my nose and forehead, like I had seen mama do. I blew myself a kiss as I left, did I look gorgeous.

Auntie Shaila gave a shriek of alarm when I opened the door. '*Hai Ram!* What is this? Looking like a rumpty tumpty dancing girl already . . .' She tottered inside, dragging Uncle Amman behind her, his smooth, polished billiard ball head glistening with raindrops. 'Daljit! Eh! Look at your daughter!' Auntie Shaila continued, peeling off her overcoat, two woollen shawls and finally a thick pair of old bedsocks, revealing a glorious emerald green sari. 'Damn English weather . . . having to hide all the time under these smelly blankets . . . Daljit!'

Mama came bustling in from the kitchen, adjusting her sari *pulla*, and stopped short when she saw me pouting back. 'Meena! What have you done to your face?' she asked.

Auntie Shaila kissed mama and handed her a box of Ambala sweetmeats, sticky yellow *laddoos* pressing against the clear cellophane of the lid. 'Happy Diwali, sister. You see what happens to our girls here? Wanting to grow up so quickly and get boyfriends-shoyfriends . . . Isn't childhood short enough, eh?'

'She was just experimenting,' papa smiled, giving a jolly *namaste* to our visitors. 'Meena, go upstairs and wipe it off, good girl . . .'

'No!' I said, shocked by the sound of my voice. 'Where's Pinky? Where's Baby?'

Auntie Shaila's two daughters were the only other girls

roughly around my age in our circle, and therefore I treated them as best friends in front of the adults, although I secretly thought they were boring and rather thick. I had planned a whole evening of ghost stories and plays in which we would take turns at playing a screaming blonde heroine being pursued by nameless wailing monsters. Auntie Shaila spoke carefully, as if addressing an idiot. 'Pinky and Baby are home with their dadima. Tonight is for grown-ups. And please no naughtiness tonight. Your mama is in a delicate way, you should be pressing her feet and asking for forgiveness. Now upstairs, and come back down wearing your own pretty face.'

After scrubbing my cheeks and lips clean with tissues, I opened my bedroom window and saw, as I had expected to, the lights of the fairground twinkling through the trees surrounding the Big House. I caught glimpses of the Octopus whirling round and round, its tentacles hung with chairs containing screaming, laughing passengers, their voices mingling with the thumping soundtrack of a pop song, *One Two Three, Oh It's So Easy, Ba-by*! as my papa began tuning up his harmonium in the room below. I could see couples drawn by the music and lights, picking their way through the rows of cars which clogged the road up to the pithead.

I could make out another crowd of people pushing their way through the fairground punters, struggling against the flow and press of bodies. This crocodile of renegades moved slowly. I saw the flash of a jewelled sandal picking its way through the mud, a glittering nose ring caught by the flare of a neon bulb, a streak of vermilion silk exposed by a winter coat whipped up by the night air, and knew the rest of our guests had arrived.

By the time I had realised no one had noticed I was sulking and went downstairs, the front room was full of my uncles and aunties, all sitting cross-legged on the white floor sheet. Mama was handing round starters of kebabs and chutney whilst papa leafed through his tattered notebook containing *ghazal* lyrics, deep in conversation with Uncle Tendon, who cradled his *tabla* like a child. 'Ah Meena beti!' they called out as one, and I did the round of *namastes* and kisses, smiling through the lipstick assaults and the over-hard cheek pinching as my suit was praised and tweaked, my stomach tickled and jabbed, my educational achievements listed and admired, until I felt I was drowning in a sea of rustling saris, clinking gold jewellery and warm, brown, overpowering flesh.

The men, as usual, had divided up into two distinct groups. There were the ones like Uncle Tendon and my papa, the dapper, snapping, witty men in crisp suits who smoked and joked and retired to women-free corners where their whispered conversation, no doubt risqué, was punctuated by huge bear-hugs and back-slapping routines. Then there was the quieter type, like Auntie Shaila's husband, Uncle Amman, self-effacing, gentle shadows who followed their wives around playing the role of benevolent protector, but well aware that they were merely satellites caught in the matronly orbit of their noisy, loving wives.

Most of my Aunties were in the Shaila mode, plump, bosomy women with overactive gap-toothed mouths, fond of bright tight outfits accentuating every cherished roll and curve of flesh, bursting with optimism and unsolicited advice for everyone's children, upon whose futures they pinned all their unfulfilled desires. Mama was in the minority group of Auntie types, the slender, delicate soft-voiced women with the sloe-eyed grace captured by the Mughal miniature paintings hanging on our front room wall. Their serenity masked backbones of iron and a flair for passive resistance of which Gandhiji himself would have been proud.

As I watched my mother trying to force another kebab onto Auntie Shaila (mama looked like one of those tiny birds who hop in and out of hippos' mouths, negotiating molars nervously) I realised what part of my problem was – I had been born to the wrong type of Indian woman. If I had been given a mother like Auntie Shaila, the fat loud type who didn't mind the patches of sweat forming under their sari blouses after a good dance, I would not have to feel so angry at my body, the way it betrayed me by making me stand with my legs akimbo, hands on hips, the way it tripped me up into the dirt, skinning my knees – it was never meant to behave like the body of a lady. But next to mama, I would always feel lumbering and clumsy. Even in late pregnancy, she moved like a galleon in full sail, stately and calm, her belly leading the way. There was another baby inside there, as much as I had tried to ignore it, and I suddenly understood that mama would not be exclusively mine for very much longer.

A ripple of recognition passed through the room as papa began singing, his rich vibrato climbed slowly up my spine. I knew this song, a romantic song, naturally, of a lover singing to his beloved, telling her he was so sick with desire that he would follow her wherever she wandered like a shadow . . . '*Mera Saaya Sath Hoga, Tu Jahan Jahan Chalega* . . .' Uncle Tendon joined in with a soft heartbeat accompaniment and a collective sigh of longing swelled the air. Papa's voice swooped and soared like a swallow above our heads, notes catching in his throat, flowers caught momentarily in brambles before being tossed into the air, every face turned inwards, remembering the first time they heard this song.

I suddenly saw Auntie Shaila sauntering along Connaught Place, pencil-thin in her chic chiffon suit, stepping between the sprawled limbs of the young men lounging at the sidewalk cafes over their cold coffees and cheese *pakore*, humming the song to herself, pretending not to notice, but knowing for certain, that every eye was upon her. I saw mama singing the song to the wind as she cycled back from her all girls college, her long oiled plaits bumping against her back, swerving around the cows and trucks on the Karol Bagh Road, duty and desire already at war for her future. I saw papa, just like in the old photographs, hair slicked back, movie star fashion, Cary Grant baggy suit and lit cigarette hanging from his fingers, standing on the street corner opposite mama's flat,

whistling that tune, blowing it through the peeling paint
shutters where mama sat bent over textbooks she could not
read because of the thumping of her heart, because that song
told her that he was waiting for her outside, and would wait
until she came. These were my versions of their stories and I
set them free during papa's songs.

Papa's singing always unleashed these emotions which
were unfamiliar and instinctive at the same time, in a
language I could not recognise but felt I could speak in my
sleep, in my dreams, evocative of a country I had never visited
but which sounded like the only home I had ever known. The
songs made me realise that there was a corner of me that
would be forever not England.

I glanced around at my elders who looked so shiny and
joyous in their best Diwali clothes. I had seen all of them at
some point in their workday clothes of English separates and
over-co-ordinated suits. But on occasions like Diwali, they
expanded to fit their Indian clothes and at this moment,
seemed too big and beautiful for our small suburban sitting
room.

Papa finished singing, the last notes faded away to be
replaced by rapturous applause and shouts of 'Wah! Kumar
saab!' He radiated joy, achievement. I'd never seen him come
home from work looking like this. He turned to me and my
stomach sank; I knew what he was going to ask me. 'Meena
beti, why don't you sing a song for your Aunties and Uncles?'

They all began clapping and shouting, 'Hah! Let's hear
your lovely voice! Come and show us how it is done.'

'No,' I mumbled uselessly. 'Don't want to . . . no . . .'

I knew I was already defeated, that false modesty was an
expected response to any social request, that 'No' always
meant 'Yes, I want to really but you will have to ask me at
least five times before I can give in graciously and not look like
a big fat show-off'. It applied to food, drink, money and
especially public performance of any kind; I had seen mama
literally force-feeding Auntie Shaila, who insisted she was not

at all hungry and then proceeded to polish off a truckful of kebabs without chewing, ostensibly to please mama, but grateful she had been given permission to stuff her face without guilt. Of course, we all understood these complex rules of hospitality; our neighbours however did not.

Mama had been caught out quite badly when she once offered a lift down to the shops to the Mad Mitchells who lived next door, on the other side of the entry. Mr and Mrs Mitchell were a middle-aged brother and sister who lived with Cara, a moon-faced dopey woman who, it was rumoured, was their incestuous daughter. Whilst the couple were loud, argumentative, and swore as naturally as they breathed, Cara never said a word. We would often spot her wandering down the middle of the road humming to herself, dragging a squeaky shopping trolley as alarmed motorists swerved to avoid her.

Mama had been helping me into the car when all three Mitchells appeared at her side, wearing buttoned-up overcoats and their usual warm idiot grins.

'New car, Mrs K?'

'Oh yes,' mama smiled. 'So useful for getting to work.'

'Ay, bloody bosting car that, ain't it ma?' Mr Mitchell sighed.

'Bloody bosting,' agreed Mrs Mitchell, who was holding Cara's hand tightly.

'So am yow gooin down the shops then?' they said in unison.

'Why, yes,' mama said, still smiling. 'Can I give you a lift?'

Now if she'd asked that question to an Indian, they would have replied, 'Oh no, we will walk, it is such a lovely day, please don't bother yourself, we enjoy strolling in the sleet, so good for the circulation . . .' etc, giving mama time to consider the request and the other room to withdraw gracefully, because if mama had not physically shoved them into the car, that obviously meant she was in a hurry and would rather not give them a lift at all.

Instead, the Mitchells said, 'Oh ta!' and piled into the back seat, leaving mama open-mouthed on the pavement. After we had dropped them off, we discovered a small patch of urine where Cara had been sitting. Mama had to scrub down the upholstery later that night, not wanting to do it in daylight where the Mitchells might see, and feel embarrassed.

'Hurry up Meena! No more pretending now, we have asked you enough times!' called Auntie Shaila, making everyone laugh.

I shuffled over to papa who shifted over, indicating a space beside him. I seethed with embarrassment and fury; what was wrong with these people? Why couldn't a No mean a bloody sodding No? Why was talking to them like trying to do semaphore in a gale?

'Which song, beti?' asked papa, running his hands over the keys, flexing his fingers in preparation.

'Any,' I said ungraciously.

Papa began an introduction to an old Hindi film song he had taught me. He paused where the verse began and nodded encouragingly. I took a breath and began, '*Yeh Raat Yeh Chandari Phir Kahan, Sun Ja Dil Ki Daastan . . .*'

I knew the song was about a sultry moonlit night in which a lover is thinking about his absent object of desire. I knew it was a romantic song, but as I sang, all I could think of was the Poet sniffing at Anita's hemline like a yard mutt. I became aware that some of the Aunties were giggling, whispering to each other behind their hands and then fixing me with long, fond stares. I could hear Auntie Shaila clearly, whispering not being one of her strong points. 'Va! She sings Punjabi with a Birmingham accent! Damn cute, really!'

I stopped dead, the harmonium carried on for a few bars after me and then breathed out and fell silent.

'I don't want to do this song,' I said to papa.

'But it sounds so lovely, really. You should sing your own songs, Meena.'

'Okay,' I said, took a deep breath and launched into a

rendition of 'We Wear Short Shorts', complete with the gyrating dance routine I had seen Pan's People do to it on *Top Of the Pops*. I flicked my hair and kicked my legs as papa and Uncle Tendon gamely tried to match a key and rhythm to my show stopper, although their complex minor key riffs and passionate drum solos did not altogether complement the song. I finished by shouting 'Yeah man!', and doing the splits, accompanied by a loud ripping noise and after a moment's pause, a round of enthusiastic applause. Mama pulled me up and examined the large tear along the crotch of my trousers. 'Did you have to do that?' she hissed.

Papa laughed, 'Leave her! It was very groovy, Meena! That was what you call a good jam-in, hey Tendon saab?'

They slapped each other's backs and hooted uproariously.

The Aunties and Uncles just loved me; they crowded round patting me like a pet, over-enthusing about my talent and charisma whilst papa shot knowing winks to mama, who was slowly melting in the face of this public approval. 'Hai, such a performer!' shouted Auntie Shaila above the din. 'So sweetly done, so er modern! Where did you learn this song, Meena beti?'

'Off the radio,' I preened. 'It's my all time favourite song at the moment,' and then added, 'It's so brilliant I could shag the arse off it.'

There was a sudden terrible intake of breath and then complete silence, broken only by the harmonium emitting a death rattle as papa's fingers fell off the keys. In a split second, my beaming admirers had become parodies of Hindi film villains, with flared nostrils, bulging eyes and quivering, outraged eyebrows. They only needed twirling moustaches and pot bellies straining at a bullet laden belt to complete the sense of overwhelming menace that now surrounded me. In my dizzy state, I fancied I saw Anita Rutter perched on a dodgem car with a fag hanging out of her mouth, and laughing in reverberated echo as the heavens slowly crumbled and fell in blue jagged lumps around her.

'What did you say, Meena?'

It was papa, in a tone of voice I had not heard before, which shot right off the Outraged Parent clapometer.

'N . . . nothing papaji,' I stuttered, noticing that the Aunties and Uncles were now drifting away. This was a very bad sign. They were not even attempting group discipline on this particular crime. I was on my own. Papa stood up slowly and strode towards me. Papa has never hit me, never hit me, I told myself over and over again and yet I flinched when mama suddenly appeared at my side, putting a protective arm around me and shoving me towards the stairs. 'You better go upstairs, Meena,' she said quietly. I did not need to be asked twice and I fled.

I did not bother putting my bedroom light on as I changed into some trousers and a jumper. I did not remove mama's diamond on a chain, I left it on, hidden spitefully beneath the jumper. The curtains were not drawn and the fairground lights provided just enough illumination and flashes of neon which danced mockingly across the walls and ceiling, reminding me of what I was missing. I sat by the window for a long time before I had enough courage to venture back downstairs. No one looked at me as I crept through the sitting room, where all the men were now engaged in loud banter whilst some of them balanced over-full plates of steaming food on their laps. I did not know if I was being ignored or if this was just the usual absorption of the elders when they were eating.

The kitchen was bustling with activity, so I stood in the doorway, trying to make myself appear smaller and sorry. My Aunties had formed an assembly line with mama at the head, who warmed up a chapatti on the griddle before passing it down the line on a plate onto which each Auntie plonked a serving of meat, rice, vegetables and yoghurt, straight into the waiting hands of the men. My usual job was water monitor; I would be sent round the circle of Uncles balancing a tray of paper cups which would be drained and placed back in front of me in a second. It irritated me that the men would hardly look up whilst I stood there waiting for them to finish. It was not that I felt they were excluding me, it was the easy confidence they had, that they could extend a hand and their water would appear as if by magic.

I decided it would be a good move tonight to volunteer for water duty, but before I could offer, I was stopped by the mention of my name. Mama was talking to Auntie Shaila as she held a chapatti over a naked gas ring. Her fingers actually lingered in the bluey-yellow flames but she never seemed to notice. In fact, all the Aunties had this talent for being utterly fire resistant when it came to cooking. I had seen all of them at some point lift up dishes straight from the stove, pat and shape dough onto smoking griddles and of course, wave cupped hands over and over again through the sacred flame of the *diyas* on their shrines. Whenever I helped mama cook chapatti, I always ended up with red stinging weals on my fingertips. I decided this talent to not burn, or at least to not feel pain, only came to Indian women after they were married.

Mama's fingers flicked the flames as she talked, or rather half-shouted, to Auntie Shaila over the hissing pans and clanging utensils. 'But really Shailaji, Meena just won't stop! I don't know what to do . . .'

Their backs were towards me; mama still had a waist, Auntie Shaila's was lost in the concertina of honeyed flesh that bulged from beneath her sari blouse.

'It's probably the baby coming that's making her so difficult,' Auntie Shaila shouted back. 'Attention-seeking, bas, that's it . . .'

'But she's been like this since she could talk!' mama wailed, unnecessarily dramatically I thought. 'If it isn't rude things it is lies, always lies . . .'

And then to my mortification, and in front of the rest of the mafia, mama actually presented an entire CV of my misdemeanours, including some I'd completely forgotten about.

'You remember, that time she told my entire staff room that she had been a bridesmaid at our wedding?' This wasn't fair!

every other girl in my class of four-year-olds had been a bridesmaid and boasted about it continually, I just did not see why I had to be left out, that was all. 'And then the story about India, when she told her class we had gone there on holiday? She told them we stayed in mud huts and killed a tiger for breakfast . . .' Well, I'd been watching too much 'Tarzan' on the TV and it was better than saying the highlight of our holiday had been a daytrip to Blackpool. And they had been really impressed. 'Then that time she attacked that boy with a milk bottle top . . .' Peter James had said my blood was not red like everyone else's , so I cut my finger to show him it was, and then stabbed his leg just to double check his theory.

Mama paused for a second to flip a chapatti over. This was my chance to clear my throat or something, but I missed it. 'And she gets into so many fights, Shailaji, comes home with ripped clothes and scratches . . . What if she starts that at school as well?' Well I already had, but luckily mama had not found out yet. Launching immediately into anyone who started name-calling was the only way to stop it becoming day-to-day bullying, as I saw happened to other kids – the fatties, the spotties, the swots and naturally, the only other four non-white children at my school. Surely mama would understand this, being a teacher . . . 'And all the times she steals money from my purse and thinks she is being clever and I don't know . . .' She had got me there. And I did not want to hear any more.

'Hello mama,' I said loudly. Mama actually jumped at my voice which strangely pleased me.

'Meena . . . beti . . .' mama said carefully, weighing up what I might have heard with what I had said in mixed company just half an hour before. 'You want to eat now?' mama continued, whilst Auntie Shaila was already reaching over her to fetch me a plate.

'Er, no, mama, I'm going to the toilet first . . . thanks,' I added and slipped out of the back door, bypassing the outside loo smartly. I flung open the back gate to our yard, snuck into the entry, and simply followed the flashing fairground lights.

It was spitting raindrops as I reached the first stall, cursing myself that I had not brought, or stolen, any money. A red-faced plump man stood guarding a pool of bobbing ducks, occasionally poking them with a long pole topped with a claw. 'Hook a duck, chick?' I smiled and shook my head. He forgot I existed immediately, looking over my head for the next punter. The noise was deafening, several pop songs blared out simultaneously from different rides, the flashing lights held back the darkness, I felt as if I was on a floating neon island in a sea of inky endless black.

The fair was full of teenagers, respectable families had long since gone home. I recognised some of the youths from the council estate near the shops a few miles away who trailed round in packs, sniffing the air for unaccompanied women, displaying their hardness by thumping hell out of the Test Your Strength Punchbag or knocking down coconuts with a single deadly throw. I thought I saw Hairy Neddy and Sandy strolling arm in arm past the amusement arcade. She was holding a huge, demented-looking fluffy rabbit whilst he fed her candy floss from a plastic bag.

Sam Lowbridge and a group of his biker mates had taken over the shooting range. He was aiming a rifle at a jungle scene where tigers, lions and occasionally a grinning black face with a bone in its nose would pop out from the foliage, daring him to fire. Sam pulled in his rifle and blew on the end of it like a cowboy, making his mates laugh. He saw me and cocked a surprised eyebrow, blowing a lock of sandy hair from his eyes. 'Alright littl'un. Yow cum to have some fun?'

I nodded airily, as if this was a fairly regular occurrence.

Sam handed me the air rifle and said, 'Goo on then. Have one on me.'

I'd never held a gun before. I'd seen the farmers up the top end of the village firing at crows, and sometimes, tramping down the hill with several furry corpses hanging from their shoulders, so I knew what I had could do some damage.

I tried to hold the gun evenly and it slipped off my shoulder. The bikers laughed loudly. Sam smiled at me lazily. He was all loose limbs and offhand gestures, almost foppish, but his body was lean and hard and ready to move and no one was fooled by the apparent indifference in those half-lidded grey eyes. I wondered how many girls he had kissed, and why he ever bothered to talk to me. 'Hee-yaar,' he said, turning me round to face the moving jungle, holding the gun for me but pressing his fingers over mine on the trigger. 'Just watch, right . . . dead carefully . . .' He squeezed my hand and I closed my eyes, recoiling slightly with the bang. When I opened them, a surly young woman, the one I had seen smoking on the caravan step, was holding a plastic bracelet out to me ungraciously. 'Yow got him right in the head, girl,' said Sam, taking the piece of tat and slipping it on my wrist. I did not want to look and see what damage I had done to the poor man with the bone in his nose. I knew it had not been me that had won the prize.

I was not surprised to see Sherrie sitting on the steps of the waltzers. She was sharing a cigarette with Tonio and was wearing his denim jacket over her mini-skirt. She saw me and smiled briefly before flicking back her hair and revealing a bruise the size of a saucer on her neck. I gasped, horrified at this deformity. Tonio stood up and shouted as he walked off, 'Gooing for a slash, chick. Don't go away!'

Sherrie sighed and pulled the denim jacket around herself, sniffing it tenderly. 'Seen this?' she demanded, pointing to the livid purple and yellow blotch. 'Tonio did it.'

'Really?' I said. 'What for?'

''Cos he likes me, you daft cow.'

'Oh,' I whispered, wondering if this abuse was part and parcel of hanging around boys.

'He wants to give me another one,' Sherrie confided. 'What do you think I should do?'

'I think you should hit him back,' I said.

Sherrie snorted and got up, wiping dirt off her bum before

tottering off after Tonio. The waltzers were spinning round giddily, each carriage containing faceless, screaming blurs whose voices were snatched by the wind and spirited away. Dave, the Poet, was standing behind one car, tossing it round and round as he leaned into the swell and dip of the wooden floor, so perfectly balanced that the ash hung suspended from the cigarette dangling from his lips. I knew Anita was inside, being thrown about. I caught glimpses of her skinny ankles scrabbling for a foothold. But there was someone else in there with her, someone in high heels and shiny tights whose feet never moved from the floor of the car, whose pudgy knees exuded bravado and promise.

When the ride finally rolled to a halt, Anita tumbled out followed by her mother, Deirdre, who patted her perm and looked bored. Anita's mother has brought her to the fair! Anita's mother actually goes on rides with her, rides that would give my mama a migraine for a week. I was completely impressed, so impressed that I forgot the day's earlier humiliation and waved to Anita madly. She waved back, and then, completely for my benefit, turned to the Poet and gave him a light kiss on the face. Deirdre tapped her on the shoulder and handed her some money which Anita took with grateful amazement. She yelled over to me, 'I'm gooing to get summat to eat! Wait there, yeah?'

I sat down on the muddy planks and prepared to wait, vaguely aware that I might be missed at home but anxious not to miss the opportunity of going round the fair with Anita. I looked up as the ride began again and wondered where Deirdre and the Poet had disappeared to. And then I saw them, only because the Octopus ride had paused in mid-air and its headlights lit up the two figures running hand in hand towards the caravans. Deirdre had taken off her high heels and was holding them as she was dragged along by the Poet. They did not quite make the door but sank down together on the metal steps, hands tugging at each other's buttons, their faces locked together as if they were trying to swallow each other whole. Deirdre broke free for a second; she was not smiling, she looked sombre almost, and pulled the Poet into the caravan where a moment later, the lights snapped off.

I felt as if the wind had frozen my face into a mask, lockjaw set in, my eyelids would not close. Anita entered my line of vision at the far end of the fair. She was walking slowly, carrying two toffee apples and two bags of chips. She had bought me dinner. I knew I should be going home, I was already in big trouble and each minute I stayed would only increase my parents' panic and the severity of my punishment. But at this moment I could not leave Anita alone. I smiled inanely until she got close enough to grab, and slipped my arm through hers, pulling her away from the caravans behind us.

'Careful! I'll drop me sauce!' she yelled, but she did not pull her arm away. 'Where's me mom?' she inquired, through a gob full of chips.

'Er, I think I saw her gooing that way . . . you know, sort of home way . . . your home I mean . . .' I was gabbling. I rallied myself, I was supposed to be good at this. 'Let's goo on some rides, Nita, yeah? I ain't never had someone to goo on rides with before . . .'

I could tell Anita was impressed by my authentic Yard accent; she appraised me coolly, absorbing the fact I was younger and yet out at night without parents, and was apparently cocky enough to assume she would want to waste some of her time with me. She tipped up the paper cone of chips (I had not touched mine), and shook a few into her mouth. She took another look behind her whilst I willed the caravan door to stay closed, and then squeezed my arm which was still in hers. 'Come on then Meena, let's goo on all the fast ones, eh?'

I cannot remember how long we were at the fair, as every stomach-churning ride seemed to last for hours. We did them all – the Waltzers, the Octopus, the Wall of Death, the Big Ship, several rounds of the House of Evil, in which we screamed and yelled and begged for mercy and never let go of each other's bodies.

It was during our last go on the Waltzers, when Anita had got down to her mom's last sixpence, that she finally asked about the Poet. 'Where's Dave gone, then?' she shouted over the ear-splitting soundtrack of The Kinks to Gary, who had made it his personal mission to try and fling our car off its coasters. Gary shrugged unhelpfully, leaning his pudgy body away from the swell of the boards beneath him. 'Tell him, right . . .' Anita yelled over her shoulder. 'Tell him to call for me tomorrer . . . two o'clock, yeah? Or he's in for a duffing!' she added and then turned to nudge me in the ribs. I laughed, nudged her back and wondered if the Poet and Deirdre were exchanging play-slaps like us right now, giggling about Anita and her silly schoolgirl crush.

It was much darker when we climbed off the Waltzers on aching, wobbly legs; night had closed its lid on the vaulted sky, pushing the stars down towards us so they lay low and heavy like milky sponges. I began to panic. They must have noticed I was missing by now, maybe they had called the police, maybe papa was out in the cornfields right now with a torch and his heart hanging from his mouth. 'I gorra go Nita,' I said.

'Not yet, I wanna show yow summat first . . .' Anita replied, pulling me with her towards the back of the fairground, where the concrete yard met the high fence of the Big House grounds.

'No!' I said, knowing we would have to pass the Poet's caravan. 'Not this way . . .'

'Yow don't know the way I know so shurrup,' Anita replied, holding onto me tightly. I actually shut my eyes as we passed the caravans, and did not open them until I felt the ridges of a fence bump against my knees. I found myself looking up at a thicket of tree trunks, solid and scaly as elephant legs. The Big House trees, which from my bedroom window looked distant and symbolic, were now almost close enough to touch. The first few rows were lit up occasionally by the passing tentacles of the Octopus, barnacled with flashing bulbs, but beyond these there was darkness, a syrupy gloom which somewhere housed a child-eating monster.

My breathing quickened as I watched Anita expertly prise apart a couple of rotting boards in the perimeter fence and begin slipping her thin body through the gap.

'What yow dooing, Nita? They've got dogs, yow know!' I whispered fiercely, quickly thinking it was much cooler to be frightened of alsatians than witches.

'They ain't,' Anita replied, her voice straining as she eased a last bit of foot through the hole. 'He's inside, chewing up babies' bones I expect. I ain't never seen a dog in here . . . and anyway, I thought yow said yow wanted to hang round with uz?'

She used the Royal We, which seemed entirely natural. I clutched mama's gold chain to me like a talisman, I could feel the diamond digging into my breastbone, a sharp sweet pain which reminded me I was still alive and breathing. Then I panicked as Anita seemed to be slowly disappearing by inches into the branches, like the Cheshire Cat's smile, and without thinking, heaved myself through the loose boards and followed the flash of Anita's white winklepicker shoes.

At first I could see nothing; the darkness had a texture so dense I fancied my outstretched hands were pushing against giant elastic cobwebs. The ground under me conspired to disorientate me. It was spongy and silent under my uncertain feet, no crackling branches or noisy heather to reassure me that I walked on the earth and owned it; I felt this forest now owned *me*. After slapping head-first into a few low branches I became accustomed to the gloom and began to pick my way more confidently through the trees, fixing my gaze on the back of Anita's shoes which seemed to glow like low, uneven landing lights. Then I suddenly realised that I could not hear the fairground any more. It had been replaced by a much louder noise, a low breathing made up of night breeze, whispering leaves, insects humming in morse code and the sporadic mournful hoots of a lone high owl.

'Hee-yaar!' whispered Anita, who came from nowhere to appear next to me and yanked my hand, pulling me after her up a pebbly rise until we were looking down at an immense black hole, which I only realised was water when I saw the moon suspended in its centre, a perfect silver disc in what looked like another upside-down sky.

'Hollow Pond!' I breathed reverently.

I had been here once before, I have a vague memory of sitting at the water's edge with someone, papa maybe, listening to him explain how this old mine shaft had filled with water and formed a natural pool. But I was not to ever swim there because it led into a huge labyrinth of other shafts and was therefore bottomless, unforgiving. There must have been a time when Hollow Pond was open to the village as I could not imagine papa sneaking around and snagging his trousers on some barbed wire to get in. But of course, since Jodie Bagshot's drowning, no one ventured here anymore.

As I thought of Jodie, I saw a flash of something from the corner of my eye, a movement in amongst the tall blurred bulrushes that could have been a child scrabbling for air. I began shivering so hard that my teeth actually sounded like castanets, which made Anita giggle. 'Come on . . . this ain't special. I'll show yow my secret . . .' I continued holding onto Anita's hand as she pulled me down the slope and around a crumbling brick wall which I realised with a shock was the actual perimeter of the Big House garden. I was too short and the wall too high to afford a clear view through the windows, tall thin windows with many concave panes like the surface of a fly's eye, all of which were dark except one. We paused by the wall opposite the illuminated square, both of us panting for breath. If I strained my neck there it was, my first ever glimpse into the Big House; two foot square of unveiled mystery, bordered with heavy red velvet curtains, and in its centre was a chandelier out of a fairy story, a huge layered crystal cake dripping with tiers of diamonds spilling off it like an over-generous filling. I felt I could taste it, taste something. It was a sickly sweet flavour that left a sharp aftertaste, it was carefree, spoiled, unobtainable. It made me hungry and resentful all at once, and in spite of my chattering teeth, I felt my cheeks flush as I stared and stared.

Anita had to drag me away, and then we were creeping around the wall into another smaller wood at the back of the house. I had not realised the land stretched as far back as this; how did it all fit in? I did quick calculations as we tramped our way through waist-high grass which was damp and squeaky. Did this wood back onto the fields opposite Mr Ormerod's shop? No, that was not possible, the view from his swinging door was flat and treeless. Where had they managed to hide a whole other forest? And then I wondered if it was one of those enchanted forests that featured in the fable and legend books I read surreptitiously, embarrassed that I occasionally needed this regular little-girl fix of goblins, princesses and spells. I ought to have been reading *Jackie* magazine by now, I scolded myself, anxious not to dwell on the prospect of entering a wood which might fade away as the sun rose, with me and Anita still lost inside it.

'There it is.' Anita was standing under a small weeping willow tree, one hand on the trunk so she looked like she was holding up a leafy umbrella. I focused my gaze in the direction of her pointing finger towards a basin-shaped clearing, but was not sure what I was looking at. It resembled a small bandstand made out of marble, a small circle of pillars topped with a cupped dome, so hidden beneath the undergrowth that only flashes of white stone were visible beneath the tangles of creeping ivy and encrusted moss. But there was something inside, mounted on a plinth, a statue or bust of some kind which was so overgrown that in the darkness, looked like a column of silent swarming bees. I moved closer whilst Anita held back.

'Am yow gooing up there?' she asked.

I was pleased to hear the anxiety in her voice. 'Yeah, I wanna see wharrit is,' I replied, already leaving her behind.

My socks and jumper sleeves caught on briars as I fought my way through the clearing, burrs and spiders' webs latched themselves onto my fringe.

And then I was in front of it, standing beneath the dome and flanked by pillars, and staring at the thing on its mount. I pulled at the creepers around it which came away with a soft ripping sound. My fingers became coated in green slime as I tugged and wrenched at the greenery until a face began emerging from the jungle. First appeared a low ridged forehead in the centre of which was a single perfect circle, then the eyes, almond-shaped and serene but sightless, and so familiar and old to me that I caught my breath. Was it him? And what was he doing here? And just as the final fronds came away in my hands and I saw the ears unfold like a handclap and the long trunk unfurl like a blessing, I heard the dog barking somewhere far away and did not have time to do as Auntie Shaila would have done, and raise my hands in *Namaste* to our smiling elephant god, Ganesha.

'Fuckin' 'ell!' Anita was already running when I realised the barking was coming closer, a mad, ragged barking which bounced off the trees so there seemed not one but hundreds of dogs ready to leap at me with snapping jaws. I stumbled after Anita, panic constricting my chest, twisting my ankle on potholes and hollows whilst thorny fingers whipped at my face and grabbed at my clothes, trying to make me stay. I could not see Anita, I simply followed the sound of cracking branches and felt the trail of flattened grass and bent bushes she had left in her wake. And then I hit a fence, or rather it hit me full in the face. I bounced backwards so fast that when I opened my eyes, I found myself lying in a thicket, looking at the stars through a cracked windscreen of twigs and wondering why my mouth seemed full of rust.

'Meena! Here!'

Anita was running on the other side of the fence, banging

on the planks so I could follow her direction. I heaved myself up, aware that the barking was now nearer and louder, underscored by scrabbling feet and a calm snuffling. I used the fence as a guide, running with my arm against it, trying to keep upright until suddenly my hand hit air and I fell forward and into Anita's arms. She set me on my feet and expertly replaced the softened plank and we were back on the pavement at the far end of the Big House, within sight of my own front door.

'God, what yow done, Meena?' Anita asked wonderingly.

She put her finger to my lips, and when she brought it back, its tip was dark red. I gingerly felt my lips. I could trace a gash running from the inside of my bottom lip which spread halfway across my cheek. I looked down at my jumper, two great tears on one sleeve and the front of it flapping open, like I had been split from breastbone to stomach. Anita did not have to say anything, we both knew how much trouble I was in. We walked slowly together the last few yards to the crossroads. I knew it was late by the height of the moon, but strangely, all the lights in my house were still blazing and the same convoy of Aunties' cars were still parked in the lane.

'Meybbe they won't have missed ya?' Anita said finally, hopefully, knowing she would have to answer to no one.

I shook my head. I knew it would not matter how many guests were still singing in the front room. I had sneaked out without telling, and worst of all, I knew, as soon as I had looked down at my ravaged jumper, that I had lost mama's diamond necklace, which I imagined lying at Ganesha's fat feet like an offering, a single glint amidst the ivy, a fallen star.

'What was it, that thing you saw?' was Anita's parting shot before she turned into the entry.

I shrugged my shoulders, suddenly weary and in pain. 'Nothing, Nita. Nothing special,' and began the long march home.

I braced myself for howls of woe and gnashing of teeth when

I saw my front door swing open and two of my Aunties appeared shivering on the doorstep. But instead they barely registered my presence, beyond a slight gesture of relief, and looked above and beyond me, scanning the horizon, waiting for something. Then one of them called inside, 'Meena is here! Don't let her see!'

I heard the catch in their throats, they turned huge sorrowful gazes at me, I could tell they were frightened for me. Auntie Shaila appeared holding a stack of towels. Wordlessly she grabbed my arm and pulled me towards the kitchen; I caught a glimpse of my father, pale and taut, kneeling in a circle of Aunties, talking softly to someone.

My Uncles were huddled together in the lounge, silent and embarrassed almost, not daring to look up. Then suddenly I was in the darkened kitchen and the door was firmly shut behind me. I stood rooted to the spot, trying to calm my breathing whilst the sounds of muffled, frantic activity continued outside. The street light on the corner outside filled the room with a sickly viscous glow, somewhere a cooling saucepan hissed softly. I heard running water and then the dreadful familiar wail of an approaching ambulance.

I heard strange male voices entering the house, papa yelling, 'Careful! For God's sake . . .' and I hurled myself at the door, yanking it open. Mama was lying on a stretcher covered with a red blanket, her eyes screwed up with pain. Papa walked beside her, holding her hand as the two ambulancemen negotiated their way through my relatives who had formed a macabre farewell committee at the door. A small pool of red lay like fallen poppies in the middle of the white groundsheet, and at the foot of the stairs, one of mama's strappy sandals lay on its side in what looked like a portion of large, black liver. I dodged various jingling manicured hands which grabbed at the air above my head and ran to the other side of the stretcher, holding onto the blanket.

Mama opened her eyes momentarily and laid her hand on my head. 'Meena, look after papa,' she said quietly. Papa rested his hand briefly on my shoulder. Then he clambered inside the ambulance which sped away, its siren wa-waaing in time to the distant fairground songs. Mrs Worrall, Mrs Lowbridge, Mrs Povey and Cara stood huddled on the corner, whispering quietly to each other, throwing me the occasional glance.

Mrs Worrall gathered her voluminous woollen dressing gown around her and wandered over to my Auntie Shaila who was now standing next to me, sniffling into the end of her sari. She jumped as Mrs Worrall tapped her lightly, 'We'll have to do a rota. For Mr K. Mek sure him and the littl'un eat and that.'

Auntie Shaila drew herself up, her triple chins wobbling in indignation. 'Oh, don't you worry. We will see to that, thank you so much. Oh *bhagwan*. What else can this bloody country throw upon our heads . . .' she muttered, trying to drag me inside.

I pulled away from her and went to stand next to Cara. I wanted to watch the ambulance until its tail-lights disappeared over the hill. Cara sang to herself, swaying with the chill wind, 'Rock of Ages, cleft for me . . . tum te tum tum la la la . . .'

6

My brother had the distinction of being the tallest baby ever born at New End Hospital in Wolverhampton. 'The child was twenty-one inches long, can you imagine!' Auntie Shaila said excitedly on the telephone, whilst papa hid his head uncomfortably in a newspaper. 'No wonder he nearly ripped poor Daljit apart . . . but it was worth it, for a boy eh? Now the family is complete, and Meena can be another little mother to her bhaiya . . .'

I disliked him on first sight, a scrawny, yowling thing with a poached egg of a face, his long fingers clinging gekko-like to mama's nightgown front whilst she held him up to me for a first sister's kiss. I brushed his cheek sullenly with my mouth, it felt downy and damp, a strange smell of custard and roses made my nostrils twitch and for a second, he stopped crying and looked straight at me with wise old man eyes. The knowledge in them made me step back a moment. He had the face of a travel-weary prodigal, ancient dust and the maps of several continents lay on his brow, he had comet trails in his nappy and sea shells crushed between his toes. He was only a day old and I knew he had already seen places I would only ever dream of.

Papa laughed. 'Look at him! He already loves you, Meena. He's saying hello to you.' Mama offered him to my arms. She looked transparent, ethereal. A long tube ran from a drip into a needle taped to the front of her hand, surrounded by a livid green-blue bruise. She could barely shift position without biting her lip and closing her eyes, as if not seeing her body would stop the pain. I shook my head, afraid I would drop this terrifyingly powerful, chicken-legged bundle.

Much later on, when mama had made every parent's transformation from semi-divine icon to semi-detached confidante, she told me the real story of the birth. How she bent down to pick up a crushed kebab from the white sheet and felt a slimy mountain avalanche down her thighs. My brother's placenta lay at her feet and in her shoes. The anaesthetic had not kicked in when they did an emergency caesarean to haul him out, already fearing that irrevocable brain damage had claimed this long-legged baby, and then when she cried out that she could feel every stitch when they were sewing her up, a sour-faced nurse told her to be grateful she was still alive and to shut it. 'But they were the same when I had you, Meena. They left me alone in a room with a dirty blanket for ten hours. When I asked for drugs, the nurse said, "Oh, you Asian ladies have a very low pain threshold." So I said, "You won't mind if I slap you in the face and prove it . . ." But you know, I *was* grateful to be alive. She was right that time, the other nurse. I did not want to leave you alone yet.'

But nothing was the same for me and mama once Sunil came to live in our house, his house. Before he arrived, papa and I spent a few glorious mad weeks together when we had tinned spaghetti hoops and biscuits for breakfast, fish and chips or jam tarts for supper, and in between I was sent to school in crumpled uncoordinated clothes, hyperactive from sugar overdose and a series of late nights of watching the television until the small white dot appeared to send us to bed with a wink. Papa let his stubble grow and spent hours in the outside toilet with his newspapers whilst I tried on all mama's make-up and occasionally slipped into her wardrobe where I would sit amongst her cardigans and saris recalling her fresh, lemony smell.

Best of all, papa never stopped me hanging around with Anita. Since the Big House incident, which thankfully had been overshadowed by Sunil's birth and therefore had few punishing consequences for me, beyond a niggle of guilt when I thought about mama's diamond necklace, Anita and I had spent every day together. One morning we met up on the park swings. I had escaped the house, already fed-up with Auntie Shaila's constant clucking, her re-organisation of mama's spice rack and her interminable five-course breakfast, most of which I had flushed down the toilet whilst she hoovered the stairs and hand-washed the blood-stained white sheet.

Anita was sitting alone, in new jeans and a fashionable skinny-rib top. She looked older, maybe because of the purple shadows under her eyes. The hated poodle was sniffing about the metal posts near her feet, looking up at her occasionally as if expecting a command. I sat down on the swing next to hers and rocked in time with her. 'My mum's in hospital,' I said.

'So's mine,' Anita replied.

'Is she having a baby as well?'

'Don't be stupid! She said my dad beat her up. He didn't. She pricked her arm with a dart to make it look like that. Dad told me. He's not picking her up. She can come home on the bloody bus, he says.'

I did not need to ask what had led to this; I wondered how he had found out about Deirdre's lustful assignation with the Poet, maybe Anita herself had told him. I did not know how I would feel if my mother pinched my boyfriend. But then I realised we did not have boyfriends, not under any circumstances, and having seen the chaos they created, I was rather glad.

'Where's Sherrie and Fat Sally?' I asked casually.

'That Sherrie's a right slag. When I get my pony she ain't riding it, no way!' Anita spat fiercely. 'Fat Sally's mom says she's not allowed out anymore.'

I knew she meant 'with me'. So Anita was a Bad Influence, that was official. And I was temporarily motherless and a proven liar and thief. It was, I decided then, a marriage made in heaven. We did nothing special, beyond strolling round the park with carefully cultivated bored expressions, exploring the abandoned pigsties with adult disdain, shimmying down to Mr Ormerod's corner shop with unimpressed faces, always aware that we were simply too big and beautiful for Tollington and making sure that everyone else knew it as well.

And then one day, when I had almost forgotten she was coming back, mama appeared on the doorstep with a cooing bundle. Monkey-face had changed into a chocolate box cherub, impossible curls, huge needy eyes and a desperate desire to be held by all and sundry whilst he deliberately toyed with their hearts. All past habits and rituals were forgotten, swept away with a swipe of a tiny fist. Days passed in a cyclone of feeds, nappies, scattered toys and endless visiting relatives bearing gifts and sweetmeats for the Kumars' new son. Days even bled into night when I would awake with a jerk to his banshee wailing, unsure whether it was sunshine, moonlight or street lamp flare on the other side of my curtains, sometimes grateful to be dragged away from my now familiar nightmare where I pursued mama through endless winding cobbled streets, calling for her to look round. She sat in the back of a taxi, staring straight ahead, the set of neck told me she was willing the driver to go faster and everywhere I placed my feet, there was nothing but clinging wet clay.

Tollington loved new babies, and Sunil became the latest local attraction; it would take us half an hour to walk to Mr Ormerod's shop, having to stop several times on the journey whilst various Ballbearings factory women would ooh and aah into the pram, carefully blowing their cigarette smoke out the sides of their mouths. Mrs Keithley gathered a whole pile of Nicky, Natasha and Nathan's old baby clothes and dropped them off one morning, three huge plastic bags full of romper suits and cardigans, telling mama, 'If I have any more kids, it'll be an act of God so you keep them, love.' Mrs Worrall presented us with ten exquisitely-embroidered matinee suits and several knitted woollies, all of which she had been making over the past nine months. I could not imagine those fat hands casting on or manoeuvring round a crochet hook, but mama was so touched she kissed Mrs Worrall's hairy cheek and later told papa, 'She never sees her own grandchildren, that is why this means so much to her. Her kids should be shot.'

I had never realised there were so many mothers in the village, and it seemed each one either came to our door or accosted us on the street, bearing gifts or full of advice, wanting to hold this scrap of new life and remind themselves of how their own babies once felt in their arms. Nobody thought beyond that reality, the snuffling body nestling at their neck, the open, searching mouth and uncontrolled, restless arms, no one wanted to think about the gangs of no-hope teenagers who already took over the nearby park all day, drinking lager and waiting for something to happen to them, trapped in a forgotten village in no-man's land between a ten-shop town and an amorphous industrial sprawl. We still lived near enough to the seasons to be fatalistic; the corn grew every year, didn't it? Winter was harsh but never stayed too long, and the spring, well it hadn't let us down yet. Summers were still endless and by September, every single child was sunburnt, scabbed and sated with stolen blackberries and a sense of freedom. We will always have the children, the village mothers said, our only investment for the future, and then they sounded exactly like my Aunties.

It was a mutual decision we made, mama and I, to forget each other temporarily and move onto other loves. She was too tired for me anyhow; she still came back from school and went straight into the kitchen, but now she came back later, having picked Sunil up from the nursery and did the cooking with him clinging onto her hip, handfuls of her hair in his hands. Of course she could not help but notice that Anita and I were now officially 'mates', as we called for each other every day; but beyond a purse of her lips and a resigned shrug, mama decided to let it go. And I was grateful to her for that.

After some detailed discussions together on the park roundabout, Anita and I decided that we had to get a gang together. We both agreed there was no point putting so much energy into posturing and looking mean if you didn't have some others around to applaud or take the blame when things turned nasty. Unfortunately, due to the existence of two other gangs in the yard, we were left with the dregs. We would all have liked to be part of Sam Lowbridges' Tollington Rebels, a group of affectedly bored bikers (well, moped riders to be strictly accurate, but the helmets looked authentic), who divided their seemingly endless time between the park swings, their patch of yard in front of the Lowbridges' back gate and the Mitre pub, near the old pithead. Favoured activities were spitting, swearing loudly, petting (there were always girls hanging around who chewed gum and laughed in coarse screeching guffaws, but they seemed to be on a rota system, changing from week to week), doing wheelies round the dirt yard and of course, stealing and vandalism, although no actual acts had been witnessed. (Except for the time Sam had been seen pissing in the red telephone box on the corner opposite our house but as Hairy Neddy had said, 'That ain't a crime. That's a bloody local custom, ain't it?') But if anything went missing or was found broken, the finger of suspicion inevitably poked Sam Lowbridge in his skinny ribs.

The other gang was made up of all the local boys who were too young to ride a moped and too old to hang around with us, all of whom went to Anita's comprehensive school some fifteen miles away (there was a grammar school some twenty miles from the village but no one had passed the Eleven-plus for a whole decade.) The Footies were led by Chris Bailey, one of three brothers each born nine months apart to a couple we called the Ginger Nuts. Mr and Mrs Bailey lived next door to the church, their sober respectability completely incongruous with their shocking carrot-coloured hair which they had thoughtfully passed on to their children. They all looked like they were wearing those novelty wigs you could hire from the joke shop in the town, and every August, one or all of the boys would go down with severe sunburn. Chris' gang were bike and football mad and you could always spot them hogging the park, the three Bailey boys were the boiled lobsters in the Wolves' football strip, testosterone timebombs whose noise and energy levels only just kept them from exploding.

Which meant we were left with Karl and Kevin, the hyperactive twins, and their docile, long suffering sister, Susan, Natasha, Nathan and Nicky, the Keithley kids, and Tracey, Anita's sister, their only qualification being they were all over five, under eleven, not fussy and most importantly, as pliable as putty. We established our headquarters in one of the old pigsties at the far end of the yard, nestled in between the various lock-up garages and potting sheds and surrounded by an angry expanse of waist-high stinging nettles. We did not devise an initiation ceremony, getting through the nettles without losing an eye was considered enough. Anita encouraged me to ransack our bike shed/bathroom and I came away with a couple of blankets, some cracked mugs and a few tins of tomatoes in case of a terrorist siege. Anita's contribution was a pile of back copies of *Jackie*, a teenage magazine which formed the basis of my sex education for the next few years.

Up till then, I had been reading *Twinkle*, a comic aimed at those who considered Enid Blyton a bit avant garde, mainly concerned with the domestic tribulations of the elf and fairy population with an occasional risky foray into stories featuring cat fights between rival gymnasts or tuck box disputes in all-girl boarding schools. But *Jackie* was all about Boys; how to attract them, keep them, get rid of them (at least, the ugly ones), how to transform a boring denim mini-skirt into a wild disco outfit by using a few of your dad's old ties and a tube of glitter, where highlighter actually goes, what Donny Osmond's favourite colour was, what kind of chick attracted David Cassidy and why having spots was not a valid reason for suicide.

My favourite section was the comic strip story where the girl-gets-or-loses-boy theme was explored in a million different scenarios, all of them featuring a limpid-eyed, anorexic, blonde heroine (brunette if she was the independent type like a secretary or a champion showjumper) who cried as neatly as she kissed, which was often. On occasions they would feel morally obliged to feature a slightly unattractive girl who would get the guy (the same nymphet with a pair of thick glasses sketched-in which she would inevitably remove to reveal her true hidden beauty), but the girls still always looked like Sherrie or Anita to me.

Our gang, which we named the Wenches Brigade, soon established a routine of sorts; we would begin with a leisurely meeting in the old pigsty, the one nearest the park, in which Anita and I would leaf through the current issue of *Jackie*, doing the quizzes on each other, 'How Do You Know If He Fancies You?', planning our wardrobes and interior decor for the flat in London we would buy together when we reached eighteen, and eating sandwiches and biscuits that the Littl'uns had been forced to nick from their mothers' kitchens. Then we would do the rounds of our kingdom, Anita leading, me at her side, and the rest of the minions in a disorganised chattering crocodile behind us. We would walk right to the end of the main village street, down the hill past Mr Ormerod's shop (where Anita would stop off for supplies), the church, the red brick school, the Working Men's Club, and back up the rise to Sherrie's farm. There Anita and I would find a space in the long grass clear of dog shit and insects, and munch on sweets and talk, whilst our lackeys amused themselves with teasing the horses with ears of corn and conducting interesting experiments such as how far a two-day-old cow pat would travel when thrown by a small snotty-nosed child.

When I said that we talked, what I mean is that Anita talked and I listened with the appropriate appreciative noises. But I never had to force my admiration, it flowed from every pore because Anita made me laugh like no one else; she gave voice to all the wicked things I had often thought but kept zipped up inside my good girl's winter coat. Her irreverence was high summer for me, it made me shed inhibitions like woollen layers until I felt naked and slightly embarrassed at the sound of my joy. 'See er,' Anita would drawl, watching one of the reverend old biddies from the Wesleyan Church Fairy Cake Committee trudge up the hill. 'Er's got a pouch under her coat full of shit . . .' She was talking about Mrs Todd who never passed me without a radiant smile, and yet I giggled uncontrollably. 'It's true!' Anita continued. 'She had this operation, right, and her bum broke down so they had to move it outside her body. Into a bag. She knits pouches for it. The bag not her bum . . .' I would gasp for air and wait enthralled for the next revelation, each one tilting my small world slightly off its axis so I saw the familiar and the mundane through new cynical eyes, Anita's eyes.

Of course it was inevitable that Anita would get round to sex; it hung round her anyway like a faint perfume, what she gave off by the tilt of her thin hips, in the quizzical arc of an eyebrow, in her constant unhurried monologues about the boys in her school who all panted after her madly and whose desperation made her laugh. 'There's that David in 5C, he keeps sending me notes like . . . and keeps paying for me chips and buying me stuff.'

'What stuff? Expensive stuff?' I asked.

'Oh yeah, rings, bracelets, last week he bought me a record . . . Judge Dredd . . . It goes, "Lie down girl, let me push it up, push it up, lie down . . ." Dead saucy he is but he's gorra face like a cat's arse so he ain't gettin any off me . . . no way . . .' And she would throw back her head and chortle whilst I pondered on the lyrics of the song and why they made me feel so uncomfortable and tingly at the same time.

Anita finally got round to explaining what those lyrics meant after the peeing competition we held one day when we were bored and feeling bad. It had started when Karl had declared he was 'dying for a widdle' and had picked his way through the nettles to find a convenient spot. Anita put her finger on her lips and beckoned the whole gang of us to follow him. I saw Karl holding what looked like a button mushroom in his right hand and aiming a steaming jet of pee at a clump of clover, making their purple leonine heads bend and dance. I squealed, Karl turned round and promptly sprayed Anita's dog (I never called him by name), who must have thought his luck was in and attached himself to Karl's leg, humping with unabashed gratitude. Kevin boasted he could hit the clover patch from ten feet and performed so impressively that we had to take shelter in the pigsty, marvelling at how versatile these boys' mushrooms were. I did not feel embarrassed at all; I had known for ages that whatever boys had 'down there' was big trouble and not to be approached, but after seeing Karl and Kevin's vegetarian-friendly offerings, I felt relieved and somewhat cheated.

Kevin was about to claim his prize of a remaining penny chew in our sweet hoard when Anita said, 'Ay! Us wenches haven't had a go yet, have we?' Susan and I exchanged horrified glances; she was shy enough in normal circumstances and I reckoned the trauma of pulling her knickers down in mixed company could push her over the edge. Susan sidled off nervously, mumbling something like, 'Me mom's calling me, honest!' and scampered through the undergrowth without a backward glance.

Anita called after her, 'Chicken chicken! Yow better not come back again, Susan Archer!' and roused us all into a half-hearted chorus of clucking which only served to make Susan run faster. Anita looked round at us, mockingly. 'I'm gooing fust. I ain't bothered.' In one fluid motion she whipped off her panties, I caught a flash of smooth white thigh under her dress, and threw them at Tracey, who held them gingerly between a thumb and forefinger, unsure whether she was proud or mortified by her older sister. Anita squatted down near the clover patch and let out a little grunt before emitting a fireman's hoseful of pee which, by arching her back and hips, she managed to direct squarely on target, laughing in triumph.

'Yow'm nearer than I woz!' shouted Kevin indignantly.

'Well! I'm a girl! I'm allowed!' said Anita, as if referring to paragraph three, section two of the Official Handbook of Mixed Pissing Etiquette, acutely aware that she had just defied nature and gravity as well as saving on a visit to the toilet. Karl and Kevin shook their heads in reluctant admiration, hands in pockets as they reassured their mushrooms that not all girls would show them up like this.

Anita slipped her knickers back on and pushed Tracey forward. 'Your go, our Trace.'

Tracey snuffled quietly, 'I've got trousers on, Nita . . .'

'Well tek um off then!' yelled Anita, tugging at the waistband. 'Don't show us up!'

Tracey backed away and began fumbling with her buttons, trying to control the trembling of her lower lip. She opened the top and edged her trousers down, the top of her legs looked like sticks of lard, thin without muscle tone, neglected. I shifted uncomfortably, I wanted to say, leave it, leave her alone, but she wasn't my sister, was she? Tracey turned her back on the boys as she bent over to tug her trousers down further, and then Kevin and Karl began giggling manically, nudging each other and pointing.

'What?' called Anita, sniffing blood. 'What?'

'Her's got a poo stripe!' yelled Karl. 'Her's got kak round her bum!'

Tracey spun round, a faint but visible skid mark neatly outlining the crack of her cheeks. 'I ain't!' she whispered. 'Stop it! I ain't!'

The boys glanced at Anita, wondering if they had gone too far, picking on the sister of their leader. Anita smiled at them and began the chant, 'Poo stripe! Poo stripe!' which they gleefully took up, doing a mad thumping dance around Tracey whose trousers had wedged themselves round her knees and were resisting all her frantic, tearful yanks. I did not join in, neither did I help her disentangle herself. I merely watched as she half hopped, half stumbled through the nettles, their green jagged edges pricking her bare flesh, leaving behind their stinging mottled red kisses. I had barely registered the state of Tracey's underwear; I wished I had not seen what I was sure I had seen, the row of bruises around Tracey's thighs, as purple as the clover heads, two bizarre bracelets perfectly mimicking the imprint of ten cruel, angry fingers.

I did not allow myself to dwell on this, I had to act quickly to prevent Anita turning on me. I squatted down, holding the leg of my knickers to one side, feeling my warm pee trickle down my leg, soak my socks and slosh inside my shoes. 'Yow daft moo! Yow'm supposed to take yer pants off!' laughed Anita, who was already eating her prize. The twins began hooting, I ran towards them making squelching noises, made a clown of myself to erase Tracey from all our minds. But they did not fool me. I had seen how in an instant, those you called friends could suddenly become tormentors, sniffing out a weakness or a difference, turning their own fear of ostracism into a weapon with which they could beat the victim away, afraid that being an outsider, an individual even, was somehow infectious.

As I wiped what I could off my legs with some dock leaves, I remember thinking that this group hostility seemed to be happening more and more in the yard recently not only amongst the children but around the adults too. They had begun whispering in corners whenever a stranger appeared, they had begun dividing themselves up into camps of differing loyalties, those who thought Mrs Keithley was a stuck-up cow, others who thought Deirdre was nowt but a fat slag. I had never noticed these undercurrents before forming the gang; all adults were open and helpful, all children potential playmates, all of us together in this cosy village idyll. This sense of suspicion had begun soon after the news that a new road would soon be running through the village, a motorway extension which would cut through the fields opposite the Mitre pub at the back of the posh detached houses and run parallel to the old mine railway.

This new road linking up the industrial estate some twenty miles away and the motorway to Wolverhampton had been discussed for years, even before we came to the village. I vaguely remember some hand-drawn protest posters appearing in Mr Ormerod's shop window and Uncle Alan knocking on doors trying to whip up solidarity for a protest march which he had christened Tollington In Turmoil! Until someone pointed out that having T.I.T. emblazoned across your front might attract the wrong kind of support. There was a march, or rather a slow shuffle as there were not many participants who could make it up the hill without a motorised zimmer frame, letters were sent off to our local MP on church-headed notepaper with the usual arguments against destruction of the countryside and levels of noise and air pollution. The authorities did not exactly quake in their shoes faced with this polite provincial request and simply waited until everyone had almost forgotten about the motorway before moving the diggers in.

Besides, they wrote, in the only letter they ever sent back, didn't we realise that Birmingham was about to explode with richness and vitality, Britain's second city which would become the nation's major conference centre once the NEC was complete, and wouldn't everyone in Tollington want to be part of this Black Country Renaissance? It seemed to me that nothing was happening in Tollington, except children were turning into teenagers, teenagers were getting married and quietly moving away to where the jobs were supposed to be. Once there had been rumours that the old mine would be turned into variously a supermarket, a leisure centre, a baby clinic and a builder's yard. But by now, most people had realised the old mine would remain exactly what it was, a crumbling monument to a halcyon past, and that the promised Renaissance had taken a diversion somewhere round Wolverhampton and missed us out completely.

Maybe it was the earth shifting under the motorway diggers that had brought all these tensions up to the surface. In any case, it certainly shifted something in Anita because after the Littl'uns had been called in for their teas and we sat together in the pigsty, huddled beneath an old bedspread, Anita told me the facts of life. I don't remember her exact words, I was too busy trying not to seem surprised or appalled whilst awful, vivid pictures of all the people I knew with children turned cartwheels around my brain. '. . . And when he's finished, he goes to sleep and yow have to wash in gin and vinegar if yow don't want to have a baby.'

'I ain't never gonna have babies,' I said quietly. 'Not like that anyway. There must be other ways yow can have babies, using tubes and machines and stuff, 'cos my parents . . .' I could not finish the sentence. I had a baby brother at home, which meant they had definitely done It within the last few years and what was worse, I must have been in the house at the time. And then there were all my Aunties and Uncles, those women who would scream and blush at any Punjabi word which might vaguely be considered risqué – items of clothing, any references to marriage, selected root vegetables, bedrooms . . . And my Uncles, those men who at the mention of childbirth or marital matters would harrumph self-consciously and gather in awkward huddles, clutching their whisky glasses like shields, silently praying for someone to crack a manly quip.

After a few nights of contemplation, when I suddenly became aware of every creak and shift in my parents' bedroom next door and took to stuffing my quilt in my ears, I decided it was all a mass conspiracy. If this sex business was all wrong and dirty and they found it so embarrassing, why did they end up doing it? Everyone from Auntie Shaila to Mrs Worrall next door had managed to do it without throwing up so, I concluded, along with all the nasty bits, there must have been something good about the experience. Armed with this knowledge, a few days after Anita's chat, I stole mama's powder compact from her dressing table and begged Anita to make me up like Babs, the blonde pouty one, from Pan's

People. She used the whole pressed circle of Honey Beige on my face, and finished it off with a smear of Deirdre's strawberry-tinted Biba lip gloss. Then we stood outside the Mitre pub and watched Sam Lowbridge and his gang down half-pints of sweet cider and flick ash at the tame geese who waddled around the pub garden, hissing like dying balloons. A couple of the lads noticed Anita and winked at her, one of them even gave her his half-eaten packet of cheese and onion crisps which she later pressed inside a copy of her mum's *Woman's Own* and kept in a biscuit tin in our den. Only Sam noticed me; he did a double take and shouted over, 'Am yow feeling alroight, chick? Yow look a bit peaky.' If only he had kissed me, he would have tasted summer strawberries on my lips.

Then I began wondering if any boy would ever notice me, the way that they always noticed Anita. I turned to my oracle for an answer, *Jackie* magazine I knew would tell me what to do. I feverishly scoured the 'Cathy and Claire' column to see if any of the other readers shared my dilemma. The *Jackie* problem page was a revelation and somehow a relief; I had no idea there was so much suffering out there. But after a few weeks, during which I could not find one letter specific to my particular dilemma, I decided to write in myself. I composed the letter in our bike shed – I did not want Anita to know anything about it – helped myself to an envelope and stamps from papa's supply which he kept in a carrier bag under the record player, posted it off all the way to London, and then waited.

My letter was published some three weeks later. 'Dear Cathy and Claire, I am brown, although I do not wear thick glasses. Will this stop me getting a guy? Yours, Tense Nervous Headache from Tollington.' The reply was not quite as detailed as I would have liked, but reading it in the gloom of the pigsty away from Anita's prying eyes, I felt thrilled that Cathy and Claire had even bothered to write back. 'Dear TNT from Tollington, You would be amazed at what a little lightly-applied foundation can do! Always smile, a guy does not want to waste his time with a miserable face, whatever the shade! P.S. Michael Jackson seems to do alright, and he's got the added problem of uncontrollable hair! Most of all, BE YOURSELF! Love, C & C . . .'

But after the initial excitement of seeing myself in print, albeit anonymously, had worn off, it was replaced by a strange new feeling for which I yet had no name. I knew that all those Desperates from Darlington and Moodys from Manchester would grow out of whatever it was that was impelling them to write, or rather that they would eventually grow into the bodies they presently despised. I had never wanted to be anyone else except myself only older and famous. But now, for some reason, I wanted to shed my body like a snake slithering out of its skin and emerge reborn, pink and unrecognisable. I began avoiding mirrors, I refused to put on the Indian suits my mother laid out for me on the bed when guests were due for dinner, I hid in the house when Auntie Shaila bade loud farewells in Punjabi to my parents from the front garden, I took to walking several paces behind or in front of my parents when we went on a shopping trip, checking my reflection in shop windows, bitterly disappointed it was still there.

Somewhere in the middle of this time, which I recall as a colour, the blue-black of a hidden bruise, my birthday happened. I was ten years old. I told mama and papa I did not want any presents or a party, which was accepted as it was a weekday and mama had a parents' evening at her school. I smiled prettily when I opened my presents before breakfast; clothes from mama in beige and grey again, sensible clothes with elasticated waistbands and growing room, books from papa, Charles Kingsley's *The Water Babies*, *Mine For Keeps*, a touching story about a girl in a wheelchair and her faithful dog, a hairbrush and mirror set from Sunil which I left unopened on my dressing table for a few months afterwards. At school, I did not bother to inform any of my classmates of my Special Day, and after a hug and a promise from papa that they would organise a party at the weekend on my behalf, I spent a few precious hours with Anita in the pigsty. I lay back on our blanket, breathing in its unique smell of fizzy pop and cat pee, and let Anita's monologues, all spark and spit, illuminate the dusk like fireworks.

The following Saturday, whilst mama was preparing food for 'my party', or rather the usual music evening with the same old crowd that they were calling my birthday celebration, I heard her discussing me with papa. She was whispering to him whilst she chopped up peeled potatoes and my brother dozed on her back. 'I think she might be jealous. It's natural. She was the only one for nine years and now it's hitting her. Be patient, darling . . . you talk to her, please. I've got enough to worry about . . .'

So papa took me for a walk, something we had done every Sunday until Sunil arrived, way past the Mitre pub where excavation had just begun on the new motorway. Papa and I walked along the rusty tracks, past the abandoned station-master's hut and into what used to be a buttercup-filled meadow but was now a deep hole filled with slow nodding earthmovers which bent their necks to the ground and rose with jaws full of mud and flowers.

Papa cleared his throat and took in a deep breath of air, 'Meena, is there something worrying you?' I shook my head, digging my hands deeper into the pockets of my high-waisted flared jeans (a grudgingly given Christmas present, whenever I wore them mama would shudder and insist on pulling down the material caught in the crack of my bum). Papa continued, 'You were always so . . . happy. You talked to me. Why have you stopped?'

Something shifted under my feet, maybe it was just the earth diggers crossing a ley line, but I felt wrong-footed and bewildered. What did he mean, talk to him? Words had nothing to do with what held us together, did they? Next he'd want to swap make-up tips and discuss the finer stylistic points of Marc Bolan's new haircut. That was Anita's job. I had never considered that anything I might do or say would change how papa felt about me, that whatever passed between us was constant, unquestioned, non-negotiable, even when I had lied and thrown hysterical tantrums around the lounge floor, even that time I had written a note saying I was running away to work with animals and hid in the bike shed, listening to mama and papa calling my name around the house and trying, I knew, to suppress their laughter. Had I ever talked to him, the way I talked constantly to Anita? If I had, I could not remember those occasions any more. Now I only thought of myself, a hurried visitor to our dinner table, picking my way round my brother's baby debris like a long-suffering house-guest, and where I wanted to belong. My life was outside the home, with Anita, my passport to acceptance.

'I do talk to you. But I've got me mates now, haven't I? I'm dead busy, me.'

Papa winced at the slang which I used deliberately. 'You mean Miss Anita Rutter?' he said archly. 'There are other friends you know. You have not played with Pinky and Baby for so long. Don't you think we have noticed how you ignore them?'

Even their names reeked of childhood, something I was desperate to wrap in rags and leave on someone's doorstep with a note, Take It Away. Pinky and Baby born a year either side of me, Auntie Shaila's daughters who displayed their medals from the debating society on their chichi dressing table laden with ugly, stuffed gonks, who fought over the privilege of handing round starters or wiping down surfaces under the proud gazes of the grown-ups, whose scrubbed, eager faces and girlish modesty gave me the urge to roll naked in the pigsties shouting obscenities. 'I don't like them. They are boring,' I said finally.

'Why?' pressed papa. 'Because they are polite and sweet and enjoy spending time with their family?'

That description fitted all the Indian girls I knew, all the daughters of friends and relatives who would land in our house after a cramped journey wedged between two fat aunties. I half expected them to bring out their passports and get them stamped at the door. I knew all of them lived in the towns or cities, I'd made the reverse journey enough times, to cramped terraced houses in streets which seemed full of nosey Indians who all knew each other and if you farted, would phone you up to complain about the smell. Or we'd pull up to a smart semi-detached in a street full of identical houses and set dozens of curtains twitching convulsively as we piled out of the car in our finery, when I always had an urge to shout, 'Thanks for putting us up, Auntie! I'll just unload the goats and steal a local child for dinner!' Or very occasionally, we would swing into the massive drive of a doctor or businessman friend, where the gardens were so big and the walls so high, you didn't have to give a damn about who lived next door and whether they liked it or not.

But whatever their dwelling, the girls were always the same – pleasant, helpful, delicate, groomed, terrifying. Nothing snapped them out of it; I tried showing them the slug trails in the entries, the laden blackberry bushes behind the pigsties, the dead baby birds rotting in our flower beds, the teeth marks in our back door made by the field mice frantically seeking refuge from the cold winter, my personal discoveries, the gifts I thought might break the ice. But these girls were never impressed; instead they would squeal or turn up their retroussé noses, clutching at their silk and satin suits, looking like I had presented them with a severed head. My only revenge was to ply them with glasses of Cresta Cream Soda and then enjoy their dismay when nature took its course and they discovered we had an outside toilet. I would wait until a victim had picked her way over the mossy cobbles to the windswept lav, lock the door from the outside, switch off the light on the exterior wall, and make suitable rodent noises until they begged to be released.

I always got told off, but I was beginning not to care. I knew I was a freak of some kind, too mouthy, clumsy and scabby to be a real Indian girl, too Indian to be a real Tollington wench, but living in the grey area between all categories felt increasingly like home. And Anita never looked at me the way my adopted female cousins did; there was never fear or censure or recoil in those green, cool eyes, only the recognition of a kindred spirit, another mad bad girl trapped inside a superficially obedient body. In fact, sometimes when I looked into her eyes, all I could see and cling to was my own questioning reflection.

Papa was giving up on getting a coherent anwer from me, so he changed tack. 'Your mama is very overworked. She could do with your help sometimes. Life isn't all ha-ha-hee-hee with your friends. They will leave you when times get bad, and then all you will have left is your family, Meena. Remember that.'

We walked back in silence, although papa insisted on holding my hand. If Anita's father, Roberto, had delivered a speech like that to her, she would have flicked her hair and said Bog Off! The words sat poised on the tip of my tongue all the way home. I did not have the courage to free them, but I imagined their effect and the image made me giddy.

I soon found out where my divided loyalties really lay, and it happened that afternoon when Pinky and Baby arrived. Auntie Shaila had decided to come early to help mama with the cooking for the evening meal, 'As she never gets any rest with that *munda* on her back all the day . . . Still, such a chumpy-sweetie pie he is . . .' What I had not bargained for was that she would drag along her two docile daughters who had once been my friends but whose presence now made me groan inwardly as they carefully got out of Auntie Shaila's Hillman Imp.

'Some company for you Meena beti!' Auntie Shaila trilled as she swept past me in a cloud of perfume and coriander. 'Why don't you show them round, huh? Go to the park, Baby loves swings, don't you, beti?'

Baby nodded shyly, hiding behind Pinky as usual, looking

to her to answer for her. Once the adults had disappeared into the house, I stopped pretending I was vaguely pleased to see them and stared at them moodily. They were in matching outfits again, pink jumpers with hearts and daisies around the neck, jeans with a carefully ironed crease running down the legs, long black hair in bunches, held together with cutesy plastic bobbles. Pinky was my age, Baby a year younger, and they looked to me like infants.

'Hello Meena. Shall we go to the park then?'

Even Pinky's voice set my teeth on edge, a soft pliant whine with a lilt of Punjabi in it, the over-pronunciation of the consonants, the way every sentence rose at the end so everything became a question, forcing you to answer and join in.

'No!' I spat back, furious that my afternoon plans of strolling up to Sherrie's farm with Anita had been ruined.

Looking at Pinky and Baby's timid, apprehensive faces, I knew Anita would enjoy snacking on their insecurities, their obvious lack of Wench potential. If anything, they were too easy a target, mere hors d'oeuvres for Anita's appetite. I also knew that if I had any sense of mercy I should bundle them both into the house and leave them in front of the television, their purity intact. But it was too late; Anita was standing at my front gate in a skirt that barely covered her thighs and one of her mum's old cardigans which had two saggy pouches at the front, like deflated balloons, where Deirdre's boobs should have been.

'Am yow comin' then, our Meena?' Anita's tone was deceptively gentle, she stood back slightly, sluttishly, and enjoyed the sight of Pinky and Baby shrinking back from her cocky gaze.

'Me cousins are here,' I said sullenly, ignoring the hurt realisation that was spreading over their faces. 'I'm supposed to look after em . . .'

I left the unspoken question hanging in the warm afternoon air. An aeroplane passed silently above our heads, unzipping the blue sky with a thin vapour trail.

'Yow'll have to bring 'em then, won't ya?' Anita said lazily, already turning away, knowing we would all follow.

I pulled Pinky to one side and hissed in her ear, 'Yow can come with uz, right, but don't say nothin' and don't do nothin' and don't show me up, gorrit?'

Pinky swallowed and nodded, and then said, 'Meena didi, why are you speaking so strangely?'

'Coz this ain't naff old Wolverhampton anymore,' I said. 'This, Pinky, is Tollington. Right?'

Anita and I linked arms and sauntered down the hill, past the terraced houses and overflowing gardens where the occasional OAP would lift her head from her sunflowers and ornamental wells to nod at us as we passed. Their gazes lingered a little longer on Pinky and Baby whom I could hear pitter-pattering behind us at a respectable distance, and to my annoyance, I could feel the pensioners sigh and beam at my cousins in approval, uplifted by this vision of pretty little sisters in matching separates and coordinated dimples. We paused, as we always did, outside Mr Ormerod's shop window and shared a reverential moment of worship, faced with the tempting array of sweets which shamelessly flaunted themselves at us from the safety of their fat glass jars. I waited for Anita to go inside, as she always did, and wondered briefly where she got the money from for the sticky picnic we would always share in the long grass next to Sherrie's paddock.

'No, yow come in as well, Meena,' Anita said. I shot Pinky and Baby a Stay There glance but they ignored it, and followed us in warily, still holding hands. Mr Ormerod was shuffling around in the back room of the shop, when he spoke his voice sounded strained as if he were lifting something heavy. 'Be with you in a tick!' he shouted cheerily. Anita quickly leaned over the shop counter and grabbed handfuls of the loose confectionery that was always laid out in a small wooden tray, each assortment in its own snug box – cherry lips, sherbet flying saucers, chocolate spanners, edible neck-laces made up of tiny pastel-coloured discs, white mice with licorice whiskers. All of them disappeared into the depths of Anita's cardigan pockets and for the first time, I realised why she wore these voluminous woollies.

'Goo on Meena!' she hissed, indicating I should help myself while the coast was clear.

I glanced at Pinky and Baby who were staring at Anita as if she'd just deposited a turd on top of the shop counter. Pinky had a whole fist stuffed in her mouth, the other hand was clamped over Baby's eyes, and both of them looked close to tears. My hand hovered over a pile of marzipan bananas. I did not know why it trembled so much. And then suddenly Mr Ormerod appeared from the back room and I confidently picked up a banana from the top of the heap and laid it before him. He examined it quizzically. It looked ridiculous and lonely, a single unnaturally yellow smear on his sparkling glass counter. He looked up slowly at me, his eyes hardening.

'This all you want, chick?'

'Yes please, Mr Ormerod,' I said confidently. I did not dare to look at Anita who was standing, legs akimbo, hands in her pockets, checking her booty, a knowing grin plastered on her face.

Mr Ormerod swivelled round to face her and his polite smile became an obvious sneer. 'Don't suppose you will be buying anything, will you, Miss Anita Rutter?'

'Nah, got no money have I, Mr Ormerod,' she grinned back.

A muscle in Mr Ormerod's cheek began twitching slightly, he gripped the edge of the counter for a moment and the tips of his heavy-lobed ears went bright red. He was looking straight at Anita's bulging pockets and she knew he was; she was daring him to challenge her. Mr Ormerod was having a moral crisis, that was obvious. He had to somehow square Thou Shalt Not Steal with Suffer the Children to Come to Me, his desperation to be the most holy and charitable man in Tollington with the strong desire he now felt to smack Anita Rutter into the middle of next week. For a horrible moment, I feared he was going to keel over, but then he exhaled noisily and turned to me briskly with an open palm. 'Ha'penny please, Meena chick.'

Of course I had not brought any money with me, I never had to whenever I went out with Anita, and I suddenly felt cheap and childish that I had lived off her for all this time and had never appreciated all the risks she had taken to keep us both in pop, sweets and comics. I shifted my feet and let my gaze wander away from Mr Ormerod's still waiting palm until it rested on a small tin can next to the cash till on the counter. It was not a proper collection box, you could tell it was a former soup can masquerading as an official charitable receptacle, and besides, the slot in the top for coins was far too big. Someone had clumsily gouged the slot with a knife, so it was just as easy to take money out as put it in . . . It was when I read the label that I decided to do it; a homemade label on lined paper in blue biro and Mr Ormerod's tense, tiny scrawl, 'BABIES IN AFRICA; PLEASE GIVE!'

'Mr Ormerod, I've just remembered,' I said clearly. 'Me mom wanted some Brasso . . . yow know, that polish stuff. Have yow got any?'

I could feel Pinky and Baby at the back of me who had suddenly gone completely still, sniffing trouble in the air, and from the side, I felt Anita's knowing smile warm up my face like a spotlight.

'Ar, I have got some . . . It's out back, just a mo chick . . .' said Mr Ormerod, his voice back in its usual chirpy chappie mode, reassured that I was buying something else besides the marzipan banana. The minute the tailcoats of his brown overall disappeared into the stock room, I plucked the can from the counter and began emptying its contents into my skirt, which Anita, unbidden, held out like an apron.

'Get the shillins! Quick, Meena!' she whispered.

I shook furiously but there was some kind of log jam round the slot. I could see a fair bit of silver inside, sixpences and florins in amongst the threepenny bits and pennies, but all that came out was two shillings and a couple of farthings. Then I heard a muffled clang from the stock room. Mr Ormerod was replacing the small foot stool he kept to get to the high shelves, so I pocketed the two shillings, grasped the tin and stuffed it down the back of Baby's soft pink jumper. She was about to squeak in alarm but swallowed it as I brought my face inches from hers. 'Yow say anythin, and yow'm dead, Baby.'

Mr Ormerod was back behind the counter, brandishing a small pot of Brasso. I handed him the two shillings and he smiled as he gave me back the change.

'Giz a couple more bananas then please,' I added non-chalantly.

As he counted the sweets into a small brown paper bag, he looked over my shoulder, from where I could hear Baby breathing heavily. 'You okay chick?' he asked suspiciously.

I turned to see large silent tears coursing down Baby's cheeks; she was standing as if someone had a gun to her back and one hand was clamped over her crotch.

'Oh, she needs the toilet, we'd better get home,' I said hurriedly and put a protective arm around Baby's shoulder, clasping the tin to her and did not let go until we were all halfway down the hill. Baby cried the whole way to Sherrie's farm, and was still snuffling when Anita and I settled down in the long grass to count our booty.

'Eighteen shillings and eight pence!' I breathed, enjoying the feel of the coins in my hand. 'We could buy all the top ten singles for that!'

'We could buy a ticket to London,' added Anita. 'We could just get up now and goo to London and no one would ever see us again.'

At this, Baby broke into fresh sobs and clung to Pinky's leg. 'Don't want to go to London, didi!' she wailed. 'Mummy will be angry! And I've got a maths test tomorrow!'

'Who said yow was coming anyway?' snapped Anita.

I could see she was getting bored of having the moral

majority following us around. Pinky finally spoke, she sounded so calm and grown up I wanted to gob on her T-bar sandals. 'The man in the shop. He will soon find out you have taken the tin. Then what will you do, Meena?'

'Then what will you do, Meena?' Anita mocked her, in a bad parody of Pinky's accent which came out as adenoidal Welsh.

'He won't know it was us. Unless you tell him,' I added, staring at Pinky.

'Us?' she blinked. 'But me and Baby . . .'

'Baby carried the tin didn't she?' I continued. 'That means you helped us doesn't it? That's what I'll tell the police anyway.' I finished off with a wink to Anita.

Pinky gulped and blinked rapidly for a few moments; I had not noticed before how long and luxuriant her eyelashes were, she looked like Bambi with a nervous tic. 'We will not tell, Meena,' she said finally. 'But we want to go home now.' And with that, she turned on her heel and led Baby through the long grass, both of them picking their way carefully through the cow pats and nettles like two old ladies negotiating a slalom.

'Hey, our Meena,' Anita said softly. 'Yow'm a real Wench. That was bostin what yow did. Yow can be joint leader with me now if yow want, you know, of our gang. Want to?' I nodded stupidly, too overcome to speak. I had earned my Wench Wings without even trying, and it had been so simple and natural, and what thrilled me most of all was that I did not feel at all guilty or ashamed. I had finally broken free, of what I did not quite know, but I felt my chest expand as if each rib had been a prison bar and they had all snapped slowly one by one, leaving my heart unfettered and drunk with space.

'Let's goo and buy summat, right now!' I said, heady with my triumph and Anita's praise.

Anita laughed wryly, 'Where? There's only one shop round here and we've just robbed it. We'd have to gerra bus into town and . . .' She glanced down the hill towards Pinky and Baby's retreating figures.

'Yeah, I know,' I sighed. 'I'd better go with em . . . you know, in case they say summat,' and heaved myself to my feet whilst checking my bum for burrs.

'Yow gonna keep the tin then . . . till we get to some proper shops?' Anita asked. 'Oh yeah, no problem,' I said, taking her arm in mine. No one would come looking for me. Only the ones who felt bad got caught, everybody knew that.

The knock at the door came just as we were about to serve supper. We kids, as usual, had been fed first and I was just wiping up a final mouthful of spinach with the favourite end of crispy chapatti that I always saved till last. The Aunties and mama were lining up a battalion of plates for papa and the Uncles who hovered around the entrance of the kitchen like hopeful domestic pets at a banquet. Pinky and Baby had not eaten anything, despite Auntie Shaila's loud protestations. 'You know how long it took me to puree this methi? Three hours, just because I know my betis like it smooth-smooth. And now you just sit there with a Pite-Moo . . .' (This was one of Auntie Shaila's favourite expressions, which meant the object of the insult had a face curdled up like the top of a yoghurt.) And indeed it was the perfect description of her daughters, who had both studiously avoided me since we had got back home.

I had hidden Mr Ormerod's tin amongst the rows of canned tomatoes in the bike shed, a perfect camouflage I had thought proudly, and had enjoyed a whole evening of being pinched and fussed over whilst opening my presents from the Uncles and Aunties. It had not been a bad haul either – the usual sick-making selection of frilly girlie dresses which all made me look like a biker wearing a collapsed meringue, but amongst these were a couple of books (*Look And Learn Compendium*, a *Jackie Annual*, a collection of Indian folk tales), and best of all, a bottle of perfume called Summer Daze, The Teenage Fragrance from Auntie Madhu. 'Now you are getting such a big lady, Meena, and maybe you won't come to my house smelling of cow's muck anymore,' she said kindly as I unwrapped it. Pinky and Baby had sat in a corner, regarding me with mournful moon-eyes and I knew they were hoping I would suddenly break down in filmy tears and confess my crime, to save all our souls. But their disapproval only made me more manic; the more they stared, the harder I giggled and quipped and chattered excitedly about nothing. I basked in their fear and bewilderment, it fed me and I welcomed it for it reaffirmed I was nothing like them, would never be them.

And then Mr Ormerod was standing at our front door and talking in whispers with papa, both of them throwing me sidelong glances, papa's face set like stone and Mr Ormerod's expression somewhere between wonder and disapproval as he scanned the glittering array of silks draped over the Aunties' magnificent bosoms.

'Please do come in Mr Ormerod,' said mama, wafting over to him holding out an empty plate, unaware of the gravity of the men's chat. 'We cannot allow a guest to leave hungry . . . there is so much food, mountains!' she continued cheerily.

'Not now, Daljit,' said papa softly, staring hard at me.

The chapatti in my mouth suddenly turned to a clump of barbed wire and I could not swallow. I hurried into the kitchen and spat out the end of my meal into the bin, running my tongue over my teeth which felt as if they were covered with a sour, greasy film.

Papa appeared at my elbow. 'Meena, I am going to ask you something and you had better not lie . . .'

I affected an innocent expression, vaguely aware of Mr Ormerod, who had advanced a couple of feet into our front room and was gingerly holding a pakora between his fingers as if it was a small, sharp-toothed rodent.

'A collection tin has gone missing from Mr Ormerod's shop, a tin full of money for charity. Charity, Meena. Do you know anything about it?'

I opened my mouth to allow the story sitting on my lips to fly out and dazzle my papa, but stopped myself when I saw how furious he was. Both his eyebrows had joined together so he had one angry black line slashing his forehead like a scar and his usually light brown eyes were now black and impenetrable, glowing dark like embers. Then the enormity of what I had done hit me and a fear so powerful that I felt a few drops of wee land in my knicker gusset. I did the only possible thing and burst into tears.

'It was Baby!' I wailed. 'She wanted sweets and I didn't have money! I told her not to take it! She put it . . . put it down her jumper! Honest! Ask her!'

I upped the volume of my wails and forced more snot out of my nose, waiting for papa to take me in his arms and tell me how sorry he was to have falsely accused me. Instead there was an endless pause and then, 'Are you lying? Because if you are . . .'

'No papa! I swear! I got the tin! I hid it and I was going to take it back tomorrow! Honest!'

At that moment, Mr Ormerod rushed into the kitchen and flung himself at the cold tap, turned it on and stuck his mouth under it, gulping like he'd just come back from a long desert trek. Mama bustled after him, wringing her hands fitfully. 'Oh please, Mr Ormerod! We do have glasses you know!' she fluttered, and then to papa, 'He bit on a green chilli . . . poor man . . .'

When Mr Ormerod stood up, there were beads of sweat on his nose and he spoke in a breathy whisper, 'Please don't worry, Mrs Kumar . . . I'll be right as rain. I mean, I eat English mustard but this has never happened to me before . . .'

'I should have given you one of the children's snacks, they don't take to chillies either. Oh I feel so bad!' mama continued, until papa whispered something to her and she backed out gracefully, shutting the kitchen door behind her.

'Mr Ormerod,' papa said in a businesslike tone, 'I'm afraid one of our friend's daughters may have taken your tin and I don't want to embarrass her parents . . . you understand.'

Mr Ormerod nodded, taking deep gulps of air, waving his hand in assent.

'But Meena said she managed to get the tin off her, so if I refund you the difference, maybe we can say no more about it, eh?'

Once Mr Ormerod had counted the contents, he told papa, 'It's just a couple of bob missing . . . Let's leave it at that, shall we?'

But papa insisted on giving Mr Ormerod a ten-shilling note, pressing it into his hand in a fervent manner that left no room for disagreement. I mentally calculated how many sherbet saucers I could have got for ten shillings and felt aggrieved.

We must have been in the kitchen for a while because when we came out, the Uncles were finishing off their meal and the Aunties whispered curiously behind papa as he bade a still perspiring Mr Ormerod farewell. Mama raised questioning eyebrows at papa but he waved her away, indicating he could not talk whilst Auntie Shaila was at her side. That was a mistake because Auntie Shaila had radar built into her sari blouse and she collared papa soon afterwards in a corner, demanding to know what had gone on. Pinky and Baby were cuddled up together on the settee, testing each other on the capitals of Europe from one of the encyclopedias I had been given at Christmas and had never read. They were completely unaware of Auntie Shaila's murderous glances and trembling gestures in their direction, but when it finally came to everyone to leave, Auntie Shaila merely threw their coats at them and shouted, 'Car! Now!' Pinky and Baby fumbled with their toggles and hoods nervously, now wide awake and alert.

Papa stopped Auntie Shaila at the door and pleaded with her in Punjabi, I caught the words for 'Gently . . . children . . . finished . . .' none of which made any impression on Auntie Shaila.

I stood shivering in the doorway, watching Uncle Amman lead them to the car which was parked a little way up the lane.

I told myself that if Pinky and Baby managed to get into the car without being told off, they were okay. The whole incident would be forgotten on the way home. I held my breath as Auntie Shaila held open the car door for them. Pinky got in first, Auntie Shaila did nothing. They were fine. Then as Baby got one leg into the car, Auntie Shaila cuffed her soundly on the back of her head, making her bangles jingle. Baby immediately burst into sobs, so Auntie Shaila hit her harder and then reached over her to slap any bit of Pinky that came within reach. 'So now you are becoming robbers? My own daughters?' Every word was punctuated with a swing, followed by a plaintive 'Mama nahin! Nahin mama!' 'So you think because you live here you can become like the goree girls? What next, huh? Boyfriends? Babies? You think you can spit in my face? Your own mother!' Auntie Shaila was still shouting over her shoulder as Uncle Amman pulled shakily away, forgetting to put his headlights on until he was halfway down the hill. I briefly saw Pinky and Baby silhouetted in the back of the car. They had their arms wrapped around each other and their heads lifted in silent wails, like they were howling at the stars.

I could not sleep that night and apparently neither could papa. I heard him tossing and turning next door, and then much later, through a hazy half-doze, heard his heavy footsteps going downstairs. The next morning he did not look at me and when Anita came calling at the back gate, he picked up his newspaper and left the kitchen, slamming the door behind him.

7

Spring was always my favourite season in the village, and as the first cuckoo sounded, almost every cottage door would swing open revealing taut-jawed women in pinnies and headscarfs brandishing an armoury of cleaning materials. You could not walk down the street without falling over some possessed female hunched over a front step with a wire scrubbing brush, choking over the clouds of dust rising from the scores of rugs being beaten to a pulp by strong sleeveless arms, picking your way through clusters of china dogs and horse brasses laid out on sheets in the watery sun, drying to a gleam whilst indoors, cupboards, shelves and cabinets were being emptied and washed down. The air filled with dust motes and the women's screeching voices, calling to each other from their upturned nests, swapping domestic hints, 'Yow want to try some lemon juice on them glass doors!', the latest gossip, 'Some big knob come down to look at the school . . . says it's too small to keep open! That's the bloody point, in't it? Don't want the estate kids coming round here . . .' and always the litany of marital woes, 'So he spends all the housekeeping, rolls into bed stinking like a brewery and says, brace yourself chick, I'm coming up! Course, I bloody walloped him! We made it up after though . . .' 'Yeah I bloody know, I live next door remember! . . .'

I loved hanging around the houses during this ritualistic skin shedding, fascinated by the objects and memories behind all those shut doors, intoxicated by the smells of disinfectant and coal tar soap which complemented the sticky new buds adorning every tree certain that something clean and brand new was about to happen.

Of course, not every household embraced the spring with soapy red arms; the Mad Mitchells next door merely chucked a few more bits of junk into their front garden, adding to their bizarre monument to kitsch. There was an old style perambulator filled with a jumble of mangy fur coats, a half-smashed fake crystal chandelier, a coal scuttle, two brand new bedpans, a car battery and two cracked wing mirrors, a hat stand, a stuffed mongoose, and a collection of rusted, unopened cans of fruit. Whilst mama tut-tutted every time we passed their house, taking in the grimy opaque windows, the tattered curtains and peeling front door, I always checked to see if there was another imaginative addition to the Mad Mitchell Collection. I thought it was like a living sculpture, each object telling a story which grew more complex with every new throwaway, charting the changing tastes and fortunes in their lives. Whose baby had gurgled in that pram? Why didn't they ever eat those tins of fruit? Was the mongoose once a dearly beloved pet? My excitement increased when mama told me that mongooses came from India, and also fought and ate snakes. Had there once been a plague of serpents in Tollington, like those pestilences Uncle Alan had talked about at Sunday School? Maybe Mr Mitchell had lived in India and brought back the mongoose to clear up the village.

It was true I had never seen any of the Mitchells travel further than the town shops. Journeys seemed to bother them greatly. They would line up at the bus stop at least a half hour before the hourly bus was due, Mr and Mrs Mitchell checking the horizon every few minutes, not seeming to notice Cara wandering down the white lines in the middle of the road, singing to herself. Mr Mitchell's favourite place was definitely his outside lav, which looked out onto the entry dividing our houses. In winter, I'd hear him straining and cursing as he rattled his newspaper, but for him, warmer weather meant he could stay in there as long as he liked, sometimes for hours on end, and not bother to lock the door. That was his version of a spring clear out, I supposed. Whilst running down the entry, I often glimpsed a hairy leg with long johns draped around the ankles, and once or twice he'd even called out a cheery, 'Bloody noice morning, Meena duck!' as I had scampered past, terrified one day a sudden breeze would swing open the door and I would face the moral dilemma of whether I should ignore or greet an elder sitting on the bog.

Later on, when I read about The Sixties, when enough time had lapsed for those two words to be headed with capital letters, I felt as if I was reading about some far off mythical country where laughing teenagers in sharp suits and A-line dresses drove around in psychedelic Minis, having sex in between chain-smoking and dancing lumpishly in the audience of *Ready Steady Go!* We owned a Mini which I was not sure had a fourth gear – that was the only point of contact I could find.

Tollington's version of the sexual revolution was Sam Lowbridge's heavy-petting sessions on the park swings, which were always cut short by a giggling audience of five-year-olds or Mrs Keithley running out of her yard brandishing a garden hose. Drugs were what Mr Ormerod kept on the top shelf of his shop, buttercup syrup, aspirin tablets in fat brown bottles, Old Sloane's Liniment Ointment, a particular sell-out item round spring cleaning time. Parties were what grown-ups had, my parents' chaotic passionate music evenings, the occasional tea dance organised by Uncle Alan in the church hall when our yard would be overrun by blue-rinsed ladies and proud old men with ostentatious cravats, whilst the local dogs would be driven barmy by the high-pitched whine of dozens of hearing aids jamming the airwaves. Sometimes, the Mitre pub would host an engagement party or stag night, playing loud rock and roll music that made the geese shit in terror and cower under the apple trees, but the music would always be switched off at ten o'clock on the dot.

But if Tollington was a footnote in the book of the Sixties, then my family and friends were the squashed flies in the spine. According to the newspapers and television, we simply did not exist. If a brown or black face ever did appear on TV, it stopped us all in our tracks. 'Daljit! Quick!' papa would call, and we would crowd round and coo over the walk-on in some detective series, some long-suffering actor in a gaudy costume with a goodness-gracious-me accent. ('So Mr Templar, you speak fluent Hindustani too! But that won't stop me stealing the secret formula for my country from where I will soon rule the world! Heh heh heh . . .') and welcome him into our home like a long-lost relative. But these occasional minor celebrities never struck me as real; they were someone else's version of Indian, far too exaggerated and exotic to be believable. Sometimes I wondered if the very act of shutting our front door transported us onto another planet, where non-related elders were called Aunties and Uncles and talked in rapid Punjabi, which their children understood but answered back in broad Black Country slang, where we ate food with our fingers and discussed family feuds happening five thousand miles away, where manners were so courtly that a raised eyebrow could imply an insult, where sensibilities were so finely tuned that an advert featuring a woman in a bikini could clear a room.

Our revolutions were quieter and often unwitnessed, I soon realised, after years of earwigging on the elders' evening chats. They had their own version of history: 'You remember, walking round Swiss Cottage, trying to find a boarding house that did not have that sign "No Irish, Blacks or Dogs?" . . . Hai, the letters I wrote home, so many lies about the jobs we had, the money we were making. My mamaji still thinks I am a college lecturer . . . You know that old trick, you ring up and get an interview in your best voice, then they see your face and suddenly the job is gone . . . Ah yes, but also these people on

Christmas Eve, they see us standing at the bus stop in the snow and drive all of us right to our front door . . . these people can be so cruel . . . some of these people are angels, I tell you . . . if only mama/papa/bhaiya/didi were here to see this . . .' None of these stories appeared in any book or newspaper or programme, and yet they were all true. But then I was beginning to realise that truth counted for very little, in the end.

I did not realise quite how starved we were of seeing ourselves somewhere other than in each other's lounges until Rita Farrier, the reigning Miss India, won the Miss World contest. This is such a distant memory that I must have been very young, but the sense of excitement and pride it awoke in my parents and their friends obviously made a lasting impression. I have a vague recollection of our telephone ringing constantly immediately after the announcement whilst the TV remained on full blast, and then our house being invaded by various Aunties and Uncles all bearing pans of the food they had cooked that evening, ready for another impromptu party. The mantra that went round the rooms stays with me too. 'And she a doctor as well!' crowed Auntie Shaila, everyone's long-held belief confirmed that Indian women were the brainiest and most beautiful in the world. If only Rita Farrier had come along when I was ten and it was Spring, and I could have taken her hand and walked down the main street in Tollington, both of us in saris, her stethoscope flapping around her long brown neck.

Sadly, Rita never made it to Tollington, but even without her, Spring in the village was always welcome, and always celebrated by our only communal, organized event, the Tollington Spring Fete. This was held in the grounds of the grandest house in the village, an exquisite Tudor mansion owned by Mr Pembridge, a local Tory councillor and businessman who did something minimal and managerial in construction. Every year, they would throw open their garden to a number of stalls from all the surrounding villages, the proceeds of which would be distributed by the local churches to a chosen charitable cause. The Pembridges lived at the posh end of the main village road, where the houses gradually became larger and more set back from the pavement. Their wrought iron fences enclosed miles of manicured emerald lawn, riotous flower beds, horse chestnut and beech trees shading an outdoor pool and a salmon fishery. Mrs Worrall told me that the house itself was at least three hundred years old and originally belonged to the Squire of Tollington, whose last remaining heir, a daredevil bachelor, had been killed in the Spanish Civil War. The ironwork on the gates delivered the motto, *Semper Eadem*, which papa told me meant, Always the Same. And indeed, the Pembridge mansion had not changed in all the years I could remember, remaining an island of grace, tranquillity and unimaginable wealth whilst the village school halted any new intake of children, preparing to gradually close down, and the neon motorway lights began slowly appearing, poking their stiff necks above the horizon.

On the morning of the Fete, most of the village gathered outside the Pembridge gates, talking in hushed whispers whilst they waited to be admitted. Not all of them were wearing hats, but if they had been, lots of doffing would have been the order of the day. The grandeur and elegance of the place affected us all, made even more desirable by its very inaccessibility. For the other three hundred and sixty-four days of the year, the Pembridge mansion remained out of bounds to us, as effectively as if it had been surrounded by electric fences and a shark-infested moat. Of course, most passers-by would feel compelled to slow down and drink it in, the women all breathy and eagle-eyed, checking for a change of curtains or new shrubs in the herbaceous borders, the men seemingly unimpressed, although their eyes would narrow and nostrils flare at the salmon lake and the blue Rolls-Royce with its numberplate PCC 1. We did catch glimpses of Mr Pembridge easing himself in and out of his car on his sweeping driveway, always in a suit with a carnation as red as his face in his lapel. And sometimes we would catch sight of Mrs Pembridge in the back seat, as they left, we assumed, for a party. She was a thin, bored woman with a head far too big and bouffant for her body, who would acknowledge our stares with a cursory flicker of a smile.

Anita and I were very excited to learn that they had a son so there was indeed a young heir to the manor, and one day he actually rode through the village on a huge skittery horse. Unfortunately, the horse was better looking: Graham Pembridge had his mother's skinny frame and his father's 'mardy' face, and when he stopped to ask us the time, he talked like he had a shilling's worth of gobstoppers in his mouth. He was obviously not a born horseman, and sat like he was waiting for it to explode underneath him. Not long after, we saw him zipping about the lanes in a bright red Porsche, which seemed to suit him better. Paula watched him burning rubber as he took a corner and sighed, 'One day some lucky cow is going to marry into all that.'

Mrs Lowbridge picked her teeth with a hairgrip and replied, 'Ar, but she'll have to marry Mr Plug-Face to get to it. Inbreeding's a terrible thing, ain't it?'

Mama, of course, had not wanted to accompany me and papa to the Fete. Nowadays, she seemed to exist in a self-contained world of nappies, cleaning, cooking and fitful twitchy catnaps, brief moments in between my brother's incessant, cheery demands. He was not exactly a naughty baby; he didn't yowl for hours on end like Mrs Keithley's Nicky used to, to a single note of whining torture which could strip paint and compel church matrons to murder. He did not throw food around or break ornaments or deposit curdy omelettes of sick on the furniture, like most of the other babies that had passed through our doors. In fact, if he had been ugly or maladjusted, at least we would have had the excuse to give him away to the Sunshine Orphanage in Cannock, whose minibus occasionally trundled through the village. We kids always rushed to wave at the vehicle with its huge painted rainbow on the side. I was expecting to see thin, hollow-eyed ragamuffins slouched shivering in the cushioned seats who would gaze at us with longing, and maybe raise a skeletal hand in timid welcome. Instead, they all appeared indecently healthy, even though their uniforms of striped shirts and brown cords were rather naff, and returned our greetings with bored indifference or, once or twice, two fat jerking fingers out the side windows of the bus.

So I did not think I was being too unreasonable when I did suggest to mama, after yet another sleepless night, if she could maybe drop Sunil at the orphanage for a trial period. Her reply was to burst into tears and rush into her bedroom where she locked the door, and did not come out until papa spent ten minutes talking softly to her through the keyhole. He then pushed me into my bedroom and told me to 'Stay there until you realise what you have just said . . .'

I was on the point of apologising until I heard Sunil laughing and gurgling as mama and papa played with him downstairs. Eventually papa called me to eat, I decided a grumpy 'sorry' was fair exchange for a meal as I was starving. But papa made me feed Sunil before he let me touch my food. It was a near impossible task, trying to get a spoonful of puréed slop into my brother's anemone mouth. He was teething; two snow white stumps had appeared on his bottom gums and as he grabbed any opportunity to chew the spoon, I could feel the hard edges of two more top teeth grinding against the plastic. Mama and papa I knew were pretending not to watch me, but mama's eyes were still puffy and I did not want another emotional collapse on my conscience. So I changed tactics; I tried aeroplane swoops, silly voices, pulling plasticine faces, I showed willing as a devoted sister although I knew a funnel and a pair of bellows would have done the trick, and all through my performance, Sunil clapped and laughed and refused to eat a morsel. Wordlessly, mama took the spoon off me and shovelled the food into Sunil's waiting, open mouth, he ate gratefully, his eyes never leaving her face, they basked in each other's adoration.

Then I knew what the problem with my brother was, he did not want anyone else except mama. I had got so used to seeing mama moving around with Sunil clinging onto her back that it was like she had grown a hump. He even accompanied her to the outside toilet (underneath a shawl she would chuck over his body, for modesty's sake), and I had long ago given up my midnight jaunts to my parents' bed, because inevitably, when I snuggled up to mama, Sunil would be sleeping on her chest, a snuffling milky mass of warm roundness barring the way to her heart. He had to be forcibly peeled off her at nursery every morning, and stopped crying only when one of the carers sang mama's lullaby to him (mama had written it down in phonetic Hindi and adapted it to the tune of 'Baa Baa Black Sheep'). If she tried to put him down, he would clamp toes and fingers to any available expanse of flesh or material and if she left the room, he would cry, not the petulant, demanding cry of the child deprived of a toy, but great gulping sobs of abandonment and terror which would bring all of us rushing to his side, wondering if he'd impaled his willy on his nappy pin or swallowed something dangerous. But once in her arms, he would become the Sunil the rest of the world saw and loved, a smiling, dimpled, chubby, bite-sized morsel of cuteness, dispensing infant largesse from his throne, my mama.

Sunil's attachment to mama even withstood a moral assault from Auntie Shaila who declared, 'The boy should be crawling, not stuck at your bosom all the time, Daljit. If you remind these men how soft and safe it is up there, they will never want to leave.' And Auntie Shaila was right, Sunil's need was so great that mama seemed to have disappeared under it. Even her usual schedule of ruthless Spring Cleaning had seemed muted and haphazard this year; mama would start on one cupboard and leave it halfway to go and wash the bedroom curtains, leave them soaking whilst she started on the bike shed, keeping up an appearance of efficiency, but actually finishing nothing properly. Her tearful door slammings and tantrums had gradually disappeared, to be replaced with long, exhausted silences or more frightening blank stares, where she would gaze at me and papa as if we were strangers. Sunil's surprised eyes would peek over her shoulder as if in parody. Mama barely looked up as papa and I told her we were off to the fete; she was removing all the spice jars from a kitchen cupboard, sheets of old *Express and Star* newspapers lay ready in a pile. I waved at Sunil who was chewing on mama's shoulder; he flashed me a heart-stopping radiant smile.

A ripple of excitement passed through the crowd as Mr and Mrs Pembridge began the long walk from their oak panelled front door to the end of the drive. The various stalls had already been set up, church tables covered with crepe paper and unsteady awnings of candy-striped canvas, everywhere handwritten tags and signs to attract the serious bargain hunters; 'Kiddies Woollies! Hand-Knitted From Local Sheep!' 'Vintage Elderberry Wine . . . Bottled in Cannock!' 'Mrs Horton's Homemade Cakes . . . Free Scone With Every One Shilling Spent!'

As you could tell by the unnecessary use of exclamation marks, competition between the stallholders was fierce. Every year, rival villages would battle it out to see who could rake in the most money, therefore ensuring that their local church would get to choose to which charity the takings would eventually go.

Uncle Alan was instrumental in setting up campaigns and fund-raising work for international charities in the parish. However, unlike Mr Ormerod and his Bibles for Africa whist drive, he did not seem keen in bringing the light to the darkest jungles of the Third World. 'Actually, Mr O,' Alan confided once to him. 'I think they should jolly well follow whatever religion they choose. As long as they can feed themselves and work their land with some independence, I feel that we will indeed have done the Lord's bidding.' Mr Ormerod looked as if Alan had suggested having a piss in the font and from that point, as much as it must have pained him to snub a man of God, gave Alan a wide berth. I once remember standing waiting to be served in his shop with papa at my side whilst Mr Ormerod conducted a heated discussion with one of the choir ladies about Uncle Alan's worrying views. 'I mean, Mrs Lacey, it's not just about giving them stuff, is it? It's about giving them culture as well, civilisation. A good, true way of living, like what we have. It's all very well just saying hee-yaar, get on with it but they'll just tek us for mugs. They'll want fans next, radios, cookers. I mean, we ain't a charity, are we?'

Mrs Lacey nodded her head and then said, 'I thought we was a charity.'

'Well, you know what I mean,' replied Mr Ormerod testily, giving her some change and turning to us with a welcoming smile, completely devoid of irony.

Papa of course related the whole episode to mama when we returned and they laughed till they wept, playing both the characters in the scene, 'They'll want cookers!' giggled mama. 'Doesn't he know we were fitting bidets into our houses when their ancestors were living in caves? Oh God!' and then she went suddenly quiet and looked hard at papa. 'God Shyam, is that how they see us? Is it really?'

Papa shrugged his shoulders. 'You take things too seriously, Daljit. They have accepted us, have we ever had any trouble from people round here? You know, like Usha had over in Willenhall, those shaved head boys shouting at them, pushing the kids around?'

Mama got up angrily, 'Just because it doesn't happen to us, does not mean it is not happening! And they leave us alone because they don't think we are really Indian. "Oh, you're so English, Mrs K!" Like it is a buggering compliment! If I hear that one more time . . .'

Then they both seemed to notice I was in the room and changed the subject quickly, as I knew they would. I thought of my Auntie Usha, all of four foot ten and as mild-mannered as a mouse, and could not imagine why anyone would even want to raise their voice to her. The image of Auntie Usha being shoved about by anonymous white fists stayed with me for ages and every time the picture formed in my mind, so detailed I could count the creeping hair on the clenched knuckles and the intricate patterns on the hem of her sari, I felt both impotent and on fire. Mama seemed to imply that there was some link between Mr Ormerod's earnest ramblings and the activities of those unnamed boys, that one was merely an inevitable consequence of the other. I could not understand this then, I simply divided the world into strangers and friends and reckoned if I stayed amongst those I knew, I would be safe. But since joining Anita's gang, I had become more suspicious of how the familiar could turn into the unknown, and what happened at the Fete revealed how many strangers did indeed live amongst us.

As Mr Pembridge opened the gate, there was a slight swell forward which he stopped, Canute-like, with his upraised hands. He cleared his throat, fingered his collar which looked way too tight and made his neck bulge like a bullfrog's, and was about to launch into speech when he seemed to discover something was missing. He patted his pockets, and then remembered what it was. He turned round and beckoned Mrs Pembridge from where she was lurking by a tombola stall, to come and stand dutifully at his side. 'Now, before I open up the ground to you all, I shall, as always, say a few words of welcome . . .' The crowd relaxed slightly, people settled down dutifully for a few more minutes of standing, although all I could see mostly was backs and necks, and a glimpse of Mr Pembridge through a gap in the bodies. Mr Pembridge continued, 'Beryl and I are honoured to be part of Tollington's proud history, living as we do, um, here, but as you know there are great changes sweeping across our lovely land. A new road is, even as we stand here, burrowing its way into um the land, as I said, and our lovely school is closing down. Do we want to ship our children five miles away? I say no. I say our lovely village is doing quite nicely thank you and a change is not as good as a rest. In this case anyway . . .'

He tailed off as he realised most people were staring at Beryl who was edging forward clumsily, her high heels sinking into the lawn. She had a sort of shift dress on, muslin with little clocks round the hem and as she clicked her teeth nervously, it sounded like ticking. She shot an imploring look at her husband who beckoned her again, becoming impatient. She eventually piped up, it was the strangest voice, which did not at all go with her body and was never the voice I imagined she would have. It was a miner's daughter's voice, all tin and rust and under the earth. 'Stan, I've gorra go in and put me pumps on. Sorry like . . .' There was a collective intake of breath. Mrs Worrall, whose massive bosom was the only thing holding me up, breathed out, 'Hark at Lady Muck! Blue blood, my arse. It's gin!'

Somebody sniggered loudly behind us, all heads turned to see who was spoiling this ritualistic moment. Sam Lowbridge and various gang members were standing across the road, leaning on their mopeds. He looked different, harder, leaner, and then I realised what he had done. His hair was gone, his sandy shoulder-length locks had been replaced by a spiky crew cut, so close that I could see the pink of his scalp underneath. The rest of the gang had done the same. Before, I had seen them going around in long, baggy green anoraks with targets painted on the back, but all of them were now wearing this uniform of short denim jackets, tight jeans held up with braces, and huge clumpy boots. They looked like a child's drawing, stick men with exaggerated huge heads and huge feet. Sam returned the crowd's gaze calmly and then gobbed on the floor, sending a ripple of disgust through the group. Mrs Pembridge meanwhile had reached the sanctuary of her front door and disappeared inside whilst Mr Pembridge battled on, trying to win back his audience.

I could see Uncle Alan chatting animatedly to one of the stallholders. He was flirting with an octogenarian, one of his specialities, and she twittered and giggled under his twinkling gaze. I was surprised that Uncle Alan was not standing to attention like the rest of us; indeed, he seemed completely unconcerned that Mr Pembridge was still struggling through his speech. 'As I was saying, this is a time when we must stick together in Tollington to defend ourselves against outside forces, if we are to preserve everything we hold dear. You can sign petitions inside against the motorway and for the school, careful you don't get your votes mixed up everybody!' He paused for laughter which did eventually come, politely, in a trickle. 'If I can end by quoting a man I am sure is everybody's hero here, Sir Winston Churchill, who said We Will Fight Them on the Beaches . . . Just like our Winnie, we in Tollington must prepare to fight! Thank you and I now have great pleasure in declaring the Tollington Spring Fete . . . open!'

As he finally pulled back the gates, he was almost knocked over by the rush of villagers who shouted and laughed at full decibel as they pushed their way through, purses already being snapped open at the ready. I felt giddy with indecision, there were so many stalls that I did not know where to start. Tables groaned under mounds of lovingly-presented cakes, 'Chocolate, fruit or fairy, dear?', homemade jams, pickles and wines battened down beneath stoppers and corks, seasons of summer fruits and hedgerow flowers compressed into their little glass worlds, bric-a-brac galore, old war medals, Coronation mugs and plates, chamber pots filled with pansies, twenties costume jewellery heavy with chunky paste garnets and emeralds, miner's lamps polished up to become coffee table conversation pieces, crocheted doilies in pastel shades ('Lovely for the dressing table or vanity case'), old gramophone records as big as dinner plates, lacquered powder compacts with pressed flowers petrified under their glass lids, huge vegetables, cartoon-like in their size and colouring, marrows like rockets, tomatoes like small red planets, cauliflowers as bumpy as the surface of the moon.

We found ourselves in front of Sandy's soft toy display where quite a few of our neighbours had gathered out of a sense of loyalty as this was Sandy's first year as a stallholder, and we all wanted one of our own to do well. Sandy stood shyly in front of a collection of stuffed toys which, at a distance, were charming, multicoloured fluffy shapes each with its own price tag attached. But on closer examination, I realised it was hard to tell exactly what each animal was supposed to be, as if they'd decided to play a joke after lights off in the Ark. This one could have been a giraffe, it had the markings, but its neck was too short and it had the snout of a pig. This one definitely looked like a horse, except for the bushy tail and pug face. There were several ears missing or extra paws attached, and Sandy stood nervously guarding her precious mutations as, gradually, the excited chatter of the Ballbearings women subsided into soft whispers.

'It's a bloody horse . . . in't it? . . . Nah, it's a lion, look at the feet, yer daft cow . . . Ooh, I wouldn't like to cuddle up to this one, mind you, anything looks good after my Stan . . .' Sandy licked her lips and patted down her hair, keeping up a fixed friendly smile. I guessed she had got up in a hurry because she had not got any make-up on, I hadn't realised how many freckles she had as they were usually hidden under a matt finish of foundation. They were the colour of what I supposed her real hair must have been, shiny copper. From a distance she looked as if she was sprinkled with pennies. But without make-up she looked vulnerable and younger, for the first time I saw the downward tilt of her large blue eyes which gave her face a soft, bewildered expression. She glanced behind to check on Mikey who was slouched in a chair pretending to read a *Whizzer and Chips* comic which he held deliberately in front of his face.

I ached for him; I knew the shame that was contracting his muscles and constricting his throat, the worst kind of shame engendered by having to hang around your parents when they were turning social embarrassment into an art form. I tugged at papa's sleeve, but he had already guessed what I was going to ask him and shook his head. 'We don't need more clutter in the house,' he whispered. Please, I silently asked him, don't put Sandy through any more of this rejection. Uncle Alan breezed past, sending a shiver of delight through the Ballbearings women and called out, 'Come on then ladies! Let's support all our brave volunteers! We're the hot tip to make the most money this year!' Anything Uncle Alan said was taken as a saucy double entendre and Hot Tip was too good an opportunity for them to miss, so they began nudging each other and breaking into snorting laughter, Sandy's stall already forgotten. But then a familiar voice boomed over their heads, slicing the laughter into slivers. 'I'll tek them two . . . no, mek it them four at the front, Sandy chick!'

It was Hairy Neddy, or a neater, washed version of him, as he was wearing a jacket and tie with his jeans which he had ironed from the knee downwards. He ostentatiously waved a ten-shilling note above the ladies' heads as he reached through them to claim his four unloved orphans. Sandy had sense enough to swallow her gratitude and look unsurprised at this gallant gesture, but Hairy Neddy was on a roll now. 'Ey Sandy, yow'll mek a packet today with these Space Gonks. Yow cor get em for love nor money down Wolverhampton. Even Beatties is sold out, they'm having to send down to London for more supplies!'

Sandy nodded uncertainly, the beginnings of panic flitting over her face. But the Ballbearings ladies' ears pricked up at this information.

'What yow mean, Space Gonks? Am they famous or summat?'

'Oh yeah!' enthused Hairy Neddy. 'Them am like these new educational toys, right. They look like lots of different animals in one, meks the kids use their imagination when they play. Me brother's kids have been killing me over getting some, still, no worries now eh, thanks to Sandy . . .'

The women digested this for a moment and then they began a flurry of purse-opening and grabbing at the toys excitedly. 'Better get one for our Lorna, what with her birthday coming up . . . Well, that's Easter taken care of. Pass us that dog thing, the blue one . . . Hey! I saw that un fust, gerrof!'

Sandy just stood and watched this a moment, her eyes brimming. As she took the note Hairy Neddy was holding out towards her, he grabbed her hand and I lip-read his words as if in slow motion, the words I had lately been dreaming that some shadowy man would one day say to me. Hairy Neddy whispered, 'Will you marry me?' and Sandy, in response, burst into tears. As the women cottoned on to what was happening, they broke out into squeals and applause, bringing curious punters from all corners of the grounds, wondering what exciting bargain they were missing. My heart was pounding against my chest and I felt as if my lungs were full of hot thick air. I had witnessed one of the most romantic moments ever in my short life and I knew Anita would be pig sick when she found out she had missed it.

I looked up at papa to see if he was similarly affected but he was concentrating on the apparently heated discussion going on between Uncle Alan and the Reverend Ince by the Raffle and Tombola stall. Mr Ince, our church vicar, a thin erect man with a shock of fuzzy salt and pepper hair, had a hands off approach to his flock. He confined himself to one sermon a week, on Sundays, and occasional outings to events such as the Fete where he could swan about in his hardly-used robes and take credit for all the backbreaking work his assistant, Alan, had put into our community. It was Uncle Alan who raised funds through sponsored events and door to door collections, who ran the Tiny Tollington's Youth and Sunday clubs, who swept the pews and arranged the flowers in the church and encouraged various groups around the village to use the draughty church hall for their dances, bingo or parties. It was part of the accepted order of things, that Uncle Alan got his hands dirty and Reverend Ince kept his clean to shake with various dignitaries, but as Alan seemed cheerful enough with this arrangement, we never thought of passing judgement.

But today, Uncle Alan was red in the face and veins stuck out in his temples, his fists were clenched at his side as he talked rapidly to the Reverend who simply kept shaking his head in response. I had never seen Uncle Alan with anything but a chipper grin on his face, and to see him so contorted with anger made him almost unrecognisable. Eventually the Reverend turned his back on Alan, whilst he was still talking, and walked over to join the Pembridges at the Homemade Wine stall. Uncle Alan took a moment to steady his breathing and then strode purposefully towards us to shake papa's hand. 'Mr Kumar! And Meena! Great to see you here today!' His voice was the same bouncy back-slapping voice he always used but there were still sparks glinting in the corner of his eyes. Papa greeted him warmly; he always seemed to relax in Uncle Alan's company and I once heard him telling mama what a 'sensitive and educated fellow' he was.

'What did you think of Mr Pembridge's speech then?' asked Uncle Alan casually.

'Oh, very um impressive. As usual,' papa smiled back. 'Although Mr Churchill is not particularly one of my heroes. But anyway . . .'

'Why not?' pressed Uncle Alan, suddenly alert, searching papa's face as if wanting confirmation for something still forming in his head.

'Well,' paused papa, feeling slightly uncomfortable, 'no doubt he was a great leader . . .'

'But?' pressed Alan.

'Well, when Mahatma Gandhi came over here to visit, your Mr Churchill described him as "that half-naked little fakir". But still . . .'

Uncle Alan interrupted papa, a bitter smile twisting his lips, 'Mr Kumar, he is not my Winston Churchill, and I thank God for that.' And then he stalked off and disappeared amongst the crowds.

Papa was pulling me gently away from Sandy's stall around which a sizeable group had gathered, mainly female, all chatting animatedly and teasing the hot and sweaty Hairy Neddy who seemed to be in shock, the realisation of what he had just done freezing his face into a dumb smiling mask. I could tell papa felt uncomfortable amongst the Ballbearings women; whenever we came across them in the village he would always come up with some lame excuse to get away with the minimum of small talk, during which the women would flirt with him unashamedly, enjoying his obvious discomfiture. 'Ooh an't he got lovely eyes, Brenda . . . Yeah, just like that Omar Sharif . . . Ooh yeah, your missus is a lucky woman, yow tell her that from us, Mr K!' Papa would always nod and smile politely but if he happened to be holding my hand, he would squeeze it so hard that my knuckles cracked together, and once we were home, he would retell his experiences to mama as if recounting a near miss in a nasty accident.

'And then that one with the big teeth and purple hair winked at me! Of course, they are nice women and all that but honestly, are there no limits? And in front of Meena as well . . .' Mama always listened to these close encounters with a satisfied possessive expression, secure in the knowledge that not only was her husband tasty enough to flirt with, but that the incident proved how lucky he was to have his own Indian wife whom he knew would never exhibit such loose behaviour in a public place. 'They are harmless, Shyamji, just having fun,' she would soothe him. 'That is just their way of being friendly.' And then papa would nod and kiss her cheek and she would wrap her delight close to her like a shawl.

Papa was jingling his loose change in his jacket pocket and I knew he wanted to make his way over to the skittle stall. Papa loved gambling; I had watched him playing rummy with my Uncles, everyone sitting cross-legged in a huge circle on our carpet, their coins and tumblers of whisky at their knees, throwing down cards with whoops of triumph or dismay. Or I had followed him into penny arcades during shopping trips, when he would slip away whilst mama was taking too long over a purchase, and would watch him feed the one-arm bandits carefully, holding his breath as the tumbling oranges and lemons spun to a halt as if expecting a jackpot win every time. Whilst papa thought of himself as a rakish risk taker, I could see how hard it was for him to gamble without guilt by the way he reluctantly handed over notes for change at the penny arcade booths, or how hesitantly he would place his bets on the carpet whilst my more flamboyant Uncles would be flinging shillings and sometimes notes onto the floor with optimistic battle cries.

Actually, papa won quite often. Uncle Amman was always saying that 'Lakshmi mata must be sitting on your right hand, Shyam saab,' as papa raked yet another heap of winnings into his lap. But for papa, every win was tainted by the memory of all those other times he had gambled and lost; this little war of sacrifice and gain plagued him every time, and I wondered why a man who had risked so much by setting foot in a foreign country with five pounds in his pocket and no friends to call on, could not simply throw caution to the wind and just let go. Later on, when mama had begun to treat me like a grown-up and had released nuggets of information about her and papa's experiences in India that would have given me nightmares as a child, this battle between desire and duty made perfect sense.

Of course, papa courted chance like an old friend; as a seventeen-year-old in a refugee camp who owned only what he wore, he could afford to decide anything on the flip of a coin because, at that point in his life, there was nothing left to lose and any gain, even the smallest *anna*, would be a victory. However, papa was not a recreational gambler, a rich man playing with his wealth for whom poverty was an unimaginable and distant maybe; he had lived, breathed and smelled it, and the prospect of returning there due to a miscalculated bet must have haunted him. It sat on his shoulder whilst he fed change into a Lucky Waterfall machine, shook its head and tutted every time he picked up his hand of cards and scanned the diamonds and hearts. And whilst his peculiar brand of fiery caution often irritated me, it was only because I had not yet realised how he, and everyone else of his generation, had taken enough risks already to last a lifetime.

But today, he felt lucky, I could see it in the spring in his step and the way he kept patting his pockets, reassuring himself that he had the money to back up his ambitions. Besides, papa had won a bottle of whisky at last year's Fete. 'Coming, beti?' he asked. I shook my head and pointed over to the fortune teller's stall, 'I'll be over there,' I said, hurrying off before papa cottoned onto the fact that Anita was already waiting for me, tapping her foot.

I was surprised to see that this year's fortune teller was not our usual Madame Rosa, alias Mrs Goodyear, a plump, ruddy newsagent's wife from a neighbouring village. Mrs Goodyear considered her job as soothsayer to be similar to that of a jolly missionary; all single girls were told they would be marrying into unimaginable wealth with a handsome upright Christian man, all married men were reassured that next year would bring them promotion, status and a batch of sturdy sons, and anyone in between was advised to 'keep working hard, read your scriptures, and all that you wish for will come knocking at your door by this time next year.' Last year Sandy had complained to her that the only thing that came knocking was 'the sodding rent man and the woodworm in my lav', but none of us could have guessed that twelve months later to the day, someone would finally make an honest woman out of her, again.

Although Mrs Goodyear had a polished, convincing patter and a few admirers who swore that she knew the most uncannily intimate details about them (strangely enough, all these punters were her best friends from the W I), she always had a bit of a hiccup when she came to read my future. As soon as she saw me approaching, she would clutch nervously at her upside down goldfish bowl and muster up a genial, almost convincing expression. 'Meena duck! I was just about to knock off . . . My psychic energy's running a bit low right now . . .' However, she never turned me away and her prognosis was always the same; 'Ooh yes, you are a decent obedient girl, although your dad's a bit strict isn't he? He's only worried love, wants you to marry well . . .' (I was all of six and a half when she first trotted this one out . . .) 'But you will . . . I see a tall man, coloured like yourself, in a white coat . . .' (Well it had to be a doctor, or the long shot could have been the director of a mental institute. And the nearest she could come to imagining a mixed relationship was a Methodist marrying a Catholic . . .) 'You will do well at school, love, I see you in an office, or possibly on a bus . . .' (I like to think she had once met an Indian conductor on the single decker into town . . .) 'And you'll make a lovely home for your husband and five children . . .' (She must have read that in the paper, that we all bred like rabbits . . .) But in her limited terms of reference, Mrs Goodyear was only telling me what she thought I longed to hear, the future I deserved, and by golly she was going to give it to me because she thought of herself as a fair-minded woman and leaving me out of her act would have been plain bad manners.

But the woman with whom Anita was chatting animatedly was a stranger, a mysterious stranger, I breathed to myself because she was dressed as if she had looked up fortune teller in the dictionary and chosen her wardrobe accordingly. She wore a floor-length purple robe decorated with silver stars and

crescent moons, her wrists jangled with thin silver bracelets
and tied around her head was a black bandana shot through
with silver thread from which a fringe of dyed black, wiry hair
protruded. She had shiny olive-toned skin and small beady
brown eyes and although her craggy hands revealed she must
have been in her fifties, her face was as smooth and unlined as
a young girl's. She made me feel nervous, and then I realised
that this was because she looked Indian enough to be one of
my Aunties and it made me want to trust her.

Anita did not seem to notice me as she was in mid-argument
with the Mysterious Stranger. 'Ow goo on, missus, you can
give me a little go,' Anita whined. 'I've only got sixpence,
honest!' The woman shook her head and spoke in a weird
lilting accent which seemed so foreign, she sounded like one of
the sloe-eyed villainesses who popped up regularly in
'Batman' on television. 'No darlink, I only work for a shillin',
you see? No more, no less.'

Anita shot me a glare which made me fumble in my
cardigan pocket; I only had sixpence for the whole Fete but
she already had her hand outstretched, expecting it. Anita
slammed down both our coins onto the ricketty card table, her
voice high with excitement. 'See? A shilling! See? Yow can do
us both for that ey? We'm only nippers, after all.'

The woman motioned us to sit, there was only one chair,
which Anita took, and then in a fit of uncharacteristic
generosity, motioned me to squeeze alongside her. The
woman cleared her throat and suddenly took my hands in
hers, turning them palm upwards and examined the clear
dark lines, some of which, I was ashamed to note, were
grooved with dirt. She nodded to herself and began, 'You hef
to watch your momma's health, is not good. But there will be
help soon. Help from over the seas, yes?' I swallowed, my
mind racing. I had not noticed mama was ill, just tired
perhaps and 'over the seas' was a pretty safe prediction to fling
around me. I began thinking of all the other things I could
have been doing with my sixpence when she continued,

'Success is written here, darlink, a good mind and a strong heart, but sacrifice too, you see, and guilt. You are under a bad influence, but you cannot break free. Soon you will hef to choose, darlink, and you will lose everythink before you can begin again. But it is for the best. Only you know what is the right think to do, you see?'

A bad influence; that sounded like a curse. Maybe she had looked right through my eyes like a telescope and seen the wicked thoughts and easy lies and bitter frustration that sometimes seemed to fill my head until it felt like it would burst.

I pulled my hands away quickly, feeling suddenly light-headed, and shot Anita what I hoped was a mocking, completely unimpressed grin. But Anita looked deadly serious; she wiped her hands down her dress ceremoniously and placed them on the table. The woman took Anita's hands in hers and drew a short breath as her eyes darted from the palms and then back again to Anita's eager, determined face.

'Don't think I can read you, darlink,' the woman said suddenly, letting go of Anita's hands.

Anita's nostrils flared, her pupils dilated until her eyes seemed black holes, 'You did her! I paid you and all! You did her, missus!'

The woman pursed her mouth and shrugged her shoulders, making the tiny coins sewn onto the rim of her bandana jingle and dance. 'Okay darlink. Is what you want. Your momma is not around anymore, yes?'

Anita sneered, 'Yeah! She's mekking me tea right now, actually! What you on about?'

The woman remained impassive. 'Okay. Is nothing then.'

'What? What do you mean? Where's she going?'

'Is nothink I say!' the woman spat back angrily, making Anita retreat. 'You want this or no?' She took Anita's silence as assent and continued, 'I see troubles for you. Married too young, babies too fast. Why you always in such a hurry eh?'

Anita said nothing, she was chewing her lip fitfully,

affecting boredom, but held her hands out as if they had suddenly become very heavy.

'Something bad is coming, in two maybe three years time, an accident, or maybe not an accident. Is up to you. You could be lucky, young lady. But why you try and spoil everything good, eh?'

Anita was now breathing heavily, her eyes blinking rapidly. She yanked her hands away and grabbed the two sixpences off the table as she stood. 'You're shit, you are!' she hissed into the woman's face. 'Yow don't know what you'm talking about! I ain't paying nothing for you!'

Anita pushed the sixpence into my hands and strolled off into the crowd, banging into people as she passed. The Mysterious Stranger watched her with detached amusement and then turned to me, fixing me with a long challenging gaze which made me feel as if all my clothes were gradually being unpeeled and falling in a crumpled heap at my bare feet. I replaced my sixpence on the table and whispered, 'Sorry about me friend, like . . .'

'Is that what you think she is, darlink?' she smiled, and tucked the sixpence away into a hidden pocket in her gown, a purple night studded with a million twinkling stars.

I followed Anita around like a shadow for the rest of the afternoon, keeping a respectful distance behind her, letting her know I was there without going too close to the dark mood that hung around her like a forcefield. By now I was used to Anita's tempers and knew how to ride them as skilfully as Uncle Hugo rode the unbroken ponies in my favourite Saturday morning programme, *White Horses*. I knew if I got too close to her during one of her wordless seething tempers, I would be sucked into it like a speck into a cyclone. Her fury was so powerful it was almost tangible, drew the energy and will from me until the world reversed like a negative and I found myself inside her head, looking out of her eyes and feeling an awful murderous hatred. But if I retreated too far she would sense my fear and detachment and turn on me, accusing me of betrayal.

Now I understood what had made Sherrie and Fat Sally do their merry dance of repulsion and attraction around Anita, for like the girl with the curl in the middle of her forehead, the good and the horrid in her were equally irresistible. I used her thin rigid back as a compass, pursuing her through the crowd as she passed from stall to stall, watching her finger the knitted baby bootees, tinker with vases and dried flower arrangements, rifle through stacks of old magazines until she finally nicked a couple of lemon curd tarts off a cake stall which we ate in quick hurried gulps. There was no need to discuss what had happened; I knew that the fortune teller would never be mentioned again.

We came across Sherrie sitting under a tree smoking a cigarette. She looked so much older than when I had seen her at the funfair; her hair had been cut in 'feather' style, layered completely from crown to ends so that from the back, she could have passed for a blonde version of David Cassidy. She wore faded jeans which ended in huge panelled flares and a tight cheesecloth top which revealed two small, but perfectly formed, buds of breasts. Sherrie nodded to us and flicked open her fag packet expertly. I was seized with panic; if papa saw me hanging around juvenile smokers, I knew he would have a fit. Luckily, Anita refused Sherrie's offer, 'I've given up,' she explained airily. 'Me too,' I said, to save her the trouble of offering one to me. Sherrie shrugged and leaned back, deliberately pushing her chest forward, screwing up her eyes against the thin blue line of smoke rising from the cigarette dangling from her lips. I thought she looked beautiful.

'Am yow wearing a bra?' enquired Anita, who then poked a forefinger into the centre of one of Sherrie's bumps.

'Gerrof yow daft cow! Course I am!' Sherrie cried, pushing her away. 'I got to, specially when I'm riding Trixie, or they wobble about like buggery.'

We all giggled, I did not know why I was feeling embarrassed all of a sudden.

'Yeah, it's dead painful, innit?' Anita continued. 'I ain't wearing mine today. Wanted to get some air on them, like. So they grow bigger.'

I had never seen Anita wearing a bra, the only straps I had seen falling out of her sleeves definitely belonged to a vest, but I held my tongue and nodded wisely, resolving to have a good look at my chest as soon as I got home to check if I needed one too.

'So yow got a horse then?' Anita said. I could hear the envy icing the comment.

Sherrie nodded. 'Trixie's so gorgeous, I kiss her all the time. Dad says he's gonna enter me for the showjumping next year. I'll have to get a hard hat though first. And a sports bra probably.'

Anita kicked at a clump of grass, I could feel some sort of heat rising from her. It was spooky, I knew what she was going to make Sherrie say and she did, faltering over her words like they were being pulled from her mouth. 'You er . . . why don't you come down to the farm and have a ride, like? It's dead good.'

Anita did not even look up, making Sherrie feel like she was doing her a favour by even considering her offer. 'Meena's got to come too,' Anita said finally, making my chest swell with gratitude. Bet I need a bra right now, I thought.

Sherrie threw her cigarette onto the grass and left it smouldering there whilst she got up and picked leaves off her bum. 'Tomorrow then, yeah? In the morning. Trix is dead frisky in the morning.' And she sauntered off, her clogs making wet slaps on the grass.

It was only when I saw that the ends of her hair were turning flaming red that I realised it was late afternoon and the Fete was drawing to a close. People were gradually gathering around the Tombola stall where every year, Mr Pembridge would tell us the exciting news of which village had managed to raise the most money. I glimpsed Sandy and Hairy Neddy clearing away the few remaining toys from her

188

stall and whispering to each other, occasionally looking up to receive someone's congratulations or to shake an outstretched hand. I saw papa chatting to a woman who I presumed was Fat Sally's mother, as Fat Sally herself hovered nearby finishing off the crust of a large bakewell slice. She was squeezed into a denim waistcoat and skirt and had the obligatory shimmery scarf fastened around her waist. She ate like she wanted to choke herself, without pleasure or pride, not even seeming to taste the food but cramming it into her mouth, willing it to disappear. And when I looked at her mother, I understood why; she was a petite, coiffured brunette in a tight-fitting trouser suit who waved her skinny arms around as she laughed and talked with my father, rather too cosily I thought. She only glanced at Fat Sally once, and then returned to her conversation whilst bringing a tissue from inside her sleeve and pushing it at Fat Sally who cleaned round her mouth with furtive swipes. I had not liked Fat Sally up until this point, but I knew what it was like to live inside a body you did not feel was yours. I wondered if we should invite her to come with us to Sherrie's farm and resolved to ask Anita's permission later on.

Papa glanced up and caught my eye, and held up a whisky bottle with a ticket stuck to its side which he waved about like a trophy. I waved back and was about to move towards him when a high-pitched whistling emanated from the direction of the Tombola Stall. Mr Pembridge was speaking into a rusty looking megaphone but none of the growing crowd could hear anything but feedback, and many cupped their hands to their ears, waving madly at him to stop. Reverend Ince was immediately at his side, fiddling ineffectually with the control knobs whilst Uncle Alan stood behind them, looking on with weary amusement. Finally the odd word began filtering through the crackles and squeals until we all paused as one to listen to Mr Pembridge's speech.

'. . . three hundred and seven pounds and eight shillings which is once again a marvellous effort, and I think we should all give ourselves a big round of applause!' Everyone complied heartily to this request and we were momentarily united in an orgy of clapping, basking in the glow of our charitable efforts. I glimpsed Mrs Pembridge swaying in the cavernous front porch of her mansion; she was cradling a wine bottle to her cheek like a child and was staring at Mr Pembridge with an expression that somehow contained both utter contempt and profound pity.

Her son Graham was standing next to her. He had obviously had something better to do this afternoon and looked as if he had just returned from safari somewhere, dressed in a mud-splattered tweed jacket and corduroys. By the way he looked at his watch I could tell he was counting the seconds until he could claim his house back as his own. He did not seem bothered by his mother's obvious emotional state. I checked Mr Pembridge's grinning red face, wondering why he couldn't feel those eyes burning into the back of his head, and when I looked back, both his wife and son had gone.

Mr Pembridge raised his pudgy hands for silence and continued, 'We have just done our totting up of all the village stalls and I am especially, um, proud to announce that this year, the largest amount raised was a wopping ninety-three pounds, three shillings and eight pennies by my home village of Tollington!' A huge screaming cheer erupted from a far corner of the grounds where the Ballbearings women were whooping and clapping their hands above their heads. In the midst of them were Sandy and Hairy Neddy and by his face, you could tell he attributed every penny of our success to his brilliant future wife and her unique needlework skills.

Reverend Ince was shaking Mr Pembridge's hand, whilst Uncle Alan stood silently at his shoulder, his face slowly turning a deep, warning crimson. Reverend Ince took the megaphone off Mr Pembridge and cleared his throat noisily before speaking in his familiar, resonant boom: 'Well done everyone, we certainly had the Lord on our side today!'

'Amen to that!' shouted Mr Ormerod, who I had not recognised out of his usual brown overall. He was leaning against the now empty trestle table where Sandy had set up stall and held a rapidly melting ice cream cornet in his hand.

Reverend Ince had a moment of panic when he thought Mr Ormerod might launch into a chorus of hallelujahs so he quickly continued, 'And now we come to how this money should be spent. You remember last year we sent most of it to our Missionary Project in Africa, a lot of paper work involved I can tell you, that kept me busy for months . . .' Everybody knew the African appeal had been pulled together by Uncle Alan, and I watched him, waiting for some kind of protest or self deprecating laugh, one of those moments he often shared with us in which he acknowledged our pity and shrugged it off with his usual modest optimism. But Uncle Alan did not even look up, his gaze was fixed on something in the far distance, his lips drawn shut.

'But,' Reverend Ince continued, 'this year we felt that maybe charity should indeed begin at home, especially considering what is happening to our village. We thought, what can we do to bring a little blessing and light into our beloved, besieged Tollington?' And here he paused for dramatic effect, the space filled by urgent whispering as people speculated on what particular form this blessing should take. 'The school appeal, of course . . . A shelter for the bus stop, it's frigging freezing there of a morning . . . A gate round the mine shaft, I dread the littl'uns falling in one day . . . Nah, a bloody big party, free booze, we deserve it . . .'

'I'd buy a pony,' Anita whispered to me, gripping my arm tightly in anticipation.

The Reverend Ince ploughed on over the hubbub. 'So we have decided that this year, the proceeds of our Spring Fete will be put towards a brand new roof for our chapel!'

Mr Ormerod burst into wild applause which was quickly taken up by other members of the church choir standing around him, and gave a huge thumbs up to Reverend Ince who acknowledged his supporter with a proud nod.

All around me mutters of discontent and resignation hung in the air like whispering fog; Uncle Alan had turned on his heel and was about to walk away when a loud barking voice cut through the air, jerking him back like he was on a leash. 'Bloody rubbish, the lot of you! Bloody crap, you lot!' We turned as one to see Sam Lowbridge standing at the gates, a smouldering cigarette dangling from his lips. The rest of his gang lounged around their mopeds smirking self-consciously, a pile of empty lager cans at their feet. 'Bloody church roof? What's that gonna do for us, eh? Wharra about us?'

Reverend Ince stroked his nose, feigning amusement, but I could tell he was seething at this public humiliation. Mr Pembridge was looking round, ineffectually, for help, as if he expected two burly minders to appear and drag this heckler off for a good pasting. I tried to spot Mrs Lowbridge in the crowd, I knew if I had made such a spectacle of myself, mama would have dragged me off by the hair by now to a quiet corner for some moral rehabilitation. But strangely, there was little reaction from the crowd; I expected the Ballbearings women to be up in arms, defending the honour of their village, but instead they all stood with crossed arms, looking from Sam Lowbridge to the Reverend, expectant, and I thought, somewhat pleased with themselves.

Sam sensed this unspoken support, he wiped his mouth with the back of his hand and moved closer, confident now, high on the sound of his own unchallenged voice. I did not care for his new haircut; it made him look like a blonde bullet, and I wondered where all the soft shadows I had so admired in his face had gone. 'Yow don't know what we want! None of yow lot! Kowtowing to the big lord and bloody master here like he's doing us a favour! Yow want to stop the motorway, ask him! He's a bloody builder and all, in't he?'

The crowd erupted now, some people shouting at Sam to 'shuttit!', others calling to each other excitedly, 'He's got a point! He could stop the diggers! Maybe they're his diggers, eh? Ask him!'

Only Uncle Alan's voice cut through the babble, 'Sam! Listen! We do understand! You're right! Maybe this isn't the best way to use the money!'

Reverend Ince grabbed hold of Uncle Alan, who threw him off with such violence that the crowd gasped and instinctively moved back, clearing a pathway between Alan and Sam. The grounds had become some great leafy arena, the air fell quiet, punctuated only by distant birdsong and a collective intake of anticipatory breath; we all knew something important was happening, epic even, and our job was to witness and listen. Uncle Alan took a step forward, ignoring the fierce exchange starting behind him between Mr Pembridge and Reverend Ince. 'Sam, a lot of people feel the same as you. This is our money. We could have a vote, yeah? A meeting, let's talk about . . .'

Sam interrupted, a sly grin curling the corners of his mouth: 'Yow don't do nothing but talk, "Uncle". And give everything away to some darkies we've never met. We don't give a toss for anybody else. This is our patch. Not some wogs' handout.'

I felt as if I had been punched in the stomach. My legs felt watery and a hot panic softened my insides to mush. It was as if the whole crowd had turned into one huge eyeball which swivelled slowly between me and papa. I wished I had stood next to papa; I could feel Anita shifting beside me, I knew she would not hold me or take my hand. Papa was staring into the distance, seemingly unconcerned, gripping his bottle of whisky like a weapon. Uncle Alan's mouth was opening and closing like a goldfish, Reverend Ince whispered to him, 'Good work, Alan. One of your supporters, is he?'

And then a rasping voice came from somewhere in the throng, 'You tell him, son.'

I jerked my head towards the sound. Who was that? Who said that? Who had thought that all this time and why had I never known about it? And then another voice, a woman's, 'Go on, lad! Tell him some more!' The sound had come from somewhere around Mr Ormerod, I stared at him, straight into his eyes. He shifted from foot to foot and glanced away.

My mind was turning cartwheels; I wanted to find these people, tell them Sam Lowbridge was my mate, the boy who had taught me how to shoot a fairground rifle, who terrorised everyone else except me. I was his favourite. There must have been some mistake. When my ears had stopped ringing and I gradually returned to my body, I could hear catcalls coming from all over the grounds; 'Yow shuttit, yow bloody skinhead idiot! Bloody disgrace, Sam Lowbridge! Yow wanna good birching, yow do! Yow don't talk for me, son! I'd be on my deathbed before that'd happen!'

Uncle Alan was half-running towards the gate, towards Sam who was strolling back to his moped to the cheers and claps of his gang. 'Wait! Sam!' Uncle Alan puffed. 'Listen! Don't do this! Don't turn all this energy the wrong way!' Sam was not listening. He was already revving up, clouds of bluey-grey smoke wheezing from his exhaust. 'Anger is good! But not used this way! Please! You're going the wrong way!'

Sam aimed his moped straight at Uncle Alan who was now outside the gates, making him jump back and stumble, and then he sped off up the hill followed by the rest of his three-wheeler lackeys, who manoeuvred in and out of each other like a bunch of May-mad midges until they were nothing but annoying buzzy specks in the distance. Uncle Alan sat heavily down on the grass and rested his head on his arms. People were now crowding round papa, offering condolences and back pats like he'd just come last in the annual church egg and spoon race. 'Yow don't mind him, Mr Ku-mar, he's always been a bad-un . . .' Papa smiled graciously at them, shrugging his shoulders, not wanting to draw any more attention to himself or what had just happened. I knew he was trying to get to me and I began pushing forward, encountering a wall of solid backs and legs.

Anita was tugging my sleeve as she held onto me. I turned round to face her, my cheeks still felt warm and taut. 'Wharrabout that then!' she grinned, 'In't he bosting!'

'What?' I croaked.

'Sam Lowbridge. He's dead bloody hard, in't he?'

'Anita Rutter, yow am a bloody stupid cow sometimes,' I said, and did not look back until I had reached the haven of papa's arms.

Papa and I walked in silence back home, ignoring the other villagers around us who were still loudly dissecting the dramatic events of the day. It was only when we approached the crossroads near our front gate that papa turned to me and said, 'If anyone ever says anything rude to you, first you say something back, and then you come and tell me. Is that clear?' I nodded my head reassuringly. After what I had just said to Anita, I knew that I would need papa on my side for the foreseeable future.

As soon as we entered the house, I sensed that something was wrong. None of the lights were on; the back door to the yard was open, even though it was dusk and the night air had begun to bare its tiny sharp teeth. The spice jars and sheets of newspaper were still on the kitchen floor where mama had left them and the pantry door was swinging slowly on its hinges. 'Daljit!' papa called, motioning me to sit on the farty settee and stay there. I ignored him; the last time he had done that to me was the night of Sunil's birth when I had been locked in the kitchen and left with my imagination.

So I followed him into our lounge at the end of the house where he snapped on the light. Mama was sitting on the sofa staring out of the window where the first few pinpricks of stars had begun to appear. Sunil was fast asleep on her lap, the material of her sleeve imprisoned in his tightly-clenched fist.

She looked up at us listlessly and then turned back to the window. 'It's the same sky,' she said finally. 'The same sky in India. It's hard to believe, isn't it?'

Papa sat down gently next to her, he seemed afraid of what she was going to say next. He tried to take Sunil from her lap, but even in his sleep he cried out furiously, holding onto mama, his eyes still shut until papa admitted defeat and let him go. 'Daljit, what is wrong? Tell me please,' papa said gently.

Mama could not tear her eyes away from the window, as if she was counting the stars in her head. 'I can't cope any more, Shyam. Back home I would have sisters, mothers, servants . . .' The stars were her family, his family, she was crossing them off one by one, naming them to keep them alive. 'I can't do this any more. I can't.' She blinked back tears as papa put his arm round her and motioned me away. This time I went willingly.

I sat in my darkened bedroom and from the window watched Mr Ormerod and various helpers carrying the last of the stalls and awnings from the Big House's grounds and onto a waiting truck. I thought about the fortune teller, and wondered what else would be coming true, and if everything that was going to happen to me had already been decided, what was the point of ever dreaming and hoping for change, for something better? It was a clear night; the few stars I had glimpsed before had turned into thousands, millions, brighter and thicker than the stars on the Mysterious Stranger's purple cloak. They vied with the illuminated front rooms and kitchens all over the village where my neighbours, even now, would be sitting over mugs of steaming tea, retelling the story which had made strangers out of friends, labelled friendly passers-by as possible enemies, at least in my eyes. Nothing was safe any more; even my own mama had talked in an unknown poet's voice which made me think that at any moment, the walls of my home could buckle and shake, and crumble slowly downwards into the earth.

When I had whispered up all those silent prayers for drama and excitement, I had not imagined this, this feeling of fear and loneliness. But tonight I finally made the connection that change always strolled hand in hand with loss, with upheaval, and that I would always feel it keenly because in the end, I did not live under the same sky as most other people. I did not need a bra or some blue eyeshadow to appear older, not tonight.

I woke up to a very weird morning; the weather was exactly like the weather in all my dreams, a cobalt blue sky with small high clouds blown furiously about by an impatient wind. I stayed in bed for hours it seemed, hearing Sunil's cries and nonsense baby talk filtering upstairs, along with dozens of loud telephone calls, hurried activity with doors slamming and cars arriving and departing. I recognised Auntie Shaila's booming tones, I knew that papa had gone out in the car for at least an hour and returned busy and full of news. I was not bothered that they seemed to have forgotten me.

I also saw Anita and Fat Sally strolling arm in arm past my house, I knew that they were going up to Sherrie's farm to ride Trixie and I also knew that they did not have to walk this route to get there. Anita affected her usual manic high-pitched tone when she was talking *through* someone and not *to* them. 'Sherrie said I could tek me best mate with me – Sally. We'm gonna have a bosting time, in't we?'

To my surprise, I did not care much. I felt leaden and sleepy today, in spite of the fact that last night I had fallen into unconsciousness the minute my head hit the pillow, and was still in my pyjamas, even though I guessed it must be at least midday. Finally, papa came into the room, all rosy and windswept from his wanderings. He sat down on the bed next to me and slapped me playfully on the back. 'Guess who's coming to stay with us next week?' I shook my head and then a phrase entered my head like a jolt as he finished his sentence. 'Your Nanima! Your mama's mama! Isn't that great news?'

Help from Overseas, my mind sang. Help, I need Somebody, Help, Not Just Anybody . . .'

'Great news,' I replied, and fumbled under the quilt for my bedsocks as my feet had suddenly gone icy cold.

8

My Nanima's arrival did not go unnoticed in the village, probably because when papa finally returned with his precious cargo from the airport, he drove up to the house tooting his horn furiously, whereupon a noisy welcoming committee made up of mama, Auntie Shaila and Uncle Amman, Pinky and Baby, myself and Sunil, all rushed into the garden shouting and waving, causing traffic to slow down and passing women to stop and squint curiously, patting their hair into place in case there were hidden television cameras in the privet hedges.

Papa flung open the Mini door ceremoniously, and Nanima levered herself out, brushing out the creases in her beige *salwar kameez* suit with gnarled brown fingers and pulling her woollen shawl around her to ward off an imagined breeze. She had barely taken a step before mama had thrown herself into her massive bosom, laughing and crying all at once, whilst Auntie Shaila sniffled to herself as she anointed our front step with oil as a traditional gesture of welcome. (It was supposed to be coconut oil but a bottle of Mazola Deep 'N' Crispy still did the trick.)

It took at least ten minutes for Nanima to reach the front door as each of us were shoved into her path to receive a blessing from her upraised hands. I was furious that Pinky and Baby got there before me, she was not even their sodding granny and there they were in the front of the queue, collecting a few more brownie points for their next life. But I reckoned since the Collection Tin incident, I could afford to be a little generous; after all, they had not mentioned it since.

Neither had they ever allowed their mother to leave them alone with me, for which I was relieved. However, I smirked to see Nanima's confusion as she patted them on the head, and felt vindicated when I saw mama whispering their names to her, explaining, I was certain, that they were hangers-on as opposed to blood relatives.

Papa held Sunil out for inspection; his bottom lip began quivering as soon as Nanima tried to cuddle him, so she laughed instead and pinched his cheek, handing him back to mama who kept up an excited monologue, 'See beti? That's your Nanima! Your Nanima has come to see you! Say Nanima! Say it!' Then I found myself looking up into my mama's face, except it was darker and more wrinkled and the eyes were rheumy and mischievous, but it was mama's face alright, and suddenly I was in the middle of a soft warm pillow which smelt of cardamom and sweet sharp sweat, and there was hot breath whispering in my ear, endearments in Punjabi which needed no translation, and the tears I was praying would come to prove I was a dutiful granddaughter, came spilling out with no effort at all.

I knew Nanima was going to be fun when she rolled backwards into the farty settee and let out a howl of laughter. As Auntie Shaila tried to haul her out, she continued laughing, shouting something to mama which turned into a loud chesty cough as she finally regained her balance. 'Meena, don't titter like that, have some respect,' papa admonished me gently. But as I handed Nanima a glass of water, one of our best glasses with the yellow and red roses around the rim, she chucked me under the chin conspiratorially and said something to papa who shook his head resignedly.

'What?' I badgered him. 'What did she say?'

'Nanima said you are a "junglee", a wild girl, uncivilised . . .' papa said. I ran around the front room whooping 'Junglee! Junglee!' and doing mock kung fu kicks at my shadow on the wall to make Nanima laugh even harder.

'Oy!' papa shouted over the din. 'It is not a compliment,

you know!' But Nanima's expression told me it was exactly that.

The rest of the evening passed in a stream of constant visitors bearing gifts of sweetmeats and homemade *sabzis*, anxious to meet one of the generation they had left behind and to catch up on the latest news from the Motherland. However, those of my Uncles and Aunties seeking the latest political intrigue in Delhi or the hot filmi gossip from Bombay ended up sorely disappointed as Nanima now resided in a tiny village in the Punjab and was not exactly equipped to be India's latest Reuter's correspondent. Most of the conversations began with someone asking, 'So! Tell us the latest, Mataji . . .' Nanima then launched into a jaunty monologue, punctuated by loud slurpings of tea and surreptitious massaging of her feet which silenced the questioner into a series of polite smiling nods.

'What did she say?' I tugged on papa's sleeve.

'She said that they are building a new road into Bessian town centre and that Mrs Lal's daughter is finally getting married to a divorced army officer . . .'

'Who is Mrs Lal?' I continued.

Papa shrugged his shoulders. 'Who knows?' he whispered back, stifling a grin.

But frankly, Nanima could have answered their continuous questions with a series of burps or simply fallen asleep mid-sentence, and every gesture would have still been received with the same reverence and adoration. For her audience was there not because of what she said but because of who she was, a beloved parent, a familiar symbol in her billowing *salwar kameez* suit whose slow deliberate gestures and modest dignity reminded them of their own mothers. Of course they would deify her, their own guilt and homesickness would see to that, but how could this small vessel possibly contain the ocean of longing each of them stored in their bellies? It was only when papa lined the three of us up for a photograph, daughter, mother and grandmother, all of us the product of each other, linked like Russian dolls, that it struck me how difficult it must have been for mama to leave Nanima and how lonely she must have been. Indeed, I had never seen mama so fresh and girlish, as if some invisible yoke had been lifted from her shoulders and she regained the lithe legs and strong back she must have had when she cycled to and from college, humming the tunes my father sang to her through her shuttered bedroom window. I vowed then that I would never leave her, this wrenching of daughter from mother would never happen again.

Of course, this would not stop me having all the adult adventures I had been planning for myself; I would still travel and cure sickness and rescue orphans and star in my own television series, I would just have to make sure mama came with me, that was all. My mind drifted into practical overdrive, as it did with all my daydreams. It was never enough to have a vague picture, such as 'I save Donny Osmond from near death and win a medal'. I had to know what I was wearing, whether it was a fire in a top London hotel or a runaway horse in a summer meadow, what the weather was like, who was watching and how my hair looked at the moment of rescue.

It was an annoying trait, I admit, and often I got bored with the fantasy halfway through, bogged down by stylistic detail when I should really have been concentrating on the emotion and wish-fulfilment side of things. But I needed to calculate how feasible it might be for mama to leave her teaching job and what make of car would be large enough to contain my vast wardrobe and yet be safe enough for mama to manoeuvre in a three-point turn. So I barely registered the click of papa's camera and in the photograph, which I still have, mama and Nanima are beaming full into the lens like similar yet not matching bookends, and I am gazing dreamily into the middle distance, as if I am merely lending my body for the pose. 'Va Meena!' papa had said when the photograph came back from the chemist's. 'You have the soulful look of a movie star!' I had not the heart to tell him I was mentally choosing my car upholstery.

Still, that evening our house seemed to vibrate with goodwill and hope, the air felt heady and rare, the food seemed mountainous and never ending, even Sunil giggled and chirruped his way through dinner from his usual position on mama's hip, trying to form passing adult words like some drunk parrot. It was such an unseasonably warm evening that every possible window was flung open as the house became more crowded and noisy, until suddenly, the front door was ajar and our guests began spilling out into the garden, still clutching their drinks and balancing plates of food. This threw me into a minor panic; Tollington front gardens were purely for display purposes, everyone knew that. And here were all my relatives using our scrubby patch of lawn like a marquee, laughing and joking and generally behaving as if they were still within the security of four soundproofed walls.

It felt so strange to hear Punjabi under the stars. It was an indoor language to me, an almost guilty secret which the Elders would only share away from prying English eyes and ears. On the street, in shops, on buses, in parks, I noticed how the volume would go up when they spoke English, telling us kids to not wander off, asking the price of something; and yet when they wanted to say something intimate, personal, about feelings as opposed to acquisitions, they switched to Punjabi and the volume became a conspiratorial whisper. 'That woman over there, her hat looks like a dead dog . . . The bastard is asking too much, let's go . . . Do you think if I burped here, anyone would hear it?'

I stood uncertainly on the front porch and watched helplessly as the Aunties and Uncles began reclaiming the Tollington night in big Indian portions, guffawing Punjabi over fences and hedges, wafting curried vegetable smells through tight-mouthed letterboxes, sprinkling notes from old Hindi movie songs over jagged rooftops, challenging the single street light on the crossroads with their twinkling jewels and brazen silks. Usually, mama and papa were the most polite and careful neighbours, always shushing me if I made too much noise down the entries, always careful to keep all windows closed during papa's musical evenings. But tonight, I noted disapprovingly, they were as noisy and hysterical as everyone else. I had never seen the Elders so expansive and unconcerned, and knew that this somehow had something to do with Nanima.

I hesitated on the porch step, unsure whether to flee indoors, dreading what the reaction of any passers-by might be, but also strangely drawn to this unfamiliar scene where my two worlds had collided and mingled so easily. There was a whiff of defiance in the air and it smelled as sweet and as hopeful as freshly-mown grass. Nevertheless, I froze when I heard the footsteps approaching the crossroads. It was two of the Ballbearings Committee, I was not sure which ones as in their Gooin' Out Outfits of tight shiny tops and optimistically short skirts, they all looked like sisters. By the way they were holding onto each other, I could tell they were on their way home from the Mingo disco, although they seemed to sober up immediately as they caught sight of our crowded front garden. Two pairs of red eyes ringed in creased blue powder took in the teeming, laughing masses and two lipstick smudged mouths broke into wide wicked grins.

'Ay up, Mr K! Havin a bit of a do then?' one of them shouted, every word sliding into each other so it sounded like a strangely musical babble.

'Oh yes ladies!' papa called from somewhere near the hedge. 'Come and join us! Whisky, yes?'

Even in this light I could tell papa's face was flushed; he was wearing that lazy benevolent expression that always settled on his face after a good session with the Uncles, who were now gathering around him, seemingly impressed that papa was acquainted with some of the local talent.

'Whisky!' the other Ballbearings Committee member shrieked. 'Hark at him! Posh or what. Not on top of Malibu, thanks Mr K. Don't wanna be picking sick out of me birdbath again tomorrer!' The women's swooping laughter met the men's bass chuckles and it really did sound like a beautiful, improvised song, as beautiful as any of papa's free-fall scales he would perform at the harmonium. 'Yow have a good time, Mr K!' the women called to papa as they staggered off. 'The world looks better when yow'm pissed, don't it?'

We got off fairly lightly after that; if any of our neighbours did object to the din, they did not tell us. A couple of passing cars slowed down to have a good look at us, and somewhere around eleven o'clock, an old man passing on his bicycle narrowly missed clipping the public telephone booth as he caught sight of our party. But by then I had got used to it, this world within a garden, and by the time papa sidled up to me and gave me a bristly kiss laced with fumes and tobacco, I felt as if some heavy invisible cloak had fallen off my shoulders and I had grown a few feet taller. Out of nowhere, papa said, 'You really must learn Punjabi, Meena. Look how left out you feel. How will you ever understand your Nanima, huh?'

I felt wrong-footed, vulnerable. It had been such a good evening and now papa was asking me questions for which I had no instant replies.

'Leave the girl alone!' Uncle Amman called out from a dark leafy corner, his cigarette end glowing and fading like a wheezy firefly. 'Now her Nanima is here, she will learn soon enough!'

Papa patted my cheek and squeezed me tightly. 'She is my jaan, my life,' he said brokenly, and went inside for a refill.

And then two very strange things happened, almost simultaneously. First of all, an unfamiliar car drove slowly past our house and parked deliberately near the entrance of the Big House, which as usual, was unlit and impenetrable. As the car door opened, the interior light came on and I saw a hennaed beehive briefly collide with a blonde male head. Deirdre Rutter climbed carefully out of the car and tapped confidently towards the crossroads as the car screeched away into the night. She broke her jaunty walk only to fiddle with a strap somewhere beneath her perpetually moving jumper. And then suddenly, Anita was on the corner, right outside our house! That head cocked to one side, that I Dare You stance of hers, one hip out, one hand on the hip, was as familiar to me as my own palmprint and only then, as I studied the back of her head, did I realise how long it had been since I had talked to her. I silently willed her to look round, I would smile at her I thought, she must have been aware of the commotion going on just a few feet behind her. But I knew the set of that back; I knew she had not forgiven me for what I had said to her at the Spring Fete. I knew she would not turn round.

Deirdre's face sagged as she saw her daughter waiting for her on the corner. I could not make out what she said, Auntie Shaila chose that moment to break into a raucous folk song which Deirdre momentarily acknowledged with an amused sneer. But whatever she said to my friend, her daughter, a few short barking phrases, they had the desired effect. For the first time ever, I saw Anita Rutter burst into tears before fleeing down the nearest entry. I barely had time to absorb this, to reconcile the anger and pity washing over me before I noticed something else that made my heart flip like a fish. There was someone in the grounds of the Big House and they were watching us. I rubbed my eyes with a fist and looked again, straining my eyeballs until they watered. A figure, huge and shaggy as a bear, was standing just beyond the fence near the crossroads. I thought I saw the wink of a torch, occasionally visible behind a veil of waving bushes, and the flash of its light seemed to throb in time to the beat of Auntie Shaila's song. '*Chal Koi Na, Pher Koi Na, Hai Koi Na,*' she sang, It Doesn't Matter, Nothing Matters, she told the watching bear. My lips felt parched. I croaked 'Papa?' I looked round wildly for him, and when I turned back, the bear had gone.

When I finally dragged myself up the stairs after the last visitor had gone, I found Nanima sleeping in my double bed, curled up in my quilt like a cocoon. As I stood there, shivering in my nightie, mama entered quietly with Sunil sleeping in her arms. She carefully placed him in his cot at the foot of the bed, a mere gesture as he would be up in a few hours time, ready for the transfer to her bosom, and led me to the far side of my bed, motioning me to climb in. Sensing my resistence, she whispered, 'There is nowhere else for Nanima to sleep. And anyway, you are so lucky. She has the warmest tummy in the world. Get in. And don't fidget or you will wake her.'

I sidled in beside Nanima, pulling in as much quilt as I dared which barely covered my ankles and knees. She was snoring gently and breathed in huge deep sighs which seemed to swell her body to twice its size, her large stomach looked like a slowly rising loaf of bread which quickly deflated with every exhalation. Then quite suddenly she let out an enormous rasping fart which seemed to go on forever and shook the quilt around her, making me collapse into a fit of giggles which I had to stifle into my pillow. Then she heaved herself fully around so that she was facing me and dragged me under her arm where it smelt yeasty and safe, tucking the quilt around me expertly, imprisoning my freezing feet in between her soft fleshy knees. Then she opened one eye briefly and said, 'Junglee!' before dropping off to sleep.

At some point in the night I had a strange dream; Sunil was crying, nothing new in that, and I heard mama's footsteps pad into the room. Then there were two voices, mama's and Nanima's which reminded me of the wood pigeons who would coo to each other under the eaves each morning. Then Sunil began crying again, for some reason he was still in the room; and then I heard a song, or rather I felt it, a lilting lullaby in a minor key which made me think of splashing stone fountains in shadowed courtyards and peacocks ululating on tiled flat rooftops, sunlight glinting off the deep blue feathers encircling their necks. And then I saw, although my eyes were closed, I saw Nanima rocking Sunil in her arms, quite violently I thought, and rise slowly into the air and circle the room, her pyjama bottoms flapping like Hermes' wings at her ankles, whilst he laughed with delight and tried to catch the sparks fizzing from her fingertips. When I woke up the next morning, I found myself looking into a pair of muddy doggy eyes. Sunil was lying across Nanima's breast, sucking his thumb contentedly whilst she snored on, oblivious. From that day on, Sunil slept in his own cot, sometimes for eight hours at a stretch, and only a few days later, sat on papa's lap for the first time ever to eat his breakfast.

Since Nanima's arrival, we had fallen into a comfortable routine. The house would be warm and delicious smelling when we opened the front door and nothing would be where we left it the previous morning. Pots and pans would be stacked neatly in the larder, cushions from the settee would be arranged in symmetrical piles at the foot of the stairs, my magazines would be behind the television and papa's shaving things would have somehow found their way into the bicycle shed. Although Nanima wanted to be useful, she had no idea where to put things once she had used them or picked them up to clean round, so she figured as long as they were in a tidy pile, she had done her bit. Mama had explained apologetically, 'She's always busy back home you see, there she has a place, a role. Don't ever make her feel she has done anything wrong.' But I admired this mad logic, and actually looked forward to the chaotic treasure hunt for our possessions on our return.

The rest of the evening would be devoted to a new activity called Entertaining Sunil. Since that first night when Nanima had applied some ancient witchery to finally cut the umbilical cord that was slowly strangling both him and us, Sunil was now anybody's, especially mine. Although he was not yet crawling, every time I entered the room he would hold out his chubby hands towards me, demanding to be picked up and played with. His eyes followed me upstairs, outside, I would even occasionally glance up from the TV screen to find him sitting next to my head as if on guard, waiting for my next command. I was not used to this, these demands on my time which I would rather have spent daydreaming on my bed or doing yet another *Jackie* quiz on How To Make Him Notice You Without Even Trying! It was a good job I was a social reject and did not have a boyfriend to whisk me off Down The Mingo, because every waking moment it seemed was taken up with my baby brother.

I found myself doing jobs I had run away from just a few weeks earlier, mashing up boiled vegetables into a runny goo for Sunil's meals, boiling water for his bottles and nappies, even carrying his incredibly stinky nappies out to the bicycle shed, albeit at arm's length, where they would solidify in a plastic bucket until mama spent a day boiling them clean, filling the whole house with clouds of citrusy steam. When I sat him on my lap after Nanima had given him a massage in warm olive oil, naked and slippery as a fish, feeling his legs bump against my knees and his tin pot dictator belly taut against my hands, I could not imagine how I ever resented him, could not even remember why. I decided that either I must be getting soft in my old age, or that Nanima was indeed some kind of sorcerer.

Most of all I enjoyed her stories, usually told by the light of the flickering TV screen when the last plate had been wiped and put away and papa was absorbed in one of his favourite programmes, *The Prisoner* or *Rowan and Martin's Laugh-In*. By now he had become an expert in stereo-speak, translating Nanima's words before they had barely left her mouth without even having to turn round. Nanima's stories never followed any pattern, and mostly she would come out with anecdotes sparked off by something on the television, to which she was heavily addicted. 'Go To Work On An Egg!' sang the advert, and Nanima would tell us of how some passing British soldiers once took away all the family's chickens claiming they needed the eggs to sustain them during a long march to visit the Rajah of Patiala. 'But the way those chickens fought and shat, they knew they were going to be eaten . . .'

Once, during an episode of *Randall and Hopkirk Deceased*, when Hopkirk, a friendly ghost, appeared at his living friend's side to offer him some tasty clues on an ongoing murder hunt, Nanima chipped in with 'My grandmother's ghost lives at the top of our house in the village. I've never seen her, I only hear her walking around, carrying the son I had who died at birth. Only one person has seen her, my sister's husband, and he has turned out to be a madman anyway . . .' She even claimed that Peter Wyngarde, the Mexican moustachioed TV detective with a natty line in flowered cravats, was the spitting image of my grandfather's brother, who tried to flee with the family assets whilst my nana (her husband), was lying supposedly on his death bed, following a terrible accident in one of his fleet of village trucks. 'No one thought your nana would survive, his leg was so badly crushed. But the doctor-saab replaced the bone with a goat's bone, cut him open after feeding your nanaji a whole bottle of whisky. You could hear his cries from the other side of the village. And just a few months later, the British came to put him in prison because he would not fight in their army. He was still limping when they took him away. I did not know he was alive for four years, until he limped back into our courtyard and I fell down in a faint.'

At first, these remembrances seemed so far fetched, so far removed from anything I recognised as reality, I wondered whether papa was having a joke at my expense and embroidering the translation when he got bored. This was compounded by my mother's reaction to some of Nanima's monologues, 'I never knew that, mama! . . . When did that happen? . . . Why didn't you tell me?' I was beginning to realise that everyone's mothers had secrets and kept them particularly from their daughters. I wondered if I would have to wait until I was a mother before mama would tell me some of hers. But gradually I got used to Nanima's world, a world made up of old and bitter family feuds in which the Land was revered and jealously guarded like a god, in which supernatural and epic events, murder, betrayal, disappearances and premonitions seemed commonplace, in which fabulous wealth and dramatic ritual was continually upstaged by marching armies and independence riots. They all put mama's rickshaw story and papa's unexploded bomb tale into some kind of context for me; my parents' near brushes with death were not one-off happenings, they were simply two more incidents in a country that seemed full to bursting with excitement, drama and passion, history in the making, and for the first time I desperately wanted to visit India and claim some of this magic as mine.

It was all falling into place now, why I felt this continual compulsion to fabricate, this ever-present desire to be someone else in some other place far from Tollington. Before Nanima arrived, this urge to reinvent myself, I could now see, was driven purely by shame, the shame I felt when we 'did' India at school, and would leaf through tatty textbooks where the map of the world was an expanse of pink, where erect Victorian soldiers posed in grainy photographs, their feet astride flattened tigers, whilst men who looked like any one of my uncles, remained in the background holding trays or bending under the weight of impossible bundles, their posture servile, their eyes glowing like coals. There would be more photographs of teeming unruly mobs, howling like animals for the blood of the brave besieged British, the Black Hole of Calcutta was a popular image, angelic women and children choking on their own fear whilst yet more of my uncles and aunties in period clothes danced an evil jig of victory outside.

Then there were the 'modern' images, culled from newspaper and television clips, where hollow-eyed skeletons, barely recognisable as human beings, squatted listlessly around dry river beds, and machete-wielding thugs tore into each other in messy city streets, under the benevolent gaze of a statue of Queen Victoria. I always came bottom in history; I did not want to be taught what a mess my relatives had made of India since the British had left them (their fault of course, nothing to do with me), and longed to ask them why, after so many years of hating the 'goras', had they packed up their cases and followed them back here.

That question was answered unexpectedly by mama one evening following an especially juicy Nanima anecdote involving two brothers, both the brightest in their district but poor with it. Their parents could raise only enough bribe money to secure a place at the district university for one of them. The successful brother went on to study law and became heavily involved in the Quit India Movement, the other brother disappeared without trace. Then one rainy monsoon night (these things always happened during the monsoon apparently), the lawyer, who was on his way to a meeting with Nehru-saab himself, was held up by a gang of *dacoits* and in the ensuing *tamasha* received a fatal *golee* to the heart. (My Punjabi vocabulary was expanding rapidly by now, *tamasha*, meaning 'fracas', made sense, the word sounded like a flurry of activity, but I still had not figured out why the word for 'tablet' and 'bullet' was the same.)

As the lawyer fell to the ground dying, there was a yelp of anguish from one of the masked bandits, who ran to the victim to cradle his head in his lap, crying and begging his brother for forgiveness. Shortly afterwards, the bad blood brother was found swinging from a neem tree, 'too full of shame and remorse to continue his life . . .' Nanima sat back with a satisfied grunt and helped herself to another doorstep slab of angel cake.

Mama shook her head sadly, 'You see Meena, what happens when someone is deprived of education? At least in this country, you can get to the top university without having to pay a thousand greedy officials to get there. That's why we had to leave, we were poor and clever, a bad combination in India.'

'But mama, you're too old to get to university now,' I said, unthinkingly, walking straight into it.

'Not for us, for you, silly! You and Sunil! Of course, if Britain had not left us in such a damn big mess, it would be a different story . . . but it's all kismet, hey mamaji?'

Nanima burped wisely, she really could do that, and I felt suddenly depressed. I knew exactly what mama was getting at; next year would be the dreaded eleven-plus, the national entrance exam which for us Tollington children, would decide whether we got to attend the posh girls' grammar school twenty miles away, or the spanking new comprehensive in the next town. Up until now, the eleven-plus had been a sort of swear word bandied about by various teachers when they were faced with yet another display of incompetence, like the time we were discussing *Othello* and Mr Williams had asked where the Moors came from, and I had put up my hand and answered confidently, 'Yorkshire, sir!'

'Woe betide you, girl, if you think this standard of rubbish is going to get you your eleven-plus!'

But now those two words took on an ominous significance; this was no longer a mere exam. If I failed, my parents' five thousand mile journey would have all been for nothing. It was not even summer, and I was already dreading next year. And then I thought about Anita; failure also meant that I would be going to the same school as her, every day for the next seven years. A few months ago, the thought of having her all to myself like this would have made me so happy. And now, it worried me and I could not work out why.

When mama, Sunil and I rushed into our front room having just completed our last schoolday before Easter, drunk with freedom as we now had three weeks of holidays stretching before us which we would share with Nanima, we did not expect to find the house empty. There were the tell-tale signs that Nanima had been there recently, a saucepan of shelled peas on top of the wooden cabinet holding our ancient record player, layers of neatly-folded clothes on the dining table, but the kitchen was bare and unloved, and the back door leading to our small cobbled yard was wide open. 'Mama! Mataji!'

mama called, dumping Sunil into my arms as she rushed outside, panic constricting her throat. She yanked open the back gate and shouted down the entry, her voice reverberating off the tall damp walls which, even in the spring afternoon haze, were gloomy and secretive. 'Mama! *Tusi Kithe ho?*' she called.

Mrs Mitchell popped her head out of her back window. She had crumbs round her mouth and no teeth in. 'What's that yow said, Mrs K?' she spluttered.

'My mother! Small woman, bit like me . . . Have you seen her?' mama shouted.

'Ooh I don't recall . . . Mr Mitchell? Yow seen anyone small like Mrs K?'

Mr Mitchell's voice came booming from the outside toilet built into the entry. Mama stepped back with alarm as the door swung open slightly and a cloud of blue cigarette smoke billowed out. 'Now! I ain't seen nobody, chick!' replied Mr Mitchell, who threw his smoking fag butt onto the floor before closing the door again.

I had followed mama out into the entry with Sunil struggling in my arms like an imprisoned rabbit, his legs and arms were surprisingly strong, and I could not prevent him dragging his hands along the entry walls until they were covered with mossy green slime. 'No! Naughty boy! *Nah ker!*' I said, hoping the Punjabi phrase would echo Nanima and shock him into good behaviour. I realised I was acting as if she had already left us, and I shivered involuntarily.

Mama looked up as footsteps tap-tapped into the entry and revealed Deirdre, who, for some reason, was wearing a headscarf and a pair of sunglasses, muffled up as if she was a terrorist off on a mission. She jumped slightly as she came face to face with mama, and the two women eyed each other up for a few seconds. Mama had not gone out of her way to be friendly with Anita's mother, since discovering how she had chosen to name their piddly poodle, but trapped in such a small space, it would have been tantamount to GBH not to at least greet each other. Deirdre nodded her head curtly, 'Alright?'

Mama smiled briefly, 'Hello Mrs Rutter. I wonder, you have not seen my mother wandering around anywhere?'

'Thought yowr mam was back in Pakistan,' she sniffed, glancing quickly behind her as if she expected someone.

'India,' mama said stiffly. 'We are from India.' The tone she used clearly said, not that you would know the difference you naughty tramp.

I gulped and shifted backwards into our yard, feeling I was somehow the cause of this icy exchange. Sunil whimpered in protest and wiped his filmy hands all down the front of my school blouse. I pinched his leg and he burst into tears. Mama shot me a hard look and continued over his wails, 'She's visiting us for a few weeks and . . .'

Before she could continue, Mrs Worrall's voice came booming from behind me, 'Ey! Am yow back, Daljeet? I've got yowr mom in here with me!'

Mama relaxed visibly and shouted back, 'Okay Mrs Worrall! Thank you so much!' and was already on her way back to the yard when Deirdre's sharp call stopped her in her tracks.

'Mrs K, have yow stopped yowr Meena seeing my Anita?'

Mama turned round slowly, wearing that dangerously patient expression that always made me want to slink into a corner wearing a conical hat with a D on it. 'Now why should I want to do that, Mrs Rutter?'

'Cos we ain't good enough for yow lot, is that it?'

Mama and I both picked up Deirdre's tone, which was one not of hostility but disbelief; she was waiting for an answer to the question that obviously deeply puzzled her and upset her, how could we possibly think ourselves better than her?

I had always been a little afraid of Deirdre, with her scarlet gash of a mouth and her backhanded conversation, but now I could see something else, something unexpected in her face – she was frightened of us. Of course it made sense; we were not one of those faceless hordes depicted in the television news, arriving at airports with baggage and children, lost and already defeated, begging for sanctuary. We were not the barely literate, perpetually grinning idiots I occasionally saw in TV comedies, or the confused, helpless innocents I spotted in bus and supermarket queues whilst they tried to make sense of their small change or the gesticulating wanderers who would sometimes stop my papa for directions, holding up pieces of paper with 'Mr Singh, Wolverhampton, England' written on them.

Mama and papa charmed people, they had bought a new car, they held parties, they did not ask for approval or acceptance but it came to them nevertheless. Deirdre had been seeking approval all her life in this village, her village, and I suppose she wanted to know why life was so bloody unfair. Mama must have picked this up, she softened slightly, 'We have been very busy with my mother lately. Anita, you know, is welcome any time.' I was so shocked that I did not even feel Sunil sinking four very sharp teeth into my shoulder. Mama had never uttered Anita's name without adding some derogatory prefix, 'That Anita Rutter' or 'Your Anita Rutter' and here she was declaring open house. Was she scared of Deirdre? I could not bear that, I did not want her to cower to Deirdre the way I had so often swallowed myself to please Anita. My parents were not supposed to make my mistakes. But mama's face told a different story, she was smiling, gracious, mama the bounty giver. She felt victorious enough to be charitable, she had won, and Deirdre knew that too.

Deirdre actually stuttered, 'Yeah . . . well yeah . . . th . . . that's okay then, in't it? I mean, the girls gorra have mates to play with. Keeps the bloody monkeys off the streets, don't it?'

Mama nodded, 'Monkeys, yes indeed!' her waving hand indicating that the meeting was over and hurried past me, scooping a now sniffling Sunil into her arms as she made her way towards Mrs Worrall's open back door. Deirdre took off her sunglasses for a moment, her false eyelashes made her look like two crows had landed for a chat on her cheeks, and squinted down the entry past me. From the road, just visible in the square of distant light at the end of the entry, a car horn tooted faintly. She replaced her sunglasses quickly and teetered past me as if I was invisible.

Mrs Worrall was bouncing Sunil in her arms whilst he chewed on a piece of rock cake. There was an open tin of biscuits on the kitchen table, its lid depicting an idyllic snowy landscape of mountains and chalets, in the foreground two cute and unreal children skated arm in arm on a glassy lake. I could not remember ever seeing 'social snacks' in Mrs Worrall's kitchen; we of course had a whole cupboard devoted to nibbles – masala peanuts, crisps, pakore and savoury vermicelli – which would be handed round as pre-starter starters to our visitors. Mrs Worrall did not have visitors, as far as I knew, and I noted that the label on the biscuit tin said 'December 1965'. She put a fat finger to her lips and cocked her head towards the sitting room. Mama was standing in the doorway, rapt.

I pushed past her and saw Nanima sitting opposite Mr Worrall whose wheelchair had been parked next to the settee. Nanima was speaking to him rapidly in Punjabi, in between scoffing large mouthfuls of still warm rock cakes. Every so often, when she paused to chew, Mr Worrall would try and open his mouth in response, his limbs jerking excitedly, the moans coming from his throat sounded almost like speech, the way the wind made words in the trees round the Big House. 'Them two been getting on like an house on fire,' whispered Mrs Worrall, not wanting to disturb the conversation.

'But what are they talking about?' I whispered back. 'Mr Worrall doesn't speak Punjabi, does he?'

Mama and Mrs Worrall didn't hear me, they were too busy eavesdropping on this meeting of minds, looking on like two proud parents whose infant had just taken its first stumbling steps. I decided there must be a language called Grunt, remembering how Nanima often asked for things or replied to questions with a series of tonal explosions which, funnily enough, we all understood, even Sunil. Watching them both huddled next to the coal fire, which burned every day in this room of perpetually drawn curtains, they did not seem to need the rest of the world.

'She's been telling me she ain't been nowhere, yowr mom. Yow should tek her out more,' Mrs Worrall admonished mama.

Mama arched her eyebrows. 'She told you that, did she?'

'Well, I can mek it out, what she means. Show her round the village, up the shops, anywhere. I'd tek her meself but, well, you know . . .' Mrs Worrall trailed off.

So it was that ten minutes later, I found myself struggling through our front gate with Sunil's perambulator, and Nanima waddling behind me, swathed in two Kashmiri woollen shawls. I had never taken Sunil out for a walk on my own before, he would not have got further than the end of the road before yelling for mama, but now he was screaming excitedly as I struggled with the unwieldy pram which looked like a waltzer car on wheels and seemed just as heavy. I tried out some of my recently acquired Punjabi on her, which I had absorbed with bad grace after realising that Nanima and I would spend our days in silence unless I made some effort. 'Nanima!' I puffed. 'You don't need them shawls. It's warm! Um, *tunda hai* . . . oh no, that's cold, isn't it . . . er HOT! Phew!' I mimed, wiping the very real sweat that was pricking at my temples.

Nanima harrumphed in agreement, gathering her shawls more tightly around herself. 'Hah beti, *bowth sardi hai*,' she said, agreeing that it was freezing, oblivious to the bees buzzing lazily around the gate post and the heavy may blossom which filled the air with its sickly sweet smell.

I checked in my pockets for the shopping list and change mama had given me. I did not want to visit Mr Ormerod's shop, for obvious reasons. Not just because of the Collection Box incident but also because of the Spring Fete Happening when some of his church cronies had added their nasty heckles to Sam Lowbridge's now notorious outburst. However, applying a boycott was useless in a village with only one shop. How could I get away with not going inside?

Nanima interrupted my reverie with a shout of warning. I turned and saw Cara, the mad Mitchells' daughter, doing her usual stint of jaywalking along the white lines in the middle of the road, whilst Shandie, the perky white terrier from a few doors down, yapped at the fraying hem of her long velvet cloak. Nanima seemed alarmed and shot off a stream of very fast Punjabi. I put a forefinger to my temple and screwed it in. 'She's a bit soft, Nanima, it's okay. Soft but Nice, yeah?' It was only when Shandie came over to my clicking fingers that I realised who was making Nanima nervous. She pulled me away from Shandie's eager tongue and wiped me down furiously with her *chunni* before aiming a swift kick at the dog who fled yelping down an entry. 'Nanima!' I gasped, frantic that someone might have witnessed this assault, 'You don't do that to dogs. Not in England! Um, *Gore Lok*, the white people, um, they love their *Kutte* . . . like *Bachhes*, like kids, see?'

Nanima looked at me as if I had grown horns and then let off one of her wheezy laughs. 'Junglee!' she said affectionately, and ruffled my hair. Sunil moaned in protest so she pinched his cheek hard which left fingermarks, but he seemed to love it when she did it.

As we passed the cottages leading up to Mr Ormerod's shop, it seemed a welcoming committee had gathered to greet us. I don't know whether it was coincidence or curiosity, but every one of the Ballbearings Women happened to be shaking out their front doormats and all of them stopped me, demanding an introduction. 'Oooh, is this your nan? . . . In't she sweet! . . . Look at that material, is it silk? . . . Lovely colour ain't she . . . She's seventy odd? Ooh, don't look a day over sixty, does she? . . . Them all her own teeth?' I half expected one of them to forcibly separate Nanima's lips to have a look, the way I'd seen them check over Misty, when she'd grazed in the field opposite our house. It was a strange kind of compliment they paid Nanima, wanting to touch and feel her like an imported piece of exotica.

'Look at them eyes . . . Oh, just like Meena's mom, eh? Just like Johnny Mathis, you mean . . . Oh, I could give him one . . . Shurrup, you daft cow, not in front of this lady . . . She doesn't understand anyway, does she? Do you love? . . . Does she speak English, Meena love? . . . Your mom and dad speak it lovely, don't they? . . .'

I felt confused. Sunil was protesting now, trying to pull himself out of his pram, aghast that his usual fan club was completely ignoring him, and I did not know whether to swat the ladies away or say thank you. I knew they were being friendly, but it was not somehow a meeting of equals, I felt like we were suddenly the entertainment, so I concluded I might as well put on a jolly good show. 'Oh, she does speak English,' I piped up, 'and French, Russian and a bit of Latin. But she's really shy, an' she's got a bit of a sore throat at the moment . . .' I bundled Nanima further into her shawls to illustrate my point whilst the women fell respectfully silent, doing a double-take on this little brown O A P.

'Russian eh? That's great, in't it, Irene? What's she over for, an 'oliday is it?' 'Oh no,' I continued, remembering how much I enjoyed doing this, 'she's looking for gold.' You could hear their collective jaws drop. I quickly pulled back Nanima's sleeve, she gave in to my insistent tugs, revealing the thick *kara* she always wore, a silver bangle denoting her Sikhism, and the two ornate gold bangles which many married women wear to denote their wealth and status. The Ballbearings Women stretched forward for a better look. 'It's what she does back in India. Precious mineral mining . . .' (Thank god I'd flicked through my oft neglected *Children's World Dictionary* last night . . .) 'But her biggest mine was destroyed by a volcano last month. She and my grandad had to flee a sea of foaming lava. They managed to save most of the jewels though. Lucky she knows how to ride a motorbike eh?'

And then my coup de grâce. I felt in my pockets and they were still there, a handful of junky glass stones Nanima had bought for me at some Indian market, dazzling but worthless, the kind of fake costume jewels the careful women wore when they ventured to weddings in dicey areas. I chose a moment when the hubbub of whispering had abated a little, and slowly brought them out, turning them over in my palm so the sunlight made miniature rainbows dance on my rapt audience's faces. 'Oh will yow look at them! . . . Worth a bloody fortune! . . . Yow can't get them here! . . . A volcano, yow say? . . . How did yow escape, Mrs er . . . what yow say yowr nan's name was?' Now everyone was firing questions at Nanima which she parried expertly with an enigmatic smile.

That would have been the perfect moment to make a dramatic exit when Mr Topsy muscled into the group, his voluminous trousers billowing with excitement. 'Alright, Topsy!' he grinned, yanking at my bangs. Last year I thought this was cute, now I wanted to poke him in the eye. Then he pushed forward to face Nanima and greeted her with a long exaggerated 'Namaste!' which made the women ooh and laugh with delight. Nanima put her hands together and politely namasted him back. I thought she might be getting bored so I took her arm but Mr Topsy stopped me. He turned to Nanima again and said, '*Mera Nam* Mr Turvey *hai!*'

So that was his name. I felt satisfied that 'Mr Topsy' – my guess – had not been too far off.

'Where did yow learn to speak Indian then?' asked one of the women, but Mr Topsy/Turvey was concentrating hard on Nanima.

'*Thusi kither rande-ho, ji? Punjab the vich?*' Nanima nodded her head vigorously and then, they actually had a conversation! I caught snatches of it, he mentioned Ludhiana, she talked about Bessian, he asked if there was still such and such a market in Delhi, she said she'd bought carrots there just last year . . . We were all stunned into silence, even Sunil stopped eating his shawl and regarded them both with disbelieving saucer eyes. I felt hot with fury. How dare he steal my Nanima from me! How dare this fat man with the ridiculous crimplene strides know more Punjabi than me! I went into a deep sulk and made a pretence of rocking Sunil's pram so I could move further away, hoping that Nanima would finish soon. She was giggling away like a schoolgirl, she's even flirting with the old sod, I thought angrily, and then she eventually gave him another long namaste and nodded her farewells.

Mr Topsy/Turvey watched her with devoted eyes. 'I served in India. Ten years. Magical country. Magical people. The best.'

'Shouldn't have bloody been there anyway, should you?' I muttered under my breath. 'Who asked you to lock up my grandad and steal his chickens?'

I was by now walking fast, making Nanima puff and trot a little to keep up, but I could still hear him shouting behind us, 'We should never have been there. Criminal it was! Ugly. You look after your nan! You hear me, Topsy!'

I stumbled momentarily, cursing as the heavy pram wheel ran over my foot. Had Mr Topsy/Turvey been reading my mind? I looked back quickly and although the women were now dispersing, deep in conversation, he was still watching us with a fond, faraway look in his brimming eyes. '*Achha Admi Si, Ohne Punjabi aandi hai,*' Nanima said breathlessly.

I slowed down a little to let her catch up. 'Don't encourage him, Nanima. He'll be coming round wanting to swap curry recipes next.'

She shrugged her shoulders. I assumed that she had not understood, but as we reached the plate glass door of Mr Ormerod's shop, she said, 'Nice man.'

'Hey Nanima!' I bumped her with my hip, the way I did it with Anita, our own method of saying "Alright!" 'That was brilliant! Give Nanima a clap, Sunil!'

Sunil obliged by crashing his palms together and then throwing up all over his yellow romper suit. As I fumbled for the tissues hidden beneath his cot blanket, I squinted through

Mr Ormerod's door and froze. I recognised the old man with whom he was laughing and chatting, he was one of the church mafia and I was sure he was also one of the phantom hecklers who hid behind Mr Ormerod to spit his poison. I could not go in that shop. I thrust the shopping list mama had written out for me into Nanima's hands and propelled her towards the door.

'*Thusi under jao*, Nanima,' I told her, 'Here, *paisa*, money. It's okay . . .' Nanima looked from the list to me and then at the money, and shrugged again before opening the shop door. I manoeuvred the pram so I could watch the shop interior through the crack in the window display, a convenient space between the Player's Cigarette sailor and the huge Marmite jar. I checked on Nanima, she was simply staring at the laden shelves before her, as if choosing something special. Mr Ormerod was wearing a fixed, patient smile, the mean-faced man was looking at Nanima with barely disguised amusement, taking in her woollen shawls, her loose fitting *salwar kameez* which to the English eye I knew, looked like pyjamas, and the men's bedsocks, crammed into her worn leather thong sandals. The Mean Man shot Mr Ormerod a mocking glance and Mr Ormerod bit his lip and looked away. I felt terribly guilty suddenly, protective. I wanted to go inside and drag Nanima out of there. But it was too late.

Nanima was still checking out the produce, so Mr Ormerod reached over the counter and gently took the list and the ten-shilling note from her hand. He read it briefly and then turned back to the shelves and disappeared from sight for a while. Nanima was pointing to something on a high shelf, and then smiled and nodded, and all the while, the Mean Man never took his eyes off her face. I could not work out what he was thinking; there was fascination there certainly, distaste, and something much more awful and unwelcome – pity.

Mr Ormerod's face came back into view and he talked so slowly and carefully that I could lip-read what he was saying.

'Do You Want A Bag, Love?' and waved a sheet of brown paper at her. I ducked out of sight and busied myself with Sunil, who was now lying on his back, sucking his toes noisily. He was hungry. I had been left in charge of my family and failed miserably; my baby brother was starving before my eyes and my aged granny was a helpless mute in front of two people I had not the courage to face myself. Then the shop bell tinkled and Nanima was beside me, clutching her booty. I took the bag from her and quickly checked off the contents against the list. It was all there, and then Nanima handed me the change. I counted it, then recounted it and checked the list and bag again. There was no mistake. I knew the price of every item written down there by heart, as I always used the leftover coppers to buy sweets. Sixpence short! Six whole pence! Mr Ormerod had tried to cheat my Nanima!

This is a test, I told myself over the hammering of my heart, these people have hurt you and now you can get them back, these lying pigs who took advantage of an old lady who could not speak English. I had never confronted an elder before on anything, but this time I had good reasons. I felt I had been waiting so long for this moment. 'Wait here, Nanima . . . *Thehro aider!*' I whispered to her, took a deep breath and entered the shop.

Mr Ormerod looked up, confusion and, I thought, guilt creasing his features. 'Hello Meena, love! Was that your nan who just came in?'

'Yes, it was actually, Mr Ormerod,' I said calmly, although my voice sounded high and forced to my ears.

'I thought it was. I'd heard you had visitors. How's she been with this weather? Must be cold for her, ey?'

'Funny, you're the tenth person to say that today, smartarse!' I thought, but actually what I said was, 'Yes, a bit.'

There was a brief silence when we all looked at each other, waiting for someone to fill the gap with some polite social chit-chat. The Mean Man was now picking his teeth with the edge of a threepenny bit. Probably my money as well, I thought, and the idea of ferret-face cleaning his gob with my Nanima's change made me suddenly burst out with, 'You made a mistake! You cheated my Nanima!'

The Mean Man stopped flossing, he raised his eyebrows at Mr Ormerod who looked at me kindly, which made me feel even angrier. 'I don't think . . .'

'You thought just because she don't speak English you could cheat her! Well she's really clever actually, she knows lots of English, I bet you don't speak any Punjabi do you?'

I was breathing hard now, I could feel tears pricking my eyes which I blinked back furiously.

Mr Ormerod came out from behind the counter, 'Well I thought I'd totted up alright, but tell me anyway, what's missing then?'

'Sixpence,' I stuttered. 'You kept sixpence back for your-selves! I expect you'll be giving it to buy that new church roof, won't you?'

Mr Ormerod's face fell. I had him now. He cleared his throat uncomfortably. 'Well now . . . I understand why you're a bit upset, love . . . Awful business that, we was all really sorry . . .'

'I don't want your sorry,' I said flatly. 'I want my sixpence back.'

Mr Ormerod coughed again and patted his pockets. 'Well now, that sixpence must have been for the chocolate bar your nan bought, Meena.'

'Chocolate bar?' I said stupidly, forcing myself not to look round at the Mean Man who I was sure would be smiling now.

'Look, hee-yaar . . .' Mr Ormerod said breezily, as he dived into a box under the counter. 'Have this on me. No charge, ey?'

He was holding out a Curly Wurly, he knew they were my favourites. I shook my head and backed away, fumbling for the door handle. 'No thanks,' I said, and fell out of the shop.

Nanima looked up as I approached; she swallowed something quickly so she could flash me a grin. Sunil was cooing noisily, his hands and face were smeared with chocolate, the last chunk enclosed tightly in his fist. He held it up to me proudly for inspection. 'Nanima!' I turned on her. 'Why didn't you tell me? *Thusi kew* . . .' I was too tired to think of the translation, I wanted to lie down right now on the pavement and curl up into a very small ball. Instead, I yanked the pram towards me, making Sunil sway and clutch the sides nervously, and heaved myself up the road, not caring if Nanima caught up or not.

I was pushing hard, concentrating on the bumps and cracks in the pavement, when my ears pricked up at a familiar voice. Uncle Alan was in the middle of one of his jocular moral chats, '. . . understand why, but just think if you could use all that energy to do some good. Find out who the real enemies are, the rich, the privileged, not the other people trying to make a living like you, not people like . . .'

As I rounded the corner, he stopped, and I looked up from my pram handles. Uncle Alan was standing next to Sam Lowbridge, who was sitting on the low wall surrounding the patch of wild ground where we hunted for blackberries in the autumn. The rest of his gang slouched in the long grass, propped up on elbows and swigging from plastic bottles of cider. I had an impression of a cluster of shaven heads, downy and vulnerable as dandelion clocks, peeking out at me from the hollyhocks and yarrow stalks. A slight breeze seemed to catch their faces, as they swung as one to face me.

I pinned myself to Uncle Alan's calm, dimpled face. I clung to it mentally like a drowning swimmer onto a buoy. I would not look at Sam Lowbridge. I would never look at him again.

'Well here's Meena! And little Sunil too! What a super chappie he's turning into, ey?'

I pitied Uncle Alan then, if you're waiting for a hallelujah chorus from that lot, I thought, you really do need help.

'He's teething,' I said uselessly, wanting to keep up this pretence that this was a cosy meet and greet chat, the kind that went on hundreds of times a day in this village. I felt a sudden pang of regret, that this small custom would be denied me from now on, that I would never be able to walk the streets without wondering if I was going to bump into Sam and his cronies, and suffer the impotent fury that was knotting my stomach muscles into cramps. In that one moment at the fete, when Sam had opened his mouth and let the cider and his single brain cell do the talking, he had taken away my innocence. There was nothing in the world I could do to him that would have the same impact, that would affect him so deeply and for so long.

Sunil yawned languorously, a cat's yawn full of indolence and self satisfaction. I was glad his eyelids were drooping and rocked the pram gently to encourage him to sleep. I did not want him awake for this.

'Sam and me were having a very interesting talk about blame and responsibility. About how easy it is to get angry with others for what's going wrong in your own life. Have you got any thoughts on this, Meena?'

Uncle Alan's eagerness was beginning to grate. I shifted my gaze slightly so I could see the metal toecaps of Sam's boots; he was bouncing his heels against the wall, I knew if I just raised my eyes a little, I would see that lopsided beam and the black pupils floating like planets in the blue sky of his eyes. I felt sharp and bright as a knife. I cut carefully. 'If I was Sam's mum, I'd feel bloody responsible. But it ain't her fault her son's a prat.'

Sam's heels stopped kicking suddenly. There was an exaggerated 'Whooo!' from the gang members who shifted onto their haunches to get a better view.

'Now then Meena,' broke in Uncle Alan. 'That's not the way we settle disputes, is it?'

'Who's we?' Sam's voice almost made me jerk my head up towards him but I resisted the impulse, although I could already feel a slow throbbing headache playing bongos on my temples. 'Are yow angry with me, Meena?' He asked me like he was asking me to dance. He was soft, yielding, teasing. I stared steadily at Sunil who was now fast asleep and tucked the cot blanket round his bare legs. 'Meena? Ain't we friends any more then?' Someone in the gang shouted out something, I could not make out what it was, but Sam rounded on them with a sharp 'Shuttit, Baz!'

What was the matter with him? Didn't he understand what he had done? Just when I thought I would faint with the heat and pain in my head and effort of looking anywhere except where I wanted to look, I felt Nanima's hand on my arm. She felt my cheek and prised the pram handle out of my fingers. I noticed that my knuckles were white.

'This your Nan, Meena?' said Uncle Alan with relief, and shook Nanima's free hand vigorously. 'Lovely to meet you. Welcome to England!'

He sounded like he was speaking underwater. I thought I heard hissing, like the geese in the pub courtyard, but louder, more stinging. The sibilance made the bongos beat faster, the pavement looked transparent and rose slightly towards me. I had to look up then, but not at Sam, I looked straight at the gang members who were on the verge of having a huge laugh at Nanima's expense. Their lips were pursed, ready to hoot or chant or gob or giggle and I was not having it.

All the pain in my head crystallised into two beams of pure energy which shot out of my eyes and which I turned on Sam's gang, expecting to see them shrivel like slugs under salt, like metal under Superman's laser x-ray gaze. I was ten feet tall, I had a hundred arms, like the goddess on top of the fridge in Auntie Shaila's house, I was swathed in red and gold silk like a new bride. I felt myself floating above them all, just like Nanima had risen up to the ceiling that first night with Sunil in her arms.

The gang fell silent. I let Nanima lead me away. I did not look back. As we reached our front door, I heard snatches of a chant that they were singing at my back, 'De de dah de, de de dah de, de dah dah dah de . . .' I dimly recognised it as the theme tune to *Laurel and Hardy* before I sank into the farty settee and gave in to darkness.

Mama said I had a very high temperature. 'She's burning up! My God!' I heard her whisper to papa who must have arrived home by this point. I let them sponge me down with warm water which felt icy cold to my skin, and opened my mouth at obedient intervals for the glass thermometer, which mama would consult and then 'tch tch' loudly at. When I finally dared to lift an eyelid, it was not Nanima lying next to me but papa. It was that strange time when night is about to bleed into morning, when the shadows look textured and grainy and you keep thinking you hear birdsong.

Papa was sleeping in his characteristic pose, head resting on his right elbow which was tucked under him. As usual, he had discarded his pillow which lay at the end of the bed like another sleeping body. I prodded his chest and he awoke with a grunt and automatically felt my forehead.

'Okay beti?'

'Water,' I croaked. My throat seemed coated with sand. Papa heaved himself out of bed, tiptoeing past Sunil who was flat on his back, legs and arms akimbo, sleeping the blessed expansive sleep of a baby. A minute later papa returned with a plastic cup which he held to my lips whilst I carefully slurped. It was warm and pungent, with a bitter-sweet aftertaste.

'What is it?'

'Hilachi tea. Nanima made it. Drink. It's good.'

I finished off the whole cup and my stomach felt bloated, as if I had inhaled a four course meal.

'Where's Nanima?'

'Sleeping with your mama. Rest now.'

I lay back and fitted my head into papa's armpit, enjoying his scent of tobacco and aftershave.

'Papa?'

'Hah beti?'

'I want to play with . . . I mean, hang round with Anita tomorrow. I want to go and ride Sherrie's pony. Can I?'

'If you're better. We'll see.'

I persisted. 'Mama spoke to Anita's mum today. They've made it up now. You can ask her.'

I did not tell him the real reason why I needed to see Anita, that image that kept coming back to me, of her thin shoulders shaking with sobs as she ran away into the night. Papa smoothed my hair from my face, a few wet strands clung to my temples.

'There was nothing to make up. Why do you worry about such tiny things, eh? That is our job. Your job is to enjoy yourself, enjoy your studies, and leave the rest to us.'

'So does that mean yes,' I yawned, hoping the sympathy factor of me being ill and emotionally insecure would swing it.

'Okay,' papa sighed. 'Now sleep.'

Later on, I could not tell exactly when, I felt Nanima sidle into bed beside me and pull my head onto her mountainous chest, which she fluffed up for me like a pair of pillows. And then she talked, and the strange thing was, although I am almost sure that she spoke in Punjabi, I understood every word. At first she did not make sense, but her broad vowel sounds and earthy consonants knitted themselves into a cradle which rocked me half asleep, then out of the rhythm came words, one or two I recognised, then phrases, then sentences, then all the stories I had been waiting to hear, the stories I knew Nanima owned and kept to herself, but I had never owned enough Punjabi myself to ever ask her if she would share them with me. And now she was, and I did not even need to open my eyes.

'My village was very modern, top class roads, electricity, fresh water, BBC on the radio. Our family home was one of the largest – tiles in the courtyard, carvings on the shutters, we only ate what we grew in our fields. Your fields do nothing. You waste them.' Maybe I told Nanima about the blackberry bushes at the far end of the park at that point. Or maybe not.

'My childhood was good but short. It was always this way for girls. I was the plump one, the beautiful one. I never went out without covering my head, I knew my beauty would bring the dogs running if I did not.' Nanima did not like dogs, maybe this explained why. 'I went to school, my father insisted. I was lucky, to read and write and learn to recite from the Granth Sabib. Never did I think I was less than a man. More than a man sometimes, this I was. To cook and clean and carry and fetch and soothe and smile and climb and fall.' My Nanima climbing trees, I grinned into the darkness. 'At sixteen years of age, two brothers were married to two sisters. I was one of those sisters. The other is your Nani Masi. We lived together the four of us. At twenty, we had four children between us.' I knew about mama's brother, the one who had died as a baby. I thought I heard tears in Nanima's voice. Then I thought about Anita who would be sixteen in three years' time, the same age as Nanima when she got married. I could not imagine Anita ever getting married. Nor myself for that matter. Ever.

'Then only stones fell from the sky; the fields were given over to English soldiers, the cattle too, the most dignified people had to eat dust when they passed, nothing we owned was ours anymore, not even our names, our breath.' I knew this feeling, I had felt it too, but did not know why. 'You know about your Dada, being taken to prison. I lived as a widow until he returned and he returned to nothing. Even the pots and pans we ate from had been sold, or taken. But after a death, what can you do but be born again? We lived. In five years, Dada owned trucks, I had gold earrings. But then came the accident . . .' Dada trapped in one of his own trucks, his own brother taking over the business assuming he would die, Dada having a goat's bone forced into his leg. Now I really wanted to wake up, the rocking became a seasickness, an ocean of heaving cinnamon-scented bosom. 'Again we lost everything and this time we were reborn in Delhi. What is there to fear when you have already lived two whole lives? And how many more to come? Your mama is on her second one, here, over here. And you Meena . . .' I forced my eyelids apart and it was morning. There was no sign of Nanima except a slight depression in the mattress and a few strands of silver hair on the pillow, caught in the cotton mesh like fine slivers of glass.

9

I did not mind leaving Nanima the next day; I knew mama was now on holiday for two weeks – the great advantage, maybe the only one, of having a parent who was a teacher. It was a hard process, convincing mama that I was now fully recovered and was not about to keel over, foaming at the mouth. I forced myself to eat two aloo rotis which came sizzling straight from the griddle onto my plate, I broke off tiny morsels for Sunil which I blew on loudly, making him laugh. I also asked for a glass of milk, which Nanima prepared by warming up in a pan, adding crushed almonds and sugar till it foamed like a choppy sea.

Then I began an exaggerated routine of tidying up my comic pile and chirpily whistling the *White Horses*' theme tune around the kitchen until mama said, 'Go on then, you're giving me a headache now. But be back for dinner, okay?'

'Nighttime dinner?' I called, grabbing my cardigan.

'No! Daytime dinner! Two o'clock or else I will come looking for you and you will get embarrassed!'

I did not get as far as Anita's yard door before being mobbed by the rest of our now defunct gang. Karl and Kevin, Susan, Natasha, Nathan and Nicky, all crowded round me like the prodigal returned and I was touched. 'Where yow been? On holidays, yeah? We cor get in the pigsty den, someone's put a lock on it. How come yow don't play out anymore?' 'Me nan's come to visit,' I told them, straining my neck to see if there was any sign of life in Anita's back yard. The curtains both upstairs and downstairs were drawn and a half-eaten bowl of very old dog food sat on the step. 'She's dead old, so I've been cooking for her, washing her and that . . . I've got a lot of responsibilities,' I continued, enjoying the open-mouthed wonder and admiration that encircled me. They all seemed so small, I felt like I was wading knee deep in a sea of midgets, Nathan was still in nappies for God's sake. How did I ever think this motley collection of toddlers and bedwetters constituted a gang?

It was Tracey who answered the door, still in her pink flannelette nightie with her finger on her lips. 'Gorra be quiet! Me mom's gorra headache!' I was momentarily wrong-footed. Tracey was at least six inches taller than when I had last seen her – the day of the Peeing Competition – and the pinched, wan features had rearranged themselves into a compact heart-shaped face of such sweetness and sorrow that I felt like gathering her up from the kitchen lino and feeding her something hot.

'Er . . . seen your Anita anywhere?'

Tracey sighed. Of course she knew I wasn't calling for her but now I wished I had at least pretended to. 'She's up at Sherrie's farm. She's always up there now . . .' she said wistfully.

'I'm gooing up there as well,' I said breezily, not thinking about what I would do if Anita chased me away with a pitchfork full of horse manure.

Tracey was already closing the door when I turned back and said, 'Yow wanna come with me?'

Her eyes widened, 'I'm not allowed. Not on me own.'

'You won't be on your own, will you, soft bat.'

Tracey slid inside wordlessly, leaving the door slightly ajar. I spent a few moments testing the crust of dog food with the toe of my shoe, it felt crumbly and light, and little puffs of dust flew up from the bowl. I heard snippets of conversation, Tracey's slight whine counteracted by Deirdre's smoke-laden bark, and somewhere the skittering of doggy feet. Soon, Tracey emerged, hair unbrushed, in a frilly summer dress and plastic sandals, her cardigan slung over her arm. She held the door open for the mangy black poodle who flew into the yard on two legs and skidded madly towards the back gate. 'Gorra tek Nigger with us,' Tracey said proudly. 'He needs walkies.'

Tracey ran her fingernails against the entry wall, changing her hands into a demon's green taloned claws. The piddly poodle waited for us at the end. He let out an impatient bark which with the echo, sounded like a baby's wail. 'The Christmas house is haunted now,' said Tracey authoritatively. 'That's why they can't get rid of it. But I'm not scared of ghosts. Mom says she'll buy it for me when I grow up and then we'll be neighbours . . .' We ambled past the park where I could see Sam Lowbridge and his gang lolling on the roundabout we called the Witches' Hat. A few younger children stood by uncertainly, waiting to claim their territory back. I looked away quickly. I had seen his silhouette, that was enough for me.

A car zoomed past, quickly followed by Blaze, the mad collie, who yapped furiously at its back wheels, missing them as always by inches. The piddly poodle watched this with interest and then swerved towards the road. 'Nigger!' Tracey screamed, running towards him and swooping him up in her arms. 'Bad dog! One of these days . . . He don't have no road sense. Yow silly Nigger yow!' she crooned, nuzzling up to his neck. He licked her face and as always, when he got excited, a slow drip began from his nether regions. That did it.

'I hate that stupid name!' I snapped.

'What?' said Tracey, startled.

'His name! It's so . . . stupid!'

'It's just 'cos of his colour, honest!' Tracey said pleadingly.

'I know that!' I retorted. 'But it's very insulting you know! It's . . . it's like a swear word.'

'Is it?' Tracey said quietly. 'I . . . I didn't know. Sorry.'

We quickened our pace and reached the end of the park where the big houses began. Tracey suddenly linked her arm in mine and said reassuringly, 'Mom chose it. Anyway, I wanted to call him Sambo.'

*

As I turned into the rough pebbly lane leading up to Sherrie's farm, I saw Anita immediately. She and Fat Sally were sitting on top of a five-bar gate around the paddock whilst Sherrie urged a brown fat pony over minuscule jumps. As the pony managed to heave itself over each six-inch bar, Anita and Fat Sally let out a whoop of joy and applauded loudly. Sherrie looked just like a medieval princess, I thought, her blonde hair streaming behind her, her sharp alabaster features focused and confident. Even though she was wearing tatty jeans and a baggy T-shirt with a faded print of Marc Bolan on it, she seemed elegant and completely in tune with her rotund steed, making him turn or speed up with the slightest nudge of her knees.

I lifted my hand to get their attention, but heard the rumble of a car engine behind me. A mud-spattered Land-Rover eased past us, the window rolled down and Sherrie's dad poked his head out to greet us.

'Alright girls! Come for a ride, then?'

'Yes, Mr Palmer, if that's okay, like!' I called back.

Sherrie's dad was so sinewy he had muscles in his earlobes. He was tall, blond and sunburned, even in winter, and every bit of him seemed to ripple when he moved.

'Seen the mess they're making of my back field?' he said, pointing to the land at the back of the house where I could make out a yellow earthdigger moving slowly like some huge shiny snail. 'Bloody slip road. They never mentioned that in the original plans.'

'Oh, that's awful, Mr Palmer! What you gonna do?' I asked, imagining how the car headlights would light the whole Palmer family up as they lay in bed.

'Oh, it's been to court already, chick. Don't worry, I shall be a rich man pretty soon. And then we're off.'

He revved up the Land-Rover and began to pull away.

'Off where?' I shouted after him.

'Lake District!'

His words were snatched away in the wind. 'Buying a

hotel . . . No slip roads for bloody miles!' he laughed loudly, and speeded up into the yard.

My feet felt heavy against the stony road. Everyone was moving away, everyone except for me. By now the girls had spotted us, and the last few yards up to the paddock felt endless. I was expecting a full-frontal verbal assault from Anita, maybe a three-pronged attack from all sides when she got the others to join in. 'What the hell's she doing here?' Anita shouted. I was about to answer her when I noticed she was looking at Tracey, who was holding up the dog to her face, like a shield.

'I said she could come. She was bored,' I replied.

'And who said yow could come anyway?' challenged Fat Sally, whose large bottom spilled out over both sides of the fence, like she had a hot water bottle under her denim shorts.

'Whose bloody horse is it anyway?' called Sherrie, who drew in the pony's reins, urging it to come to a gentle halt near the hedge, and threw Fat Sally a hard glare.

'She's my mate, so she can come. Is that right, Shez?' said Anita, who looked me up and down coolly, enjoying my amazement.

'Ar,' said Sherrie, finishing the conversation and dismounting with a grunt. She patted the pony's haunches and ran her fingers over its smoking muzzle, 'Good girl, Trix! Wharra good girl you are, yes . . .' she crooned. Trixie pricked up her ears in pleasure and snorted, spraying Fat Sally's bare legs with spit. Fat Sally squealed and almost fell off the gate in her haste to get away, the rest of us howled till our bellies ached.

It felt so good to be back here and to be laughing at someone else. Anita and me bumped hips and laughed some more. I was not sure when or why she had forgiven me, and I was not going to press for an explanation. But the fact that I had apparently got away with it made me feel light-headed and free. Maybe now things would be different; I would no longer be Anita's shadow but her equal, just like the slogan on

Mrs Worrall's tea towel that said, 'Do not walk behind me, I may not lead, just walk beside me and be my friend.' She had bought it for herself on Mr Worrall's behalf as her Christmas present from him, which I thought was sad as Mr Worrall didn't walk anywhere.

Sherrie's shout interrupted my reverie. She was pointing at Tracey imperiously. 'What's that bloody dog doing here! Get him away from the horse now!'

Tracey had been waiting at the paddock entrance all this time, and visibly jumped at Sherrie's command. 'I . . . I can't send him home! Not on his own! He's daft round cars!' she stammered.

'You'll be sorry if Trix kicks him in the head, won't ya?' said Sherrie.

I didn't think that would be such a tragedy, but Anita took over, snapping her fingers at Fat Sally who was wiping down her thighs with clumps of hay.

'Ey, Sal, giz us your belt!'

'No! Why?' moaned Fat Sally.

'Just giz it now!' Fat Sally looked like she was going to cry; reluctantly, she undid the shiny green scarf tied around her middle and handed it over to Anita who yanked it from her to make a point.

'That's a Biba scarf, that is!' Fat Sally protested. 'My mom got it from London!'

'Well tell her to gerranother one then! She's gorrenough money, ain't she?' called Anita, who was striding purposefully towards Tracey.

At first I thought she was going to truss up her sister, but instead she quickly pulled one end of the scarf through the poodle's collar, joined both ends together and tied him to a branch in the privet hedge running along the side of the lane.

'There. He cor get out of that. Stupid dog,' muttered Anita, as the poodle began to whine pitifully and pull against his haute couture leash.

'He's gonna get strangled!' yelled Tracey, running towards him.

'I'll strangle you if yow don't come here now!'

Anita's tone was quietly threatening, all of us recognised it and all of us unconsciously stood to attention. Tracey sniffed loudly, gave in, and slowly lowered herself into a corner near the gate, occasionally throwing the now-chastened poodle long, apologetic glances.

'What do you mean, my mom's rich?' Fat Sally demanded.

Sherrie and I immediately looked away, I busied myself with stroking Trixie, enjoying the sweaty velvet of her back. Anita's nostrils flared slightly, momentarily giving her the alert, challenging look of a wary horse.

'Yowr mom wears dresses all the time, even though they look like someone's been sick down them . . .'

Fat Sally gasped audibly, I could tell no one had ever dared criticise her mom's dress sense before.

'And anyway,' continued Anita pleasantly, 'she's sending yow to that posh slags' school, in't she? How much is that costing her?'

'It's not a slags' school!' shouted Fat Sally, trembling now. 'It's Catholic! So there! And we aren't . . . I mean ain't rich. We just work hard and save hard, we make sacrifices so I can have a good education!' Although she was obviously repeating verbatim one of her parents' lectures, this was a familiar mantra to me, any one of my Aunties could have said that. I wondered briefly if Catholics were anything like Hindus and that maybe Fat Sally also had an army of overpowering female relatives who made regular inspections of her homework books and sent her crash diets cut out of women's magazines through the post.

Sherrie looked up, interested suddenly, 'Ain't yow coming to Bloxwich Comp with us?'

'Nah, she's too good for a comp,' sneered Anita, taking Sherrie's arm. 'Me and Sherrie are the cocks of the school and yow'm gonna hang round with a bunch of bloody nuns.'

Fat Sally moved closer, her fists clenched. I had never seen her so enraged before, I did not think those soft fleshy features capable of anything but bad moods and wounded pride. She spoke through gritted teeth, I fancied I could hear her molars grinding with each syllable. 'They are not bloody nuns! They are decent women who have given their lives to God!'

Anita and Sherrie both tittered in stereo. 'Yow mean,' Anita hiccupped, 'they're too bloody ugly to get sex! Yow should be in good company then!'

Before anyone knew what was happening, Fat Sally threw herself onto Anita with a strangled scream, grabbing handfuls of hair and pinning her squarely to the ground. Sherrie, Tracey and I all cried out in unison and Tracey dived straight into the tangle of kicking, biting, scratching bodies but was caught on the chin by a stray foot and reeled back onto her knees. The piddly poodle went mad, yapping hysterically and jumping up, trying to escape, repeatedly being hurled back on itself by the scarf which was gradually entangling itself round its neck. Sherrie just kept screaming, 'Stop it! Stop it, you two!' running round them helplessly, trying to .identify a recognisable limb she could maybe grab onto and haul one of them out. I stood transfixed, not even daring to interfere, because I was concentrating on Anita's face. It was clearly visible, poking out from behind one of Fat Sally's wrestler's shoulders. Fat Sally still had a bunch of Anita's hair in each fist and was pulling so hard that the skin on Anita's temples was lifted up from her scalp and any moment, I expected to hear an awful ripping sound. Fat Sally kept up a constant impassioned monologue as she pulled harder and harder, 'You bloody slag! Your mom's a slag! Everyone says so! You'll end up in the bloody gutter! Everyone says so, slag!'

But Anita did not even register these curses; she had her fingernails sunk firmly into Fat Sally's cheeks, just below her eyes, and there were already tiny bubbles of bright red blood seeping from under them. And whilst words poured out of Fat Sally like messages from a fairground medium, Anita remained completely silent. She did not utter one word, emit one moan, her breathing was steady and her muscles relaxed, all her energy focused into the ends of her fingers and triumph glazing her eyes and twisting her mouth into a good-humoured grin. What really troubled me was her quiet acceptance, her satisfaction at being pummelled. She seemed to be saying, I made you do this, I knew you would do it, and I have been proved right. I could not work out if this made her a bully or a victim, but I knew I could not stand by and watch this any longer. 'Stop them Sherrie!' I shouted pathetically. Sherrie was now bashing Fat Sally on the back with her riding crop; it was like pinging an elastic band at a yeti. 'Get me dad!' she shouted.

I shook myself and ran towards the gate, the piddly poodle's barking had turned into a single wailing note of anguish. Just as Tracey picked herself off the floor to attend to him, at the very moment I shinned the five-bar gate, the dog suddenly broke free of the hedge, was catapulted forward by the impact and shot down the lane, the Biba scarf dragging in the dust behind him, and disappeared from view.

'Nigger!' screamed Tracey.

'Dad!' screamed Sherrie.

'My scarf!' screamed Fat Sally and let go of Anita's hair, heaving herself unsteadily onto her feet. Sherrie and I simultaneously clamped our hands over our mouths in disbelief. Fat Sally had a semi-circle of bloody indentations under each eye, like the bite marks of some large peckish animal. She was crying, although unaware of it, and walked like a drunkard, swaying slowly up the lane in the dust trail of the missing dog. 'My scarf . . .' was the last thing we heard her say. Tracey was already at the end of the lane, sobbing brokenly as she scanned the horizon, too afraid to venture further on her own. She slipped in behind Fat Sally and they both turned the corner and were gone.

Anita was still lying on the ground. Trixie had ambled over and was snuffling at clumps of her hair that lay about her head like a broken halo. Sherrie stood over Anita, who was gazing straight up at the scudding clouds, with a calm, faraway face. 'Yow alright . . . shit! Yow've got bald patches, Nita! What yow gonna do?'

Anita got to her feet in one easy motion and brushed the dirt and hay stalks off her back. 'I'm gonna ride Trixie,' she said.

If Sherrie was a good horsewoman, Anita was a centaur; she rode Trixie like she was her bottom half, clearing all the jumps in one at full gallop. She did not have Sherrie's style, she did not rise to the trot or even hold the reins, preferring to bury her hands in Trixie's mane and hug her flanks tightly with her thighs, leaving the stirrups empty and swinging free. But she moved with joy, as if she possessed the best and deepest secret, and she rode better than anyone else because she truly had no fear.

Watching her was the best antidote for the ugliness we had just witnessed, my heart slowed down to the regular thump of Trixie's hooves. Even Sherrie relaxed enough to feel impressed at Anita's skill. 'She's a natural. Can't wait until her mom gets her that horse. She can stable it here, dad says. We'll just spend all day riding and grooming. Dead good.' Sherrie did not even know that her parents were thinking of moving, Sherrie and Anita did not know what I suddenly realised now, that Deirdre had no intention, ever, of buying Anita a horse. Sorrow flooded me until it rose up to my eyes and made them sting. Anita, the same skinny harpy who had just narrowly missed gouging out another girl's eyes, was now whispering lover's endearments into a fat pony's ears. She needed me maybe more than I needed her. There is a fine line between love and pity and I had just stepped over it.

I never did get to ride Trixie that day. I had literally got one foot in the stirrups, had the reins in my hands ready to haul myself up onto that broad furry back when we heard a car horn followed by a screech of tyres and the endless pause after it, finally punctuated by a shrill, inhuman scream. Anita and Sherrie simply dropped whatever they had in their hands and began running at full pelt down the lane. It took me a few moments to untangle my foot and lead Trixie to her trough where I left her slurping gratefully before I closed the gate behind me with deliberation and set off at walking pace after them. I did not want to go any faster; the birds had suddenly gone silent.

As I rounded the corner onto the main road, I saw them huddled around the body. Tracey sat crying noiselessly on the kerb, her lanky legs stretched out before her. 'The car didn't stop!' she choked. 'It was a red one. It drove away!' Anita and Sherrie were looking down at the piddly poodle's crumpled body which lay in a misshapen heap across the broken white lines of the tarmac. Although his eyes were closed, his hind legs were twitching intermittently and his diaphragm rose and fell in short rapid pants. 'He's still alive . . . Oh shit,' Sherrie said, backing away. Anita blinked once and wrapped her arms around herself, swaying slightly. We instinctively all shifted to the pavement as a car coughed slowly towards us, its gears crunching loudly. Hairy Neddy's three-wheeler shuddered to a halt in front of the pathetic body. Sandy, who was doing her lipstick in the wing mirror, paused with her hand up to her mouth as Hairy Neddy got out, hitching his jeans over his belly.

'Who done this then?' he demanded accusingly, as if it could have been any one of us. Tracey's sobbing began again in earnest, 'Dunno!' she cried.

Hairy Neddy knelt down next to the dog and gently felt its abdomen, shaking his head.

'He's still alive, in't he?' Tracey asked hopefully.

'Ar, but not for long, poor little sod,' he replied, and then turned sharply as he heard Sandy letting herself out of the passenger door. 'Stay inside, chick!' he called to her, in the tone of a fire chief faced with a towering inferno. 'Yow'll only get upset!'

Sandy smiled at him gratefully, thrilled that someone cared enough to think for her, and sat down again with a pleased, resigned sigh. There was a brief pause when we all stood over the furry victim wondering who was going to end this misery and take control, and then Anita strode over to a rockery at the edge of one of the posh houses' gardens, picked up a football-sized rock and held it out with both hands towards Hairy Neddy. 'Kill him,' she said. Tracey stood up shouting, 'No! What you doing! You . . . you cow!'

Hairy Neddy backed off, shaking his head, glancing behind him to check if Sandy was a witness to this sudden change of heart. 'I cor, love,' he said. 'I know it ain't fair on the poor bugger, but not me.' Anita snorted, such a belittling noise that Hairy Neddy seemed to shrink a couple of inches, and then calmly strolled over to her family pet and raised the rock over his head, taking aim. Hairy Neddy and Sherrie moved together, he got there first, gripping her arms by the elbows and gently lowering them to her sides. The rock fell to the road with a heavy thud, splintering slightly before rolling into the gutter. Anita went as limp as a rag doll and fell heavily against Hairy Neddy, who led her to the back of his three-wheeler, opened the hatchback and settled her in amongst the old newspapers and rolls of electrical flex, coiled thickly like shiny black snakes. He then dragged out an old tartan blanket and carefully wrapped up the now barely breathing dog inside it until nothing showed but the tip of his dull pink snout. He jerked his head at us to follow him, muttering, 'I'm gonna miss me warm-up now. I hate playing be-bop without me finger exercises . . . Must be getting soft.'

As I entered my house, the sound of deep-frying greeted me. I felt each bubble and pop of fat like a mini explosion in my head, under my breastbone, the ends of my fingers and toes. I did not remember walking back from Anita's house, I even felt surprised to see Nanima standing in the doorway of the kitchen with Sunil kicking in her arms. 'You're early!' called mama. 'But sit! You eat first, huh? Did you have a nice ride?'

'Yes, thank you,' I replied automatically as I made my way

to the kitchen table. Each step triggered an image, frozen poses caught in the pop of a flashbulb, the piddly poodle skittering round my heels, his stupid grateful bark, Tracey kissing his soggy snout, the convulsions of his twisted back legs, and how often I had wished him dead. I had blamed him for what he was called, not what he was, had made him the focus of my resentment and hatred, knowing he was in no position but to accept it. Sam Lowbridge and I had that in common at least. I had always felt stupidly connected to him and despite our recent confrontation, I knew that it was not finished yet. Mama placed a plate in front of me; lying across its middle like two exclamation marks were a pair of freshly-fried lamb kebabs. It was not your fault, I told myself, and then decided to add another word to my expanding vocabulary. 'Can I have something . . . vegetarian for lunch?'

10

Deirdre walked out a few days before the start of the big holidays. The six week summer break aged us all like an extra birthday as we matured from third to fourth year, or metamorphosed completely from junior school grubs to the glittering butterflies soon to flit around the nation's hothouses – the senior schools.

Anita, of course, had been a 'comp wench' for a couple of years now. All the comprehensive school girls shared the same indolent walk and bored stare that distinguished them as effectively as a uniform. In fact, I could not imagine Anita as a bouncy junior school pupil; she always seemed older than her peers. But when I spied her sitting alone on the park swings, from a distance, her crumpled face and hunched shoulders turned her momentarily into a little old lady. She was in the standard comprehensive school uniform of shiny green sweater, grey pleated skirt, white blouse, grey and green striped tie and knee-length pristine white socks, but the socks were the only things that vaguely fitted her. The cardigan sleeves had been turned up several times and the skirt rested below her knees, even though she was sitting down, swinging gently to and fro. 'Wow, yow look bosting!' I called out, tumbling down the grassy slope towards her. Anita barely looked at me. At first I thought she was in one of her moods and automatically began racking my brains for what I could have done wrong the last time we met. I had said sorry about her dog dying, hadn't I? But as I got closer, I saw that her eyes were red and crusty, and there were tiny snail trails of moisture and dirt running to her mouth.

'What's up?'

She cracked a hard smile. 'Nothing. Got me third year uniform today.'

I nodded stupidly, thinking it was a good job she had not passed the eleven-plus as I could not imagine her in the girls' grammar school uniform, an all-in-one shapeless blue smock accompanied by a droopy tam-o'-shanter. 'Me mom's gone,' Anita said flatly.

'Oh,' I said. 'Where?'

'Dunno. She left a note, only dad read it. She's gone off with a butcher from Cannock. Dad says she'll feel at home with the other scrag ends and good riddance . . .' I did not know what to say. I knew if mama had run away leaving a note, I would now be rolling around in hysterics tearing my hair, the way they did in the Indian films, and then I would have followed the butcher in a car with darkened windows and stabbed him with his own cleaver while his back was turned, I would have emptied mama's wardrobes and set fire to all her clothes and danced round the flaming saris vowing vengeance. I would not have sat calmly swinging and picking lint off my new school skirt.

'These came this morning,' Anita continued in that same matter-of-fact tone, indicating her outfit. 'She must have ordered them ages ago. She must have known she was going.' Anita plucked at her sleeve hanging from her like a bat's wing. 'And look, silly cow still don't know my size . . .' I thought back to that chance meeting in the entry, when Deirdre was so subdued and secretive, kindly almost, and had given her stamp of approval to my relationship with her daughter. It was her way, I decided, of asking me to look after Anita after she had gone. I then did something I had never done before, swept away by a surge of protective tenderness. I put my arm around Anita and kissed her, whispering, 'Sorry, Nita, I really am.' She pushed me away so violently that I almost fell off the swing.

'Whassup with you?' Anita shouted, wiping her cheek furiously. 'Am yow a lezzie or summat?'

'What's a lezzie?' I asked.

Anita rolled her eyes and sighed, 'Yow don't know nothing, do ya?' I know you won't be getting a bloody pony now, I thought. 'Bet yow don't know what a virgin is neither!' she continued, rattling the swing absent-mindedly.

'Yes, I do!' I said, at least I knew that Jesus' mother was one.

'So am you then?'

'What?' I said suspiciously.

'Am yow a virgin then?' Anita's eyes glittered dangerously; I swallowed a marble of anger, I was supposed to be looking after *her*, I didn't understand how she managed to turn the tables so quickly.

I racked my brains furiously to think of what I and Mary, mother of the King of Kings, might have in common. She was not from England anyhow, that might be a clue, but then she was much older than me. She rode a donkey, she was married – no obvious connections there. I tried to recall how Anita had said 'virgin' – did it sound like something you wanted to become, or a dreadful disease you would be ashamed to have? I took a gamble; Mary did give birth to someone pretty important, therefore virgins could not be all that bad. 'Yeah, I am one actually,' I said confidently.

Anita shrugged. 'Me too,' she said. 'But not for long, eh?' She winked at me and giggled slyly. I laughed back wittily, resolving to ask papa about it when I got home.

Papa dropped the spoon he was holding which fell into his plate of homemade yoghurt with a soft plop. 'What did you say, Meena?' he asked quietly. Something was terribly wrong. Mama held a plate of fresh chapatti in mid-air, her eyebrows had taken refuge somewhere around her hairline, the terrible silence was broken by Sunil's insistent angry shouts, 'Ma-ma-ma-pa!' and Nanima firing off a question to mama who shook her head and looked away mournfully. I told myself to keep calm and play the innocent, it was too late to pretend they had misheard so I repeated the question, 'I said, am I a virgin? I mean, what is one? Of them?' Papa's mouth opened and then shut again slowly, he looked at mama for help. She slammed the plate down onto the table, stuck her hands on her hips and said, 'I suppose you have been talking to that Anita Rutter again! Such filthy things from such a young mouth, *hai ram*! *Thoba thoba*!' Mama did a quick translation for Nanima who immediately held the lobes of her ears to ward off the evil eye and muttered a silent prayer.

'Do you know what you are saying? I hope not!' papa barked at me. He pushed his plate away, spilling some of the yoghurt onto the newspaper upon which he always ate in front of the television. He was showing me the depth of his disgust. I had made him lose his appetite and then mama would drag me into the kitchen and tell me off again for sending my father to bed hungry. 'It doesn't matter,' I mumbled, backing away, but I was stopped by papa grabbing onto my arm. He pulled me towards him and made me stand inches away from his face. He wore a filmy moustache of white which made me want to laugh out loud, and somehow he caught the beginning of the smirk and yanked my arm again to pull me to attention. Even mama sensed that his famous temper was about to erupt and came and stood watchfully at his side, the moral committee could now convene in full.

'I do not like what you have become, Meena,' said papa slowly. 'I have watched you change, from a sweet happy girl into some rude, sulky monster.'

Mama laid her hand on his shoulder but he brushed it off, irritated. 'No, Daljit! You moan about the same things to me and then you let her get away with it the next day!'

'It is not her fault, darling,' mama said placidly. 'We cannot control what she hears on the streets.'

'No,' papa said finally, softening a little. He let go of my arm. I hoped he had left some bruises so I could make him feel guilty after he had cooled down. It was always the same pattern, this fierce outburst and snapping confrontation, followed by repentant cuddles which I made sure I milked to the full. Papa sighed deeply and rubbed his eyes. 'Maybe you'll listen to me now, Daljit. She's not picking up the right influences here. So many good children to play with and she always finds the bad ones. I said we should move . . .'

I did not hear the rest of the sentence, the blood was crashing in my ears and I inhaled sharply, my own breath sounded as loud and furious as a gale. Leaving Tollington was something I had planned on my own terms, in my own fantasies so many times. But not like this, slinking off in semi-disgrace, leaving behind people whom I had yet to outgrow, missing out on all the summers I was still young and free enough to enjoy. How would I ever make new friends? Where would I hang out? How could I possibly recreate this tiny, teeming and intimate world somewhere else? I, who had longed for change and chaos, buckled under this revelation, that if we left, things would never be as good, never be the same. Mama was talking now. I tuned into her monologue gradually. '. . . after the eleven-plus, if all goes well, then we'll just move closer to the girls' school. That would make sense . . .' So they had already decided that I would pass the exam with flying colours, were building their future plans on this dodgy premise.

'Anita's mom has run away,' I said, eager to change the subject. Mama and papa stared at me sharply.

'Meena, if you are lying again . . .'

'She left a note and went off with a butcher. Anita was dead upset, crying and everything. She did not know what she was saying, I reckon . . .' Well, I would have believed it.

Mama sat down heavily on one of the high backed chairs at the table. 'That poor poor girl,' she said softly. 'She did not deserve this . . .'

Papa pulled me, gently now, to his side and enquired, 'Who is looking after her?'

'Them,' interjected mama. 'She has a little sister – Tina?'

'Tracey,' I said, in the tone of a funeral director discussing casket size.

Mama continued, 'I mean, they need to eat, the house needs keeping, the father works, what will happen?' Mama was worrying weeks ahead on their behalf, she was already on her feet. 'I'm going to chat with Mrs Worrall, maybe we can set up some kind of rota . . .'

Papa raised his hand, 'Daljit, no. Sit a minute.'

Mama hesitated. Nanima meanwhile was squirming with curiosity, Punjabi machine-gunned round our heads whilst mama and papa tried to continue the conversation. '*Ik minute, mataji,*' papa reassured her. 'Daljit, we can't interfere . . .'

'Oh my god, that is such an English thing to say! You have been living here too long! There are little children involved.'

'I know that,' papa continued. 'But we are not their family. They would see it as . . . well, rude. Patronising even. If they ask for help, that is a different matter, but we can't just take over the way we do with our friends. Think about it please. They have their pride.'

Mama stood in the doorway, chewing her lip. She suddenly scooped up Sunil and smothered him with passionate kisses whilst he protested loudly. 'You are still my baby, you naughty *munda*! Keep still!'

Nanima was getting annoyed now, and rattled off another loud enquiry to mama who replied back in a suitably scandalised tone. Nanima understood, shook her head and carefully screwed a forefinger into her temple, apeing what I had taught her months back. 'Meena,' papa said, stroking my neck. 'Ask Anita if she wants to come and eat with us. Any time. And her sister. Don't force her though. She might want to spend some time with her daddy right now . . .'

'Can I come tonight?' said Anita when I knocked at her back gate half an hour later. And so it was that the Day of the

New School Uniform also became the Guess Who's Coming to Dinner day.

Anita turned up alone and empty-handed, wearing her new school jumper with a pair of flared jeans. 'Tracey didn't want to come,' was the first thing she said to my parents who stood by the door, as they did for all our visitors, ready to take her coat. 'Oh, that's okay, darling,' said mama, ushering her in and waving at papa to remove one of the place settings from the dining table. I had insisted that we sit at the table, something we never did with Indian guests since we usually ate in shifts. But tonight, I had set the table myself, even putting Sunil's high chair next to mama's place, and told her, 'Don't just run to and from the kitchen burning your fingers like you normally do. I want us to sit and talk, you know, like you're supposed to do at dinners.' I could have asked mama to tap-dance on top of the telly wearing false boobs and playing the spoons and she might have considered it, so anxious was she to mop the brow of our motherless guest.

I knew Anita well enough not to expect a great display of mourning, but even I was surprised by her complete lack of emotion, or indeed, social graces. She watched *Top of the Pops* through all papa's attempts to engage her in friendly chit-chat, during which he steered clear of anything that might possibly be connected with Mothers. 'So Anita . . . um, how's school?' Anita grunted and turned up the volume control, shifting away from Sunil who was edging towards her holding the edge of the sofa, desperate to make friends with this new face. 'Your par. . . your father, does he take you or do you go by bus?' Anita stifled a yawn and reached for another crisp from our nick-nacks bowl, as mama called it, which was now almost empty.

Mama had gone to the trouble of preparing two menus, which was fortunate considering Anita's reaction when the serving dishes of various curries were placed in front of her. 'What's that!' she demanded, as if confronted with a festering sheep's head on a platter. 'Oh that's mattar-paneer,' mama said proudly, always happy to educate the sad English palate. 'A sort of Indian cheese, and these are peas with it, of course . . .'

'Cheese and peas?' said Anita faintly. 'Together?'

'Well,' mama went on hurriedly. 'This is chicken curry . . . You have had chicken before, haven't you?'

'What's that stuff round it?'

'Um, just gravy, you know, tomatoes, onions, garlic . . .' Mama was losing confidence now, she trailed off as she picked up Anita's increasing panic.

'Chicken with tomatoes? What's garlic?'

'Don't you worry!' papa interjected heartily, fearing a culinary cat fight was about to shatter his fragile peace. 'We've also got fishfingers and chips. Is tomato sauce too dangerous for you?'

Anita's relief made her oblivious to his attempt at a joke. She simply picked up her knife and fork and rested her elbows on the table, waiting to be served with something she could recognise. 'I'll have fishfingers, mum! Um, please!' I called out after her. I could tell from the set of mama's back that her charity was wearing a little thin. Although I had yet to cast Anita in the mould of one of the Rainbow orphan kids, I did wonder if food was a problem at her house after seeing her eat. Any romantic idea I had about witty stories over the dinner table disappeared when Anita made a fortress of her arms and chewed stolidly behind it, daring anyone to approach and disturb her concentration or risk losing an eye if they attempted to steal a chip. She looked up only twice, once when my parents began eating, as always, with their fingers, using their chapatti as scoops to ferry the banquet of curries into their mouths.

Anita stopped in mid-chew, looking from her knife and fork to mama and papa's fingers with faint disgust, apparently unaware that all of us had a great view of a lump of half masticated fishfinger sitting on her tongue. It had never occurred to me that this would be a moment of controversy, it had never occurred to me because I had never eaten Indian food in the presence of a white person before. In fact, I only then realised that Anita Rutter was the first non-relative to sit and break bread with us, and the same thought had just hit my parents, who had gradually slowed down their eating and were eyeing a nearby box of paper hankies with longing. I snapped to attention, I would not have Anita play the same games with my parents that had made me dizzy and confused. The girl had not even said a simple thank you yet. 'We always eat our food with our fingers,' I said loudly to Anita. 'Like in all the top restaurants. Bet you didn't know that, did you?' For the first time that I could remember, my parents caught a lie flying out of my mouth and threw it right back at me with a cheer. Mama and papa both looked at their plates, their mouths twitching, until Sunil broke the moment by emptying his plate of rice over his head. Nanima lumbered into action with the box of tissues, pushing past Anita clumsily and leaning over her to reach Sunil with no regard to English body language rules.

In fact, whilst my parents did their dance of welcome around Anita all evening, my Nanima remained singularly uninvolved and unimpressed. She stood in front of the television, apparently unaware of Anita's sighs and craning neck, she slumped next to her on the settee, making Anita sink into the cushions, and gradually edged towards her until she gave up and moved to the floor, allowing Nanima to lie at full stretch, massaging her feet which she occasionally waved under Anita's nose, making her jump and hold her breath. I only began to suspect her exaggerated old lady behaviour was perhaps deliberate when she made Anita look up for the second time from her food, by letting fly the longest, loudest burp I had ever had the privilege to witness. I swear Anita's blonde bangs flew up in protest against the velocity, and even mama uttered an involuntary '*Hai Ram*, mama!'

Anita looked like she was waiting for an apology, so papa hurriedly chipped in with 'We often take a good burp as a sign of a good meal, Anita. Also, you know old ladies are a bit freer with their . . . um . . . expressions. Does your granny suffer in this manner?'

Anita thought for a moment and said carefully, 'Me dad's mom died ages ago. Mom's mom used to leave her toenail clippings in our plant pots though.'

I sighed with relief, now we were equal, and just to prove it, Anita finished her last chip, steeled herself and finally did thank my parents with a window-shattering belch. Mama did not bat an eyelid. 'My pleasure, darling,' she replied.

By the end of the meal, it was obvious to me that Nanima had not taken to my best friend. She talked over Anita to my parents in loud Punjabi. I recognised one or two phrases which were usually applied to me when I'd done something wrong, and Anita soon picked this up. 'Is she talking about me?' she whispered fiercely.

'Who's She?' I spat back. 'The cat's mother?'

'No, your gran,' she continued. 'What's she on about?'

'Oh, just saying how nice it is to meet one of my mates,' I said, fairly confident this was one porkie I could get away with. But Nanima's glowering looks and the way she wiped around where Anita sat with a wet cloth, made me feel we should perhaps move somewhere else, especially when I remembered that she might have a Kirpan concealed about her person, but it was now far too dark to go out and where else was there?

'Let's go up to your room!' nudged Anita.

'Okay, I'll ask . . . tell me mom,' I replied, hoping mama would say NO loudly. I desperately did not want Anita to see my room. I had seen hers, a teenage den of old laddered tights, make-up, posters of pop stars, locked diaries, all of which she had lost the keys to, even a few records, in other words, a proper girlie hang-out with all necessary accessories. My bedroom, on the other hand, was a place to sleep, bereft of fripperies such as cosmetics (not allowed, tarty), posters (not allowed, plaster hazard), records (only had one, a single of 'Chim Chim Cheree' from *Mary Poppins* which came free with a pound of Stork margarine) and worst still, I shared it with my baby brother and my old gran.

Unfortunately, mama said yes, and I found myself leading Anita up the dark winding stairs, trying to think of excuses for my lack of taste. I could tell she was disappointed when she saw there was no lock on the door, and cast a critical eye over the functional dressing table and the stacks of *Treasure* comics I had preserved in a pile near the huge double bed. But Anita's boredom turned to amazement when she flung open my wardrobe door and found my entire collection of Indian suits. 'Bosting clothes, Meena!' she shouted, immediately pulling the suits and scarves off their hangers, as silks and satins and cottons of deep purple and sea green and saffron yellow and cinnamon brown unfurled a world of possibilities before her. 'Oh I love this one!' she said, shaking out a cerise *salwar kameez* with gold embroidery at the cuffs. 'All you have to do is cut this bit off, it'd make a fab mini-dress!' She really liked the *dupattas*, the long flowing scarves which accompanied every suit, a supposed veil of modesty which you had to drape over your bust but which I had discovered made excellent slingshots or in an emergency, skipping ropes, also.

'Look at these! I mean, they'm miles better than Fat Sally's poxy Biba scarves . . . How come yow never wear these then?'

'Oh I do,' I told her. 'I mean I ain't gonna wear them to ride a horse, am I? I just wear them for special occasions . . .'

'Oh, and we're not special enough, is that it?' she remarked, draping at least ten of them around her head and shoulders, holding them up to the light, making them sparkle and breathe – she looked as if she was wearing a constellation of stars as a hat. For the next few hours, we tried every suit and *dupatta* on, posing in front of the fly-blown bevelled mirror, practising our catwalk style, giving each other marks out of ten for poise, charm and sexiness. The bold colours that suited me, often drained her face completely, yet the pastels that made me look sallow and old, lit up her skin and threw her features into defined relief. There were at least ten suits she recommended that I should never wear again, and as I had no further use for them, it seemed natural to give them to her.

We would have got away with it had it not been for mama's social graces. Anita was wearing my old green duffle coat, ('. . . cos she'll get cold on the way home, mama.') and came down the stairs carefully, planning to make a quick exit through the back door. But mama was waiting at the foot of the steps with her arms outstretched. She clasped Anita quickly to her and said, 'It has been lovely to have you here, Anita. Do come again soon . . .' Anita's shock at finding herself in another mother's bear hug must have broken her concentration. She opened her mouth to say something but nothing came out, just a sort of feeble croak which, for some reason, moved mama so much that she hugged her again and that's when all ten suits, carefully rolled up, came tumbling from beneath Anita's coat. I was as surprised as mama was, because accompanying them were a bundle of my *Treasure* magazines, my Chim Chim Cheree single, a silver choker I thought I had lost last year and, unaccountably, a pair of my blue wool netball socks, none of which I had included in the official booty.

'I was borrowing them,' said Anita quickly. 'Meena said I could!'

'Well, Meena should have asked me first then,' said mama, a hint of flint in her tone. 'Could you put them back please? Except the magazines which you may borrow for a while.' Mama had on her infants' teacher's voice, pleasant enough with no room for argument. This was not a good move as Anita reacted to the slightest sniff of authority with mindless violence. Anita glared at mama and stamped her foot hard. 'Now, Anita!' mama said, incredibly. I closed my eyes and waited for this Clash of the Titans that I had been torturing myself with since the day I met Anita. When I opened my eyes, Anita had gone, and emerged a moment later down the stairs again, clutching a single *Treasure* magazine. 'I'll have this then,' she said moodily.

'Of course, darling. See you soon . . .' Anita had already gone, I heard the back door slam defiantly. 'Well Meena,' mama said, turning to me. 'That was fun.'

'Can we ask Anita to come again,' I asked.

'Um, of course,' mama replied carefully. 'But let Anita call you over to her house first. That's how we do it with your Aunties, take it in turns so everyone is treated fairly. Yes?' I thought this was a good idea and dropped several hints over the next few days about the kind of food I liked, none of which Anita ever picked up.

11

If I had known what was going to happen in my tenth summer, if the Mysterious Stranger had forewarned me that my childhood would begin ebbing away with the fall of the autumn leaves, I could have prepared myself better. I would have taken photographs, pressed significant trophies in a scrapbook, been kinder to some people and harder on others, I would have kept a diary. Instead, I treated time with my usual jaunty contempt and let the days drift by unmarked, content to bob aimlessly along in the current, not bothering to appreciate the landscape because I assumed it would always be there.

But for a while, that summer was idyllic and papa was the first to be blessed, coming home late one evening singing loudly to himself and carrying a bag of sweets in one hand and a bottle of perfume in the other. Mama seemed to know that he would be delayed, and had primped and fussed over the meal and the house, tidying and arranging furiously like a VIP was coming to visit. As papa entered, mama rushed to him and flung her arms around his shoulders, which made Nanima snort and shade her face with her *dupatta*. They had a brief tender exchange in Punjabi and then papa handed round his goodies, the French perfume for mama of course, I think the sweets were meant for me and Sunil but Nanima grabbed the bag and hoovered up half the contents before I could stop her. 'Your papa has just got a promotion,' mama beamed proudly. 'What's that?' I mumbled through a handful of jelly babies I'd managed to salvage, just missing losing a finger to Nanima's chomping jaws. I looked up at papa who had slightly deflated faced with this question, and then it struck me that I still did not know what exactly my father did for a living.

The nearest contact I had ever had with papa's place of work had been five years ago, when mama had bundled me up in my best red woollen coat one frosty morning and told me excitedly, 'Now you are five, you can go to your papa's party!' I felt extremely proud that my father was so powerful and popular that a party was being held in his honour as we pulled up outside a Victorian swimming baths on the outskirts of Wolverhampton where several other similarly swaddled children were being hauled out of cars by twittering, fussing parents. 'Is it a swimming party, papa?' I asked as we negotiated the wide stone steps to the entrance whose festive decorations stretched to an anaemic strand of tinsel and two pinched balloons.

'No, beti,' papa smiled. 'This is a Father Christmas party. You want to meet Father Christmas, don't you?'

'I thought this was your party!' I wailed. 'Mama said it was!'

'Your mama,' said papa, tight-lipped, 'says too much sometimes.'

I had expected a welcoming committee of some sort; a row of men in suits clapping papa as he brought me in to show me off, streamers falling from the ceiling, a big chocolate cake with sparklers fizzing on top and letters in white icing which said, 'MR KUMAR! THE WORLD'S BEST BOSS!' But instead, I found myself in a huge draughty hall, standing in a long queue of moaning children which led up to a bare stage upon which I could just make out a fat white man in a bad false beard. Through the planks beneath my feet I detected movement, glimpsed the rise and fall of a smooth black skin, and only then I realised we were standing above the covered swimming pool. I reached out for papa, who was talking to a man in front of us. 'So Bill,' papa said matily. 'Looking forward to the break, eh?'

'Oy ay, Mr K,' said Bill, who was squat and short, and had carefully brylcremed his few remaining strands of hair into an interesting thatch pattern over his pink shiny dome. 'Cor wait, two days away from that bloody place ain't long enough though, know wharr-I-mean? Mind you, I do bloody rivets in me sleep, me missus says . . .'

Papa smiled faintly. 'My wife says I do long division in mine. What can you do?'

Bill grunted companionably and glanced down at his daughter who had not stopped staring at me during this exchange. She looked like one of those porcelain dolls I had seen in Beatties in Wolverhampton and longed to own, all blonde ringlets and peachy smooth skin. She had on a curiously old-fashioned coat with a high velvet collar and complicated fabric buttons, but what really impressed me was her hat. It was not like the hats mama forced onto me, functional suffocating contraptions which continually moulted fine fluff and made me sneeze. This was a hat to be looked at, a bonnet with bows and ribbon ties which sat on top of the glossy curls at a self-satisfied angle, useless in a Tollington gale and proud of it. The little girl slowly extended one chubby pink finger and stroked the only inch of flesh I had exposed, where my glove did not quite meet my sleeve. Maybe it was the sense of ownership with which she touched me, maybe it was the regret and resignation in papa's voice when he talked about his work to Bill, but when she extended her forefinger for the second time, as I knew she would, I bit it as hard as I could.

Papa shouted at me, he kept asking me Why? Why? to which I simply answered Because Because. By the time we finally trudged up onto the stage to meet Father Christmas, I was in no mood for social chit-chat. 'So, chick, what would yow like for Christmas then?' I shrank back under the acrid gale of Santa's bad breath; his forehead was shiny with perspiration and his beard, which was flecked with ash, had slipped slightly to one side so he appeared to have half a mouth. 'I wanna bike,' I said sullenly, edging away from his embrace. 'Well, if yow'm a good wench, yow get one, but for now, have this,' he said quickly, reaching into a big bag at his side and handing me a present which was the same shape and wrapped in the same paper as the one given to the blonde girl before me. I had unwrapped it before I got to the end of the stage. It was something called Little Misses Beautiful Hands, which comprised a cardboard sheet wrapped in cellophane upon which rested a fake bottle of nail varnish and ten rubber fingertips all topped with perfectly manicured, tapered nails. I did not try them on until I was sitting in the car where I held up my hands to the window. I looked as if I had been the victim of some awful mad doctor's experiment, holding up ten brown fingers topped with pink, latex skin and bright red talons. 'I hate my present!' I cried as I threw them out of the window. 'I hate your party, papa!' But papa was not angry with me, surprisingly. And when he asked me the following year if I wanted to go to his office party and I declined, he never got angry then either.

The memory of this filled me with a sudden surge of affection and I said through a mouthful of jelly babies, 'Promotion is dead good, isn't it, papa? What do you get for it?'

'Well, it means more money, a bigger office . . .' mama butted in quickly.

'Are we going to be rich then? Can I have a pony?'

'Hah!' said mama. 'We will never be rich, Meena, we're too honest. But we will always have enough to buy all the important things, food, heat, a car . . .'

I began to switch off. I did not want mama to remind me of all the things we had for which I had to be eternally vigilant and grateful, I wanted us to have enough money so that we could be selfish, ungrateful, and spoil ourselves shamelessly without having to do rapid sums in our heads as if we were permanently queueing at some huge check-out till.

But papa cut her off mid-flow. 'Of course we will have some

fun with the money, that's what it's for, eh?' Mama pursed her lips and sighed inwardly. 'What shall we get first, Meena?' he continued. 'A bathroom, or a trip to India?'

'India! India!' I shouted, jumping around him madly as Sunil waggled his head in imitation.

Mama grinned in spite of herself. I knew she must have been as thrilled as I was, I knew that my parents had not been back there since before I was born, that was obviously a lifetime and a half to me. 'But when, Shyam?' mama said. 'I mean, the holidays have started already. I only have one week half-term, then three weeks at Christmas . . .'

'Christmas,' decided papa emphatically. 'We will take Nanima home ourselves.' I felt strange that he used that word 'home' so naturally, did that mean that everything surrounding us was merely our temporary lodgings? But this note of disquiet melted into the symphony of anticipatory joy we all felt now, and we recalled the tune and hummed it to ourselves secretly for the rest of the holidays.

Sunil was the next beneficiary of this seasonal good fortune. A few days after papa's promotion, Sunil was left on his own in the back yard, whilst mama, Nanima and I pottered amiably around the house. Mama often plonked him out in the sunshine with some toys, having swept and cleared the yard of small foreign bodies and dirt, locked the back gate and alerted Mrs Worrall to his presence, leaving Sunil to crawl about in his own private playpen, his knees gathering moss and dandelions on the way. At first we thought the noises were coming from some kids passing through the entry, or maybe from the Mad Mitchells' radio which was always tuned to the World Service and left at full volume on their kitchen window sill. But then Nanima came and fetched mama and me, her finger on her lips, and we all crept onto the back step and marvelled. Sunil was focused on a large spider which was sitting in the middle of its web hung between the drainpipe and the wall, shiny and flat as a button. He had a handful of grass in each fist which he offered to his confidant as a gift, chattering all the time. 'Pider . . . eat . . . good . . . aja . . . chaat! . . . Na-mi-naa . . . papa . . . mama . . . Meen-ee . . .'

Mama clutched my arm, her eyes welling foolishly. My brother was not even a year old. 'Now tell me my son is stupid, you bloody doctor-saab!' mama whispered intently to herself.

I was most impressed that Sunil was a bilingual baby and suffered a few pangs of regret that Nanima had not been around when I was learning to talk. After we had fussed and cooed over Sunil and telephoned papa with the good news, I caught Nanima creeping round my now sleeping brother with a woolly black thread dangling from her fingers.

'What . . .'

Nanima shushed me and carefully lifted Sunil's wrist and tied the thread around it, murmuring a *Wahe Guru* for good measure. It was almost lost in the bracelets of plump rolls, and glistened in between them like a knowing, slitty eye. I decided that this must be another of Nanima's spells and trusted her brand of magic too much to question her further. But mama noticed it the next morning when she bathed him and said, 'Mama! *Tusi e Kala Dhaga Paya Si?*' Nanima harrumphed a 'yes' and mama rolled her eyes.

'What?' I pestered her.

'Oh, these silly habits!' mama sighed. 'People think if your child is too beautiful or clever and gets praised too much, this thread protects you from the evil eye. Something on the body to make it less than perfect, you see? I never knew your Nanima was so superstitious . . .'

But I noticed she did not take it off, and later on, feeling mortified at my own vanity, I raided mama's needlework basket and tied some black cotton around my own wrist, as no-one else seemed to think I needed one.

Mama and Nanima were also blessed with good influences, and rolled the long summer into a ball which they tossed between them lazily, going on outings nearly every day to the shops, the gurduwara, friends' houses, wherever their whimsy led them, leaving me, I was overjoyed to discover, to entertain myself. The first time the two of them set out in the Mini on a major expedition to Wednesfield, my heart skipped a beat, seeing my poor unsuspecting Nanima squeeze herself into her seat, unaware of the ordeal she was about to suffer as a passenger in mama's car. I comforted myself with the thought that mama never went above the average speed of a bullock cart and Nanima might actually enjoy getting a long careful look at the stunning industrial scenery. However, when they returned some five hours later, it was mama who was flustered and fatigued whilst Nanima fairly skipped out of the car, her trousers barely creased by the ordeal. 'Your Nanima is a very naughty lady,' said mama breathlessly. 'Always telling me to go faster . . .' Nanima rattled off a rapid Punjabi reply which I thought mentioned 'angry people' and 'big hill', and then repeated the new phrase she had picked up today, I feared, through constant repetition through a side window. 'Bloody women drivers!' she said.

As for me, the summer had never seemed so deliciously long, so wonderfully hot, so blissfully carefree. I spent practically every day at Sherrie's farm with Anita, and Tracey when Anita was in a good enough mood to let her attend, and learned how to groom Trixie, what tacking meant, how many 'hands' she was, where her withers were, why you had to stand up in the saddle when she stopped for one of her gushing steaming pees, and how to call her from the other side of the paddock with a soft sibilant whistle. In fact, I did everything for that horse except ride her; I don't know why I had suddenly got cold feet, maybe it was a lingering memory from the last time I had got as far as the stirrups, just at the moment when the piddly poodle had met his messy end. But I was in no hurry to force myself into the saddle, I was quite content to watch Sherrie and Anita trot, canter, jump and gallop their tensions away. I could not even feel jealous of Anita; my contentment had made me benevolent, and so poetic was she on a horse, watching her was almost an act of worship. I don't remember us quarrelling at all that summer, in fact we hardly talked at all, preferring to share a companionable silence as we raked hay or attended to Trixie or simply lay on our backs, chewing grass stalks and watching the larks perform their scimitar swoops of joy.

I had expected Anita to undergo some sort of emotional crisis since Deirdre's departure but she remained as brassy and belligerent as ever, somehow managing to delegate her trauma workload to her little sister, Tracey. Whilst Anita grew taller, browner and louder, Tracey became shrunken, hollow-eyed and silent, seeming less like a sibling and more like a fleeting shadow attached to Anita's snapping heels. Whilst Anita took any opportunity to be out of her house – she'd been spotted eating toast on the swings as early as half past seven in the morning – Tracey began to prefer alcoves, entries and staying inside whenever her father was home. Her body clock adjusted to Roberto's timetable, she would only venture outside after she had seen him onto the bus with the Ballbearings Women, and would suddenly excuse herself from whatever we were doing when it was time for him to return from work. She did not need to use a watch, she sniffed the air or checked the position of the sun and would march off without as much as a 'see ya!', duty and instinct pulling her home.

I had assumed that Tracey and I had established some tentative bond, recalling how she sobbed into my shoulder in the back of Hairy Neddy's van when we drove home after the farm incident. But she shyed away at my jolly attempts at conversation, and my offers to let her hold Trixie's reins when I groomed her. Whilst I was a happy spectator, secure in my role as Trixie's beautician, Tracey never enjoyed her sideline vigil. She stood apart from us resentfully, a silent, wet blanket ready to douse our flames, her eyes never leaving Anita's sun-kissed, fiery face.

Everything started falling apart the day mama discovered that her diamond necklace was missing. She and Nanima had decided to spend a day clearing out the bulky suitcases that had sat on top of her bedroom wardrobes for as long as I could remember. I had always assumed this was some kind of ancient Punjabi custom, this need to display several dusty, bulging cases overflowing with old Indian suits, photographs and yellowing official papers, as all my Uncles and Aunties' wardrobes were similarly crowned with this impressive array of luggage. Once, after I had heard papa and the Uncles getting very angry over someone they referred to as 'That Powell Bastard with his bloody rivers' and had added, 'If he wants to send us back, let him come and damn well try!' I had asked mama if the cases were ready and packed in case we had to escape back to India at short notice. She had got very upset, not with me but with papa whom she took to one side and hissed at. 'You should not discuss all this politics-sholitics business in front of her,' and then sat me down and explained, 'We just keep all the things in the cases that do not fit into these small English wardrobes, that is all.' However, I had noticed that everything in those cases had something to do with India, the clothes, the albums, the letters from various cousins, and wondered why they were kept apart from the rest of the household jumble, allotted their own place and prominence, the nearest thing in our house that we had to a shrine.

But it was only when mama had been through all the suitcases that she realised what she had assumed was missing, was in fact lost. When she asked me if I had seen her diamond necklace, '. . . the one your Nanima gave to me when I got married . . .', all I could do was shake my head dumbly. Out of all the bad, mad things I had done, losing mama's necklace had been the worst, and the one I had dwelt on the least. I could handle being a thief, a liar, even a ruthless exploiter of my timid female cousins, for in all these scenarios, I had little sympathy for the victims of my crimes, but losing something that meant so much to mama, which I knew I would never be able to replace, cut me deeply. 'You don't think . . .' Mama was slowly sifting through a snake's nest of necklaces spread before her on her bed. 'You don't think . . . that night Anita was here . . .'

'No!' I answered, a little too quickly. 'She wouldn't do that.'

'She tried stealing almost everything else in your bedroom,' mama said softly, and then sighing said, 'No. I am being unfair. She is a naughty girl, but not a wicked one. So it's gone. *Bas.*' *Bas.* The Punjabi word for finished, over, the end. Mama said something to Nanima who shrugged her shoulders resignedly, and then fixed me with a baleful stare. Nanima is a witch, I reminded myself, She knows. She knows.

So it did not surprise me when the room began vibrating. Nanima is growling, I thought to myself, now she will grow until her head crashes through the roof, pick me up in a fist the size of a cow and shake the truth out of me until it hurts. But Nanima was looking beyond me, through the bedroom window at the sky. Now we could all hear it, a far-off rumble, as distant and rolling as thunder, but unbroken, and getting louder. We were expecting to see heaving grey clouds heralding the start of another sudden summer storm. But all we saw was the clear blue canopy above us, suddenly filled with the flapping of hundreds of starlings who had taken hurried flight from the woods round the Big House. The Big House, in whose grounds somewhere, a diamond necklace adorned the feet of a pot-bellied god with an elephant's smiling face.

The grumbling sound seemed to come closer. Mama rushed to the window with Nanima following, scooping up a dozing Sunil from the bed on her way and gasped, 'My god . . . what's happening?'

Nanima sniffed the air unconsciously, then muttered a silent '*Wahe Guru!*' to herself as they appeared over the crest of the hill, the yellow motorway diggers as shiny and solid as tanks, a whole convoy of them whose caterpillar tyres seemed to chew up the road and spit it back out as they ate their way towards the centre of the village. 'The school!' mama breathed and I pushed past her and rushed downstairs.

In less than a minute, it seemed the whole village had

congregated on street corners, in gardens, hanging from windows and leaning on doorposts, to watch this unannounced metallic invasion. Everyone knew where the diggers were headed and there was no welcoming committee, just this awful silent resignation marked by folded arms and closed-off faces. Mr Topsy/Turvey spat on the pavement as the diggers rumbled past his gate. One old woman whom I rarely saw out and about, who was so ancient she looked like a pickled walnut with a white mop on her head, clapped and waved at the machines with great excitement. 'Go on our boys!' she shouted, and began a reedy warble of 'It's a Long Way to Tipperary!' 'She thinks it's the army, poor old biddy . . .' said the Ballbearings women to each other. 'Still stuck in the war. Her old man never came back, you know . . .'

Then another note joined the mechanical symphony, a buzzing staccato which counterpointed the diggers' ponderous bass, and Sam Lowbridge's moped gang phut-phutted into view, accelerating until they caught up with the diggers, weaving in and out of them like lazy horseflies, making the faceless drivers in their cabs shake their fists and mouth voiceless obscenities. Some of the villagers began cheering this showy sabotage, Mr Topsy/Turvey shouted, 'Goo on, lads! Make em crash!' Others, like Glenys, Sam's mother, and some of the Ballbearings women, tutted and looked away in shame, unsure which of these two evils they ought to boycott. Then Anita was jumping and yelling herself hoarse next to me. 'Kill em, lads! Put the boot in!' And then halted momentarily and whispered to me, 'Where's Sam?' I had been thinking the same thing; I recognised all of the other shaven heads, Craig and Baz and the ferret-faced one with the earring, but where was their leader?

As if in response, an exhaust backfired spectacularly as Sam rode into view. He had souped up his moped with extra wing mirrors and Union Jack stickers, and had cut off the end of the exhaust pipe so it looked like a sawn-off shotgun and made an ear-splitting angry honk every time he accelerated. Anita had given up on the cheerleading, instead she was completely focused on the girl sitting on the back of Sam's moped, the girl who had her arms firmly around his waist. I did not recognise her, she looked too groomed and posh to be from one of the surrounding villages, with her shiny auburn hair and pink pouty lips and skin-tight tailored jeans. However, she had obviously picked up some tips on local customs as she continually blew huge chewing gum bubbles which burst in sticky pops onto her face, and which she licked off with a pointed agile tongue. 'Who's the tart?' enquired Anita.

I shrugged. 'Dunno. Don't care neither.'

'Come on!' said Anita, shoving past me. 'Let's go and see what's happening.'

I shouted an explanation to mama who shouted back that I was to 'keep right away from the machinery and stand by a grown-up!' and joined the growing throng of curious villagers trudging down the hill.

The tiny redbrick school building, still with its former pupils' drawings taped unevenly to some of its windows, had been cordoned off by a barrier of white tape. There were quite a few bystanders, not just from Tollington, lots of mothers with prams and toddlers, some openly upset with hankies at the ready. There was a sprinkling of men also, some I recognised as the unemployed husbands of the Ballbearings women, who seemed to be unused to the bright sunlight and blinked rapidly like creatures emerging from hibernation.

And then I saw the television camera, a bulky awkward contraption on its unsteady tripod legs, which stood next to a van with BBC OB written on the side. 'Look!' I nudged Anita. 'That's Gary Skip from the telly!' Gary Skip was one of the reporters on *Midlands Today*, our BBC regional news programme. He was wearing a smart sky blue suit with huge lapels and a high-collared shirt, open at the neck.

'Ooh, he's dead short. He looks bigger on the telly,' whispered Anita.

'That's probably why he's wearing platforms,' I whispered back, noting his heavily stacked cowboy boots which were already caked with grey-green mud. Gary was lighting a cigarette and offered one to someone I presumed was his cameraman, who declined and busied himself with checking his tripod and donning a pair of earphones.

Then I did a double take; behind the white tape stood several burly workmen in donkey jackets and bright yellow hard hats; their foreman, a stocky jolly man, was deep in conversation with a bespectacled bank manager type in a suit, who was holding a clipboard. And he was Indian. He looked a little like my Uncle Amman, the same stooped body, slightly hooked nose, but much more hair, a surprisingly luxuriant quiff which was too rock and roll to be matched with a three-piece suit. There was a moment when he looked up and seemingly straight at me, although I could not be sure as his spectacles caught the sun and turned his eyes into fiery balls. But there was a sniff of recognition, a curious acknowledgement of passing strangers who might have once been friends.

I turned round to tell Anita, but she had gone. I scanned the crowd quickly and spotted her picking her way across the mud towards Sam Lowbridge and his gang, who were all parked on a nearby street corner and making themselves comfortable on someone's garden wall. 'Nita!' I shouted over the rumble of the diggers. 'Come here!' I was furious; she knew how I felt about Sam, hadn't he been the cause of our first and only falling out? If Anita had heard me, she did not care, for she was already holding a semi-shouted exchange with Sam. But he heard me alright; he looked up towards my voice and I just caught the beginning of a broad smile when I jerked my head away. I had not looked at him properly, I had still kept my promise.

Sam was calling me now. 'Meena! Ay, Meena! Over here!' A few of the mothers stared at me, unimpressed. I did not want them to think I had anything to do with the gang so I moved further away, closer to where Gary Skip was lining himself up in front of the camera lens, adjusting his fringe in its round unblinking eye. 'Ready, John?' he called to the cameraman who was now looking through an eyepiece, his brow furrowed in concentration, and gave him a thumbs up. 'I'll do me opening piece and then we'll cut to the building being crushed or whatever. Get some weeping women if you can, yeah?'

The Indian Bank Manager was leaving. He passed Gary Skip with a polite nod and began walking down the narrow leafy lane which ran down the side of the school. I wondered where he was going, and then remembered the bus stop about half a mile down that road where the fast double-deckers to Wolverhampton stopped. Why didn't he have a car when he owned a suit? I did not like the idea of him sitting on a manky bus seat, getting discarded bubble gum on his pristine trousers. If papa had been with me, he would have gone up and asked him his name, where he was from in India, thrown out acquaintances they might possibly have in common. I had seen papa do this with many Indian passers-by on the street. But I did not have the language or the courage to carry on this ritual, so I let the Bank Manager go.

Sam and his gang paused their shoving and horseplay for a moment whilst they watched the Bank Manager turn the corner and disappear from view. Something caught in my throat, a dust mote, an insect maybe, for a second I could not swallow. And then I jumped as the diggers' engines started up with a muffled roar and the onlookers herded together instinctively, pulling their children closer to them, hunching their shoulders against the increasing decibels of noise. Gary nodded to the cameraman and began talking to the lens, muffling himself up exaggeratedly against the bellowing machines. He paused as Sam's gang started up their mopeds. Their noise was a mere annoying buzz against the roar of the diggers, and he shot them a hard warning glance. 'You get in the way lads, and I'm not going to be a happy bunny, okay? In three, John . . . three, two . . . I'm standing here in the little village of Tollington, a picturesque former mining village which today, becomes another victim of the local authority's drive towards streamlined education . . .' He paused dramatically as the diggers began rolling forward, their huge shovelling arms raised in a mock farewell salute. Gary quickly stepped sideways, knowing the camera would follow him and capture the drama unfolding behind him. He raised his voice, his tone urgent and alert, '. . . And as I speak the machinery is moving in to raze the Primrose Primary School to the ground, a school that has been standing in this lovely spot for nearly a hundred years . . . for many of the local parents, who have been waging a ten-year campaign against the closure, who now have to send their children to another school some nine miles away, this is a sad, if inevitable day . . .'

His words were obscured by a gigantic crunching thud as the first digger made contact with the school and a whole wing crumbled in slow motion to the ground, throwing up mushroom clouds of grainy red dust. At precisely the same moment, the sound of revving moped engines seemed to encircle us, it was impossible to tell through the haze and flying stones where it was coming from, and suddenly, emerging through a dustcloud like a divine apparition, albeit on a scooter, Sam Lowbridge rode roughshod over rubble and mudslides, skidding and screeching and sounding his horn. He drove right at Gary Skip, making him leap for cover, then manoeuvred close up to the camera lens and yelled, 'If You Want A Nigger For A Neighbour, Vote Labour!' before hurtling away, the rest of his gang in his wake like midges following a storm.

Afterwards, I could not find Anita anywhere and felt too tired and dispirited to bother to call at her house. Sam's words remained with me, I felt as if I had been spat at, that there were gobs of bile hanging off my cheeks, the ends of my hair, and I had to be on my own to wipe myself clean. I made my way to the abandoned pigsty from where Anita and I had once commanded a makeshift gang, which we had gradually abandoned as we formed a mutual admiration society with only two members, ourselves. There were still remnants of our little empire, a few mouldering copies of *Jackie* in the corner, a pile of empty Coke bottles, the old tartan blanket which when shifted, sent silverfish shimmying into corners like mercury.

The television news was just finishing when I finally arrived home. Nanima was feeding Sunil a bowl of rice, sugar and milk as he played with her *Kara*, making satisfied sucking noises, whilst mama and papa sat on the settee, absentmindedly playing with each other's fingers.

'It was on the news, what happened to the school,' mama said without taking her eyes off the screen.

'What? What was?' I said, ready for the onslaught of insults about Sam Lowbridge and the general standard of low life that I insisted on hanging around with in the Yard.

'The diggers, you know, just a few seconds it was . . .' Mama trailed off, and I took the opportunity to slink away to my room.

I sat on my window sill for a long time, watching the sun set as it always did, over the roof of the Big House. My favourite part was when the sun dipped behind the old pithead and became a rosy disc imprisoned briefly in a gilded cage before it sank thankfully into the horizon. I needed someone to talk to, I needed to talk about Sam. Anita, being my best friend, should have been with me. But I knew, as I thought this, that she would not have understood that there were some things that we would never be able to share. I climbed into bed and for the first time in years, said a prayer. I told God I was sorry for blaming Pinky and Baby for stealing Mr Ormerod's tin and I wished fervently that they were lying next to me in their matching pyjamas and co-ordinated bed socks, listening to me telling them about Sam, because I knew that they would understand.

The next morning, the cracks appeared which would finally

split open the china blue bowl of that last summer. They began when papa read out a report from our local paper to mama over breakfast. It was tucked away on page eight, under the headline MAN ATTACKED IN TOLLINGTON. 'The victim, a Mr Rajesh Bhatra from Tettenhall was found in a ditch on the side of the Wulfrun Road. He was suffering from head injuries and broken ribs and had been robbed of his suitcase and wallet. Mr Bhatra cannot recall anything about the assault and is presently in a stable condition in Tettenhall Hospital.'

For a while there was silence in the kitchen, save for the sizzling of a *parantha* on the griddle and Sunil's stage slurps as he downed the last drops of milk from his bottle. Nanima asked for a translation, but papa shook his head and told her, '*Kuchh Nahin hai Byi, Kuchh Nahin Kas.*' Nothing special, papa said. But mama, papa and I knew just how special this was – we betrayed ourselves in the way we avoided each other's eyes. This was too close to home, and for the first time, I wondered if Tollington would ever truly be home again.

It all started because of Anita's new bra. We were sitting in the stable whilst Trixie chewed at a bag of oats – she actually preferred the bag to its contents – and all four of us lounged on the musty hay sharing crisps and a big bottle of Creme Soda. Anita lay back languorously, bubbles still fizzing on her lips, and as she went down, her chest seem to rise up and say hello.

'Nita!' shrieked Sherrie. 'Yow'm not!'

Anita smirked and slowly, slowly, rolled up her T-shirt to reveal a contraption that resembled two paper doilies strung on an elastic band, and beneath them, two barely discernible poached eggs.

'Ooh, fab!' sighed Sherrie. 'What size am yow?'

'Thirty A,' said Anita airily.

'Oh, I'm thirty-one B,' sniffed Sherrie, whilst Tracey and I exchanged peeved looks, annoyed that they were now exclud-ing us by using these technical terms.

'I went down to Larsons on me own and just bought it. I woz fed up of em flying in my face when I'm riding Trixie,' said Anita.

'Oh I get chafing me, after a day's riding,' said Sherrie. 'I probably need a bigger size.'

Now I knew they were simply showing off and I flipped away from them, lying on my front in case they started asking me breast-related questions which I knew I was not qualified to answer. 'I love them cups,' said Sherrie, leaning over Anita for a better look. 'Am they poly-cotton or nylon?' and she fingered one of the straps curiously. Tracey jumped forward and slapped Sherrie's hand away, the thwack made Trixie start a little and shift in her stall. Sherrie was holding her hand to her stomach, too astounded to speak.

Anita shouted, 'What yow do that for, yow silly cow?'

Tracey's voice was so intense, so vindictive, it made my neck crinkle. 'Don't yow touch my sister, Sherrie!'

'Yow gerrof my farm now!' Sherrie said, a catch in her throat. She was scared too and I felt relieved.

Tracey actually took a step towards her, 'Don't touch her I said!'

'Who am yow, me mother?' Anita hissed back, shoving Tracey up against the side of the stall, pinning her scrawny neck under her strong tanned arm.

'I've seen yow,' Tracey choked. 'Seen yow with him! Yow let him touch yow as well! I'm telling . . .'

She was silenced by Anita's hand which clamped over her mouth, squashing her words. 'Yow say one more word, our Trace, and I swear I'll kill yow.' She pushed her into the hay where Tracey landed on her knees and yanked her head up defiantly. For one terrible moment, I thought she was going to get up again and I was poised to throw myself in between them because I believed both of them capable of anything at this moment. Instead, Tracey burst into loud retching sobs and ran out of the stable, whilst Sherrie went over to Trixie who was stamping about fitfully, her ears up and swivelling like radar. No one spoke for a while, Anita gulped down some more Creme Soda and forced out a belch which no one laughed at. Eventually Sherrie asked the question that had been whirling around my head, making me dizzy and disorientated. 'Who's He then? Gorra fella have ya, Nita?'

Anita raised a forefinger and tapped it slowly against the side of her nose, the way we always said, 'Mind it, yow!' But her smile told me everything I needed to know.

Now Anita's recent absences made sense. My best friend in all the world really did have a boyfriend and had never told me. My best friend was sharing me with someone else and I knew whatever she had been giving me was only what she had left over from him, the scraps, the tokens, the lies. I had fought for this friendship, worried over it, made sacrifices for it, measured myself against it, lost myself inside it, had little to show for it but this bewildered sense of betrayal. Now I knew that I had never been the one she loved, I was a convenient diversion, a practice run until the real thing came along to claim her. I got up unsteadily and muttered, 'I'll just see if Trace is okay,' and walked slowly out of the stable. I sat with my back to its cool damp wall and wished it would rain.

Anita and Sherrie must have thought I had followed Tracey home. They were still talking and although Sherrie's voice was a muffled drone, Anita's was high and sharp with excitement and I could hear every word. 'So I just jumped on and went with him . . . he asked me too, cheeky bugger. I knew he'd always had his eye on me . . . And we went Paki bashing, it was bosting! This Paki was standing at a bus stop, he was in a suit, it was dead funny! Nah, I only watched, the lads like did it, you know, and us wenches, we just shouted and held their lager . . . They really did him over and you know what, the stupid bastard didn't do nothing back! He didn't even try, he just sort of took it . . . and after we kissed and kissed and kissed, with tongues and all . . . Nah you silly cow, not me and the Paki. Me and Sam. Sam Lowbridge . . .'

I remember retching quietly into the open drain outside the stable and watching lumps of chapatti sailing slowly away from me in the dirty water. I don't remember fetching Trixie from the stable, I must have passed Anita and Sherrie but if I try and recall whether they looked surprised or guilty, I see nothing except my shaking hands as I fastened the bit into Trixie's foam-flecked mouth. I smoothed out the hair on her back before placing the saddle carefully, tightened the girth gradually so the tension was just right over the drum of her belly. Trixie stood patiently as I mounted her, encouraging me to settle myself and to feel for the stirrups with my plimsolled feet.

I pressed my knees into the soft sofa of Trixie's haunches, the way I had watched Anita do it a hundred times, and she responded so immediately, so trustingly, it intensified my sense of loss. 'Hey! Meena! Hey! You daft cow, gerrof!' Sherrie's voice was already being whipped away by the rushing of air which filled my ears, my eyes and nose, entered my open mouth like a flock of birds, my cheeks flapping in time to their wings. The reins felt heavy and stiff in my hands. I loosened the slack; Trixie felt the surrender in the gesture and speeded up from a trot into a gallop, the fields and farmhouse and tarmacked road, the distant motorway lights and the rooftops of my village all sped by like a revolving painted backdrop, time rushing past me again, but this time I was going to catch it up. I yanked hard on the left hand rein and Trixie swerved sharply towards the series of jumps leading up to the paddock fence where Anita and Sherrie now stood, their arms jerking in terrified semaphore. My feet were slipping in minutes off the metal stirrup bars, my backside had not made contact with Trixie's back for several years, the first red-and-white-striped jump bar was coming up, at least a century away.

But one single thought kept repeating itself over and over,

All that time I wasted waiting for something to happen, when all I had to do was make something happen, it was waiting for me, it was as easy as this. I held onto Trixie's mane but she knew before I did that we would be parting company soon. She scrambled to a halt, inches from the jump, her hair streaming through my hands like a waterfall. I clutched air, then metal, then slapped palms with dark solid ground and heard a sharp loud crack. There goes the jump, I thought, and opened one eye, how heavy it was, to see the striped bar swinging in its grooves, complete and unbroken.

I should have been in a film; in a film everything would have dissolved into hazy lines and I would open my eyes to the sound of distant birdsong and my tear-stained but relieved loved ones in a circle around my bed, a stage sticking plaster artfully arranged on my temple. But no, I was awake for every awful painful moment; I saw Anita and Sherrie shimmering around my head. 'Oh fuck, seen her leg? It's pointing the wrong way . . . Fuck . . .' I sent a message to my body to get up and only my mind obeyed, I smelt my own pee and the clover stalks tickling my nose which I could not turn to see or lift a hand to brush away, I saw feet running towards me, mixed up with Trixie's skittery hooves, felt calloused hands on my head and a scratchy horse blanket adding to the layers of numbness settling slowly over my limbs, I heard crying, I knew it could not be Anita's, I endured strangers telling me 'lie still, chick', as if I had any choice, I closed my eyes to a familiar car engine racing dangerously up the narrow lane, I wished I could have had my hands back to block out the voices I knew so well, which were distorted with horror and false courage. 'Meena, beti? Meena!!' I better let them know I'm not dead at least or they'll go crazy, I thought, and was surprised to discover that I could no longer control my eyelids to oblige them.

12

I was in the Good Hope Children's Ward, whose peeling yellow walls sported Mickey Mouse posters and cardboard cut-outs of various soft fluffy creatures whose mouths emitted balloons with sayings like, 'Helga the Hippo Says Get Better Soon!' and 'Duncan the Duck Says Smile!' Luckily I did not have a full frontal view of these annoying creatures as my bed was at the far end of the room near the isolation booths.

On my left side was a dopey looking girl called Angela who had something wrong with her liver and whose skin tone varied from bloodless white to pansy yellow, depending on the time of day and what medication she had swallowed. On the other side was Robert in his glass walled isolation room, who on my first day breathed on the window and wrote 'Hi!!!' backwards for my benefit. The worst part was when I woke up from the operating theatre, still woozy from the anaesthetic, and saw my leg encased in plaster from toes to thigh, lashed to what looked like a four-poster bed made of dull grey metal. 'Alright, Mary?' shouted a sharp featured female doctor into my face, making me jump. I was about to correct her pronunciation of my name when she barked, 'Can't say your real name so Mary will do, ha ha! Can you feel this?' she said, jabbing what felt like a small dagger into my plaster-clad toes. I yelped in reply and she nodded, satisfied. 'Lovely. You'll be out of this by Christmas, if you're lucky. Tell nurse if you want to use the bedpan . . .' and she marched off, ticking me off on her clipboard.

I thought I must have misheard her – Christmas was over four months away! Maybe she had meant my Christmas,

Diwali. That was only eight weeks away or so, round about Sunil's first birthday which we had planned to celebrate with a big party and round off what had been, up until now, a very successful year for our family. But mama's ashen face when she came to visit confirmed my worst fears. 'Meena, oh my beti,' she said, stroking my hair, trying not to look at my leg, which was difficult as it was propped up at a forty-five-degree angle and took up most of the bed. 'Meena listen, it was a nasty break, but you must not worry, it will heal. But it is going to take some time, the doctors think that anyway . . .' Tears were already sliding out of the corner of my eyes, dropping quietly onto my starched pillow. Mama swallowed and gently tried to stem the flow, it was useless, I could have cried an ocean. 'Don't worry about school,' she continued jauntily. 'I have spoken to your teachers, I've got your curriculum books and we'll study together every day. Good job I am a teacher as well, hey?'

I let out a stifled sob; mama taught four-year-olds. I had visions of her bringing in flashcards and stickyback plastic, and me sitting on the bed crayoning laboriously with my tongue stuck out in concentration. 'What . . . what about . . . the eleven-plus?' I juddered. 'Sunil's birthday . . . Nanima? . . .' And then it hit me, the awful bitter consquences of my moment of madness: 'India? We were going to India!' and I gave in to a loud howling fit which brought a nurse scurrying to draw the curtains hurriedly around my bed. Mama held me as well as she could around the wires and pulleys and supports. She was calm now, in control, she would not let me down. 'We will all come and visit you, we'll take it in turns. We can cut a cake for Sunil right here, and bring his presents as well . . . India is not going anywhere. We can always go next summer, and Nanima . . .' She hesitated, and then added, 'Nanima is coming tonight with papa! Okay?'

But the thought of Nanima's visit did not console me. For days there was no room in my head for anyone except Anita, and my need to relive my last glimpse of her. She was sitting on the gate, watching me being stretchered into the back of the ambulance and was nonchalantly swinging her red patent heels, the way Sam Lowbridge had swung his boots against the crumbling village wall. I thought of those boots smashing into the skull of the Bank Manager, I imagined those red heels skittering in the mud at the side of the ditch, jumping for joy. Anita and I had never been meant for each other: Sam and Anita, Anita and Sam, it sounded as natural as breathing. And me and the Bank Manager, we both lay in hospital beds whilst the boots and the heels rode the highways of Tollington together, turning us into drunken, boastful anecdotes. Whilst Sherrie and her parents had seen me off with gentle words and concerned expressions, Anita had merely looked bored. She did not speak to me, she did not even wave me off, she closed her face like the end of a chapter in a long epic book, a dying cadence, a full stop.

For the first few days of my confinement, I blamed her so totally for my state that whenever I thought of her I shook hard enough to rattle my metal cage. But a few hospital meals of runny mashed potatoes and gristly pies soon broke down my resistance, as did the deadening routine of being washed and bedpanned and jollied along by the brisk, efficient nurses, and always the throbbing pain in my suspended limb, as if tiny sharp-clawed creatures were trapped underneath the plaster and scrabbling to escape. After a while it took a huge effort simply to recall Anita's features, or her catchphrases, or the way she shimmied when she walked. I began to realise I could use this enforced separation wisely, I could gradually erase her like a child's pencil drawing, begin with the top of her head and work my way down – today I'll rub out her eyebrows, tomorrow the bridge of her nose, next week I'll remember nothing but the hems of her summer dresses and by the end of four months, I calculated, she would be nothing but a smudge, a faint outline caused by an inexperienced, un-co-ordinated hand.

My nearest neighbour, Angela, was not a chatty person at

the best of times; she would lie on her stomach across her bed eating family-sized packets of crisps mechanically whilst she flicked through magazines. Our longest conversation went like this; 'When's your birthday, Mary?' 'July the sixth,' I said, and she nodded her head wisely. 'Typical Cancerian you are.' 'Oh yeah?' I replied, interested now, maybe she had already picked up my acute sensitivity and vivid imagination. 'Fat,' said Angela. 'I'm Gemini so I'll never put on weight . . .'

I turned my face to the wall, as much as I could do to get away from her, and became aware of an insistent tapping at my right shoulder and shifted myself to see Robert banging on his window with a hospital spoon. His painfully thin frame held up a pair of stripey pyjamas but his face, framed by curly brown hair, was illuminated by a pair of energetic, electric blue eyes. He breathed onto the window and began writing, 'Is . . . she . . .' and then changed his mind and dived out of sight for a moment, reappearing with a sketch pad and marker pen. He wrote down his message quickly and held it against the glass. 'Is she driving you mad?' I nodded wildly and rolled my eyes. He laughed, wrote again, this time the message said, 'Has she told you she's a Gemini yet?' I nodded again, infected by his soundless chortle. It startled me, the realisation that he was not only handsome but that he was talking to me. He does not have much choice, I told myself. He's bored, you're the nearest. Trust you to end up next to a dishy bloke when you're in your oldest nightie with no lip gloss and your leg in the air. But I was definitely feeling better, feeling something which was not boredom or pain or misery, all of whom were my bedfellows at night when the radio was finally switched off and I lay awake longing for my own bed, my family, my freedom.

I scrabbled around for a pen and paper; mama seemed to have brought everything in the house except for those two items. Food, comics, books, puzzles, knitting ('Now's the time to learn!' mama said. I never did.), photographs of everyone I loved, even yesterday's *Express and Star* with the crossword half-completed in Mrs Worrall's large uneven capitals. 'No paper!' I mouthed to Robert who wagged his finger at me mock-angrily. 'Tomorrow!' he mouthed back and eased himself back onto his bed like a very old man.

When mama and papa came to see me that evening, I made them promise to bring me a large supply of pens and paper on their next visit. I could tell that they were thrilled at this request, they made a big fuss of noting carefully what kind of paper exactly, whether I wanted pens or crayons, notebooks or loose-leafs, as if getting this right would be a miracle cure. And it was only then I noticed how much weight mama had lost, her usually moon-shaped face was all angles and shadows, she and papa had saddlebags of dark under their eyes, papa's rosy complexion had given way to a sallow tinge, as if he had been indoors for too long.

They had asked me about the accident, of course, and I had told them I had simply fallen awkwardly. I knew it had been a deliberate act, as deliberate as any of the lies I had told. Uncle Alan had been right all along; sin always had consequences, whether it was his vision of fiery pits or Auntie Shaila's prediction that I would come back to earth as an insect. I decided there and then to heal myself, both in body and mind. It was time. I asked mama to bring in all my school books to prepare for the eleven-plus, I would grow my hair long and vaguely feminine, I would be nice to Pinky and Baby and seek out their company willingly, I would write letters to India and introduce myself properly to that anonymous army of blood relatives, I would learn to knit, probably, and I would always always tell the truth.

So when mama's next question was, 'Why do you need all this paper?' I, of course, pointed to Robert and told her about my new friend. Robert was sitting up in bed chatting with his visitors, whom I presumed were his grandparents; I saw grey hair and the stems of reading glasses poking out from beneath their surgical masks. Anyone who wished to enter Robert's glass cubicle had to dress like they were entering a radioactive zone, masks and gowns and gloves sometimes, and floppy green wellies cut off at the ankle. I had not seen anyone visit him besides these two old people and a small battalion of faceless doctors, but I assumed he must have been popular as his walls were covered in Get Well cards and funny drawings (no flowers or fruit, they were not allowed apparently), and pictures of footballers and pop stars.

I was also beginning to build up quite a collection from wellwishers: my class at school sent a card and books; several Aunties and Uncles dispatched toys I was far too old for and Indian food in tupperware containers which the nurses always appropriated and ate themselves (I could smell Auntie Shaila's pickle on their breath at ten paces); Mrs Worrall sent fairy cakes and a crossword book; Sherrie's parents sent me photographs of Trixie; and there were several cards from various Tollington old people. But nothing from Anita.

'He must be quite ill, poor boy,' mama said, glancing over at Robert. 'What's wrong with him?' 'Dunno,' I shrugged. I had never asked, I actually did not want to.

As soon as mama and papa had gone, more optimistic than I had seen them for ages, I dived for the pen papa had given me from his breast pocket, with BENSON LOCKS in gold letters down one side, and ripped a page out of a magazine that had a decent-sized white border on it. I wrote a message to Robert quickly and threw a grape at his window to attract his attention. He was twiddling with one of the knobs on his portable radio and came to the window, still holding it in one hand. He squinted as he read, mouthing the words to himself, 'Tomorrow I get supplies . . . Know how to play Hangman?' He raised a thumb to me like a soldier, message understood, and I saw that the nail above the knuckle was splintered and black.

I had often dreamed of having a Boyfriend, as opposed to a mindless crush on a pop star or American TV detective. The boys I fantasised about were invariably white, clean shaven, tall and yet insubstantial, exactly like the cartoon heroes in the romantic comic strips in *Jackie*. They were car mechanics who wrote novels, racing car drivers who loved animals, surgeons who sculpted in their spare time: they inevitably spotted me across a crowded room and fell instantly, and I always resisted them until the last moment when I would swoon into their arms reluctantly. We kissed a lot and never spoke except in greeting card cliches: 'You are the one I've been waiting for, Meena . . . Meena, I was so afraid that I'd lost you . . . marry me, Meena, or I'll die . . .' In these scenarios, words were secondary, unnecessary; physical contact and smouldering looks were all. So it was very strange that my first and most intense relationship with a boy was conducted via scribbled messages on scrap paper through a pane of glass blend where you could look but not touch, understand but not hear – a true hospital love, sanitised and inevitably temporary.

At first we stuck to the obvious channels, word games, jokes, gossip about the rest of the ward, then we progressed to swapping autobiographical details; I found out the two old people who visited Robert were his parents, he was an only child, born to people who had been told long ago they would never bear children. 'I'm a medical miracle!!' he wrote. I did not write a reply, I just nodded stupidly in agreement, my throat full, my chest singing. Sharing our past inevitably led to sharing secrets and we naturally had to develop a code; we decided that we would insert extra letters between every letter in the word we wrote, and in alphabetical order. So 'How are you?' became 'Haobw Acrde Yeofu?' 'I've just had a good dump' became 'Iavbe jcudsft hgahd ai gjokold dmunmop' etc. The first few days were incredibly frustrating, as if two old friends had stopped speaking after a stupid row, or one of us had just brought back a new spouse after a torrid, whirlwind holiday romance and discovered our future partner only spoke and understood an obscure East European dialect.

Pretty soon, we reached a stage where we did not even need to complete our unpronounceable sentences, I would begin a phrase and before I had reached the full stop, Robert was holding the same question, or in a few spooky cases, the answer to something I had been about to ask him. Now to get his attention, I simply had to look up, shift my body, or if his head was turned towards his wall, casually wave my hand over the anglepoise lamp I had trained on his cubicle and my shadow would bring him to me. Even when we switched off our respective lamps, I could still hear him talking, although I had never actually heard his voice, and still see his black-nailed hands whizzing off messages which I read like braille in the dark.

When, one evening, my whole family descended upon me bearing gifts, a birthday cake and Sunil in a new outfit several sizes too large, I was temporarily dumbfounded. The logical part of my brain, the seriously underused section since I had been in hospital, told me that it must have been Sunil's birthday and therefore Diwali tomorrow and so it must be somewhere around the end of October. But the rest of my body went into emotional shock upon realising that I had been prone in this bed for over six weeks, that summer had handed over to autumn and that winter was standing in the wings sucking a throat lozenge and waiting for his cue. A new school year had started, leaves had fallen, duffle coats and mittens on strings would now be the *de rigueur* yard-wear, and I was six weeks older and a lifetime wiser.

Nanima was not her usual ironic self; she sat huddled into the folds of her shawl on the end of my bed regarding me with moist mournful eyes. I knew there was something drastically wrong when she refused the sweetmeats and Milk Tray being waved enticingly under her nose. 'What's up, Nanima?' I joked. 'You've always beaten me to the caramel whirl . . .' Nanima wiped her eyes with the end of her shawl and mama and papa swapped a You Tell Her Darling look over my head.

'What?' I said, patting the bedclothes to attract Sunil to me who was toddling now around the metal frame legs, singing some weird off-key song to himself.

'Meena,' papa began. 'Your Nanima has decided to go back to India.'

I blinked rapidly for a few seconds and from the corner of my eye I thought I saw Robert look up sharply and heave himself to his knees. 'When?' I asked casually, a chasm cracking open somewhere.

'Tomorrow,' papa said gently. 'She wanted to stay longer but now we're . . .' He was going to say, Now We're Not Going To India but as that was all my fault, he changed it to '. . . now she's feeling homesick, and the cold weather is coming . . .'

'Well, keep her inside!' I screamed in my head. 'Buy her a fur coat! Leave the heating on all night! Strap a sodding hot water bottle to her bosom and force feed her rum!' But I chose to nod understandingly and flash Nanima a bright, reassuring smile. I was a grown-up now, I had seen my parents swallow down anger and grief a million times, for our sakes, for the sake of others watching, for the sake of their own sanity. It was not so hard to do, this sacrificial lark, it came with the territory. 'Anyway,' I chirped, patting Nanima's gnarled hands which I would mourn forever, I knew it, 'we'll be coming to India soon, eh? And next time, you can teach me how to sing this in Punjabi!' and I launched into an overloud and unnecessarily bouncy rendition of 'Happy Birthday, Sunil' which made him stare at me with a frightened owlish face.

I wanted many more years with Nanima, more than that I passionately wanted back all the years I had already missed with her, all the other birthdays and accidents and door slammings and apologies that so many other children had at their disposal and treated as disposable. But I did not crack, even when she said goodbye and leaned over me, smoothing my hair back into the horrible centre parting she thought suited me, whispering her familiar prayer, '*Wahe Guru Satnam* . . .' And then, even more quietly, 'Meena . . . jewel . . . precious . . . light . . . bless you . . .' and she was gone, shuffling after mama who held the swing doors open for her and touched her lightly, motherly, as she passed through.

I lay back on my bed and waited for the nurses to do their final rounds before lights off. I could not lift my head to look at Robert, it felt heavy and leaden, full of water and stones which swished about on an irregular tide. After so long of living in that dusk where my fantasies almost met reality, where longings could become possibilities, where I tortured myself sweetly with dramatic scenarios of near-disasters and doomed love affairs, I was having to learn the difference between acting and being – and it hurt. I had enacted loss and departure so many times and thrilled to the tears I could make myself shed, but now, I could not cry at all. Robert and I sent no messages that evening. We did not make eye contact although I knew he was watching me, even in the darkness. And I woke up comforted, my fist warm and curled where he had been holding my hand.

One day, the nurses dragged in a six foot high mock pine tree, with nylon branches and a bright red plastic stand, and I realised with a start that it was a Christmas tree. The Horse Face doctor entered with a wake of eager-eyed students, and at the same time I looked over automatically to Robert's cubicle and saw that it was empty. I sat bolt upright as the flock of medics perched round my bed expectantly.

'Hello Mary, how are we today?'

'Where's Robert?' I demanded.

Horse Face cracked her first smile ever, I could tell she'd strained a muscle doing it.

'Where is he?' I asked again, sharply.

'Robert's having some tests today. He'll be back. But what about you? Leg still hurts, does it?'

I slumped back in relief onto my pillow and regarded my leg spitefully, this alien, useless liability stuck to the end of my body. 'It's fine. Just itches a lot.'

Horse Face whispered something to her disciples who

looked over my leg with sudden interest, one of them tapped his pencil on the plaster cast which was no longer brilliant white but grey and mottled, with a dirty band like unwashed neck skin where my toes met fresh air. 'Will Robert be leaving the same time as me?' I demanded. The nurses paused at the now erect tree, arms loaded with bright red tinsel and tiny icicles hanging from their fingers.

I wanted Robert to see the tree and lobbed a half-eaten tangerine at his window which landed with a soft splat and inched down the pane like a sleepy snail. He did not look up; I could see the top of his tousled head, he was lying on his back with the sheets drawn right up to his neck, his arms slack at his sides. He was not asleep, I could feel him blink, so I eased myself up onto my elbows for the first time in weeks and was able to bring my head right up to his cubicle. The silly face I had started to pull slid off the end of my chin; his face was papery and chalk white, there were two bruised holes in the centre of each hand, his drip marks, which looked like stigmata, and he was crying. 'Robert!' I shouted. It was strange to have to use my voice for him. 'Rob! Please!' He deliberately swung his head away from me but his shoulders still moved in tiny judders. 'Nurse! Quick!' Nurse Sylvie stepped to my side.

'What's wrong with Robert?' I gulped. 'He won't speak to me!' Sylvie sighed, patted her paper hat into place and sat down easily on the bed. I liked Sylvie best of all the staff, with her oval boyish face, mad frizzy hair and perpetual air of bewilderment, she reminded me of a flickering lightbulb about to blow a fuse.

'Robert had some very painful tests today. He's feeling a bit low, sweetheart,' she said.

'What tests?' I asked. 'Good tests? I mean, to make him better?'

Sylvie chewed her lip and glanced over her shoulder to check whether the Staff Nurse was snooping about. 'He's not a well little boy at the moment, sort of two steps forward and one back. He gets very tired, you know? Depressed. But we're doing our best, don't you worry.'

Robert and depression did not go together in the same sentence. I had a selfish desire to march in there, slap him round a bit and tell him not to be so stupid, because if he didn't get better, neither would I.

On December the twentieth, I packed my spongy vanity case myself as soon as I got up, distributed my comics and magazines to various other patients and said my cheery farewells, gave away my remaining fruit and juices and was all ready to leave by ten o'clock. Sylvie appeared clutching a surgical gown, mask and one green wellie and said, 'Come on then, I nearly got sacked for asking this favour for you.' Sylvie handed me my crutches and stood back to admire her handiwork; I checked my reflection, a strange hunched figure swathed in shiny green grown-up clothes, a stupid smile stretching the mask across my mouth like a gag.

We entered an anteroom with a huge sink and several empty pegs where Sylvie made me wash my hands, and then she heaved open a door marked 'Authorised Visitors Only!' which opened with a vacuum-filled pop. I limped inside and automatically sat down on the metal chair next to Robert's bed, the door closing with a sigh behind me. 'Well, don't you look fetching,' said a voice I had never heard before, surprisingly adult, posh even, only a hint of Black Country twang which sat upon the last G of his sentence. 'Hiya Robert . . . how'm you feeling?' I said, lost. Robert broke into giggles, they sounded exactly as I had imagined, rude farty bubbles in a bath. 'Ey up, yow'm a real Midland wench, our Meena! I thought you'd sound a bit more exotic than this!' God he was thin, the length of his body stretched out like a flattened skin in the sun, interrupted only by his knees and elbows.

He propped himself up on his elbows, most of his fingertips

wore helmets of gauzey bandages, the two exposed to the air were dead and coming away from the skin. 'I'm unwrapping like the Invisible Man,' he said. 'Seen that film, the old black and white one?' I shook my head, as tongue-tied as if he'd cornered me on a sweaty dance floor and was trying his luck for a grope. (I'd never been to a disco, but this was what I always imagined happened to girls like me, the favoured beauties would get whisked away by the hunks, I would get landed with the guy with acne and tomato sauce down his tank top . . .)

'Well, you're better company with sign language, our Meena,' Robert sighed. 'But I suppose we already know everything about each other anyway. What else is there to say?' I drew in a breath, he interrupted me, 'I know. Before you go, we've got to tell each other something we haven't told each other before. Something new, yeah?'

I nodded. 'Um, I'm getting a bike!' I said brightly.

'Yeah?' he said. 'So you can fall off it and break the other leg? I'll tell them to hold onto your bed, eh?'

'Rob, when will you be better?'

Robert paused and then said carefully, 'Now that's something I don't know. I've got my O levels next summer, so . . .' It wasn't an answer, but he had set himself his own time limit which I understood and respected. He continued, 'Now, what don't you know about me?'

I had nothing to lose. I could hear clocks ticking and see pages of a calendar being ripped away by a strong breeze, film titles like 'Never Say Die!' and 'The Last Chance Saloon!' inexplicably dancing across my vision. 'Okay Rob, I don't know if you've got a girlfriend or not,' I said loudly.

'Yeah, I have,' said Robert quietly and took my hand in his.

I was breathing so fast that the green mask over my mouth panted up and down like a diaphragm and I suddenly felt foolish in this medical garb. I became aware of the bones in his hand and the rough edges of his bandaged fingertips and was gloriously complete for the time it took to gather up my crutches and heave myself to my three feet. 'I'll be in soon for physio, yeah?' my voice sounded coated and subdued through my mask. 'Mind the road!' he called to my back.

I was still smiling as we drove up the one main road leading into Tollington. The familiar fields were brown moon surfaces coated with ice, the trees stark against the dark sky like charcoal skeletons, but as we turned around the corner upon which our house stood, my smile faded. The horizon glowed a sticky neon yellow, the fields opposite our house had been marked out with white sticks and tape which snagged in the breeze and there were motionless yellow diggers in what was the old mine yard next to the Big House. The crumbling low-roofed office was gone and slabs of concrete ripped from the yard lay in a haphazard pile like slices of old Christmas cake, even though there were five days to go.

'What's been happening!' I cried, furious that neither of my parents had mentioned that Tollington was being carved up in my absence.

'What?' said papa, confused and then cottoned on as we drove past the violated fields towards the entrance to the communal yard. 'Oh, well the motorway is open now, you knew about that didn't you?'

'But,' I stammered. 'Everything else . . .'

'Oh, right,' papa continued. 'Apparently Mr Pembridge has sold some of the land opposite us, don't know what for . . . There's been talk about new houses but it's just a rumour . . .'

Anita's back gate was shut and barely recognisable, a few slivers of paint remained clinging to the exposed wood and I noticed that the back upstairs window was cracked and held together with sellotape. Sam Lowbridge's moped stood in its usual space, but looked unused and rusty, its Union Jack flag was just a rag which drooped morosely from the aerial at the back. A few items of frozen underwear hung stiffly from a washing line and Blaze, the mad collie, sniffed at a pile of old newspapers, his orange and white fur the only slash of colour in this black and white landscape.

I never remembered it all looking so shabby, so forgotten. There was not even any evidence of the usual Christmas fripperies, no flashing lights at anyone's window, no tinsel trees squashed into back porches or holly wreaths hammered into back gates. It was as if everyone had given up, or was waiting for something to happen.

'Glad to be home, Meena beti?' papa said, helping me out of the car and handing me my crutches. Before I could answer, Hairy Neddy's back gate swung open and he appeared shivering in the doorway, buttoning up his sheepskin jacket whilst Sandy handed him a pack of sandwiches wrapped up in silver foil. They both saw me and waved excitedly. 'Meena chick! Noice to see ya!' Hairy Neddy called over, and then kissed Sandy absentmindedly before getting into his three-wheeler and backfiring out of the yard.

'They are married now,' papa said, reading my confusion.

'Oh. When?' I was getting less surprised at each new revelation.

'About two months back.' Papa was supporting me as I balanced myself, taking infinite care. 'Neddy's working in a shop now, he's stopped the band. See what happens when you get a wife?' papa joked.

'Huh!' called mama from the driving seat. 'It was about time he grew up!' and reversed expertly into our parking space near the pigsties.

The whole village had aged behind my back, I decided, as I struggled up the entry, noticing the litter and the dog shit and the bomb site which made up the Mad Mitchells' back yard. I could see Mrs Mitchell sitting at her kitchen table slowly peeling an apple, staring into space. The door to their outside loo was flapping open, a smell of urine and stale cigarette smoke hit me like a hot gust and made me gag.

'Okay Meena?'

I nodded, careful to not put the rubber tips of my extra legs onto any mossy patches.

'Oh, by the way,' papa murmured. 'If you see Mrs Mitchell, don't ask about Cara. She's um . . . she's gone to some home for treatment. I'm sure she will be back but . . . they're upset, obviously . . . it wasn't their decision . . .'

The thought of poor daffy Cara pacing around a padded cell brought a sudden spill of tears which froze immediately on my eyelashes. If anyone needed the open road it was her, even if it was only to wander along the broken white line singing Methodist hymns.

I finally reached our back gate and paused, hearing mama's light quick steps coming up the entry, waiting for her to catch up. I was sniffing in all the old smells I missed from the kitchen, hot, buttery, smoking griddles, potatoes frying in cumin seeds, onions simmering in garlicky tomatoes. I could taste my dinner in the air and felt ravenous. But papa was far away for a moment, taking in the cobbled yard, the padlocked bike shed, the grainy wooden door to our outside loo. 'It's home, it really is, but we can't stay here forever, Meena . . .' he said quietly, and then welcomed mama inside with a protective arm.

Later that evening, when I was trying to get changed, cursing as I juggled crutches and armholes and trousers over my cast, I heard the loud vroom of an engine screech past my window.

Sam was on a brand new motorbike, a proper motorbike not a moped, with a large fat engine and mirrors with a wing span of five feet across and a big leather saddle with enough room for three people to sit comfortably. Sam drew up under the street light next to the phone booth, his hair was now so short that he looked almost bald and I fancied I saw a scar running from his eye to his cheek which glinted under the neon. He turned round to his passenger whose skinny arms were wrapped firmly round his waist and gave her a long aggressive French kiss. Anita responded with gusto, not resisting as he slipped one hand under her jacket, and when they drew apart, Sam was wearing her lipstick.

In the limbo days between Boxing Day and New Year's Eve, papa drove me back to the hospital where I spent a useful hour trying to pick up a pencil with my plaster-encased toes. The second the session ended, I made my clumsy way down to the isolation ward like some heat-crazed, long-legged insect. Robert's bed was empty; Sylvie told me he had gone for more tests, this time to another hospital, and would not be back until tomorrow. I spent half an hour composing a light-hearted letter which I left on his pillow with a *Wolves* Annual and a book I had tried to read and found too dense, but which had recently won some big prize in America and was supposedly a great learning experience. Papa waited patiently in the corridor as I finished off with a P.S. – 'Hope you like *To Kill a Mockingbird*. I will test you on chapters four, five and six when we meet next year. Meena. X.'

When I still had not received a reply by January the fifth, I telephoned the hospital to find out where Robert was. I did not manage to track down Sylvie and some weary receptionist told me she could not give out such information over the phone. But I was never worried, I knew for certain that Robert would get in touch when he was ready, and was thrilled when a few days later, a letter arrived bearing an Aldridge postmark. I ventured out by myself for the first time and sat on the swings in the deserted, chilly park where I tore it open and read, 'My dear Meena, We are sorry to tell you that our dear son Robert left us on the last day of December. The hospital sent your sweet letter to us. We wanted to thank you for making Robert's time in hospital so happy. We know you will miss him too. With many thanks again, God Bless You, Yours faithfully, Mr and Mrs Robert Oakes.'

13

I spent a lot of time on my own that year. I had the perfect
excuse, that I was recuperating, that I needed peace and
rest, that I was often worn out from travelling to and from
physiotherapy, and people understood and mostly left me to
it. My days as a yard member were over. In fact, those days
when hordes of children hung around the dirt arena looking
for companionship and diversion were effectively ended by
the closing of the village school. Now, all those children who
used to have lazy hours to fill after lessons were finished,
following a sprint down the hill from classroom to back gate,
spent those same precious hours stuck in buses and cars,
travelling from the new combined infants and junior school
that had been built in the middle of the steadily growing
Bartlett estate.

I saw them arriving home in weary groups, dragging
school bags and shoes on the ground. In the winter months
there would only be a few hours of daylight left, and most of
my old friends preferred to spend them defrosting in front of
their television sets. With the children otherwise engaged in
this commuter hell, the village turned into the Pied Piper's
Hamelin; without the children around wreaking havoc with
bikes and balls and skipping ropes, playing 'Tick' between
our corner and Mr Ormerod's shop, the streets were empty
and unloved, populated only by old widows on church duties
and unemployed men on secretive errands.

It was not, however, any quieter; before the motorway
opened, the village had its own soothing background noise –
never silent, it was an uneven tune full of birdsong and

women's voices and the odd car rumbling through, sometimes the wind in the trees around the Big House played percussion and in summer, there was always the somnolent undertone of meandering bees. But all these notes became indistinct and fuzzy when pitched against the constant low roar of the motorway traffic which now rose each morning above the fields and hung over our houses like an unwanted, stifling cloud. Even the stars had changed; I used to be able to look out of my window and trace the studded curve of the Milky Way, point out the Pole Star and Venus as bright and clear as headlights. Through hours of sitting with my elbows propped on the window sill, staring into the night, I learned that darkness is not one colour, that there are shades upon shades within black – midnight-blue black on the horizon, pearly opaque black encircling the moon, the heavy wet green-black of a stormy night sky. But against the yellow lights of the motorway which stitched up the horizon like a cheap seaside necklace, the subtle washes of the sky and the diamond clarity of the stars simply faded away. Only the most gaudy constellation survived the neon fallout, and against it, black was no longer a colour in its own right, but simply an absence of light.

I began to notice more strangers hanging round Tollington now. The park, once the domain of the under-tens and curious stray dogs, became a hang-out for various groups of teenagers who took over the swings and roundabouts, smoking and flirting together in separate clans. Mrs Worrall told me about how the Bartlett estate had now spread as far as the edge of the cornfields and that 'all these townies get on the bus to come and sniff our fresh air.' One of my earliest memories was of standing with papa at the edge of one of these fields; I must have been tiny, as my arm was at full stretch holding his hand and the corn stalks were high enough to tickle my nose with their hairy ears. And all we could see, both of us, was miles and miles of unbroken green, and far in the distance, if we squinted, we could just make out the tower of the ballbearings factory. Now the cornfields were the only stretch of land separating us from the 'townies' we so often mocked, the day trippers, the girls in their high heels which kept sinking into the muddy edges of the pavements and the lads all swagger and brash, jingling their loose change and scaring the birds.

Sam and Anita were often in the park, their gang was not difficult to pick out. Most of the other youths were dressed in panelled flares, flapping in the wind like elephant ears and huge platform heels which left square craters in the grass. The girls favoured midi skirts and crocheted waistcoats, or flowery maxis, peasant blouses and big floppy hats. They brought sandwiches and portable radios and passed round plastic bottles of sweet cider. But Sam, and I suppose now Anita's, gang were always in denim and leather and braces and lace-up Doctor Martens, heads shorn like summer sheep, chewing gum like cud, swigging cans of lager and crushing them in clumsy fists, smoking with attitude and deliberately sitting apart and above everyone else – a colourless, humourless island in this sea of change. I never stopped for more than a cursory glance. I would just back pedal my bike for a second, long enough to absorb those familiar profiles, and continue my wheelies around the dirt yard, knowing they would not approach me and did not expect me to trouble them.

I was not the only one watching their display; whenever I glimpsed Sam and Anita, Tracey was always there, some-where in the background keeping a silent vigil. She had not spoken to me since the first day I had ridden my new bicycle, which had been languishing in the now appropriately named bike shed next to our outside lav. It had been sometime in early Spring, the tops of the trees had just begun to sprout a fine green stubble when papa drove me into the yard and I got out on two legs instead of four for the first time in seven months. The cast had been removed in mid-January, a traumatic experience as I had not been back to the hospital since Robert died and thought I had finally got over the sickness and grief which overwhelmed me every time I had tried to recall his face. But as soon as I smelt that hospital cologne of disinfectant and cabbage, he came back to me and stayed for hours.

Papa audibly gasped when the cast was finally peeled off my leg like an old crusty pod; my poor limb looked withered and unused to sunlight, a skinny brown stick streaked with dirt and tiny white flakes of plaster, like dandruff. 'My God . . . they are two different sizes!' papa said. It was true; I pushed my legs together and saw that my previously confined foot was a good inch smaller than its partner. 'So what are you going to do about it?' demanded papa, seeing a promising dancing career fly out of the window. 'Oh, it always happens with kids,' the nurse said airily. 'They grow so fast you see, the other one will catch up, don't worry.' It never did.

But nevertheless, despite mama and the doctors' advice to wait a few weeks before attempting anything more strenuous than a walk, a week later I wheeled my not so new Christmas bicycle into the yard for a first try-out. Maybe a good few months of pedalling would make me symmetrical again. I managed a wobbly, careful circuit of the yard and as I passed the entry next to the Christmases' abandoned house, I almost fell off my bike when I saw the ghost hovering in the dark maw of the tunnel. On closer inspection, the thin white figure was Tracey. The last time I had seen her, she had been a shadow in Anita's wake, now she was nothing less than transparent. Her hair was as fine and see-through as gossamer, her body a cobweb hung out on bones, her skin so pale I thought I could see the blood pumping slowly through her veins.

'Oh hiya Trace! Yow bloody scared me half to death!' I said jovially.

She just stared at me, I was waiting for her to do the polite thing and ask where I had been for most of the last year but saw at once that she was beyond social niceties. 'Our Nita's gooing out with Sam,' she said blandly.

'Yeah?' I said, a little too defensively I thought.

'Her's gonna turn out just like me mom. Fucking bitch.' It was chilling to hear this bile come out of that sweet cupid's bow, and the mundane tone she used. 'Yow are her best friend. Yow tell her to stop it now.'

'Was,' I corrected her, annoyed that this word stabbed me somewhere soft.

'So yow ain't gonna do nothing then? He's a pig. A thick shit-eating pig.'

'Yeah, so what?' I said, beginning to wheel my bike away. I could not listen to much more of this. 'I don't give a toss what your sister does, Tracey. Yow can tell her that from me.' But when I turned round, the alley was empty and she had somehow walked the length of it without the trace of an echo.

Spring bloomed into an early hot summer – by May everyone was wearing sunhats and shorts and the children began taking over the yard again, making the most of the lengthening evenings. But the park was out of bounds after sunset as it became the unofficial haunt of every teenager within a five-mile radius, and they turned every evening into a noisy outdoor party. Everyone in the yard felt their privacy invaded and there were several complaints, both in writing to the council and verbally to the offending youths. But the letters were never acknowledged and the youths merely hurled back obscenities and turned up their radios even louder. Apart from the nuisance of stationary cars and bikes outside our house and snatches of music drifting in through our open windows, we were not too badly affected, being on the corner of the road and furthest from the park.

Mama and papa, who I thought would kick up a big fuss, seemed completely unconcerned by this new invasion, as if they had already mentally moved into the four-bedroomed bungalow mama so often sighed about whenever they talked about 'the future'. They also did not seem to notice the brand new building that had sprung up next to the Big House, windowless still but structurally completed, nor that the fields opposite our house were regularly marked out with triangles of white tape by faceless men in cheap shiny suits, picking their way distastefully through the abandoned soil. Nothing escaped me, however; I saw all these metamorphoses and more. I knew that Sherrie's family had already moved away and that their farm was up for auction, that the bomb site left after the demolition of the village school had already been acquired by a supermarket firm and that as a result, Mr Ormerod had developed a grumbling, if not a bloody angry appendix.

But none of these changes touched me. I was in my own cosy world, my days divided up between solitary bike rides, my eleven-plus studies and quiet evenings in front of the television when I read stories to Sunil or pottered about the kitchen with mama, chopping and tasting when I could. But if my parents had noticed that their wayward tomboy had suddenly become a walking cliche of the good Indian daughter, they did not remark on it to me, fearful perhaps that by naming their good fortune, they would break the spell. Or more likely, that I would be so horrified to have something in common with my cutesy cousins, Pinky and Baby, I might run naked through the village screaming 'Bugger!' just to prove them wrong.

I did once overhear them discussing me in guilty whispers in the kitchen whilst I was putting my bike away in the shed, my T-shirt stuck to my back in Friesian patches and my healing leg tingling with renewed hope. '. . . used to be such a happy child!' I froze at papa's urgent tone, carefully leaning my bike against the wall and deadening its slowly turning spokes. 'She is happy, Shyam!' mama hissed back. 'You still expect her to jump onto your lap and pull on your nose hairs? She's not a little girl anymore, of course she's going to get a bit more serious about things, and so she should! We should put the house on the market now . . .' 'Let her pass the exam first!'

papa said, his voice getting louder. 'She will pass it, no problem. She's my daughter,' mama replied. I could hear the grin in her voice. There was a brief pause, some movement and a sigh, I realised with amazement that they had just kissed. Was it like Sam and Anita kissed, mouths clamped together, tongues drilling each other's cavities? Was it this that endured through fifteen years of marriage and welded people together?

'But the accident,' papa said finally. 'It definitely affected her. And that boy she was sweet on, she's never mentioned him since. Do you think . . .' 'Oh don't be silly, Shyam! She's much too young to be bothering about such things. She doesn't even know what a boyfriend is.' Papa's silence told me how much better he knew me than mama, at this point.

Ah, my darling parents, how much they had tried to cushion me from anything unpleasant or unusual, never guessing that this would only make me seek out the thrill of the dark and dramatic, afraid of what I might be missing, defiant that I would know and experience much more than them. And now I was reaping the karma of all those lies and longings; I had lost a Nanima, a soul mate and temporarily, a leg – enough excitement for a lifetime already. If mama and papa knew the whole picture, they might have called it punishment. But this was the oddest thing, this is what I realised, standing in the yard, a sweaty eavesdropper holding my breath, that at this moment, I was content. I had absorbed Nanima's absence and Robert's departure like rain on parched earth, drew it in deep and drank from it. I now knew I was not a bad girl, a mixed-up girl, a girl with no name or no place. The place in which I belonged was wherever I stood and there was nothing stopping me simply moving forward and claiming each resting place as home. This sense of displacement I had always carried round like a curse shrivelled into insignificance against the shadow of mortality cast briefly by a hospital anglepoise lamp, by the last wave of a gnarled brown hand. I would not mourn too much the changing landscape around me, because I would be a traveller soon anyhow. I would be going to the posh girls' school where I would read and argue and write stories and if I wished, trample the mangy school uniform tam-o'-shanter into the mud. After all, I had never promised to be good, had I?

As it turned out, my two weeks of revision for the eleven-plus became a fourteen-day siege. At first it started with catcalls as I flew past any corner where Tracey was standing guard. She would watch me trundle past with hard unblinking eyes, and just as my back wheels passed her feet I would hear it, soft enough to be friendly, sharp enough to be a dart: 'Meeeee-naaaa!' It was an androgynous voice, too low to be a woman's, too knowing to be a man's, and I wondered if the two of them were so close that they had blended into the same person – Sam-ita, Sam and Anita, who else could it be for Tracey's mouth was always a tightly locked door. Then came the stones; I would be sitting at my open window poring over a multiple choice paper or testing myself on European capitals and a shower of pebbles would land on my book, too tiny to hurt me but thrown hard enough to sting. I never saw anyone actually throw the stones, but sometimes I would hear a low, stifled laugh or catch the heel of Tracey's bony foot disappearing around the entry.

I began closing my window and losing my concentration. Then came the notes, always left where I alone would find them, pushed into the spokes of my bike or hidden in between the pages of my *Jackie* when it was delivered every Thursday. They were written on jagged scraps of plain paper, in the kind of anonymous capitals that adorned all blackmail letters in films, and contained strangely conflicting messages, always encompassed in a few short words. One day it would be FAT COW, the next day, NICE TITS, the day after, SILLY BITCH, and then SEXY LEGS, reminding me of the sherbet messages written on love heart sweets which were supposed to tell your fortune for the day. One of them even made me laugh, the one I found curled up inside an empty milk bottle on our front step. Whoever it was, they were, had tried to write chapatti, there were three versions of it all scribbled over angrily, SHUPAT . . . CHUPIT . . . CHARPUT . . . and then the final defeated version, SHITTY ARSE.

I don't know how my parents ever avoided discovering these missives, maybe it would have been better if they had and maybe . . . but how was I to know then how it would all end? I stopped my bike rides, not out of fear because I thought he/she/they intended to physically harm me – they had plenty of opportunity to do that effectively – but because the suspense of what they would try next was ruining my revision. All the facts and figures I had assumed were fixed forever in my memory lost their solidity and melted into one amorphous mass of nonsense. If the notes had been obviously threatening, predicting dire accidents and a messy end, I would have known how to react, I would have taken action. But their sweet-sour flavour whetted my appetite somehow; they made me alert, confused and curious because I knew they were merely the first course of some showdown which I felt hungry for, which I had been waiting for as long as I could remember.

And naturally, when it came, it took me by surprise. It was the night before my eleven-plus exam, and my parents had been fussing over me all day. As soon as I got home from school, a tense expectant day in which everyone reacted hysterically to the slightest incident, mama ran a bath for me in front of the fire in the TV room and left me in there with a cup of tea, giving papa and Sunil strict orders to keep out until I had finished. The rest of the evening took on a ceremonial air, mama laid out my pyjamas and dressing gown, even though it was barely seven o'clock, and sat me in front of my favourite meal of paratha and homemade yoghurt, watching me eat as if every mouthful would go straight to my brain and plug a hole to stop a European capital from falling out. Then she massaged my hair with coconut oil whilst I ate chocolate ice cream, made me sit with Sunil on my lap with papa next to me whilst she settled down at my feet.

Sunil struggled away from my grip. 'No, didi!' he shouted crossly. 'No like! Stopitt now good boy!'

'Sunny, be nice to your didi! She has a very important day tomorrow!' said mama, relieved that she was able to mention the eleven-plus in what she thought was a casual, unconnected way.

'I'm fine, mama,' I said cheerily, and I really was. I knew when I got into the hall tomorrow and turned over that dreaded exam paper, I would not be able to remember my name, never mind the square root of ten or the difference between an adjective and an adverb. I knew how much was riding on this paper – my parents' hopes for my future, the justification for their departure from India, our possible move out of Tollington. None of this was ever said directly to me but I knew them well enough to read the conflict in their attentive faces: 'Don't worry about this but you'd better pass . . . so what if you fail but please don't . . . you'll still be our darling daughter but you'd look so lovely in a tam-o'-shanter . . .'

And then the telephone rang; mama went to answer it and came back looking drained and older. She told papa in Punjabi that Uncle Amman had had a heart attack, that Auntie Shaila had just rung from the hospital very upset and could we please go over and sit with her until he came out of the operating theatre. Mama was doing her old trick of disguising bad news by using Punjabi, perhaps forgetting that since my year with Nanima, she and papa had very few secrets left. Nevertheless I let papa translate the whole crisis into English, selfishly more concerned at this point by the distress on my parents' faces than the thought of sweet Uncle Amman lying on an operating table with his generous heart exposed to the air.

'I'll go,' said mama, reaching for the door. 'You stay with Meena, she needs her rest tonight.' 'Nay, Daljit,' papa stopped her. 'How will you drive all that way in the dark?'

This was a genuine worry, mama had only ever driven in the day and still found roundabouts a traumatic experience. There were several roundabouts on the way to the hospital, not to mention a couple of flyovers and the notorious Coal Hill. Papa was reliving the whole journey in his head, I could see his nostrils twitching with alarm as he imagined mama in various night-time scenarios on her own, sailing right over the island of a roundabout, reversing up a slip road the wrong way. He stopped himself when his imagination reached Coal Hill, it was too horrible to continue. 'You go with mama,' I said to him, 'I need to work anyway.'

Mama and papa looked at each other for a decision. Papa checked his watch.

'If I take Sunil with us,' mama was thinking aloud, 'he'll fall asleep in the car anyway . . .'

'Tell Mrs Worrall to come and sit with Meena, if she doesn't mind,' papa said, searching for the car keys.

'But we don't know when we'll be back, Shyam!' Mama was changing her mind now. 'I mean, she can't leave Mr Worrall too long . . .'

'Look,' I said firmly, finding the keys under a cushion and tucking them into papa's trouser pocket. 'I'll lock the doors, I'll have the telly on, I'll just knock on Mrs Worrall's door if I need anything . . .'

Papa was convinced, he was already bundling Sunil into his ski suit. Mama chewed her lip fitfully, 'You promise not to open the door to anyone? ANYONE?'

'Yes! Now go on, I'm fine.'

It felt good to be seeing them off for a change; as they drove away in the sputtering Mini, I had an image of me as a mother standing in the same doorway with a child holding onto my knees, waving two old people off, mama and papa with grey hair and Nanima's slow shuffle, overwhelmed with protective love, shouting after them to button up tightly and mind the road. Mind the road. The last thing Robert had ever said to me. I held onto that, it comforted me as I went around all the three downstairs rooms, switching off lights and sockets, checking for chinks in the curtains, glad that I'd already been for a wee and did not have to venture out again into the close summer night.

The knocking awoke me with such force that I literally fell out of bed and found myself tangled in a duvet nest, my heart hammering twice as fast as the blows coming from the front door. Mama and papa have got a key, I reminded myself as I fiddled with the stair light switch and crept downstairs. I recognised the silhouette through the frosted glass of the porch door, amazed that she was solid enough to cast a shadow. It is okay, I told myself as I unfastened the Yale lock, I know her, at least I used to. Tracey stood shivering in a dress I recognised as Anita's summer cast-off, her cardigan hanging off one arm, her face contorted with grief and fury as she sobbed incoherently at me for a few seconds. 'What?' I said, grabbing hold of her arms which felt like twigs in my big hands. 'I don't understand . . . Where's your dad? What's going on?' 'He . . . he's killing her! He's g . . . g . . . going to kill her!' she hiccupped, wiping a hand across her face which made no impression in the slime of her snot and tears.

So that was it! It made sense of everything, their dad was beating her up, Roberto was a child beater and that's why Anita was so cruel and mixed up. These ramblings filled my head as I threw on some clothes in my darkened bedroom, Tracey's wailing calling me like a siren. When I slammed the door behind me, I remembered I did not have a key and knew that if my parents returned and found me missing, I would set off a police hunt, complete with helicopters and tracker dogs. I glanced at Mrs Worrall's window; the light was always on but I knew she would be watching *The Champions* repeat till late. I had time. It was only when I felt the cool air hit my face and inhaled the scent of the sleeping may blossom, that I realised I had abandoned every promise, every good endeavour in a second to accompany the sister of the girl I had sworn to renounce forever. But at the same time, I had a strong feeling of déjà vu, as if I always knew it would come to this, whatever it was.

Tracey was already running ahead of me as noiselessly as a fox. Although the sky was bright with stars, a near-full moon and the yellow glow of the motorway lights, I had the feeling she could follow any trail in pitch darkness; she moved like a nocturnal animal. I was ready to turn into the entry that led directly to Anita's house when Tracey veered off across the road and towards the Big House, which was, as always, shrouded in darkness. 'Tracey!' I called, thinking maybe her distress had made her confused. She paused for a moment, only to beckon me furiously with an imperious hand, and continued running until she reached the old pit yard where the new low-roofed building now stood, its windows still without glass, vacant like empty eye sockets.

'Trace!' I called weakly. She had pushed through a gap in the fence which was buckled in places from the building work, and waited for me in the gap, her head poking out impatiently. I was trotting right past the Big House gates – I thought of the witch that was supposed to live there, the same witch who had drowned Jodie Bagshot in the tadpole ponds and drained every last drop of blood from her body, leaving her blue and lifeless in the water. I thought of the huge silent bear that had watched us from the shadows whilst my Auntie Shaila sang her Punjabi lament to the night sky. I thought of mama's diamond necklace being examined clumsily in fat scaly paws and coming to rest on a thick furry neck. I began to mutter the old prayer to myself, 'For what we are about to receive . . .' and then swallowed it down, refusing to give in to these ancient superstitions from another era, from my childhood. If I started to believe in just one of them again, I would have to believe in everything else I had tried to discard or disprove. I would not go that way again, I had an exam tomorrow, that was my mantra and I repeated it over and over again. I Have An Exam Tomorrow. Tomorrow I Have An Exam . . .

'Quick!' Tracey pleaded. She had stopped crying but was trembling so much that her teeth chattered as loud as castanets. I unthinkingly whipped off my sweatshirt and pulled it over her head; she did not help or resist me, a mannequin enduring my tugs. I could have turned back then, Roberto was twice my size, what could I do? Why had Tracey called for me? And then she was off again, sniffing her trail through the scaffolding and piles of bricks, and when she took the dirt path which ran to the side of the old pithead and through the small gravelly hills of shale, I knew where we were headed. The ponds, the tadpole ponds. I Have An Exam Tomorrow, Tomorrow . . .

We reached the top of the rise which looked down over the largest pond, one of a series created naturally over the years by the rain filling the old mine shaft, fringed with bulrushes which housed thousands of tadpoles, wriggling commas you could scoop up by the handful. But not in the dark. Now the bulrushes stood on silent guard, furry bearskins around the still water, water with no end, no bottom because the shaft ran into a whole labyrinth of tunnels and if you fell in, you were lost forever.

Tracey did not need to grip my arm so tightly because I could see them in the clearing, a patch of scrubby grass on top of an overhang, a favourite picnic spot where you could sit on the rocky ledge and scare yourself by dangling your legs in the air above the deepest part of the pond, a straight drop of fifteen feet into nothingness.

He was on top of her, moving slightly, and pulled away almost immediately, zipping up his flies in short sharp jerks. Anita was lying motionless on her back, her knees up, her eyes closed, her knickers around one ankle. I squinted through the gloom, willing the moon to shift position because I could not see her breathing. Tracey began to sob in her throat, her fingers loosened their grip on my arm, defeated. 'No,' she said.

And then, 'Is she . . .' I was lost completely for a moment, because the moon had heard me and brushed a cloud from her face and threw a silver spotlight upon his. He was lighting a cigarette now, the flare picked out the tips of his stubbly scalp, and I was right, he did have a scar, a neat crescent running from temple to cheek.

How had he earned that? I pondered. Was he really Sam Lowbridge the Hero, as I had secretly cast him all these years, the misunderstood rebel with a soul? Was he sliced by a mugger whilst he ran to rescue a fragile old lady from a beating? Was he caught by the flailing claws of a fox he had whisked from under the huntsman's hooves? He exhaled noisily and I knew suddenly how he got his warrior mark: Sam the Drunk, staggering round the back of a pub with half a broken beer bottle in his hand; Sam the Idiot, playing ball with his own flick knife, throwing it against a wall and catching it with his face; Sam the . . . why couldn't I say it, Sam who cornered someone like my Auntie in a urine-soaked alleyway and unravelled her sari, laughing himself sick, her resistance leaving no mark except the crescent scar where her diamond wedding ring caught the soft skin of his cheek.

Sam took another drag and kicked Anita's leg with the toe of his boot, her body rolled away uselessly from the blow, her head lolled on her neck, her eyes remained shut. 'Gerrup you tart,' he said. He kicked her harder and she lurched onto her stomach, spreadeagled now, still. 'Oy! Nita!' Sam's voice had an urgent snap to it. He went to kick her again and the night became a long murderous scream as Tracey ran down the hill towards him, teeth bared, eyes wild, nails out like claws. 'Bastard!' It was then that Anita opened her eyes with a jerk, her first reaction anger because her joke had been spoiled. I ducked down instinctively behind a tree stump and held my breath. Anita jumped up and then fell over again, entangled in her twisted knickers. Sam caught Tracey by her hair and picked her up like a rag doll, jumping back from the manic, chopping limbs.

'Yow stupid cow!' Anita shouted, managing to get her legs in the right holes and finally yanking her pants up. 'When yow gonna stop following me around, eh?'

'Yow are the stupid cow!' Sam chuckled back. 'What yow pretending for? Did I shag yow out that much, eh?'

Tracey's movements became slower, weaker, Sam plonked her onto the ground and she ran immediately to Anita, arms outstretched. 'I thought yow were dead!' she shouted back.

Anita side-stepped her angrily, catching her arm and twisting it round her back. 'Yow go home now or I'll kill yow!'

Tracey ran a little way off and then picked up a large stone and hurled it at Anita, missing her by inches. 'Right!' screamed Anita and ran after her, which is just what she had planned, judging by her whoop of triumph, and they disappeared into the bushes, their cries becoming fainter and further apart.

Sam flicked his cigarette butt into the water where it died with a sharp hiss. I began inching my way from the tree stump, already calculating how many hours of sleep were left tonight, because Tomorrow I Have An . . .

'Meee-naaa!' Every hair on my neck stood up one by one in a long, lazy prickle. 'I knew yow was there, Meena! Come out! I ain't gonna hurt yow, promise!' I stood up slowly, my arms felt numb now and I remembered that Tracey had gone off wearing my sweatshirt. Sam beckoned me over with a nod. I stumbled automatically down the slope of the rise and climbed another to join him on the overhang. He would not hurt me if I showed any fear. Tomorrow I Have . . .

I sat down casually although my knees shook slightly, so I drew them together, a prissy maiden aunt pose – he would expect that. 'So where you been, Meena?' he asked in that soft drawl, as familiar as if we'd been chatting over the garden fence this morning.

'I still live here,' I said, and then I added, 'You haven't driven me out yet.'

Sam arched his eyebrows, genuinely surprised, 'Me?' he asked. 'Wharrave I done?'

'Oh, I got your notes,' I spat at him. The cold was gradually dulling every sensation including fear. 'Supposed to frighten me away, were they?'

'No,' said Sam. 'To bring yow back. I only wrote half of 'em, the nice ones mind. Anita did the others, wouldn't let me send mine on me own. She's dead jealous you know. About us.'

Sparks of recognition momentarily flew between us. I knew that weary bewilderment in his face, the resignation in his voice – all the consequences of getting involved with Anita, wondering why you hung around for more when every sensible part of you was saying get the hell out. But Sam under Anita's spell? Surely it was the other way round? There were still traces of his weird magic in the droop of his eyes right now, in the curve of his scarred cheek, but with every passing second, the illusion faded, revealing strings and sleight of hand. For all his bluster, I had the feeling that Sam was truly nothing more than a puppet and the knowledge that he would never have the character to cut the wires made me furious, for the waste, for his cowardice, for both of us.

'Those things you said at the spring fete, what were you trying to do?' I tasted grit, maybe I had ground my molars into dust.

Sam shrugged and dragged his heel along a muddy edge. 'I wanted to make people listen,' he said finally.

'You wanted to hurt people, you mean!' I yelled at him. 'How could you say it, in front of me? My dad? To anyone? How can you believe that shit?'

Sam grabbed me by the wrists and I sucked in air and held it. 'When I said them,' he rasped, 'I never meant you, Meena! It was all the others, not yow!'

I put my face right up to his; I could smell the smoke on his breath. 'You mean the others like the Bank Manager?'

Sam looked confused.

'The man from the building site. The Indian man. I know you did it. I *am* the others, Sam. You did mean me.'

Sam gripped my wrists tighter for support. 'Yow've always been the best wench in Tollington. Anywhere! Dead funny.' His face darkened, maybe it was another shift of the moon. 'But yow wos never gonna look at me, yow won't be stayin will ya? You can move on. How come? How come I can't?' And then he kissed me like I thought he would, and I let him, feeling mighty and huge, knowing I had won and that every time he saw another Meena on a street corner he would remember this and feel totally powerless. It lasted five seconds and then we heard the splash in the water behind us, then another, then a rock hit my recently broken leg and I gasped in pain. Anita was standing below us near the water's edge, mechanically picking up rubble from the ground and hurling it wildly at our heads. Sam pushed me out of the firing line and I slid halfway down the overhang on my bottom towards the ground.

'Nita,' he shouted. She was muttering to herself scrabbling round urgently for more missiles. 'You wanna chuck me for her? Her! Yow like her better? Her! Her?' A rock hit Sam full in the face, he staggered back slightly, his boots slipping over the gravel, holding a hand to his nose and registering the warmth of his own blood. 'NITA!' he roared and raced towards her with his fist raised. And then there are only freeze frames: Tracey appearing from nowhere, leaping at Sam like a terrier; Anita following her up towards the overhang; Sam backing towards the edge, laughing at this absurd challenge; Tracey flying through the air, suspended in the moonlight, arms outstretched like wings, Sam dodging sideways; and then that terrible splash which sucked in half the night with it – and silence.

'Trace?' Anita said softly, after a pause. 'Trace?' Then frantic watery leaps, wading through mud and bulrushes, Anita's harsh sobs, muffled as she fought off Sam. 'Get her,

Sam! She can't swim!' 'Nor me! Nor me! Where's she gone?'
'Trace! Our Trace!' 'Somebody!'

I was already running, cracking my head on branches and
snagging my bare arms on brambles. Where was the path,
who was nearest, phone the police somebody, which was the
way out, every moment on dry land is another one underwater, I Have An Exam Tomorrow . . .

I reached the front door of the Big House, retching for
breath, spasms gripping my leg. There were no lights on but I
put my finger on the doorbell and kept it there and even if a
woman with a warty chin and a broomstick opened it, I
decided I would still ask for help. A soft glow appeared
somewhere behind the huge oak door, I could see it approaching through the stained glass panel just above my head which
depicted a mine with a pithead behind which a red sun was
rising.

'Oo is it?' A witch's voice, strangely accented and croaky.

'Please! Please, a girl's fallen into the pond! Please help!'

There was a fumbling, then a series of about ten different
locks being unbolted and eased back stiffly, then a pause and
the witch's voice demanded, 'Oo are yoo?'

'Meena . . . Meena Kumar! I live . . .'

I could not speak any more, but the last bolt slid from its
casing and an apparition appeared – a tiny woman who
barely reached my shoulders was holding an old-fashioned
oil lamp in her delicate hand. She looked eternal rather
than old, carefully styled blue hair, spots of rouge on the
still prominent cheekbones, a dainty mouth which bled
pearly pink lipstick and those eyebrows, not her real ones,
they had obviously been shaved off years ago, but two
heavily-drawn lines which swooped right up to her hairline
like two ironic question marks. 'Ah, Mee-naa.' She sang it
rather than said it. 'You live in the corner house, is it not?
'ow is your leg, better?'

I was too dumbfounded to reply, it was too much to take in,
this designer witch who seemed to know everything about me.

The house in which she stood which was now taking shape in the shadowy gloom behind her.

The nearest equivalent I could think of was a house we had once visited in Ironbridge which had been preserved as a museum, with all the original fittings and decor from the turn of the century, and bad actors in suspiciously modern costumes and too much make-up, pretending they were the original Ironbridge family, and serving us tea and biscuits. The witch's house was a veritable time warp; old, clumsy wooden furniture cluttered every available bit of floor space, ancient oil paintings and tapestries adorned the walls and the floors were dull wooden parquet which gave off a faint lavender smell. I did not see one electrical fitting anywhere, just occasional lamps standing on sideboards and a massive, ornate chandelier with unused candles sitting in its golden cups. No television, no radio – that meant no telephone.

I began hyperventilating again. 'Please, we have to get some help! Phone the ambulance, the police . . .' The witch was walking away from me, taking the light with her. I stood in the dark of the doorway and wondered if I should just run home now, remembering that there was a phone booth opposite the house. And then I heard her talking in low tones to someone, there was a heavy click and I turned round to see her replacing an old-fashioned bell receiver into its cradle which hung on a wall. 'They are coming, emer-gency I told them.' She walked across to the foot of a large sweeping staircase which appeared to rise up in a graceful arc into thin air. ''Arry!' she called up, beckoning me to come into the hallway and close the door behind me. ''Arry! Accident at the pond! Bring Belle with yoo! Just like that other girl, what was her name,' she muttered as she set off towards me.

Jodie Bagshot. The name had been spinning around my head for the last, how long had it been, ten minutes, ten hours? Poor little Jodie who was pulled dead from the pond to the clicks of cameramen and the howls of her waiting parents who moved out of the village the very next day. That was when the rumours started, about the lifeless, mysterious Big House and the ghouls who haunted it, waiting for the next child they could pounce on and drag down to a watery grave. Now I really did want to leave. I inched backwards feeling along the grain of the door for a handle, touching only steel bolts and heavy link chains. ''Arry! 'urry!' the witch ordered, and I looked up and saw him, emerging from the shadows of the hallway.

He must have been the former mine owner, he must have owned a lot of something as he walked erect and slowly, exuding an air of authority and gravitas, but the crags and jowls of his face showed he was also connected to the earth, a miner made good perhaps. He had a workman's face and philosopher's eyes, and in his shovel-sized hands he held the lead of a jumping spaniel. But all of this became secondary when he finally spoke. '*Chup Kar Kure, Thahar Jao Ik Minut!* Get me a torch, Mireille.'

My miracle was complete. The Big House boss was an Indian man, as Indian as my father, and he spoke Punjabi with a village twang to his dog. He was brown as a nut and possessed that typical North Indian Roman nose, and the gold signet ring on his little finger sported the Hindu symbol 'OM'. 'Namaste, chick,' he said as he passed, patting me clumsily. He let the spaniel off the lead which shot off into the night, and he followed in lumbering pursuit like a grumpy bear.

Mireille, a rather elegant name for a witch I thought, snapped into action and led me into a side room in which a hearty fire crackled and spat. She forcibly sat me in a high-backed leather chair and tucked a blanket around me which smelt of wet canine coat. I could make out that we were in some kind of study as a vast mahogany desk sat in a corner, piled high with papers and letters, some of them air mail blue, and an ancient typewriter sat in the middle of the mess, a half-finished memo in its jaws. And then I saw the books, thousands of them lining the walls from top to bottom, an armoury of paperbacks, hard covers, some leather-bound with cracked spines, others cheap and cheerful off an airport stand. Every one of them wore their dog ears and thumbed covers with pride because this was proof that they had all been read and appreciated.

Envy and admiration swept over me; so this is what it was like to be rich. I had never been in such an opulent house before. I did not count my parents' business friends whose detached show homes we sometimes visited; they had money alright, but it was spent on gold bathroom fittings and imported village objets d'art. Their books were glossy, on display and untouched. But this was how I would spend my money, hoarding books greedily in a quiet room where I could go and gorge myself without being disturbed, enjoying the privilege of never having to return a cherished, newly-discovered book back to a library again. 'Yoo like the books? My 'Arry is mad on them,' Mireille smiled, placing my hands around a cup of hot cocoa. Harry did not sound a very Indian name to me; then I spotted the soft shiny briefcase propped up against the typewriter, the gold letters on the side caught the fingertips of the fire. 'Harinder P. Singh.' So 'Er 'Arry was a Sikh like mama.

I jerked open my sleepy eyes. Mama and papa would be back now, they would be frantic with worry. To my shame I had not thought of Tracey since I entered the library. I had to get up, I had to get back to the outside world and face all the consequences of this terrible and strange evening. But when I tried to move, my body refused to co-operate; shock and cold had closed it down for the night and however loudly I shouted at it, it simply blew me a raspberry and turned over for a doze. And there was also Mireille's voice, she had launched into a sing-song monologue which soon became a lullaby, she rocked me gently with her stories which came spilling out after so long with no one to talk to except 'Er 'Arry.

''Arry, he was so happy when your family moved here. 'E said he was tired of being the only local colour . . . 'Arry is so witty, yoo know. He did law at Cambridge, I was over from Paris studying Chemistry, we met and that was that as they say . . .'

I wondered drowsily why this glittering international couple had ended up running a mine in the Midlands, and the mention of Cambridge reminded me that Tomorrow I Had An Exam . . .

'Poor 'Arry, 'e was so brilliant and no one wanted him here, he got offered clerical work, can you imagine it?'

Then I remembered that I still did not know what my papa did for a living, and that I really ought to be getting home.

'And then his mad uncle, some maharajah type died, we went *fou* with the money, mad, cars, trips, furs for me, books and theatres and parties for him. Then 'Arry and me we drove through this place one day, we were lost looking for Stratford-upon-Avon, and for us it was paradise.'

How long ago that must have been, for Tollington to seem like heaven.

'The mine was almost dead anyway, the owner saw us coming. 'Arry tried to make it work but it broke him, and me also. But we did not want to go back to our families, we 'ad travelled too far, we could not go back as . . . as failures. So we stayed.'

Her voice was an echo at the end of an entry now. I wanted to prise open my eyes and ask her was it just shame then, that had kept them so hidden for all these years, wasting their gifts and zest for life instead of sharing them with people whom they could have inspired and entertained, for whom they could have been living proof that the exotic and the different can add to and enrich even the sleepiest backwater.

'We 'ave lived you know, through all of you, so fascinating, the tiny things that happen every day. We felt proud, like parents. There are not many places left like this now . . . And in here, we only needed each other. 'Oo else would have understood us, strange creatures like us?'

'Meena! Meena! Meena . . . Meena . . .' Mama was

shaking me so hard that I could feel my eyeballs banging against their sockets. She looked more angry than I had ever seen her, wild madwoman's hair and scarlet-rimmed eyes, and then she broke into low moaning sobs and crushed me to her, wanting to absorb me back into her body where I was safe, where she could find me. I heard snorting from somewhere. I saw papa slumped onto a chaise longue, he was wiping his face with a hanky, bowed like an old old man, drained with relief. I was still in the library chair, but it was daylight, now I could see the faded flowers in the wallpaper and the dust motes rising from the thick velvet curtains. 'Tracey,' I said. 'Have they found her?' Mama nodded and burst into fresh weeping, burying her face in my shoulder now. 'She . . . she was wearing your sweatshirt . . . oh my god, your sweatshirt . . .'

Tracey had been pronounced clinically dead by the ambulancemen when they arrived at hospital. They had found her by following a single flashing torchlight beckoning them through the undergrowth, and discovered a strange brown man standing over his soaking wet spaniel and Tracey's sodden body. She had been so insubstantial somehow, the current had rejected her like a piece of litter and she had snagged in the bulrushes, waiting to be dragged out by a dog's strong jaws. 'But they put her on this machine . . .' You heard the same story being broadcast on every corner, over every wall and fence, every intimate detail shared out even to strangers, this near tragedy reuniting Tollington for one last brief affair. 'And you know, gave her shocks like, electric ones, and her heart started up again. They thought there'd be like brain damage, but the water was so cold, it like shut her down for a bit. Like when you pop a joint in the top bit of the fridge. All they did was thaw her out.'

Even if the village gossip had already reduced Tracey's brush with death to a recipe card in the *People's Friend*, the press saw it as nothing less than a modern-day miracle. 'Tot Comes Back From the Dead!' 'Tracey Died For An Hour!'

'Tollington "Angel" Refuses to Die!' By the time my parents had got me home, the village was already crawling with reporters and photographers who had set up camp in the Mitre pub, ordering lavish fried breakfasts and kidnapping any passing body for some juicy quotes and anecdotes about Our Tracey, as she was now known by everyone, especially those who had written her off as one of Deirdre's no-hope daughters.

I saw the whole giddy parade from my window, saw the Ballbearings women rush indoors when they spotted the reporters coming, and rushing out again, having quickly done their hair and slapped on some make-up, and then taking up casual poses in their gardens or on their front steps, as if they always did the dusting or weeding in their eyeliner and best frock. It seemed that the whole village had an opinion or theory as to what had happened, everyone stood around waiting to be asked or simply providing an audience to the lucky few who were chosen to comment.

I heard snatches of these sound bites as I lay in bed, waiting for the violent shivering that had plagued me since I had realised that today I was supposed to have been sitting my eleven-plus.

Mama and papa became alarmed at these shakes that began to rack my body. 'It's delayed shock! Get the doctor!' mama had whispered to papa, but I could have told them it was blind, incoherent fury. I hated Tracey for coming to my door, hated Anita for speaking to me all those years ago when I sat on my front step eating stolen sweets, hated Sam for not being cruel to me so that I could have dismissed him long ago, and mainly hated myself for having completely forgotten all about it. How could I have been so stupid, to forget the chant that had carried me through last night, to miss this only opportunity to completely change my life? I saw everything crumble around me, every single daydream of wandering through the grammar school cloisters citing poetry, of my parents wiping tears away as I went up on a platform to receive yet another prize for Debating Skills or Most Graceful Netball Player, of sitting in the garden of our new bungalow being applauded by my Aunties and Uncles as the first family member to win a university scholarship and meet a future husband on the same day – all that potential, all that hope, all gone because I made friends once with Anita Rutter.

The next morning began with the unexpected arrival of two letters. I recognised the writing of the one addressed to me, the same careful capitals, except this time, she had chosen to seal the note in an envelope. 'Meena, come and talk to me about last night. DON'T talk to Sam! VERY IMPORTANT!!! Anita.' I had foolishly supposed that she and Sam were locked somewhere in adjoining cells, trying to coordinate their stories through iron bars under the watchful gaze of a violent warder. But she was at home, a few familiar doors away. I tore up the letter into tiny pieces and flushed them down the toilet.

Papa's letter was much more interesting; the envelope was silky and expensive looking, the postmark local, the handwriting in ink was large, ragged, intriguing, the address said only 'Mr Kumar (Meena's Papa), Corner House, Old Cottages, Tollington.' It was not our official address, it was as if someone had written down the way he or she would describe how to get to our house to a lost traveller, and made perfect sense. Papa ripped it open and stared at it incredulously. 'Daljit!' he called. Mama came out of the kitchen holding Sunil at arm's length; he was covered in cereal and looked proud of it. 'Look at this,' he said, showing her the letter. It seemed to be written in astrological symbols, all half moons and flying dots like comets. 'Hindi?' mama asked. Papa nodded and began to read. I could tell he was dragging up some old half-buried skills by the way his finger carefully followed the lines.

'I'm rusty,' he said mournfully to no one in particular, and then finally, 'He has asked me to come for tea.'

'Who? Who has?' mama said, craning her neck to see the letter.

Papa looked over to the Big House. 'Harinder P. Singh. All this time we have had a brother around the corner . . . all this time.' Papa had to repeat himself several times and eventually take mama through the letter word by word until she finally absorbed the enormity of this information. Then she and papa both sat on the settee together, a curious wash of pride and betrayal sweeping over them. Finally mama asked me, 'An Indian gentleman lives in the Big House, Meena. Isn't that amazing?' I could have told her then about meeting Ganesha in the forest, but that led onto the loss of her necklace and anyway, I realised it was better that my parents think they had been the first to know. 'Arry had somehow let them down by remaining a secret for so long. 'Amazing,' I replied.

All morning we had loud men in macs banging on our door and telephoning incessantly for an interview with me, some of them offering money, all of them paranoid that maybe I had spilled the beans to someone else and that their scoop was already yesterday's news. I heard them calling through the porch door to papa. 'Mr Kumar? Has she told you what happened? Is it true she was the only witness? Did she mention that it was not an accident? Did she say she saw anyone push Tracey into the water? Mr Kumar?'

It was only when papa eventually let someone in and I saw the police car parked outside that I began to feel nervous. And when papa crept into my room, the set of his jaw confirmed my fears.

'Meena, beti, the police want to talk to you. Did . . . did you see what happened?'

I nodded my head, regretting the moment when I had opened the door to that silly moo, Tracey.

'Um, there is a bit of a complication you see,' papa said carefully. 'Tracey is saying that someone pushed her in.'

'It wasn't me!' I cried.

Papa grabbed my hand and squeezed it. 'No, no, I know, she's not saying that. She is saying it was Sam Lowbridge or her sister.' I wondered why he did not call Anita by name. 'And they are accusing each other. So . . . well, so what you saw is quite important.' I nodded again, a curious elation swelling inside me. 'You just have to tell the truth, Meena,' papa said gently.

How many times had mama and papa begged me to do just that? And how many times had I laughed at their pleas and abused their renewed trust after every occasion when I had been caught and vowed never to do it again? Even now I could see a tiny seed of doubt planting itself in papa's brain, he so much wanted to believe that I would not be foolish enough to lie, romantic enough to embroider the occasion to suit my own dramatic desires. But the truth was, every little fabrication that went before, every extra twist in the tale and gilt on the lily, had merely been the rehearsal for the show which was about to begin. I had lost my best friend to someone who could have been a friend and lost himself, and between them, they had caused me what I thought was agonizing pain, until I met two other people, Nanima and Robert, who had thrown all previous self-pity into stark relief. But I hated Sam and Anita even more then, for making me believe that the power they had exercised over me was important, everlasting. I had been planning a spectacular revenge for so long and now, finally, I was ready.

Up until this moment I had been supremely prepared, going over every fine detail of what I would say, how Sam and Anita caught Tracey spying on their lovemaking (that was not the right word, far too kind a term for what they had been doing), that they flew into a rage, chased and caught her, egged each other on to push her into the water (I did not see who dealt the final shove, the important bit was that they both knew what they were doing), that I watched helplessly from my hiding place in the bushes, ('No, officer, I was too scared to stop them. They both picked on me all the time, ask anyone . . . What was I doing there? Tracey asked me to help her. Tracey was always more my friend anyway.'), and then ran for help as soon as I saw my dear friend hit the water, ('And the worst bit was the way they laughed at the splash . . . I felt sick.')

'Now don't be nervous Meena, we just want to ask you a few questions.' I had expected two burly thugs in dirty macs with dog-ends hanging out of their mouths, like the two detectives in *The Sweeney* on television. I had even prepared myself for the Nice Cop, Nasty Cop routine, deciding I would burst into tears if things got too hairy. But these two were soft-cheeked rookies, their hats looked too big and they ate all of mama's snacks within a minute of sitting down, suggesting that their own mums had got up too late to feed them their usual fry-up. They opened their notebooks (pick up your pencils please), they turned to a page of notes (no turning over the exam paper until I say begin), and as they began their enquiries, I gradually drifted far away until I was outside my body, watching a fat brown girl chew her lip and talk in faltering sentences.

Yes, I went because Tracey called for me, said the girl. Yes, she knew the way, she had been watching them all night. Yes, they were . . . they were having sex. I saw the girl's parents hang their heads and grip the side of their chairs, but the girl herself, well, she was completely unperturbed, a natural. Yes, there was a fight, kind of, Tracey ran at them . . . yes, she did start it. And then. And then? And then I flew right through the roof of my house and I saw everything: I saw the Ballbearings women haring down the street and grabbing life in their hands with every short barking laugh, I saw Mrs Worrall eating her daily treat of a lemon puff and feeding the best bit to Mr Worrall with devotion, I saw Tracey fuming in her hospital bed, reunited with her anger, I saw Sam polishing his bike, avoiding his own reflection in the chrome, I saw Anita at her kitchen table eating toast which she had burned just like her mother and she liked it that way, I saw Mireille laying out a tea table with her best china and 'Arry watching her quick delicate movements with quiet joy, I saw that Tollington had lost all its edges and boundaries, that the motorway bled into another road and another and the Bartlett estate had swallowed up the last cornfield and that my village was indistinguishable from the suburban mass that had once surrounded it and had finally swallowed it whole. It was time to let go and I floated back down into my body which, for the first time ever, fitted me to perfection and was all mine.

'Tracey went for Sam and missed him and fell into the water.' 'Come again?' The police-boy was staring right at me, disappointment already flushing his face. I knew he wanted to get Sam, with a previous record as long as his arm and that Rutter girl, well maybe it would stop another kid having yet another kid who would live off the State. He was telling me I could put them away if I wanted, but I'd had my revenge, I was leaving them to themselves and I believed utterly now in the possibilities of change. 'It was an accident. I saw it. Tracey's lying if she says anything else.'

I sat the eleven-plus in my headmaster's office the next day. It felt like a mere formality as I had replayed it so often in my head. I had peaked far too early, what could I do? So I was surprised to see papa hammering in a FOR SALE sign in our front garden when I got home.

'Meena, beti! How did it go?'

'Okay. Not as good as you think it went,' I said, smiling at the sign.

'Oh this! Well, I had a tip-off.' Papa patted his nose and tipped his head towards the Big House. So that's what they had talked about, property and money. I was disappointed. Mama came out onto the step, Sunil charged in and around our legs with a banana for a gun and one of mum's hairbands on as a helmet.

'This whole field,' she said, gesturing to the view opposite. 'It's going to be houses soon. Mr Singh told papa.'

'How does he know?' I asked.

'He owns it,' mama said. 'That new building next to his house, that is the show-home office or something.'

'Is he moving too?' I wondered aloud. I could not imagine Mireille and 'Arry living next to a pretend home which would be full of dreaming strangers every day, oohing over the carefully chosen fittings and making plans around as yet empty plots of land.

'I don't know,' papa said. 'I didn't ask him that.'

'What a shame you did not get to know Mr Singh before,' sighed mama. 'All that time we were here . . .' She did not finish the sentence, we each filled in our own stories in the pause.

Papa broke it by fumbling in his jacket pocket and handing mama a small velvet pouch. 'Oh Shyam, a present? What for? Why did you spend so much . . .'

'I didn't buy it,' interrupted papa. 'And it's yours anyway.'

Mama gasped as she pulled out my Nanima's diamond necklace from the velvet folds. 'How . . .'

Papa shrugged. 'Harinder-saab said he found it.'

'Do you think . . .' mama began.

'Daljit, leave it,' papa said finally. 'It's come back. That is enough.'

Only Mrs Worrall was invited from the village to our leaving party. We felt we had already said goodbye to everyone else. Auntie Shaila had brought us all presents to mark this next reincarnation in our English life cycle. She gave mama a metal OM to hang above the door of our new bungalow. 'Don't worry about someone taking it. Now you're in a nice area and half your neighbours are Hindu so they'll have one of their own.' Papa received a car cleaning set, a shampoo, chamois leather and plastic scraper for an icy windscreen. 'Now you have a garage, Shyam-saab, please keep your car a little nicer. And anyway, you will be using it much more now we will be living so close to you . . .' For Sunil, she brought a tricycle so he could work off some of his increasingly manic energy in our new, large, landscaped garden. And for me, a beautiful ink pen with my name engraved on the side. 'For all those top-class medical essays you will be writing at your grammar school!'

I already knew I wanted nothing to do with bodies and breakdowns, but I thanked her wordlessly with a hug. No false protestations or promises to get fitted for a stethoscope straight away, I opted for a gracious silence and kept my options open. I used the pen that night, wrote a short note and pushed it through the appropriate letter box. 'Dear Anita, We're moving on Saturday. I'm going to the grammar school, so at least you won't be around to tease me about my tam-o'-shanter! See you around. Meena.' She never replied, of course.

To

Nan,

Have a great time,
remember me, and

don't forget to show
them your bowling
tactics —

love,

Jy .